Books by Elisa Braden

Midnight in Scotland Series

The Making of a Highlander (Book One)
The Taming of a Highlander (Book Two)
The Temptation of a Highlander (Book Three)
The Wickedness of a Highlander (Book Four)–Coming soon!
The Love of a Highlander (Book Five)–Coming soon!

Rescued from Ruin Series

Ever Yours, Annabelle (Prequel)
The Madness of Viscount Atherbourne (Book One)
The Truth About Cads and Dukes (Book Two)
Desperately Seeking a Scoundrel (Book Three)
The Devil Is a Marquess (Book Four)
When a Girl Loves an Earl (Book Five)
Twelve Nights as His Mistress (Novella – Book Six)
Confessions of a Dangerous Lord (Book Seven)
Anything but a Gentleman (Book Eight)
A Marriage Made in Scandal (Book Nine)
A Kiss from a Rogue (Book Ten)

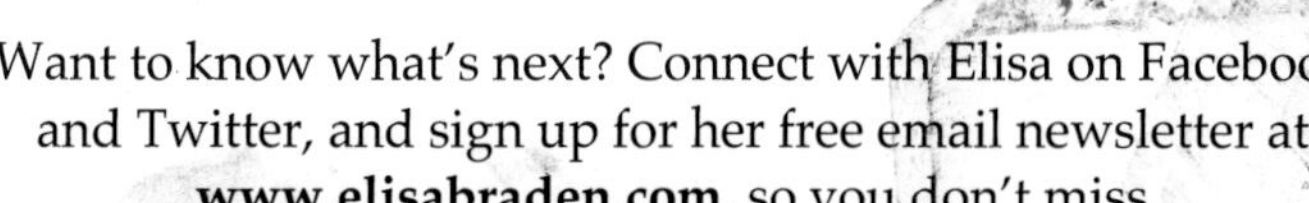

Want to know what's next? Connect with Elisa on Facebook and Twitter, and sign up for her free email newsletter at **www.elisabraden.com**, so you don't miss a single new release!

THE TEMPTATION OF A HIGHLANDER

ELISA BRADEN

This is a work of fiction. Names, characters, places, and incidents are products of the author's imagination or are used fictitiously and are not to be construed as real. Any resemblance to actual events, locales, organizations, or persons, living or dead, is entirely coincidental.

Cover design by Dar Albert at Wicked Smart Designs

For more information about the author,
visit www.elisabraden.com.

ISBN-13: 978-1-950805-09-9

Prologue

December 14, 1826
Ellery Hall
Cambridgeshire, England

"Dash!" Clarissa Meadows chided the velvety gray ball of fur sprawled belly-up across her writing desk. "You've had more than enough petting. Now, shoo."

A lazy feline tail twitched toward the inkwell.

"Dash," she warned. "Don't you dare."

Waving tauntingly like a flag, the tail danced and gave a little shake before suddenly dipping. Drops of ink flew.

"Oh, for pity's sake!" Clarissa plunked her bonnet onto a chair and lurched toward her infuriating companion. Before the tail could dip again, she took hold of it. Dash swatted her hands and rolled to-and-fro like a skiff at sea.

"Rowl," came his scratchy, disgruntled reply. Copper eyes blinked in objection to her dabbing his tail with her now-ruined handkerchief.

She clicked her tongue. "This is why I named you Dash-It-All, you absolute rascal."

"Mrow."

"Being adorable is no excuse. Look at the mess you made." She held up the stained linen—then noticed her stained sleeve. "Blast."

"Been at the inkwell again, has he?" asked Clarissa's grandmother. Rosamond Brightwell Stimson, the Dowager Countess of Darnham, entered the small library cradling a cup of tea. Her shawled shoulders were hunched against the chill.

Clarissa scooped Dash off the desk, kissing his head before depositing him on the floor. "Naughty boy. Go do something useful for once."

In his usual contrary fashion, the round-faced cat purred loudly, rubbed his shoulder against her ankle, then abruptly sprinted out of the room as though he'd been stung by a bee.

Clarissa examined the ink stains on her sleeve. Faded and dingy, the gown hadn't been properly washed since they'd been forced to dismiss Clarissa's lady's maid. The three maids remaining at Ellery Hall lacked the girl's laundering skills.

"We'll have to find the funds to hire the washing done," she muttered, plucking the account book from the shelf and fetching a chair for Grandmama, who settled beside her to peer at the dismal numbers. "Especially given Darnham's demand that we reduce the staff at Ellery Hall to one footman and two maids. Apparently, male servants are more costly for taxation purposes. That leaves us with poor Geoffrey."

Grandmama shook her head. "Poor Geoffrey."

"Yes. He hasn't been the same since the mopping incident."

"Certainly, he won't find employment elsewhere. We'll have to keep him on."

"Perhaps I can tempt the Peabody family to lease another acre of the south garden. They acquired geese, you know."

"Geese?" Grandmama scoffed. "Ducks are a far better choice. Quieter, certainly. I shouldn't like to have geese in the south garden."

"Agreed. But it may be necessary."

Grandmama fell silent, her shoulders slumping. "Perhaps it is."

Unfortunately, Grandmama depended upon Rupert Stimson, Grandpapa's nephew and the current Earl of Darnham, for her income. Before Grandpapa's death, Rupert had promised to let her remain on the estate where she and her husband had raised their three daughters. After the death of Clarissa's parents, they'd raised her at Ellery, too. It was home.

Yet, slowly over the past ten years, Cousin Rupert had siphoned the estate's income and tightened budgets to such an extent that Clarissa had been forced to close off three-quarters of the house and lease acres of parkland to their neighbors for grazing sheep. Meanwhile, Rupert had purchased a townhouse in Brighton and renovated his country house in Shropshire twice, all while demanding that Grandmama make do with a fraction of the funds he'd promised.

Rupert's callousness toward the Dowager Lady Darnham made Clarissa's blood boil. But she had little recourse. He was an earl. Clarissa was a poor relation who, until this year, had been the oldest, dustiest wallflower in the marriage mart.

"Have you decided whether you'd like another season, dear?"

Clarissa sighed and plucked up a pen. "Does one have a *tenth* season? I should think such longevity warrants a more grandiose term. Jubilee, perhaps. We could arrange confetti."

"Oh, pooh. Numbers are unimportant. Last season, you were a spectacular success."

Yes, after years of spectacular failure. But she didn't bother pointing out what they both knew. Instead, she brushed a silver wisp from her grandmother's wrinkled cheek and replied gently, "I don't see how we can afford it, Grandmama."

Smile-shaped creases curved into a grin. Blue eyes that resembled Clarissa's warmed and sparkled. "Easily. We'll visit Darnham first."

Clarissa chuckled. "If you keep pawning his silverware, he'll discover it missing and be very cross. He may even shrink our budget by another ten percent."

"*Hmmph.* Anything I've taken originally belonged to me and my dear, sweet Alfie," Grandmama grumbled. "I'm simply reclaiming my property and putting its value toward a more worthy endeavor."

"My doomed search for a husband remains *worthy* in your view?"

"'Doomed' is too severe." Another sip. "I prefer 'invigorating.' Like a bracing night swim in uncertain waters. Ah, those are exciting, dear. One is never gladder to be alive than when one is hopelessly adrift, only to reach firm ground, exhausted and shivering and curious where one's drawers have gone."

Clarissa snorted with laughter and made a note beside the tea expenses. She suspected they could find a better price at the shop in Huntingdon.

"Firm ground awaits you. And when you find it, all your struggles and lost garments will be forgotten." Grandmama paused. "A good marriage would solve *many* problems, Clarissa."

"Yes," she murmured.

"It is hardly your fault gentlemen took no notice of you until this year."

"Hmm. Perhaps we could speak to Mrs. Johnstone about taking in our laundry. And we'll reduce our coal deliveries to every two weeks instead of one. The coal man adds a fee to each billing, you know."

"Young men are blind. They chase dazzling lures whilst overlooking far more *substantive* options dangling beneath their very noses. Appalling state of affairs."

Clarissa slanted her a teasing look. "Substantive. Is that how we're referring to plumpness, now?"

Grandmama huffed. "You were not *plump.*"

She glanced down. Full bosom. Trim waist. Lean thighs and arms honed by a love for dancing. Not slender, perhaps, but pleasingly shaped. No, at present, she wasn't plump. But before last year? "Plump" would have been a kindness. Still, Clarissa didn't argue. Grandmama had always been her greatest champion.

"And if you were, what of it? Many girls are plump. It only means you'll last longer in a famine."

Clarissa gestured wryly to the accounts. "Or a budgetary drought?"

Grandmama set down her tea. "Let's go up to London for another season, dear. Firm ground is waiting for you to land upon him."

"One vexing task at a time, hmm?" She tapped the column for household staff. "We've a decision to make about the maids first."

With an impatient sigh, Grandmama threw up her hands. "I cannot possibly dismiss any of them. Those girls all have families to support. They've worked tirelessly—"

"We must, Grandmama."

"A generous husband would rescue you from this drudgery, you know."

Clarissa smiled. "And you. I would insist."

"You're a good girl."

"I'm pleased you think so."

"You deserve a good man. With a *substantial* fortune."

"I'd settle for a slim fortune," she retorted dryly. "Emaciated, even."

"No, no. He must be well positioned. A man of means and strength. A man who offers his wife a proper home. Protection."

Feeling her own failures keenly, Clarissa propped her chin on her knuckles and sighed.

Grandmama's voice thinned. "Safety, Clarissa. That's what the right marriage will bring."

She placed the pen back in its holder. A dark chill stalked her skin. "I know."

"Is it London that worries you? I should think you'll be safer surrounded by friends."

She didn't wish to discuss this. It was enough that she never ceased thinking about it. "H-he's promised to stop. In his last letter, he apologized for everything."

Grandmama shook her head and covered Clarissa's wrist. "And I pray he is sincere. Regardless, you must marry."

Clarissa didn't know how to answer. She'd failed to find her "firm ground" for nearly ten years. Ten years of swimming in the dark, only to encounter monsters that wanted to pull her under. She was lost. Exhausted. Yes, a husband would solve … everything. But thus far, she'd scarcely managed to keep from drowning.

"Now, then," Grandmama continued. "I believe I have a brooch that may be worth something. It won't fetch a fortune, but perhaps it will see us through winter."

The brooch was stored in a small, hinged box somewhere in the northeast wing, which had been closed up for several years. After they finished with the household accounts, Clarissa quickly settled her grandmother in the parlor, donned her cloak, and retrieved a lantern. As she entered the corridor to the northeast wing, she fought a deep shiver. It was dark. Cold. Her breathing sounded eerie in the echoing silence.

She searched three bedchambers, the billiard room, and the music room with no luck. The room she entered last—her grandfather's old study—smelled of dust and the pipe tobacco he'd smoked until the day he'd died. The scent was a comfort.

Her lantern cast a bronze glow over the windowpanes and the canvas-shrouded desk. After removing the canvas and coughing at the cloud of dust, she searched the drawers quickly before turning to the oak cabinet behind her. Halfway through a set of tiny, labeled boxes, she found the brooch.

"Huzzah," she murmured, holding the clustered diamond beauty up to the light. The gold setting shimmered in the lantern light. "Thank heavens. You, my lovely, will be put to good use."

She was pocketing the brooch and closing the cabinet when she heard a sigh.

It wasn't hers.

Every hair on her body stood on end. Her heart stopped then pounded painfully. Spinning until her back pressed against the wood, she peered toward the door she'd left open to a lightless corridor.

"Dash?" She waited. The cat shouldn't be in here. She'd closed the door to the main wing behind her, and there was no other way in.

"Who's there?" she called out, wondering if one of the maids or a footman had followed her.

No answer.

Outside, wind blew fat tufts of white against a darkened window. She scarcely heard the soft patter over her pounding heart.

"Answer me, if you please. Who is there?"

Nothing.

Her nerves sang at a soprano pitch. Frantically, she scanned every corner of the study—the tall cabinets and long bookshelves, the canvas-covered wing chairs and large crate of Grandpapa's paintings.

That was when she noticed the anomaly. A large, dustless shadow marred the carpet beside the crate, which should have been two feet further from the window but was instead positioned beneath it. As though someone had moved it recently.

Ice flooded her veins.

"If—if anybody's there, you should know I'm armed!" Shaking, she scrambled for Grandpapa's letter opener, which he'd always kept in his top desk drawer. Cool silver slid into her hand, offering faint reassurance. "I've no qualms about defending myself. Any blood spilt shall be the price you pay for trespassing. Consider this a warning. I'm being quite generous, you know."

Still no answer, merely the wind, the snow, and the flickering darkness.

"One of my footmen will be along shortly! I recommend fleeing before he arrives. He's big! *Huge!*" Was her embellishment sufficiently threatening? Perhaps a bit more was in order. "Practically mad. And he'll kill you without compunction. We've had the constable out thrice to subdue him. Vicious, violent man. Still, he's very useful for certain tasks. We're quite fond of him, really." Good God, what was she saying? Pure nonsense.

The only response was silence. Had she imagined the sigh earlier? Perhaps the crate had been moved by one of the servants.

Perhaps she was a perfect ninny, shouting at an empty corridor and letting foolish fears turn her into a bloodthirsty madwoman.

"Hallo?" she tried again.

Nothing.

Swallowing hard, she drew the canvas back over the desk, gripped the letter opener with a slick palm, and lifted her lantern high. "I'm going to leave this room, now. Be warned that if you have not vacated the corridor, I shall demonstrate my displeasure with piercing directness."

Perhaps she should clarify.

"I shall stab you." She slowly edged around the desk and approached the doorway. "Repeatedly!" She squinted as the light revealed nothing but white walls and oak floors beyond the door. "In dreadfully tender parts! I'll have no mercy!"

Sidling along the casing, she gathered her courage. *No choice but to brave it,* she thought. *No choice. Must go.* With a deep breath, she thrust herself into the corridor, frantically looking right and left.

Empty.

For a moment, air flooded out as relief flooded in. But her nerves continued singing. She sprinted to the main part of the house, locking the connecting set of doors at the end of the passage.

After ensuring her grandmother was safely sipping her evening chocolate in the parlor, she questioned the footmen and maids. None of them knew anything about the repositioned crate, and none of them had seen anything suspicious around the northeast wing. Clarissa assigned the two footmen to guard the connecting doors.

Even with all her precautions, she didn't sleep that night. Partly, it was her nerves, which jangled like a vibrating bell until all she could manage was pacing and wondering whether her "intruder" had been imaginary. But her sleeplessness had another cause.

She couldn't find Dash anywhere.

Normally, the cat curled up on her bed after dinner, waiting for her to tell him about her day. For all his mischievous ways, Dash was a keen listener and, when the mood struck him, a secret cuddler. He'd slept beside her every night since she'd plucked him from a neighbor's woodpile as a kitten.

But not this night. He didn't meow demands at the kitchen door. He didn't leave paw prints in the garden. She searched everywhere and found nothing but dread—sick, cold dread. Her heart screamed that something was wrong. Had he gone hunting and been caught out in the snow? Had he been startled up a tree by their neighbors' boisterous spaniel? Was he in pain?

Morning arrived slowly. The world's new layer of white brightened the cloudy air and muffled sound to a hush. Jittery with exhaustion, she roused the two sleeping footmen slumped in front of the doors and sent one of them to fetch the constable. The other she assigned to search the main house. Then, she gathered two maids in the kitchen and gave instructions for finding Dash.

"We'll begin in the stables. That's where he likes to hunt. If you find him, bring him here immediately." Clarissa swallowed a lump. "He'll be c-cold. We must have blankets at the ready. And warm milk."

Grandmama, who had kept Clarissa company for half the night before succumbing to exhaustion, looked on with a worried gaze. "Any signs of him in the garden this morning, dear?"

Clarissa pressed her lips together and shook her head.

Grandmama squeezed her arm. "Go join the search. I shall warm the milk and greet the constable when he arrives."

With a quick, grateful hug, Clarissa gathered her cloak and led the maids outside. Each of them took a different direction, one maid to the stables, one to the western wood, and Clarissa to the walled garden near the groundskeeper's cottage.

She had to shove open the rusty iron gate, as untended vines fought her entry. The dry crackle of dead leaves resounded oddly inside the enclosure. Carefully, she sidled through the opening. The ground was white. Pristine. No paw tracks or signs of intrusion. She ventured further, noting the old well at the center sounded like it was dripping. It seemed too cold for the snow to be melting already, but perhaps that was simply her dread. It sharpened with every step.

She searched beneath the rose bushes in the far corner before rounding back toward the apple tree. A few waxwings were feeding on rosehips, and a squirrel ran the length of the southern wall. Otherwise, no signs of life occupied the garden. A harsh, icy wind gusted through, billowing snow beneath her cloak.

She turned back toward the gate. The wind died.

The well was still dripping. *Drip. Drip. Drip.*

Sensation trilled over her as if she had metal between her teeth.

Drip. Drip. Drip.

The well bucket should not be dangling that way.

Drip. Drip. Drip.

She'd told the maids a dozen times if they left it hanging through the winter, it would be worthless come spring. But it moved as though it was … full.

Drip. Drip. Drip.

Her heart stuttered.

The rope creaked. The bucket swayed. The drips were not water.

Not water. Not water. Not water.

The drips were dark. Red.

A hard, choking gasp wheezed queerly from her throat. Light flickered. Black spots danced. She blinked and groaned. Blinked and hoped her eyes were wrong. Blinked and prayed she was dreaming.

Please be wrong. Please. Please.

She staggered forward. Pleaded with sobbing wretchedness. Looked inside.

Saw gray fur. And red.

Her stomach thrust itself into her throat. Choking. *Choking.* She sprinted for the gate. Yanked as hard as she could. Stung her hands and scraped her shoulder. She'd just managed to slip through when she lost control, bending in half to empty her stomach of the tea she'd forced down that morning.

The spasms went on forever, but she couldn't waste time. She must return to the house. She must find Grandmama, protect her. She must fetch someone. Who? The constable, perhaps.

Time passed in a haze of running, slipping. Her vision misted. Warped. Her breath was white smoke.

Sound wore down to a faint thread amidst rushing water. Nothing was real. Nothing was real.

Nothing.

She didn't realize she was sobbing until she raced into the parlor.

Grandmama was there conversing with a dull-faced, thick man. Startled, both rushed to her side, asking what had happened.

"The walled garden," she choked. "The well." She choked again, covering her mouth and bending in half.

Grandmama hugged her shoulders and tried again. "What is it, dear? What did you find?"

The constable glowered his confusion but told her to stay there while he looked over the grounds.

He returned an hour later—most of which she spent sobbing into her grandmother's shoulder. His eyes were grim. "I emptied the bucket, Miss Meadows. I know it gave ye a dreadful fright. I'm sorry for that."

She knuckled away her tears and nodded. "What do you intend to do?" Her voice was a ravaged croak.

He frowned. "Do?"

"About the … about the man who … killed him."

His head snapped back. He shot a nervous glance out the window. "I'm afraid I don't know what ye mean."

Grandmama answered for her. "We had an intruder last night, Constable. My granddaughter heard him. She saw that a crate in my late husband's study had been moved. I explained all this to you earlier."

He nodded, fidgeting with his collar and straightening his coat. "I recall what ye said, m'lady."

"And? Did you search the entire house?"

"We did. No signs of an intruder were found. Ye've said ye haven't noticed anything missing. 'Twould be an odd sort of thief to break into a fine house like this without botherin' to nick anything." He rubbed his nape. "Perhaps one of yer servants has been playing 'lord of the manor' and didn't want ye to know."

Grandmama straightened and tightened her arm around Clarissa's shoulders. "Young man, are you implying we are *imagining* a threat where one does not exist?"

"Ye were frightened. Only natural, ye bein' ladies and all."

Clarissa's temper caught. She kept her eyes on the constable while addressing her grandmother. "Did you show him the letters, Grandmama?"

"Indeed."

"And what did he say?"

"He thought you must be quite lovely to garner such *passionate* regard from a suitor."

Shaking her head, Clarissa glared at the constable until his cheeks turned a rusty hue. "Lady Darnham has explained precisely whom we suspect has been lurking about. And now my …" She lost her air for a moment. "My cat has been …"

"Dreadfully sorry, miss. I truly am." The constable gave an infuriating shrug. "But that might've been done by a fox."

Her chest tightened. Burned. "A fox."

"I've seen what they do to hens."

"Really? And do they deposit hens neatly inside a well bucket when they're finished with their day's work?"

Another uncomfortable shrug. "Even if you're right, there'd be nothin' I could do. Nothin's been stolen. Cats ain't livestock. And there's no laws been broken. If he attacks ye, perhaps—"

"If he attacks me," she snapped, "I'll fare no better than what you found in that bucket, Constable."

He grimaced. "I'm sorry."

Grandmama lost her patience and ordered him to leave. When he was gone, she spent several minutes denouncing the feckless failures of British policing while vowing to write the magistrates at her earliest opportunity.

Clarissa wrapped her arms across her body and rocked. She did it automatically, as she'd done in the months following her parents' deaths. She'd been eleven at the time. She remembered how Grandpapa would wrap her in a blanket and put her on his lap. He'd smelled of pipe tobacco—a blend of spice and smoke, rich and faintly floral. More than once, his patient strength had lulled her to sleep. The rocking hadn't comforted her. He had. But he'd been gone for ages.

"I've known two of the three magistrates since they were in leading strings. I'll give them a thorough dressing down for this appalling—"

"We must leave, Grandmama," she whispered. "We're not safe here."

A pause. Then, a gentle hand stroked her hair. "Where shall we go?"

Clarissa's heart squeezed as she clasped her grandmother's delicate fingers. "North. We'll sell the brooch. Hire a carriage. Francis suggested spending Christmas with Kate. He promised to join us. I wasn't certain we'd wish to do more traveling in winter, but I think it's best."

Another stroke of her hair and a kiss at her temple. "Very well, dear. We'll go." Grandmama slid her hand over Clarissa's and squeezed.

She barely felt it. Couldn't feel anything, really. Everything was … numb.

"We'll go to Scotland. And pray he never finds us."

Chapter One

February 16, 1827
Rowan House
Glenscannadoo, Scotland

The handsomest man she'd ever seen spun Clarissa Meadows around the drawing room like a dandelion on an elegant breeze. Golden hair, laughing blue eyes, and perfect features filled her vision while a waltz lifted the air around them.

How long since she'd been this happy? Not for months. Not since London.

"Shall we dare a scandalous embrace, my darling?" Francis waggled golden eyebrows.

She clutched his upper arms dramatically. Together, they spun and spun, approaching the pianoforte. He clasped her waist firmly with one arm. They linked hands. The waltz reached a crescendo. Clarissa's face, hot with joy and exertion, paused near his cheek. He flourished with one hand while presenting her with the other. On a whim, she rose up on her toes and spun, arms extended and head aswirl.

The final, pounding notes of the waltz played while she ended her spin in a deep, sweeping curtsy.

Francis crowed and applauded loudly. So did Kate, their dearest friend, who'd been playing her new pianoforte so that Clarissa and Francis could enjoy a dance.

Others in the room—Clarissa's grandmother and Francis's valet—joined in the applause. Clarissa's cheeks prickled more than usual at the praise.

"Well done, indeed!" Francis's grin was blindingly beautiful. "You've been practicing without me, I see."

"Oh, no," she replied breathlessly. "That is, yes, I have. But only because you were unavailable. You must know you are my favorite partner."

Clarissa only practiced ballet alone, for it was a foreign sort of dancing unsuited to London ballrooms. But they weren't in England. They were in Scotland.

And Clarissa hadn't felt this free in a long while.

Kate rose from the piano bench to loop her arm through Clarissa's. "Now, you must teach me."

Concern tugged at Clarissa's heart. "Are you certain? You're paler than you should be."

It was true. Before she'd become Kate MacPherson, Lady Katherine Huxley had been the daughter of an English earl, raised in the genteel warmth of her family's home in Nottinghamshire. Last autumn, she'd come to Scotland to visit her brother, John Huxley, who'd married a funny, fiery Highland lass named Annie Tulloch MacPherson.

Through a series of unusual circumstances, Kate soon found herself married to Annie's stepbrother, a scarred, towering Scot named Broderick MacPherson. And while Kate had fallen madly in love with Broderick, and he with her, he'd been locked in a battle with a dangerous enemy. The man who'd once falsely imprisoned and tortured Broderick had escaped jail, fled to Edinburgh, and eventually sought to use Kate to further torment Broderick. The villain had abducted and nearly killed her before Broderick and his brothers came to her rescue.

Three months had passed since Kate's horrifying ordeal, which she'd recounted to Clarissa upon their arrival on Christmas day. The thought of slim, lovely Kate being sealed inside a cask and left to die alone in the dark still gave Clarissa nightmares. She couldn't imagine how Kate must feel.

Well, perhaps she could. Terror had a familiar tinge.

Kate waved away her worry. "As I explained to Broderick this morning, my pallor may be blamed on my Huxley ancestry. We are notoriously milk-skinned and prone to flushing. Vigorous exertion can only do me good."

Francis chuckled. "Vigorous exertion. Is that what you told him? Little wonder you were late to breakfast."

Kate swatted his elbow. "Oh, do stop teasing. George!"

The brown-haired valet reading beside Clarissa's grandmother raised his head.

"Come play for us, won't you?" Kate beckoned. "We must have music, and you play better than Francis."

As the valet crossed the room and sat on the bench, Francis's gaze fixed upon him with glowing regard. Clarissa's heart warmed at the sight. She'd waited years to see her dear friend in love.

Kate tugged her to the center of the room between two tartan-upholstered sofas. "Now, show me what you've learnt from Mademoiselle Durant."

Clarissa glanced around the room. Only Grandmama watched them, and as usual, she nodded encouragement. Clarissa swallowed before daringly raising her blue gauze skirts above her ankles and tucking fabric into the sash at her waist. She found a downbeat in the music then rose up on her toes and executed an arabesque followed by a pirouette.

"Position your feet just so. You see?" she instructed. "If you center your balance properly, the transition into your next step is a simple matter." She demonstrated again, and a third time.

Kate attempted to mirror her spin twice but lost her balance both times. Clarissa steadied her then performed the combination again. "Proper positioning enables a full turn." She added a second turn. "Or more."

Blowing upward, Kate tried again, only to stagger and collide with Clarissa halfway through. They both laughed helplessly.

A deep voice came from the doorway behind them. "Ah, ye're a bonnie sight with that color in yer cheeks, *mo chridhe*."

This time, it was Clarissa who stumbled. Together, they spun to see Kate's husband entering the room.

"Miss Meadows is a fine instructor," he continued. "But mayhap ye should let me help steady ye, eh?"

Broderick MacPherson was a foot taller than most men, wide-shouldered and heavily muscled. And scarred. Badly scarred. One eye was covered with a leather patch. The rest of his face bore slashing ridges and jagged lines. Yet, his remaining eye was as dark and beautiful as his hair. The brown-black gaze glimmered with heat whenever it landed upon Kate.

Broderick, however, was not the man who made Clarissa gawp like a moonstruck girl. Broderick didn't make her heart stop and start again at twice the tempo. Broderick wasn't even the tallest man in the room.

No, that man was his older brother, Campbell, who entered behind him like a great, mountainous shadow.

With fluttering fingers, Clarissa tugged her skirts free to fall to their original length. Then, she brushed a blonde curl from her eye and tried with all her might not to look at him.

Looking at Campbell MacPherson, she'd learned, erased her good sense.

Kate, meanwhile, dashed across the room to greet her husband, leaving Clarissa awkwardly stranded.

Grandmama came to her rescue. "Clarissa, dear, might you pour me another cup of tea? I fear I've caught a chill."

Pressing her lips together, she nodded and crossed to where Grandmama sat beside a window. Unfortunately, she passed within a few feet of Campbell. His nearness made her insides heat and quake.

He was impossibly huge—nearly nine inches above six feet and as muscular as a thoroughbred trained for Ascot. He had his brother's brown-black hair and eyes, similarly heavy bones, and broad frame. But whereas Broderick was scarred and the other two MacPherson brothers, Rannoch and Alexander, were quite handsome, Campbell's face resembled a granite cliff. His jaw was too square, his brows too heavy, and his expression too forbidding for true handsomeness.

So, why did the sight of him reduce her to blithering idiocy? She hadn't the faintest idea. All she knew was that when he was nearby, she was better off saying nothing.

She poured Grandmama's tea and sank onto the chair beside her.

"Broderick said ye wished to move the pianoforte," Campbell said to Kate. "Where would ye like it, lass?"

Oh, heavens. How that low, resonant, brogue-lilted voice made her toes curl.

Kate answered, but Clarissa scarcely noticed. A mountainous shadow crossed the floor in front of her. She inhaled the scents of pine, wool, rain, and some earthy spice. Moments later, she heard his calm instructions from the corner near the pianoforte.

She couldn't help herself. She glanced up—and gasped.

He was lifting the blasted instrument by himself.

Very well, not *entirely* by himself. He had help from Francis, George, Broderick, and the ginger-haired footman, Stuart MacDonnell. But half of the weight rested in Campbell MacPherson's massive, capable hands.

Clarissa's heart pounded. Her belly trembled as she watched the muscles in his thick neck and bulging arms work. Veins stood out. A hard jaw flexed. The weight of the thing clearly strained him, yet as gently as a mother lowered her babe into a cradle, he placed his sister-in-law's prized pianoforte into her preferred position two feet closer to the fireplace.

Kate cheered and thanked the men. Broderick teased Kate that he'd demand a steep price for his services. Francis joked about having done most of the work. George shyly suggested adding casters to the fluted legs.

Campbell, as usual, said nothing.

Clarissa stared, tracing his heavy brows and square jaw, admiring the size of his hands. They were unusually large but not clumsy, as one might expect. Long fingers and thick wrists were balanced by sensitivity of movement. She'd watched him carve a bird from a piece of wood once. The memory made her tingle until she squirmed in her seat.

"Have some tea, dear. It will help."

Vaguely, she nodded to her grandmother and fumbled with the pot on the tray. She sloshed scalding water on her thumb. "Drat," she hissed. Yet even the pain was not enough to distract her.

"I once painted a portrait of my dear, sweet Alfie," Grandmama said, sipping her tea. "Watercolors." Lately, Grandmama enjoyed sharing fond recollections of her marriage to Clarissa's grandfather.

Clarissa murmured, "I thought you hated watercolors."

"Oh, I do. Messy business. Too imprecise. In the end, his face resembled a trampled peach and his hair a lazy caterpillar."

Clarissa blew cool air on her stinging thumb, debating how many yards of gray wool it had taken to make Campbell MacPherson's coat. It was well-fitted. Sturdy. Far from dandy-fine, but impressively made. Like him.

"Of course, my work would have been better if I were more *attentive*. And I might have been more attentive if I had been less *infatuated*. Do you intend to drink that tea, dear?"

Dutifully, Clarissa raised the cup to her lips without looking. Fortunately, it had cooled since scalding her thumb. She watched Campbell speaking with

Broderick. He murmured something and clapped his brother's shoulder before striding toward the entrance.

Toward her position.

Directly in her direction.

Oh, dear. Her eyes widened. Her cheeks burned. She dropped her gaze to her cup.

"Lady Darnham," he greeted as he passed. "Miss Meadows." His low rumble sent heat shimmering through her middle.

For pity's sake, the man scarcely knew she was alive. Why did he make her so nervous? She forced herself to meet his gaze. It was a long way up.

"Mr. MacPherson," she murmured after clearing her throat. "We were just admiring your capable hands." Oh, God, why had she said that? "Capable of lifting an enormous instrument." Her cheeks burned. "That is, such a sizable instrument must be a strain." Drat! It was happening again. She must stop. *Must. Stop. Talking.* "So much wood." She couldn't stop it. "But you've large hands and … handled yourself … quite well."

His mouth quirked and a brow twitched. But he simply nodded as though she hadn't mortified herself before him yet again.

She tried one last time to salvage a shred of dignity. "I'll certainly know whom to call upon, should I require hands of superior size to position me properly for playing my own instrument."

Grandmama coughed on a sip of tea.

Campbell blinked.

It took several seconds for Clarissa to realize what she'd said. Her eyes flew wide. Her entire being lit on fire—cheeks, throat, bosom, soul. Damn her foolish mouth!

Grandmama attempted a rescue. "Are you staying for dinner, Mr. MacPherson?"

He answered, but Clarissa couldn't digest the response. She suspected her brain had been damaged by the inferno of embarrassment. He exited the room. Several moments passed before she managed to breathe.

"Well, now," Grandmama said casually. "Rarely have I encountered a man less flappable. Perhaps the Duke of Wellington. But I often wondered if his grace's aplomb was simply deafness caused by cannon fire. Do you suppose Mr. MacPherson was a soldier? War does harden a man." She paused. "No, dear, not in that sense."

"Dear God, Grandmama." Clarissa's groan wheezed past a tight throat. She covered her eyes with shaking fingers. "It happened again."

She patted Clarissa's arm and pushed her hand back to her lap. "He scarcely took note of it. Unflappable

Scotsman." She shook her head and sipped her tea. "A rare breed, indeed."

It took a half-hour for Clarissa to recover. By then, she and Francis were the only ones remaining in the drawing room.

Francis sat beside her, drinking tepid tea and musing about whether Clarissa looked better in blue gauze or pink satin. "I know we chose the pink for your ballgown, darling, but the blue does wonders for those glorious eyes of yours." He pulled a squinting expression. "Blue satin. It is the only satisfactory compromise."

She rested her head against his shoulder. "I humiliated myself again, Francis. I don't know what's wrong with me."

"Nothing whatever. Apart from your distaste for German opera. That is pure madness."

"I've never had such trouble conversing with a man."

"No, indeed. If anything, words flow from your sweet lips in rather greater abundance than most women."

"Are you saying I talk too much?"

"One man's flood is another man's trickle. Besides, it is not the quantity but the content of your conversation that has you fretting, yes? What was it this time? No, no, let me guess. You made reference to his expertise in plowing again. 'Deep, hard furrows' and 'hot, driving stamina.' Wasn't that what you said across the breakfast table last week?" He chuckled. "Still trying to puzzle out how you acquired your expertise in … farming."

"Do be kind, Francis. It has been a trying day."

"You worry far too much about what one oversized Scot thinks of you. He's your friend's husband's brother. You have a firmer connection to your grandmother's daft footman."

"Hmm. Fair point."

"Besides," he murmured, kissing the top of her head. "You're going to marry me. So, none of it matters."

She squeezed his wrist. "Grandmama doesn't think it's a good idea."

"I know."

"I'm not certain I do, either," she whispered.

Silence. Then, he laced his fingers through hers. "I adore you, my darling."

She smiled. "And I you."

"You must marry. So must I."

"Yes."

"I refuse to leave you unprotected." His tone hardened as his hand squeezed hers. "Not when my name could mean the difference between your safety and—"

"What if he comes for you?"

"I may not look it, but I'm excellent with a rapier."

"Francis," she chided. *"I* can defeat you with a rapier."

"Nonsense. The incident with my pantaloons was pure chance. One more button, and I fear we both might have been left red-cheeked. In more ways than one."

She laughed until her belly hurt. Then, her throat abruptly closed, and she had to cover her mouth to keep the sobs at bay.

Francis gathered her into his arms. "Shh. Everything will be grand. You'll see."

Tears leaked forth, spilling without her permission. "I can't do this to you and George. I won't allow you to make such a sacrifice for me."

"Don't be foolish. You'll be safe. That's the important bit."

"We don't *know* that." She pulled back, aching as she saw the stubborn affection in his eyes. "Trading your safety for mine is a poor bargain. And what if our marriage spoils your happiness?" She shook her head. "No. I waited too long to see it."

Indeed, she'd waited years. Four, to be precise. Back then, in Clarissa's sixth London season, she'd been friendless, plump, and pitiful. Her grandmother and her cat had been her closest companions. Her next closest had been the walls of assembly rooms and drawing rooms across Mayfair—until Francis Prescott, Viscount Teversham, had delivered her a cup of dreadful orange punch, sat beside her on a blue settee, and remarked as though they were long friends, "If Mrs. Witherspoon wishes to discourage drunkenness at her ball, perhaps she should offer more palatable lemonade." He'd emptied a flask of brandy into his own cup and taken several sips.

Unaccustomed to male attention, Clarissa had glanced around to see if he'd meant to play a jest. Handsome young lords simply didn't approach orphaned spinsters with few prospects and the stingiest of dowries.

"I—I believe it's meant to be Seville orange punch." She'd discreetly sniffed the cup he'd handed her. He'd added brandy. "Mrs. Witherspoon grows them in her orangery."

"Ah. That explains it. Only an imbecile would add ground mace to lemonade. But then, only an imbecile would neglect to offer brandy. Intoxication enhances both flavor and frivolity. Everyone knows that."

She'd found herself chuckling at his droll tone. "Everyone except Mrs. Witherspoon, evidently."

He'd smiled a tragic, dazzling smile. "Miss Meadows, yes? I'm Teversham." He'd clinked the rim of his cup against hers. "Pleasure."

For the rest of the season, they'd been boon companions. Francis had kept her company while slyly commenting on this countess's coiffure or that baronet's mistress. He'd insisted on dancing with her at least once per party—even the ones without music. Together, they'd defied the ton's expectations, enjoying one another so thoroughly that speculation about marriage had begun to spread.

The following year, Kate Huxley had joined Clarissa along the wall and promptly befriended them both. Matchmaking speculation had shifted immediately to Kate and Francis, but the three of them had only ever been friends. The best of friends.

Because Francis didn't want either of them.

His disinterest in Clarissa had been understandable—by then, she'd had seven seasons and no offers. Attic trunks were less firmly on the shelf. But Kate? Kate was lovely. Bright and pretty and kind, her only sin had been her sister's scandal a few years earlier. With curling brown hair and dancing eyes, a slender shape and charming laugh, Kate should have been the diamond of the season. She should have drawn

Francis's eye like a glimmering jewel drew a thief. Instead, she'd become another platonic companion.

At Kate's insistence—and to Clarissa's delight—the three of them spent most afternoons practicing dances in Clarissa's drawing room. Kate had even arranged for Clarissa to receive private lessons from a French ballerina, Mademoiselle Durant. With so much additional exercise, Clarissa's figure had slimmed until she'd required new gowns. Francis and Kate had helped with that, too, advising her to hire a new dressmaker and choose more flattering colors. Before long, Clarissa was drawing attention from suitors who'd never before glanced in her direction. Kate also gained popularity as her sister's scandal faded from memory.

Yet, never once did Francis look upon Kate or Clarissa—or any other woman—with male interest.

Clarissa had been confused at first. She'd watched him carefully at the German operas and Shakespearean plays they attended, noting how much more raptly he admired the male performers than the females. The implications had shocked her. But once she'd realized how lonely such peculiarities must make him, she'd grown determined to see him happy.

Because, despite his brilliant smiles and lively humor, he hadn't been. Not in all the time she'd known him.

Then, last spring while they were enjoying tea in his garden, she'd noticed the way his eyes trailed after his footman, George Parker. And the longing she'd expected to see aimed toward Kate had finally emerged. Clarissa had pulled Francis aside and advised that he elevate George to be his valet.

Startled, Francis had turned ruddy and asked why.

"Because a valet's duties place him always at his employer's side. I suspect Mr. Parker would shine in such a role. And his … attentiveness would surely be a boon." She'd paused, wondering how much to leave unspoken. Finally, hating the turmoil and misery in his eyes, she'd edged toward plain speaking. "I should like to see you happy for once, dearest Francis."

His brow had crumpled on a grimace. "I don't know what you mean."

"Yes. You do."

A fortnight later, with Kate adding her encouragement, Francis had named George his valet, and within a month, the shadows had left his eyes. At last, his brilliant smile had been genuine.

Was she eager to be the fifth wheel in Francis and George's happiness? Not if there was any other way.

Now, Francis's mouth tightened into a grim line. Blue eyes a shade lighter than her own narrowed with protective anger. "I'll call him out. Old-fashioned, I grant you. But he'll face me or be hunted forever."

"You cannot."

"I will."

"No. He is an expert marksman. Legendary, in fact. You'd either be shot or charged for dueling."

"I don't give a bloody damn."

She gripped his hand in both of hers. "I do. If you were harmed, it would devastate me." A tear slipped free. "I couldn't bear it, Francis."

He cursed beneath his breath and offered her his handkerchief. "Has it occurred to you that I feel much the same? God, Clarissa. Had I known what he was doing before I left England, I'd have married you straight away. Or he'd be dead. Likely both. I might not be much of a shot, but I have funds, and those can pay for men with better aim and fewer scruples."

She started to answer that she wouldn't want him to commit murder on her behalf, but Kate's housekeeper entered with a letter for Francis. As he opened it, Clarissa helped Mrs. Grant tidy up the tea tray. By the time she turned around, his face was stark white.

"What is it?"

His mouth was grim. "My father."

Francis's father was the Earl of Medford. Lord Medford despised his son, and if it wouldn't have caused a massive scandal, he likely would have disowned him long ago. Of course, he'd done much worse in Francis's youth.

"What's he done now?" she prompted.

"He—he's dead."

She collapsed onto her chair. "How?"

"Apoplexy. He was at the hunting lodge in Yorkshire. Housed one of his mistresses there, if I recall."

"He had more than one?"

Francis rubbed a hand over his mouth. "Several. I always thought the blackguard too cruel to attract anyone. After my mother … well. Astonishing what a title compensates for."

Clarissa's heart squeezed and ached. She slid her arms around him and drew him close. "I'm so sorry, Francis."

He nodded against her shoulder.

"I'll fetch George, shall I?"

"I must return to England."

"Yes, but—"

"Come with me. We can marry here before we depart. I'll keep you safe—"

"You have enough burdens without adding mine. You must settle your father's estate. Speak with his solicitors. See to the duties of your new title." She paused. "Your mother will need you."

For the first time since the letter arrived, his calm cracked. He breathed heavily and groaned. "Mother. Oh, God."

"She'll be fine. Better, even. With Medford … gone."

His eyes squeezed closed.

"And you mustn't worry about me," she continued, forcing her voice to steady. "He hasn't found us here. It is still winter. He's probably lost track of us. Perhaps it will be enough. Perhaps the threat was over the moment I entered Scotland."

"Stubborn, darling girl. We must marry." He glanced at the letter and grimaced. "I'm an earl, now. Earls need an heir."

"Perhaps. But we needn't be hasty about it."

"Why wait?"

"Because when you read about your father's death, you longed for one person at your side. Only one. Who was that?"

His jaw flexed. "George."

"Quite right. Let's douse one fire at a time, hmm? Now, I shall go fetch him. Then, the two of you will pack your belongings and return to England. I assure you, you'll travel faster without a spinster and her aged grandmother in tow."

He kissed her forehead and whispered, "If I am to have a wife at all, she must be you, for I cannot bear the thought of being leg-shackled to anyone else."

Her heart squeezed. "Heaven knows I can think of no better man to stand by my side. And perhaps we will marry eventually." She nudged him with her shoulder. "Or perhaps you'll decide you want no wife at all. And your cousin will inherit the title. And you must endure a long, blissful existence with the one person who brings you happiness. How dreadful."

His smile was brief and sad. "Very well. I'll go without you—for now. Once I've settled matters at home, I'll return to fetch you. But I have one condition."

"Yes?"

"You must tell Kate and Broderick everything."

She winced. "I can't. They've already suffered—"

"I'll not leave you unprotected. The MacPhersons are good at this sort of thing. There are four of them, five if you count their father, along with dozens of loyal men who work for them. They can and will keep you safe, but only if they understand the threat. Now, I'll have your promise, or I'll have your hand in marriage this very day. Which shall it be?"

Sighing, she squeezed his hand. The day Francis Prescott had handed her a cup of revoltingly sour punch was the day her life had transformed for the better. "I shall tell them everything." She kissed his hand before rising to fetch George.

"Before dinner!" he called after her.

But she didn't answer. She was too busy wondering how to tell a woman who had survived one horror that another had already begun.

Chapter Two

Clarissa intended to tell Kate and Broderick everything at dinner, but Grandmama was feeling poorly, and Clarissa spent the evening tending to her. The following day, she tried again at breakfast, but Kate complained of nightmares and, judging from her glassy-eyed pallor, further distress would have been a cruelty.

Twice more Clarissa tried and failed to tell them the truth of why she'd come to Scotland.

Why she hadn't left after two months.

Why the very thought of returning to Ellery Hall made her stomach draw up in a nauseous quake.

Nearly a week after Francis and George's departure, however, fate forced her hand.

"Here we are, yer ladyship," said Mrs. Grant as she served Grandmama a steaming bowl of soup in the cozy parlor that overlooked the loch behind the house. "A fine bit of Scottish fare'll have ye feelin' braw in nae time."

Grandmama sneezed into her handkerchief and attempted a brave smile. "You're a dear, Mrs. Grant."

The stout, rust-haired housekeeper beamed. "That's McInnes's best skink, now. He only cooks it for his favorite lasses."

Grandmama took a careful bite. "Ah, splendid."

Mrs. Grant nodded her approval and left the parlor to fetch more tea.

Clarissa paused in opening her correspondence to fuss with Grandmama's lap blanket. "You can't taste it, can you?"

Grandmama's sniff was clogged, her sigh wheezing. "Not a jot."

Worry sank tight claws around her heart. "The physician's tonic doesn't seem to be helping. Perhaps we should accept assistance from Mrs. MacBean." The ancient Scotswoman with the wild shrub of hair and milky left eye claimed to be a "maker of potions and cures for ailments of every sort." She'd seemed slightly daft and possibly mad to Clarissa. But she was a friend of the MacPhersons, and Kate assured her that Mrs. MacBean knew what she was about.

"I'll be fine, dear." Grandmama sneezed, and her cap slid to the side. She tugged it back into place and attempted another bite of soup. "What does Darnham have to say?"

Clarissa glanced down at Cousin Rupert's letter and sighed. "He'll be spending the summer in Brighton with a friend who has shown interest in purchasing Ellery Hall."

Grandmama stiffened.

"Perhaps I should have accepted Francis's offer to wed straight away," Clarissa murmured, folding Rupert's letter and reaching for the next envelope in the basket by her hip. "He'll take excellent care of us both."

A soggy sniff. "My dear, sweet Alfie once traveled to Luxembourg to negotiate the sale of a frigate he'd won in a hand of whist."

Well accustomed to Grandmama's non sequiturs, Clarissa replied, "Isn't Luxembourg a landlocked region? A frigate would be rather a large ship for a place without a seaport. Or a navy. Or even the need of a navy, given how small—"

"Your grandfather was a superior negotiator. France and England were at war, as usual. The crown valued his services. That is all you need know, dear."

Grandmama dabbed her nose and continued, "In any event, he was absent for three months." She shook her head. "Longest months of my life."

Struggling to understand the message Grandmama wished to convey, Clarissa dropped an unopened letter back into the basket, folded her hands in her lap, and waited.

"Nine months after his return, your mother was born." Another stuffy sniff. "And I never again permitted him an absence greater than a fortnight." Grandmama narrowed watery blue eyes upon her. "A good marriage is more than pleasantries over breakfast and a mutual fondness for waltzing, Clarissa."

She sighed. "I know, Grandmama."

"Wedding a man whose *absence* would not be three months but, rather, a lifetime is hardly a fitting solution to your woes."

"What would you suggest, then?"

"Marrying a man you fancy."

Clarissa braced against the urge to squirm. "I don't fancy anyone." She avoided Grandmama's dubious gaze. "And even if I did, he'd have to be mad to take me on."

"Some men have broad shoulders. Perhaps such a man only needs a bit of encouragement."

"I'm eight-and-twenty. No dowry to speak of. No important connections. I've nothing to offer a man apart from burdens and risk." She shook her head. "No, Francis is the sensible choice."

"It only seems that way now because of your circumstances. Perhaps the answer lies in changing them."

"How?"

"The Bow Street runner you spoke with at Lady Wallingham's house party last summer. Mr. Hawthorn. He seemed a capable sort. Could we not hire him?"

"With what funds?" Clarissa gestured to Rupert's letter. "As matters stand, we'll be fortunate to remain at Ellery. For a Bow Street runner to do what we require, the cost would be grand, indeed. Mr. Hawthorn is a charming man, but I doubt he'd spend months away from his new bride to offer me protection free of charge." She huffed out a despairing chuckle. "Assuming he accepted the assignment rather than suggesting I'm imagining things."

Grandmama sighed, her shoulders curling inward again. She resumed eating her soup.

Clarissa had won the argument, but she wished she hadn't. Grandmama was right—marrying Francis might be a dreadful mistake. But what choice did she have? They couldn't remain Kate's guests forever. They couldn't afford to hire anyone. She couldn't ask Francis to pay for a Bow Street runner when he'd already paid for all her new gowns, along with the lady's maid she'd been forced to dismiss for the girl's own safety. How much more could she ask him to do for her sake? He'd already given her too much.

At least if they were married, she'd feel less guilty about accepting his help. Husbands provided for their wives, after all.

Kate entered the parlor, looking fresh and pink-cheeked following her morning ride. After inquiring about Grandmama's health, the brunette beauty declared, "Scottish winters are too long. There. I've said it."

Behind her entered the half-blind Mrs. MacBean wearing a green tartan gown beneath a wool wrap and a belted leather pouch. The old woman lowered the wrap off her wild shrub of hair and blinked, her eyelids out of rhythm with one another. "Dinnae go complainin'. Ere long, the midges will be swarmin', and ye'll be whinging about the itch."

Behind Mrs. MacBean hovered the solemn, long-nosed Magdalene Cuthbert. A friend of Broderick's from Edinburgh—Kate had been vague about the connection—Miss Cuthbert had accompanied the MacPhersons back to the glen after the dreadful incident in December. She'd been helping tend to Broderick's wounded brother, Alexander, ever since. From what Clarissa had gathered, Alexander could try the patience of a saint, so it was a good thing Magdalene Cuthbert had such a nunlike air about her. If his occasional bellowing from the attic bedchamber was any indication, she'd need the piety.

Now, Miss Cuthbert's concerned gray eyes settled on Grandmama, who coughed miserably. "Forgive me, my lady, but that cough still sounds dreadful."

Clarissa answered, "The physician gave her a tonic, but it hasn't helped."

While Miss Cuthbert fussed over Grandmama, Mrs. MacBean harrumphed. "The doctor from Inverness?"

Clarissa nodded.

"Och, lass. He'll do naught but feed ye laudanum then bill ye for the nap." The old woman dug inside her leather pouch. "Here." She thrust a small brown bottle beneath Clarissa's nose. "Tastes vile, but 'twill quicken yer womb, sure as tomorrow's sunrise."

Accepting the bottle automatically, Clarissa blinked when she realized what Mrs. MacBean had said. *Quicken her womb?* "Er, I … I am unmarried, not in need of … that is, we require a tonic for my *grandmother's* ailment." She nodded to where Miss Cuthbert murmured gentle questions and pressed a wrist to Grandmama's forehead. "Even with the laudanum, she's scarcely able to sleep."

Mrs. MacBean sat on the adjacent settee and squinted into the distance. "He willnae be easy at first, ye ken." She tapped her own head with her knuckles. "Stubborn as bedrock, aye. But he needs ye more than ye need him. 'Tis good ye've come, lass."

Clarissa glanced across the room at Kate, who was pouring tea. No help from that quarter. Was the woman referring to Francis? But then, Francis wasn't stubborn. He'd always been quite reasonable.

She met Mrs. MacBean's peculiar gaze. The milky eye wandered away from its sharper companion. Often, the woman appeared either daft or disoriented, as though she was listening to two conversations at once and finding both incomprehensible.

Clarissa tried again. "I'm afraid I don't know who 'he' is, Mrs. MacBean."

"Aye, ye do. Ye kenned him straight away." The sharp eye fixed upon her, flashing strangely beneath a frown. "Ye'll need all his strength. The wolf's found ye."

A trilling sensation, cold and ominous, made her straighten. "W-wolf?"

"The animal's mind is purely dark, now. It cannae see what's true. The chase has it in a frenzy."

Oh, God. How did she know? Clarissa still hadn't told Kate, and she'd certainly never said anything to Mrs. MacBean. "Is he nearby?" she whispered.

The old woman shook her head as though waking from a nap. "Who?"

Clarissa wondered which of them was the mad one in this conversation. "The wolf."

"Och, lass. There are no wolves in Scotland." She blinked again then dug into her pouch. "Here." She dangled an ivory charm on a leather string. "Best ye wear it 'neath yer bodice for now. If yer man catches a glimpse, he'll resist ye harder. We cannae have that. Nae time to waste. Ye're near thirty, I reckon."

Clarissa paused, wondering what the devil they were talking about. "Eight-and-twenty, actually."

"Aye. Best ye wear it *all* the time. Good for quick breedin'." The charm swung wildly as she waved a finger to indicate Clarissa's hips. "Quick birthin', too. Ye'll be thankin' me for that soon enough. Many, many bairns. Some men wait too long for supper and gorge themselves like starvin' beasties. Aye, ye'll be occupied with that one for a goodly while."

Reluctantly, Clarissa accepted the oddly shaped charm. It wasn't wood, but bone or perhaps antler. The two-inch triangle had a set of curving horns with rings around them. In the center was a face, but it resembled a goat more than a stag. And some kind of worm wrapped around the whole design.

"Thank you?" Clarissa struggled for a polite smile. "It's … lovely."

"Nae need to fib. 'Tis far from the bonniest of the lot, but for begettin' wee ones and keepin' yer flock safe, ye cannae do better."

Clarissa was almost relieved the woman was daft. For a moment, at the mention of a wolf giving chase, she'd thought perhaps … but no. Mrs. MacBean was just a kindly old Scotswoman with good intentions and addled wits. The talk of quickening wombs and hungry men should have told her that much.

Out of nine seasons on the marriage mart, she'd had five serious suitors and two offers of marriage. One of the offers had been from Francis. The other had been from a madman.

Her prospects for imminent womb-quickening were rather bleak.

Kate delivered her a cup of tea and settled beside Mrs. MacBean. "You're not frightening her, are you, Mrs. MacBean?"

"Och, no. I didnae say a word about what it's like when yer man's delayed the tuppin' too long."

Kate's eyes rounded. Her cheeks pinkened. "Oh." She shot Clarissa a nervous glance. "Oh, dear."

"Though, butter can be a help."

"Dear God."

"Aye, and a nip of whisky. Ye *drink* the whisky, to be clear. The butter, on the other hand—"

Kate shot to her feet. "Mrs. MacBean, would you care to have a look at our new pianoforte? Broderick had it shipped from Edinburgh."

"She'll discover the truth sooner or later, lass." The old woman leaned in close to Clarissa. "A proper soak'll fix ye right up. Dinnae fash."

Miss Cuthbert beckoned Mrs. MacBean to speak with Grandmama, and Kate apologized to Clarissa.

"The first time I met Mrs. MacBean, it was similarly perplexing." Sinking down upon the settee, Kate winced and drank her tea. "I'd hoped you'd experience a bit less of her … eccentricity."

Clarissa tried to smile, but it was a shaky effort. "If she can help Grandmama, she may give me all the charms and fertility tonics she likes."

Kate froze, her cup hovering near her lips, her eyes rounding over the brim. "She gave you a charm?"

Clarissa held out her hand.

Kate released a breath and set her tea aside. Then, she eyed the charm as though it might come to life and bite her nose. "Did she, by chance, say whom you will marry?"

Clarissa tucked the items into the basket of correspondence. "Marry? No. She seems keen for me to bear children, but—"

A sharp, wheezing cough burst from the corner where Miss Cuthbert and Mrs. MacBean fussed over Grandmama. Before Clarissa could rise, Miss Cuthbert calmly explained, "All is well, Miss Meadows. Her ladyship will recover. But I think a wee bit of rest would be a good idea."

After Miss Cuthbert took Grandmama up to her bedchamber and Mrs. MacBean left to gather ingredients for a "proper tincture," Clarissa sighed to Kate, "I cannot lose her. I simply cannot."

"Oh, dearest. You shan't. She has the best of care, and the two of you may stay as long as you please."

Clarissa squeezed Kate's hand and knew it was time to tell her friend the truth. She opened her mouth to do just that when Mrs. Grant entered, asking about dinner. Kate excused herself to speak with the housekeeper, and Clarissa glanced down into the basket. Perhaps she should finish reading her correspondence.

Anything to delay.

Gritting her teeth, she nudged aside Mrs. MacBean's strange, triangular charm and Rupert's galling letter then gathered up the last three envelopes.

The first was from Mademoiselle Durant, a lovely message of encouragement accompanied by sketches of new ballet combinations to try. Clarissa made a note to write her later that evening.

The second letter was from Francis. She gasped as she read his account of a mishap on the road outside Glasgow. Apparently, a stray shot had fired into their coach, grazing George's arm. Francis assured her George was well, and that it was likely "careless hunters outsmarted by Scottish fowl." But the incident made her queasy. Cold.

The third letter, buried as it was beneath the others, didn't alarm her at first.

Then, her fingers brushed the looping swoosh of the "M" leading her name. The first ripple of horror bloomed.

Miss Clarissa Meadows

Glenscannadoo, Inverness-shire

Every muscle froze. Her eyes felt stuck open. She stared down at the simple, looping script. The letters were small. Tight. Every so often, there was a thick drop of ink, as though he'd paused while his tension built.

In her ears, silence whooshed like wind through a cavern.

She forced herself to break the seal. Red wax neatly pressed. Fine paper, crisp and soft.

She forced herself to read his words. Knowing what was to come. Knowing this was the end.

My darling Clarissa,

Your vanity must want stroking, fair one. When we marry, you'll cease these coy games. Oh, the fire you light in me. How it rages in defiance of all who stand between us. One day, they will be gone. One day, you will be mine completely.

In name. In flesh. In law.

On that day, you must wear red. Your skin is—dare I say it?—splendor itself in red satin. Red upon white ravishes a man. You must have known.

She closed her eyes. Heard the paper crumple in her hand.

Heart pounded. Pounded. *Pounded.*

She'd worn red satin the night they'd left for Scotland.

Surely, had you wished to hide, you should have worn white. The color of snow. The color of moonlight. The color of your bared skin behind glass.

But you wore red for me. Ah, you wished to be seen. And I did see you, my dearest love. I always do.

I fancy a visit to the Highlands. Did you know? What a clever girl you are, Clarissa. Weddings are simpler in

Scotland. Perhaps we shall be wed before spring. Perhaps all those who stand between us will be vanquished by then.

And I shall hold you so very close. You shall whisper your sweet affections to me, and I shall kiss the very breath from your body.

Forgive these fevered musings, sweet Clarissa. My love grows more consuming with every day we remain apart.

Your most ardent admirer,
S.N.

"… is the matter? Clarissa! Dearest, you've gone positively ashen."

Clarissa fought the frozen stillness. She fought the heaving rebellion of her stomach. She lifted her head.

Kate was gazing at her with wide, worried eyes. "Are you ill? Please say—"

"He found me." Clarissa's whisper was soundless amidst the rushing in her ears.

Kate's confusion crinkled her brow.

"He found me," she repeated. "God, Kate. I … I should never have come here."

"Don't be silly, dearest. Why would you say such a thing?"

"After everything you suffered. The cask. The nightmares. And I've brought you another. Broderick will hate me. He'll want me to leave." A sob gathered. Terror made her head spin.

Kate's lovely brown eyes rounded in bewilderment. "Please tell me what's happened," she demanded, squeezing Clarissa's hand and crinkling the paper.

Slowly, Clarissa withdrew. Straightening her spine, she flattened the letter against her thigh. Then, she handed it to Kate.

As her dearest friend read the words of a madman, Clarissa wrapped her arms around herself as though that might hold the pieces together. It wouldn't. She was falling apart.

Kate glanced up, her mouth open, her eyes dawning with the first stirrings of true fear. "I don't understand."

Tears gathered. Light liquified. Her chest felt crushed. "I'm so sorry, Kate. I've brought the wolf to your door."

CHAPTER THREE

Campbell MacPherson swung down from his horse's back and cursed the sodding rain. Icy water trickled past his coat's collar. Mud slicked his boots.

Scottish weather was pure misery much of the year, but this winter seemed bent on punishment. He'd spent the previous day traveling to Inverness for supplies. The wagon had mired repeatedly before floodwaters had nearly carried it off into a ravine. He'd reversed the slide by wedging himself between his wagon and a fallen log, adding his own muscle to that of the horses.

He'd nearly lost the load. His back bore dents from the wagon's rails. He'd had precisely two hours of sleep. And his ballocks had yet to thaw.

His father, Angus, had a term for this mood: MacPherson black. It wasn't Campbell's usual shade. Angus and Alexander were better known for their unruly tempers. But God, it had been a shite few days.

Handing his horse to Broderick's stable lad, he glanced up at the house he'd helped build, a house much finer than his own.

Not that it mattered. Broderick had long been the more polished brother. He *should* have the more polished house. For years, Broderick had represented the MacPherson Distillery with a mediator's diplomacy. He'd needed this grand, symmetrical box of stone and glass to impress the lofty sorts. Perched amidst the glen's wooded foothills, it was a bonnie house fit for a gentleman.

By contrast, Campbell was the brute. Always had been. The largest and oldest of four MacPherson brothers, he'd never bothered to play civilized for the government men. Hell, he scarcely bothered smiling for his wee stepsister, Annie. And she was the heart of them all.

No, Campbell's rough, empty farmhouse suited him fine—though, lately, the contrast between his house and Rowan House sharpened every time Broderick summoned him for a visit. That had happened much more frequently since Kate's finespun guests had arrived.

Lord Teversham and Lady Darnham were pleasant enough, as English aristocrats went. But Miss Meadows was … confounding. Bonnie, to be certain. Beautiful, in fact, with pale-gold hair, full, bowed lips, abundant curves, and eyes as deep and blue as a loch on a clear day. Aye, she was a lovely thing. And the strangest mixture of breathless chatter, fiery blushes, awkward silences, and obscene boldness he'd ever encountered.

Perhaps his size was to blame. Some lasses found him intimidating, he supposed.

He shook off his wandering thoughts and entered the house, greeted by the ginger-haired footman, Stuart MacDonnell.

"Everybody is waitin' for ye in the drawing room, sir."

Campbell nodded and handed the lad his dripping hat before heading in that direction. The doors stood open, allowing him to take in the whole room at once. Broderick stood with his back to the fireplace, wearing a deep scowl. Kate sat in the chair next to him, looking whiter than porcelain plates and clutching her husband's hand with both of hers. The elderly Lady Darnham occupied one of the sofas. She was coughing into a handkerchief. The cough did not sound good.

Lastly, there was Miss Meadows. Blonde curls gleamed softly as she stood at the watery window. Only ten days ago, she'd been dancing with Kate, giving breathless instruction and gliding into graceful poses that should be bloody outlawed. Of course, the moment she'd seen him, she'd turned crimson and rushed to her grandmother's side. He'd think her shy if she hadn't then made it clear she'd been eyeing him like a Highland bull at auction.

Hands of a superior size, indeed.

This morning, she appeared smaller. Fragile. Her gown was loose around that curving waist. Beneath a knitted shawl, delicate shoulders shuddered. A wad of paper was crushed in her hand.

"I shall leave straight away," she murmured to the glass. "I—I'll go west. To Ireland, perhaps."

"Lass," Broderick began.

But she wasn't listening. "Then, America. Perhaps you could lend me funds for my passage? I shall repay you once I've landed. Doubtless it will take some time to secure a position, as I've never before had one, but—"

Lady Darnham interrupted with, "Don't be foolish, dear." Ragged with illness, her admonishment trailed off into another harsh cough.

"He fired upon Francis's coach," Miss Meadows continued. "He shot George."

"A graze. Teversham's note said George is recovering well. And who's to say it wasn't simply a hunter's stray shot—"

"You know better, Grandmama. We both do."

Broderick glanced in Campbell's direction. "Brother. My thanks for comin'."

"What's happened?" Campbell noticed Miss Meadows's shoulders tense, but she didn't turn his way.

"We've a wee spot of trouble." Broderick drew him forward then lowered his voice to a murmur. "Teversham sent word from Yorkshire. His coach was fired upon south of Glasgow. Clarissa believes the shooter is a man she kens."

"Who?"

"A rabid dog with a taste for the hunt," Lady Darnham rasped, casting him a watery blue squint. "Last spring, he developed a *tendre* for my granddaughter. The sentiment is far from mutual. Yet, he has continued to pursue her with a fervency that may only be attributed to madness. Unfortunately, he is a Northfield." She waved her handkerchief with disgust. "Prominent family. Good society. They've refused to do anything about him, despite my numerous warnings."

Campbell frowned, glancing between the old woman and her granddaughter. Miss Meadows clutched her shawl tighter and continued staring through the glass.

"'Tis the job of a man to put rabid creatures down. Have ye no male kin, m'lady?"

Lady Darnham sniffed. "A nephew. He inherited the Darnham title from my dear, sweet Alfie."

"And he hasnae dealt with the problem ere now?"

"He does not consider it a problem. Or any of his concern."

He noted the tension in Miss Meadows's shoulders. Her cheek and nape had the sheen of pearls in this light. What a soft, gentle beauty she was. He could imagine a suitor becoming overzealous. Obsessed, even. But violent?

"Why target Teversham?"

Kate sat forward to answer, "Francis is Clarissa's closest male companion. Last season, although she had many suitors, he was the one she danced with most. Northfield might consider him a rival for her affections."

Campbell nodded. Teversham's tastes ran toward males, but he was openly affectionate toward both Kate and Miss Meadows. A jealous man who'd lost his head over a woman could mistake their friendship for more than it was.

Kate continued, "Northfield has pursued Clarissa relentlessly for the past ten months." She cast a concerned glance in her friend's direction. "He has gone to great extremes to advance his suit. Some of them have been … distressing. And his letters to her grow ever more threatening. I very much fear for her safety and that of Lady Darnham. He—he's quite mad, I suspect."

He looked to his brother. Broderick's posture angled protectively close to Kate.

"What do ye need from me?" Campbell asked.

Oddly, Broderick hesitated. "I wouldnae ask this of ye, brother. Not after all ye did for me in Edinburgh."

Campbell sighed and ran a hand over his face. Edinburgh had been a nightmare. Necessary, of course. But they'd almost lost Kate. Alexander had nearly died. It had been much too close.

God, he was tired. "Just say it. Ye want me to put him down?"

"No!" The hoarse shout came from Miss Meadows. She'd finally turned around, and now he could see the black shadows beneath her eyes, the whiteness of her full lips. He could see her fear. "I refused to let Francis do … that." A dainty chin tilted up. "I certainly would never ask it of you, Mr. MacPherson."

Something in her expression made him want to kill the man regardless. Inside enormous blue eyes lay terror he hadn't seen since the battlefield. It twisted his gut into a hard knot.

Aye, he could hunt this Northfield blackguard and put him down—rabid dogs deserved no better. Problem solved. He didn't require her permission.

He turned to Broderick. "Say the word."

Broderick's jaw flexed as he glanced down at his wife. "Kate and I would be obliged to ye if ye'd agree to guard Clarissa."

"Guard her?" Campbell frowned.

"Aye."

"Here?"

Another hesitation. "No."

His frown deepened as he realized what Broderick was asking. "Dinnae say it."

"She needs to be where he wouldnae think to look for her."

"Bluidy hell, brother. She cannae stay with me."

"'Twould only be for a month or two. Long enough to find him and do what must be done."

"I've nae housekeeper. I've nae bed for her—"

"We'll send supplies with ye—"

"Are ye out of yer bluidy mind?" He felt a growl building in his chest. Unless she was content with being ruined, an unwed English lass living with an unwed man for any length of time meant marriage. And he had no intention of marrying anybody, let alone a soft-as-thistledown *lady* with a peculiar interest in the size of his hands.

"She cannae stay at the castle," Broderick continued. "Annie's birthin' time is too close. Da's house is fine enough, but I willnae ask Clarissa to put up with his bellowin'. Alexander returned to his house two days ago, but he's still healing. Rannoch's been traveling for distillery business of late. And he's … Rannoch."

Indeed, she needed protection, not seduction. Rannoch had plowed his way through two counties and was working on a third. A woman as bonnie as Clarissa Meadows? Their youngest brother wouldn't think twice.

Campbell blew out a frustrated breath. His eyes burned. His head ached. Bloody hell.

"We need her safe, Cam. We need her hidden. Then, we need to send a message to the mad bugger who's chasin' her—either he gives up or he dies."

"Or we simply kill him," Campbell grumbled. "Save ourselves a lot of bother."

Miss Meadows abandoned her vigil at the window. "You mustn't do that, Mr. MacPherson. Please. His family has great influence. They would not hesitate to charge you with murder." She pressed a small, white hand over the center of her bosom as though her heart needed calming. "He will be difficult to find and difficult to defeat. Additionally, he is an extraordinary shot."

Lady Darnham hummed her agreement. "That line of Northfield men always was. Master marksmen, the lot of them."

"He is dangerous," Miss Meadows murmured. She clenched the wad of paper harder. Whatever color she'd had vanished, leaving her skin translucent white. "I cannot ask you to risk yourself for my sake."

His gut hardened. Burned. "Ye didnae ask. Broderick did." Instinctively, he moved closer, bending his head and lowering his voice. "What's that in yer hand, lass?"

Her breathing quickened. She clenched her fist harder and wouldn't meet his eyes. "H-his letter." Barely a whisper. She scarcely moved.

"Give it to me."

A jerky shake of her head.

"Lass. Give me the letter."

"N-no. I—I don't … I can't."

As gently as he could, he lifted her hand and uncurled her fingers. The muscles in her arm were stiff, her knuckles white, her hands frigid. Slowly, he loosened the paper from her grip. She wasn't fighting him, precisely. Rather, she seemed too frozen to comply.

He pulled the paper free, straightened it, and began reading.

By the time he finished, his decision was made.

"Do ye ken now, brother?" Broderick said softly.

Campbell met his gaze, recognizing the fury there. His own was similar, yet bigger. Mountainously bigger. "Aye." He folded the letter and tucked it into his coat pocket. "She'll require a maid."

Miss Meadows sputtered nonsense objections and demanded he return her letter. He ignored her.

"And a bed. I've none but my own."

Broderick nodded. "I'll send men with ye, as well."

"Nah. I've enough lads. Is Lady Darnham to accompany us?"

"She may be a second target. Splitting his focus could give us an advantage. Besides, she's been ill. We thought it best she remain here."

"So, no chaperone."

"We could ask Magdalene."

Kate interrupted. "Magdalene has been taking care of Lady Darnham since Alexander left. Her ladyship would prefer to keep her here until she's recovered."

Lady Darnham sniffled and nodded. "Miss Cuthbert has become indispensable to me. Lovely young woman. I cannot bear to part with her."

Broderick confirmed, "No chaperone, then." He turned to Campbell. "Are ye agreeable?"

Miss Meadows cleared her throat pointedly.

Campbell ignored her. "Aye."

"Mr. MacPherson," Miss Meadows snapped. "Would anyone care to ask if *I* am agreeable? To *any* of this?"

Slowly, he tilted his head and raised a brow. She had a bit of color in her lips and cheeks again. Good. He didn't want her swooning on him. "Ye're agreeable, lass."

"You don't know that."

"Aye, I do."

"You haven't asked—"

"No need. Ye've a mad dog on yer heels, and I'm offerin' protection. Ye're nae daft, so I assume ye're agreeable. Am I wrong?"

She sputtered and flashed Kate and Broderick a glare. Then, she locked eyes with her grandmother, who gave a gentle nod. Finally, she wrapped her arms around her middle. "No. You're not wrong."

"Right. Then, ye'll do as I say and give me nae trouble." She started to sputter again, and he ignored her again. "Go pack whatever ye can fit in yer trunks, Miss Meadows. Ye'll need all the comforts ye can get."

Chapter Four

Clarissa's first glimpse of Campbell MacPherson's home came after a long ride in a heavily laden wagon. First, they descended Rowan House's drive through the forested foothills, exiting woodlands of birch and pine into the misty glen. Then, they followed the river southwest past Angus MacPherson's lovely stone farmhouse. They skirted the humble village of Glenscannadoo, which stretched along the shore of a steely loch. Finally, they took a rougher road west, ascending between two naked hills to enter a series of undulating valleys. By the time she saw a single blessed structure, she felt as though she'd never find civilization again.

Because here, there was nothing. Simply nothing. Just rolling grass, mossy rocks, heather, and wind. In time, she glimpsed the odd, lonely tree here and there. Stretched along one side of the road was a meandering trickle of a brook. Eventually, it narrowed and disappeared into the grass.

Wind numbed her cheeks. Heavy gray clouds matched her mood. At least it wasn't raining.

A fat drop splatted on her skirt.

Drat.

"How much farther, Mr. MacPherson?" she called to the giant, silent Scot riding ahead of the wagon.

He didn't answer.

Beside her, Stuart MacDonnell—likewise a man of few words—offered, "Nae far now, miss. Another quarter-hour or so."

In fact, it felt like centuries before any structures came into view. Even then, she thought they were outbuildings. Surely, the low-slung hovel sprawled haphazardly on a shallow rise could not be his *house.* Angus MacPherson's farmhouse was a palace by comparison. Even Rowan House's stables were finer.

Stuart guided the wagon onto the narrow dirt drive branching off the main road.

Her heart sank. Indeed, the odd patchwork cottage of timber and stone was Campbell's house. And she'd be living here for at least a month—or however long it took Francis to return to Scotland.

The wagon slowed as icy rain blew sideways, spraying her face with a needling blast. She tucked her head. Beyond her bonnet's brim, she examined her temporary home, which appeared to have begun as a humble farm cottage then expanded over time. The roofs of the various sections were all thatch, some darker and some lighter, some with dormers and some without.

The main cottage was two stories. A single-story wing branched off at an odd, southwesterly angle. Several chimneys dotted that roof. The kitchen, perhaps? Another two-story wing on the northern side was twice the length of the first wing, jutting along the rise before ending in a T.

A separate wooden structure stood thirty feet beyond the second wing. Clarissa supposed it might be the stables, though it seemed too large for that purpose. A barn, rather?

Yes, now that she had a chance to truly look, she spotted several woolly cows grazing in the distance. Kate had mentioned the MacPhersons raised cattle in addition to running their distillery.

There were no gardens and scarcely any trees nearby. Nothing much at all, really. Just a three-pronged structure and a few outbuildings perched amidst barren fields, rail fences, and stone. If Rowan House was a splendid manor in a magical woodland, this place was its bleak opposite.

"I'll secure the horses, miss," said Stuart as he drew them to a halt near the front door. "Then, I'll help ye down."

Her face was too frozen to reply.

"I have her." The low rumble came from behind them. She twisted to see Campbell dismounting. The man was so tall, he made his deep-chested hunter look like a pony.

He approached her side of the wagon with a grim look. "Come, lass."

Scooting to the edge of the bench, she started to rise. But before she could gather her skirts, massive arms scooped beneath her. He lifted her high into the air the way she might lift a child.

Carried her nearly seven feet off the ground.

Cradled her tightly against hard, muscled man.

Frantically, her arms clasped his neck. Good heavens. Her senses were spinning too much to squeak, let alone protest. It felt like floating.

His face was so close to her lips, she could feel the heat from his skin. It was … tingly.

She closed her eyes and inhaled. Cold air. Wet wool. Warm skin. And the faint scent of wood and spice. Something about the way he smelled made her belly quake.

"Ye're all wet," he murmured.

Yes. Yes, she was.

He carried her inside the cottage. The scents she associated with him were stronger here, particularly the wood and spice.

Gently, he lowered her feet to the floor. She blinked up at him, clinging to his arms. She didn't want to let go.

"The fire will warm ye while the lads and I prepare yer bedchamber."

She nodded, though she didn't know why. Nothing made sense. All she could see were his rain-wet lips. The flexing muscle in his jaw. His deep, dark eyes shadowed by a heavy brow.

"Are ye well, lass?"

A tiny moan escaped her throat.

He frowned. Inched closer. "Ye're safe here, ye ken." His big hand slid from her shoulder to her elbow.

She knew his touches were meant to comfort, nothing more. She knew he was only doing this as a favor to his brother. But her body didn't care about his reasons. It wanted his nearness more than her pride could bear.

She pressed her lips together to prevent any humiliating outbursts.

"Let me unload and tend to a few tasks. Have a look about, eh?"

Another nod. Gestures were better than speaking. Less likely to spin out of control.

He withdrew and ducked through the main door, back out into the blasting rain.

She breathed deep, wishing he would hold her again. Having someone else's strength to rely upon would be heavenly. But she had only herself now.

Only herself. She must remember that.

Campbell was a good man and, as Kate had assured her a dozen times while they'd packed her belongings, more capable than any Bow Street runner she might have hired for the same purpose.

He'd been a soldier in his younger years, according to Broderick, part of a Highland regiment. Campbell had seen battle. He knew a great deal about tracking, hunting, weaponry, and war. He knew about killing.

Clarissa was grateful for the protection he offered. She was.

But she could not expect him to give her comfort. Certainly, she could not expect him to feel the same attraction. Over the past two months, he'd made it obvious he did not. Only look at how affected she'd been when he'd lifted her from the wagon. And how impersonal he'd remained.

The contrast was embarrassing.

She shuddered and forced stiff fingers to loosen her bonnet's ribbon. Then, she glanced around the room where he'd deposited her. A parlor, perhaps? Running the width of the front of the cottage, the room was narrow and long. The ceilings were lined with rugged wooden beams. She noted the stone fireplace and heavy, soot-stained mantel. Four small windows offered dim, watery light. Plain wood paneling lined the walls, and wide planks lined the floors.

There was only one chair. It was large. Heavy. Made of wood—as everything here seemed to be. An overturned crate sat beside it, topped with a knife and a lantern. The rest of the room was empty.

She frowned. *Empty.* Was this how he lived?

With her bonnet in hand, she drifted toward the doorway leading to the rear of the cottage. The passage was poorly lit and cold. She paused to let her eyes adjust before glimpsing a narrow set of stairs winding upward to her right. As she ventured further, the planks squeaked and wind whistled through unseen crevices. At the rear of the cottage lay a dining room with a long, rough-hewn table and four mismatched chairs. Across the passageway lay another small chamber that must have once been a scullery or garden entrance. Now, it functioned as an antechamber leading to the single-story wing with, she presumed, the kitchen.

When she smelled bread baking and heard distant chatter, she took her first easy breath and quickened her pace. Inside, a surprisingly spacious kitchen bustled with activity. Two boys dashed about, tending the fire and hauling water. Two maids worked at the massive hearth, stirring pots and chattering about the *"dreich"* weather. A thin, bearded young man stood at the center table preparing fish.

One of the maids turned. "Miss Meadows! I didnae ken ye'd arrived." The plump, plain-faced girl skirted the table to take Clarissa's bonnet. "Ye must be chilled. Would ye care for tea?"

Her chest tightened. Perversely, she wanted to weep. When had she become so weak that simple kindnesses broke her composure? She couldn't say. All she knew was that being cold and damp and alone made the familiar warmth of a busy kitchen feel like paradise.

"Yes," she rasped. "Abigail, isn't it?"

The girl's eyes brightened. "Aye, miss."

Abigail and a second maid, Jean, had been sent here ahead of them to prepare the house and help with cooking. Clarissa wondered if Kate had informed them of the risks.

"Ye're fair shiverin', ye poor, wee thing." Abigail bustled into the scullery and returned with a woolen blanket, which she draped around Clarissa's shoulders. "There, now. Willnae take Mr. MacPherson long to furnish yer bedchamber. 'Til then, where would ye care to wait—"

"Here." Clarissa swallowed, tying the blanket's corners across her bosom like a makeshift cape. "I'll help prepare dinner, if you like."

Abigail's cinnamon eyebrows arched so high they disappeared beneath her cap's ruffle. "That—that's kind of ye, miss. But I wouldnae ask—"

"Please." She held the maid's gaze. "Please, I've no talent for cookery, but I chop very well. At home—Ellery Hall, that is. My home in England. It's in Cambridgeshire. Do you know where that is?"

Abigail nodded then shook her head.

"Oh, well, it doesn't matter, really. My point is that, at Ellery Hall, I like to help with small tasks round the kitchen. I've even been known to assist with the washing from time to time. Only so much embroidery to be done in one household, you know." She drew a shuddering breath. "I like to stay busy and … useful."

She was rambling. This happened when she was nervous. Or tired. Or tipsy. Or excited. In truth, it happened a lot.

"Aye, then." Abigail's smile was kind. "Let's find ye an apron."

A half-hour later, she'd learned that Jean had a "braw lad" waiting to marry her when he returned from working on the Isle of Skye; Abigail aspired to become a cook one day, though she still felt she had "much to learn about sauces and oatcakes"; and the slim, bearded man was a MacDonnell cousin named Daniel who had worked for Campbell for six years.

"He expects much from his lads, 'tis true." Respect beamed in the young man's eyes. "But naebody works harder than he does. Of that ye may be certain."

Clarissa wasn't surprised. Even among the MacPhersons, Campbell was revered. His brothers spoke of him with something approaching hero worship. She'd heard his father boast on several occasions that "my son's unmatched in the caber toss. Lad could hurl a bluidy mountain all the way to London, if he were of a mind."

To this, John Huxley—Kate's brother and Campbell's brother-in-law—had taken umbrage. "I bested him at last summer's Highland Games. You were there, Angus. Don't tell me you've forgotten."

Angus had shaken his head in a pitying fashion. "Pure luck, lad. Doesnae count."

As usual, Campbell had merely raised a brow at their nonsensical argument. There'd been no need to say anything. Everyone knew his strength, his competence, his quiet command. Everyone understood—especially Clarissa. Her foolish infatuation rarely let her forget.

Even now, as she listened to Daniel's account of Campbell righting a loaded wagon with sheer brute strength, a shivery thrill ran from her nape to the base of her spine. She kept her eyes lowered on her task—peeling potatoes—lest she reveal her fascination.

How was she to spend the next month or more living with the man? She didn't know. Kate remained oblivious to Clarissa's dilemma. And Grandmama had been no help when they'd discussed the matter earlier.

"Do be sensible, dear," she'd sniffed. "He would intimidate Goliath himself. I fail to see the problem."

"I'll be ruined. Not that it matters. Francis won't mind having a scandalous wife."

Grandmama's expression had turned mutinous. She still did not approve of Clarissa's plans to wed Francis.

"But what if I fail to control my babbling again?" Clarissa had whispered the shameful worry out of desperation. "What if he thinks I'm trying to … entice him?"

Oddly, Grandmama had been unsympathetic. "All the better, I'd say. Perhaps he'll be tempted."

She'd stared at her grandmother for long seconds. "You cannot mean—"

A clogged sniff. "You could do far worse, Clarissa. He is unwed, has land of his own, a full head of hair, and no *valet* whatever. A prime catch, given your circumstances."

She'd felt abandoned, left to her fate. Of course, that had been a childish reaction. Likely Grandmama was out of sorts because she was feeling poorly. Clarissa must keep her dignity and behave like the lady her grandmother had raised her to be.

And she would. All she had to do was keep her mouth shut whenever Campbell MacPherson was present. Simple enough.

As Daniel MacDonnell scaled his last fish and chuckled over Jean's complaints about drink-addled men, a cold draft and a quiet clamor came from the scullery. A door shut. Quiet bootfalls and rhythmic tapping sounded. Clarissa glanced up and stiffened.

It was Campbell, looking as forbidding as the weather. He carried a small cask on one shoulder and a basket of bread beneath his arm. Even bending down to place his load beside a cabinet, he dwarfed the room.

Beside him stood a creature she'd never seen. It appeared to be a dog but much, much taller. Lean and long and covered in wiry gray hair, it halted at his side. And its dark eyes fixed upon her.

Her heart flopped. Thudded. Squeezed.

Carefully, she set her knife on the table. Wiped her hands. Lowered her gaze.

She'd stopped looking in the dog's direction, so when she felt a nudge at her ribs, she gasped. Twisted to see. And there it was, its back higher than her waist. She was average height—two inches above five feet—but the lanky animal made her feel tiny. Its long snout nuzzled and sniffed. Calm, dark eyes gazed up at her soulfully.

Her heart clenched until she couldn't breathe. She lurched backward. Spun on one foot. Rounded the table.

The dog followed, its tongue lolling as if she'd issued an invitation to play.

"Fergus," Campbell said quietly. *"Trobhad."*

She assumed Fergus was the dog's name. The second word had sounded like "true-it." It must have been a command, because the dog immediately halted, gave her a plaintive look, and trotted back to its master's side.

Only after it sat across the room from her did she realize she'd retreated behind Daniel.

"Fergus is gentle as a lamb, miss," Daniel assured her. "Ye've naught to fear from him."

She swallowed, her chest tightening. He was wrong. There was everything to fear.

"I—I was startled. That's all."

Campbell frowned and murmured another incomprehensible command. The dog retreated back through the scullery.

"Come, lass," he said, nodding toward the passage to the main cottage. "I'll show ye to yer bedchamber."

She swallowed. Nodded. Reminded herself that she must *not* speak. Gestures only. And for God's sake, nothing lewd.

Campbell lit a lantern and led her upstairs without a word. She didn't know what she'd been expecting, but the upper floor of the main cottage housed only two chambers and a single, narrow corridor. At the end of the corridor was a third door that led to … more corridor.

She frowned. It had to be the upper floor of the second wing, though she didn't dare ask. Asking meant speaking. And speaking to Campbell MacPherson while the giant Scot was leading her to a bedchamber spelled disaster.

Indeed, when she followed him through the second door on the right, and he remarked, "The door we passed is mine, so if aught frightens ye, knock," her first thought was to wonder what he wore to bed. A shirt? Drawers? Nothing?

She eyed the breadth of his shoulders and sighed.

"Will this do for ye, Miss Meadows?"

"Hmm?"

"The bed."

What would he look like unclothed? So many muscles. Such large bones and *substantial* hands. Her curiosity begged to be satisfied.

"Lass."

Her gaze flew up to meet his. "Yes?"

The faintest crinkles appeared at the corners of his eyes. "I'll keep ye safe, ye ken."

Heart stuttering, she pressed her lips together then nodded.

"This isnae the sort of comfort ye're accustomed to." Bracing his hands on his hips, he glanced at the dark wood bed with its green tartan coverlet—the finest object in the room—then briefly at her three trunks and a small dressing table in the corner near the window. Everything had been brought from Rowan House. "But 'tis only for a time. Just until Northfield is …" His jaw muscles flexed. "Dealt with."

She wandered deeper into the room. Carefully skirting around Campbell, she noted a rug from Rowan House's guest chamber had been placed beneath the bed, and her valise with all her toiletries rested neatly beside the dressing table. The dormered window was small—only four panes—but it looked out upon rolling fields that she imagined would be glorious when the heather bloomed.

No, this wasn't the comfort she was accustomed to. It was better. She would sacrifice every marble tea table and china teacup at Ellery to feel safe again. She'd sleep on the floor like a dog to ensure that her grandmother and Francis and everyone she loved would be protected.

"There are rules ye must follow," he said. "Ye may object. But they're necessary."

She turned. Sucked in a breath. He was running a hand through his hair, leaning against the bedframe, and looking … devastating. "Rules?"

"Aye." He ticked them off on long, thick fingers. "Dinnae go outside unless ye've a man with ye. Preferably me."

Her cheeks heated.

Another finger. "If aught alarms ye, tell me as soon as it happens. Nae more waitin' until ye've a letter from the wee bastard."

For some reason, her foolish mouth clarified, "He's not wee."

The intimidating glower deepened. "Eh?"

"Northfield. He's not a small man. Above six feet, actually. And rather … fit." Why was she talking? God, why were words coming out of her mouth?

Campbell crossed thick arms over his chest. "That so?"

She nodded.

"Is he bonnie, too?"

This time, she frowned. His voice had softened, yet there was a dark edge to it, like sarcasm or resentment. "Well, yes, I suppose. Most Northfield men are reasonably handsome. Fine eyes. Good chins. I confess I was flattered by his interest, at first. He was considered an excellent catch."

Campbell's jaw flexed. "Right." His gaze shifted above her shoulder briefly before he continued with his third rule. "Ye must do what I tell ye without question or hesitation. If I tell ye to lie flat on the ground, down ye go. Dinnae ask why. Dinnae delay. Just drop. Clear?"

She nodded.

"Tomorrow, we begin trainin'."

"Training of what?"

"Of ye, lass."

"Me?"

"Ye must learn to protect yerself. Do ye ken how to handle a weapon?"

Her throat tightened until her voice was a thread. "I swung a rapier once. Francis lost his buttons and very nearly his dignity."

An instant before he swiped a hand across his mouth, she thought she saw a smile. But that was silly. Campbell MacPherson never smiled.

She continued, "If you're referring to guns, no. I've no experience with those."

When he didn't immediately reply and his gaze turned assessing, her nervousness grew.

And her mouth grew restless. "But I'm certain you'll be an admirable instructor. And I will be your rapt pupil. You may teach me whatever you like. Proper grip. Proper aim. Locating the tenderest center and hitting it with all one's prowess. Consistently. Repeatedly. Again and again." A raspy, involuntary chuckle escaped her throat. "I shall gladly surrender my virginity to your capable tutelage."

His brows arched.

Oh, dear God. What had she said? She'd been rambling—again. And she'd said something about …

Dear. God.

Violent heat flooded her face. "I—I didn't mean—"

"Calm yerself, lass."

"I was referring to firearms."

"I ken. Dinnae fash."

"*Firearms* virginity. I am untried, you see." She winced. "What I mean to say is I have never touched a long gun. Or a short one. Actually, no guns of any sort have been fondled by these fingers."

"Miss Meadows."

"And furthermore, I should like to point out that Mr. Northfield is extremely adept with his gun. I daresay, his skills might surpass yours. Though, certainly, he cannot match your size. No, indeed. Whilst he is larger than average, your size is incomparable, Mr. MacPherson."

"Lass."

"This is only to say that training me to handle a weapon may be a waste of your time, as he will always be the superior shot at long range. And close quarters? I've no chance whatever. I am quite small compared to him and positively tiny compared to you." Another chuckle. Perhaps she should shut her mouth. "Why, I'd wager you could lift me like a pillow, bend me in half, and toss me over the mattress, should you fancy it."

Yes, she should definitely shut her mouth.

"Not that you would."

She mustn't mention his hands. Whatever she did, she must not mention—

"But if you decided to bend me to your will, I've little doubt you'd handle me superbly. For such a powerful man, you have the most remarkably gentle hands."

Silence fell. One of those strong, gentle hands rubbed the back of his thick, powerful neck. Finally, he sighed. "Did ye ever speak like this with him, lass?"

Her skin throbbed with mortification, but somehow, in her latest hellish bonfire of unintentional innuendo, she'd managed to burn away an important threshold. The threshold of shame. She'd finally done it. She'd passed beyond embarrassment, beyond the point of retreat. It felt … freeing.

She squared her shoulders. "No. Mr. Northfield and I conversed primarily about his family and my preference for pineapple ices. Oh, and dancing. He did not approve."

A frown. "Of dancing?"

"Of *me* dancing. Particularly with any man other than him." She cleared her throat and folded her hands at her waist. "It was among the reasons I declined his suit."

"Dancing means that much to ye." He didn't phrase it as a question, but rather, an observation.

She paused, feeling his understanding glow between them. There, in the shadows of her makeshift bedchamber, she saw herself reflected in his dark eyes. "Yes," she whispered. "It does."

He nodded. "I'll keep ye safe."

"I know you will."

"Ye must follow my commands without askin' why I've made them. Can ye do that, lass?"

"Yes."

"I'm nae much for explaining."

She couldn't help smiling. "You do splendidly, Mr. MacPherson. If only I possessed your talent for verbal restraint."

He didn't reply, merely gazed down at her with a curious expression.

She decided perhaps she should reassure him. "In any case, you shan't be forced to suffer my presence for long."

His eyes narrowed. "And why is that?"

"I intend to marry Lord Teversham." She forced brightness into her voice. "Francis has offered, and I … I believe it may be the best course. He must attend his duties in England first, naturally. Then, he'll return to collect me. We may even marry here in Scotland. Won't that be lovely?"

His silence stretched. Deepened. His jaw turned hard. His nose flared faintly.

Under most circumstances, reading Campbell MacPherson's expression was an exercise in futility. He rarely smiled. He rarely showed pain or grief or joy. His eyes were occasionally revealing, and he frowned a lot. But otherwise, one was hard-pressed to guess whether the man was gratified, horrified, pleased, thirsty, or bored senseless. He simply did not reveal emotions the way others did.

However, if Clarissa were asked to identify Campbell MacPherson's present mood, she'd have said he was displeased. Very, very displeased.

The question was why.

"Dinner will be ready soon," he bit out. "I'll leave ye to get settled." Abruptly, he strode to the door. There, he paused to add, "Oh, and lass. The privy is behind the barn. My rule stands. If ye leave this house, ye must have me or one of my men with ye. No exceptions."

She blinked. "You can't possibly mean—"

"Aye." His mouth quirked at one corner. "I can. And I do."

Chapter Five

Clarissa had spent too many years sitting. She'd sat beside Grandmama watching other ladies waltz. She'd sat with her tea and biscuits listening to other ladies gossip about their suitors. She'd sat in overdressed parlors embroidering patterns she'd seen on other ladies' hems. She'd sat and sat and sat while other ladies formed affections then marriages then families. Two years ago, she'd forced herself to change. To move. To dance. And that had changed everything.

Now, if she didn't find something to do, she'd go mad.

So, on the third day stuck inside Campbell MacPherson's creaky, drafty house, she set herself a task: She would repay him for his trouble. It was only fair. He didn't want her here. He couldn't have made it plainer that guarding her was a bitter duty.

At dinner, he scarcely glanced her direction. Twice in two days, he'd barked commands at her to avoid standing near the windows. This morning, she'd asked whether he'd had his coffee. He'd grunted and left the house without a word—and without his hat. It had been raining buckets at the time.

Clarissa might be a spinster well past her prime, but she wasn't useless. Now, as she donned an apron and examined the cottage's front room, new energy surged. "Is there any spare furniture?" she asked Daniel MacDonnell. "Anything will do."

The lean, bearded man lifted his cap and scratched his head. "Aye. A few auld pieces in the barn. But they're meant for kindling."

She clicked her tongue. "Let's have a look before we toss them in the fire, hmm? We'll need more chairs. Tables." She glanced toward the chair near the fireplace. Beside it, the overturned crate held the beginnings of a bird sculpture. She'd seen Campbell carving the cracked, whorled log the previous evening. He'd stopped the moment she'd entered the room. She'd asked for permission to make some changes to the house. Giving her a strange look, he'd agreed. Then, he'd barked at her to go to bed. The man obviously resented her presence, which was why she'd avoided asking him for help and relied instead on the mellower Daniel.

"I'll need my largest trunk brought down from my bedchamber," she murmured to Daniel now, eyeing the wavy, dusty light shining through the glass. "We must do something about these windows."

Abigail entered carrying two buckets. A sharp tinge of vinegar wafted with the steam. "Here ye are, Miss Meadows. Jean's bringin' the rags and spare blankets."

Clarissa nodded. "Right. Let's get to work."

It took them most of the morning to clean the main cottage. By the time they'd finished, Clarissa's back was sore and her hands were forming blisters, but the results were noticeable. Brilliant sunshine shone through the glass. The floors were cleared of dust and wood shavings. And the hearthstones bore significantly less soot.

Next, while the maids reorganized the larder, Clarissa and Daniel ventured outside to the barn. Deep in the farthest corner lay a neat stack of old, broken furniture.

"Most of it was here when Mr. MacPherson took possession of the house," Daniel explained. "Auld Rob

Robertson had nae sons. Never wed, in fact. Just lived alone up here with the sheep for all his days."

She began picking through the pile, lifting a chair from atop a small table. One leg was cracked, but not beyond repair. "I haven't noticed any sheep. Mr. MacPherson raises cattle, yes?"

Daniel moved to help her, pulling down a bench and an uneven footstool from the pile. "Aye. Highland coos thrive here. Particularly with Mr. MacPherson managin' things. He has a way with the beasties."

She didn't doubt it. He had a way with everything—his scruffy, oversized hound, his horse, his men. Her.

She waved toward the two chairs, bench, and stool they'd set aside. "This should do for now. Would you mind carrying these to the house?"

He hesitated. "I shouldnae leave ye alone."

She glanced over her shoulder at the open barn door. And there he was—Fergus. The hound rarely missed an opportunity to follow her. He kept a polite distance, but every time she stepped outside, she noticed him. And every time she noticed him, her heart squeezed a demand. As usual, she ignored the pang.

"I'm not alone, am I?" she murmured. "Go on. I'll finish sorting through the pile and await your return before I leave the barn."

Reluctantly, Daniel left with the two chairs. Behind her, she heard Fergus rustling the straw. The dog was determined; she'd grant him that.

Focusing on her task, she rounded to the rear of the pile in hopes of finding a table or desk. Did Campbell do much writing? She didn't know. She'd seen him reading by the fire once or twice. Still, a proper desk would be a good addition to any man's home.

Unfortunately, the largest item in the pile was a crate. It sat along the back wall, covered in dust and bits of old straw. Likely empty. Could she use the wood? It was sturdy enough and had only one water stain on the corner. She searched the barn for a tool to open it.

When she turned around, Fergus lifted his head. Soulful eyes caught her in their net. Her heart squeezed painfully. She grunted out a breath. "Stop," she whispered. "Please. Just stop."

His patient stare felt like compassion. Adoration.

She closed her eyes. Shook her head. Turned back to the crate and bent to examine the fastenings. When she saw they were already loose, she clicked her tongue at her own foolishness and tugged the crate's top panel. It came free without trouble. But the crate wasn't empty.

Nestled in the straw were several wooden carvings. One was a raven. The wood grain had been fired black to enhance the feathers of its outstretched wings.

Another was a stylized fish amidst a crisscrossed net of rune-like symbols. The runes resembled water. Both carvings were breathtaking in their detail and workmanship. Both fairly resonated in her hands. She carefully placed them back into their nests.

Then she saw the third carving. It wasn't large—perhaps eighteen inches long and ten wide. What caught her eye was the face. A woman's face. Exquisite. Clarissa brushed aside the straw and lifted the carving into her hands. The wood felt ancient, its weight lighter, its gnarls twisting like a stormy wind. The woman's hair had been fired black like the raven. Her eyes were closed and her expression serene. But all around her was chaos. He'd used the natural forms of the wood to portray a near-violent burst of leaves, fabric, and ropes.

She traced a fingertip along the woman's cheek, smoothed to a high polish. He'd carved every eyelash, the subtle parting of the lips, even a tiny beauty mark near her brow. Heavens, this was a masterpiece.

She'd no doubt it was Campbell's work, though it appeared much older than the birds. "Who are you?" she whispered to the carving. An answer came swiftly: someone he loved. It was obvious from the work.

She felt like she'd been kicked. Her chest ached. Her stomach hurt. Carefully, she placed the carving back into its nest.

He loved someone else. At least, he once had.

Perhaps that was why he resented Clarissa so much, why he'd shown little response to her outbursts of unintentional flirtation. Most men would see them as an invitation. Most men would show an interest. Not him.

She knew Grandmama would prefer she marry Campbell. Only yesterday, Stuart MacDonnell had delivered a note in which Grandmama had sung the praises of Miss Cuthbert's kindness and Mrs. MacBean's lung tonic before inquiring whether Clarissa had pondered the benefits of low-cut bodices for enticing difficult men.

Obviously, she was feeling better—a positive development. But Grandmama didn't understand. She couldn't possibly.

Campbell MacPherson didn't want Clarissa. He'd had ample chances to make his interest plain, yet he hadn't. Now she knew why. This carving explained everything.

The ache in her chest hardened into a knot. She returned the carving and replaced the crate's top. A warm presence appeared near her hip. Without thinking, she ran her palm over his wiry fur and long neck. A lanky, heavy body leaned against her.

She closed her eyes, picturing the woman Campbell must have loved. A black-haired beauty with perfect lips and long lashes. A woman he'd wanted to remember, so he'd sculpted her face into a work of art.

Blast, this wasn't helping. She must focus on getting through the next few weeks. Mooning over a man who had no interest beyond keeping her safe would bring nothing but more heartache.

She sniffed and petted Fergus absently, drawing comfort from his warm weight. Then, she realized what she'd been doing. Again, her heart twisted. She glared down at him. "Sly devil," she chided.

He gave her a silly smile.

She forced herself to withdraw just as Daniel returned. She picked up the stool while he carried the bench, and they exited into the yard. Fergus loped after them then galloped off toward the kitchen wing.

As they crossed the muddy space, male shouts echoed from beyond one of the sheds. She slowed, drifting closer to the uproar. Past the shed's corner, it came into view. And her knees went wobbly.

Grim and thunderous, Campbell climbed down from a long cart hauling an enormous, prone cow. The cow's coat was similar to other cows she'd seen on Campbell's land—rusty brown and woolly. But presently, it was smeared with blood. The animal's belly was distended, and the poor creature appeared near death. It only moved to gasp.

"Dear God," she murmured. "What happened?"

Daniel propped the bench on the ground and frowned. "Dinnae ken. That's one of the early breeders. But it shouldnae be her time yet."

They watched as Campbell issued sharp commands to his men. He stripped off his gloves and coat then swiftly rolled up his sleeves. He stroked the animal's woolly head and spoke softly in Gaelic. The cow's panting slowed. Campbell moved around to the side of the cart, pressing his hands along its flank. The animal jerked. He said more incomprehensible words in a voice that made Clarissa drift closer against her will.

The blood was coming from a gaping wound near the cow's spine.

Her stomach lurched. Her heart pounded. She swallowed against the urge to retch. "Can't we … can't we do something? We must help her," she babbled. "Blankets or water. Anything." Her stomach cramped at seeing the animal's distress.

Daniel clasped her elbow to halt her progress thirty feet away. "No, Miss Meadows. Ye must keep yer distance. Mr. MacPherson kens what he's about. Trust him to do what's best."

She swallowed. Nodded.

Campbell had shifted behind the animal. He lifted the tail, said something to one of his men about seeing hooves.

Her eyes widened. "Does he mean … the calf is coming?"

Daniel looked grim. "Aye. If he can pull it free."

For long minutes, she watched Campbell pull steadily on the calf's legs. In time, he even tied ropes to the poor creature, yanking with impressive force. Finally, the calf jerked free in a sudden burst. It was covered in fluid and stretched out lengthwise. It wasn't moving. Campbell swiped the fluid away from its mouth and snout. Then, he did the oddest thing: He picked up the calf by its hind legs and swung it back and forth like a pendulum. The motion seemed rough and strange. He laid the calf on the ground, accepted a large bucket from one of his men, and poured water on its head.

"That's to help the wee beastie start breathin'," Daniel assured her. "It must start soon, else it will die."

She stood there, clutching the old wooden stool to her chest, and watched Campbell MacPherson struggling to save a newborn life. Throughout, he moved with complete command, utter calm, and steady urgency. He crooned in Gaelic to the poor, injured cow that still panted in the bed of the cart. The cow mooed and tried to lift her head, but it seemed too much for her.

Finally, with more of Campbell's swiping and swinging, the calf twitched and began to move.

Clarissa's heart leapt. Squeezed. "It's alive! Look, Daniel. He saved it."

A pause. "Aye."

She didn't like his reluctance. "It will be all right, now. It's breathing, see?"

Another pause and a gentle, "We should return to the house."

Tearing her gaze from Campbell, presently rinsing his hands and arms in a water trough, she frowned at her companion. "Why?"

"This willnae be pleasant for ye, miss."

She darted another glance toward the cart. Campbell stood near the cow's head, stroking her neck and speaking Gaelic. She didn't understand his words, but his tone was clear. He was saying goodbye.

A breeze came up from behind her. Campbell's head lifted. He turned. Dark eyes fixed upon her beneath a fierce frown.

She swallowed as the moment lengthened. Her heart wanted to run toward him. Perhaps a man who raised cattle felt nothing for them in time. Perhaps he viewed them as a product no different than grain that must be harvested and sold at market. But she would have sworn sadness laced his expression like blue threads inside black wool—scarcely noticeable until one looked closely.

"Go inside," he rasped harshly across the yard.

She shook her head and started forward.

"Daniel!" he barked. "Take her inside. Now!"

Daniel tugged her away.

Inside the house, she tried to distract herself with placing the furniture and consulting on dinner. But only minutes passed before she heard the loud crack of a shot being fired. She jolted.

Daniel caught her gaze. "'Twas necessary," he said quietly.

She nodded. The cow had been suffering. And she didn't doubt Campbell would have spared the animal's life if he could have done. Recalling the sadness she'd glimpsed on his face, she instructed the maids and kitchen lads to prepare a hot bath for him before dinner.

Then, she resumed rearranging furniture with Daniel. "What will happen to the calf?" she asked before she could think better of it.

He hesitated.

She sighed. "Just tell me."

He shot her an amused glance. "Would ye care to see instead?"

Her chest clenched. She nodded.

He led her outside to the shed where the cart had been parked. It was gone, along with any traces of the cow. She sighed in relief. Daniel led her to the shed's opening, where rail fences formed an enclosure with two stalls. In one stall stood a large cow with a fringe of rusty fur covering her eyes. She'd been tied and was presently munching away at a bin of feed. In the adjacent stall, Campbell was pouring milk over the top of the small, trembling calf. He reached into a sack of what appeared to be salt. Then, he rubbed a handful over the calf's coat, focusing on the head and backside.

She blinked. What in blazes? Was he making butter? If so, he was going about it all wrong.

Daniel leaned close. "Keep watchin'," he whispered.

The little creature was still damp, shaky, and miserable. Would it survive without a mother? Campbell lifted it in his arms and carried it into the next stall. Then, he placed it on the ground near the cow's udders, teased the calf's mouth with his fingers, and transferred it to the cow's teat. The calf latched on. The cow scarcely noticed.

Campbell gave her a pat and crooned something incomprehensible. The cow turned her head briefly, giving him a woolly blink. She could have punished him with her horns. She could have kicked his knees or injured the calf.

But she didn't. Rather, she mooed and resumed munching. In time, the calf finished his meal and wandered closer to her head on wobbly legs. The cow, now full of feed, sniffed the calf's head. Gave it a lick. Paused as if confused. Tried again. Soon, she was licking the calf with vigor. The poor mite even took a tumble once or twice. The cow kept licking.

Daniel explained, "Now, she'll see it as hers, ye ken? If all goes well, the wee beastie will fatten up thrice its size ere spring is gone."

Campbell watched the pair closely as he left the stall. He wiped his hands on a blanket hung over the rail and finally glanced in Clarissa's direction. Dark eyes shone with something like joy. Relief. Peace. Or a blend of all three.

She rocked beneath the urge to move closer, to touch him and feel those strong, capable arms around her. Thank heaven the fence stood between them.

"Miss Meadows."

She trembled with pleasure at the rumble of his voice. Why must he affect her this way? Steadying herself, she clasped her hands at her waist. "Mr. MacPherson." She nodded toward the calf and its new surrogate mother. "Quite well done, there."

He didn't reply. Instead, he examined her hair, face, and gown with a dark expression. "Mind ye dinnae dirty yer frock. A farm isnae always a civilized place."

Her temper sparked. She feigned wide-eyed wonder. "Really?"

"Aye."

"This is shocking to a lady of my delicate sensibilities. The tenants at Ellery Hall made farming sound idyllic. Perhaps English sheep farms have somehow been spared the vagaries of nature. I must inform them of their good fortune upon my return."

Seeming annoyed by her sarcasm, he crossed massive arms over his massive chest. "There's a difference between collectin' rents and managin' livestock, lass. Rents dinnae leave yer hands dirty."

True vexation set in. Did he think she was nothing more than a pampered fribble? "And here I am without my silk gloves. Silly me."

The corner of his mouth quirked. "Mayhap ye should return to the house. Less cow shite there."

"Fewer boors, certainly."

He rested his elbows on the top rail and leaned closer. "Have ye been keepin' clear of the windows?"

"No."

He frowned. "Why not?"

"They needed cleaning."

The frown deepened. He rolled his shoulders. "The lads clean them in spring."

"Well, this year, we cleaned them early."

"We?"

"Yes. The maids and I. Daniel helped, as well."

His gaze shifted to a wary, wide-eyed Daniel and narrowed before shifting back to her. "Been mighty *helpful* to ye, has he?"

"Oh, yes, quite." She gave Daniel a bright grin, which seemed to increase the young man's alarm. "I don't know what I'd do without him."

Daniel swallowed visibly and shot a furtive glance at Campbell. "Nae trouble at all, miss. 'Tis my job."

She clicked her tongue. "Much too modest. You're also superb company—a quality I find indispensable."

Oddly, Daniel hadn't taken his eyes off Campbell. He retreated several steps and swallowed again before adjusting his cap.

She frowned between them. Campbell was glaring daggers, though she couldn't understand why. She tried changing the subject. "I was thinking about installing a kitchen garden. Daniel said many things grow well here, even with the short growing season: broccoli, cabbage, spinach, parsnips. Leeks and potatoes for your favorite soup. He knows a good deal about—"

Campbell interrupted with a low, grumbling, "No."

"Whyever not? Every home benefits from a—"

"The less time ye spend outside, the better." His glare darkened upon her. "Have ye forgotten why ye're here, lass?"

A chill washed over her. "I never forget, Mr. MacPherson."

"Good. Now, return to the house. Stay clear of the windows." He shoved away from the fence to retrieve his coat. "If Northfield is about, best he sees me and my men before he catches a glimpse of ye."

Reminded of how much trouble Campbell had taken on to keep her safe—for no reward whatever—Clarissa's chest ached as she watched him shrug on his coat and give the cow one last pat.

"Right," she murmured. "I shan't trouble you further, then."

She turned on her heel and headed toward the cottage. Daniel fell in alongside her, though he kept glancing behind him as though expecting an attack. Her own neck was tingling, but she refused to look back.

"Daniel, I have a list of seeds to acquire. I shall need your help with that."

"Er, miss?"

"A man needs a proper home. And a proper home has a garden."

"I'm nae certain—"

"I am." She raised her chin and strode faster. "Mr. MacPherson may object all he likes. But if I'm still here when spring arrives, I'll be leaving him something to remember me by. Whether he approves or not."

Chapter Six

Campbell awakened covered in sweat. The fire was down to a smolder. Night still reigned beyond his window. Near the door, Fergus snuffled and whined. The dog trotted to the bed, nudging Campbell's hand.

He gave him a pat. "All's well, lad. Just another bad dream."

Dreams had been the bane of his bloody existence for the last three months, cutting his sleep into two- or three-hour intervals and driving him mad. Some tormented his body. Those, he craved more than he should. Others tormented his mind. Those, he fought to no avail.

He scraped a hand down his face and forced himself from the bed to wash and dress.

The darker dreams weren't new, of course, but they'd never been this bad. Indeed, back when the woman he'd once loved had first visited him this way, the visions had been a comfort. He and Isla had conversed about everything—the distillery, his brothers, her mother.

His longing to die.

When he'd joined a Highland regiment for that very purpose, she'd railed her displeasure. When he'd been sent to the Continent to fight, she'd warned him of dangers to come. In time, she'd convinced him to live on without her, to fight for his own life, and to cast off his vow to remain true to her.

"I've been dead two years, Campbell," she'd chided, her black hair shining like a crow's wing in the misty light. "Ye cannae remain faithful to a dead lass. It's nae right." Isla always had been practical. "Besides, we were never together like that. Ye only ever kissed me once."

In the dream, he'd replied, "Ye were too weak for aught else, Isla."

He almost smiled, remembering her reaction. She'd bristled. "So, ye're blamin' me, are ye? That's a fine way to treat a lass who's crossed all manner of mystical boundaries to have a blether with ye." She'd tilted her head to a familiar angle. "I'll nae have ye die a virgin like me. Yer brothers would never cease the mockery."

She'd grown serious, her voice resonating deeper, sounding layered. "Ye've a whole life waitin', Campbell MacPherson. I was part of it, aye. But only a wee part. There's more, ye ken? More and better."

In the early days, she'd brought him solace, eased his grief. Then, he'd realized he'd never move on if he continued allowing himself such an indulgence. So, he'd resisted the dreams, forcing himself to wake whenever they began. Shortly thereafter, they'd stopped.

He hadn't seen Isla again until three months ago, when she'd appeared to him in a white mist wearing her *arasaid* as a cowl, her face in shadow.

She hadn't spoken a word. Unlike the dreams from sixteen years ago, in these nightmares, she kept a silent distance. First would come a sense of loss. Then, he'd feel the ground collapse beneath him, and he'd plunge underwater. He'd fight to the surface on the edge of drowning, only to discover night had fallen. She'd be there, mist curling the ends of her hair. She'd open her mouth to speak. And nothing. She'd clasp her throat. Struggle. He'd be saturated with fear he'd never felt before. Deep, abiding dread. He'd fight to reach the shoreline. He'd beg her to tell him what was coming.

For, that was what this felt like: a warning akin to those she'd given him before battles. But a warning of what?

It had been too many years. He'd built too many barriers. Whatever she wanted to tell him, he'd lost his ability to hear her.

He finished shaving and donned a shirt and trews. Only then did he notice Fergus hadn't gone back to sleep. Instead, the deerhound sat in front of the bedchamber door, emitting occasional sighs and the odd whine.

Shrugging on his coat, he frowned. *"Wheesht."*

Another whine.

The behavior was quite unlike Fergus, who was usually reluctant to leave his pallet at the foot of the bed.

Campbell opened the door.

Fergus wedged through and loped to the adjacent door.

Miss Meadows's door.

There, he sat and gazed at the latch. More sighing. More whining.

"Ah, laddie," Campbell whispered. "She wants naught to do with ye, I'm afraid. Nor me."

In the week she'd been here, in fact, the lovely English lass had offered a kind word, sweet smile, and delightful conversation to everybody she'd encountered—the maids, his men, the young lads who helped with hauling water and tending fires.

Everybody except Campbell. No, *him* she avoided like he'd been rolling in horse shite.

Whenever she needed a man to escort her outside, she sought out Daniel. Whenever she had a question about the household, she asked Daniel. Whenever she needed a trunk moved or a pitcher fetched from a high shelf, she begged prettily for assistance from Daniel.

Bloody, bearded Daniel.

He'd meant to begin her training last week, but she'd asked instead for his permission to make changes to the house.

"What sorts of changes?" he'd asked.

She'd looked everywhere but at him before answering, "Oh, this and that. Little things, really. Curtains. Perhaps adding a few chairs here in the front room. A bit of comfort to thank you for … your hospitality." She'd bitten her lip as though stopping herself from saying more.

He'd granted her request, thinking curtains might add security. The bastard who hunted her liked to spy on her through windows, after all.

The thought had reignited his fury, so he'd left her to her "changes" and focused on establishing patrols, securing fences, and setting traps in the surrounding hills. A good rifle had a range of several hundred yards, and Miss Meadows had said Northfield was an excellent shot.

Campbell intended to have the upper hand, come what may.

Which was why he'd wanted to train Clarissa in a few basic skills. But she was forever avoiding his company. The only creature she avoided more was Fergus. And the dog was *pining* for her.

"Trobhad." Campbell uttered the command twice more. Fergus's head lowered as though he understood he was being disobedient but refused to move from his spot. Campbell approached the door, intending to move him bodily if necessary, when he heard the sound.

Whispery, feminine moans. Then, a tiny whimper.

His gut hardened. Lantern in hand, he ordered Fergus to stay put and opened the door. Inside, it was dark and too bloody cold, but there was no intruder. Just a soft woman lying in the bed alone. He turned to leave her in privacy.

She whimpered again.

He halted. Fergus whined.

"No," she panted. "Pl-please."

He ran a hand over his face. God, he shouldn't be doing this.

The bed creaked as bedclothes rustled. "Don't. Don't hurt him." Her sob was tight and wrenching. "Whatever you want. Don't hurt him."

He closed his eyes. "Lass," he uttered quietly.

"Pleeeaase." More rustling.

A shudder ran through him. Bloody hell.

He moved to the bed, placing the lantern on the floor. Her lower half was twisted up with the blankets. Her upper half was …

Air whooshed from his lungs. She wore only a thin shift, which did nothing to shield his view of her breasts.

God Almighty.

"Lass." He forced the word out, louder this time.

Her back arched high. In the faint light, she was … breathtaking. But she was also writhing in distress.

Drawing her blankets up over her shoulders, he crouched beside the bed. Silvery tears streaked her cheeks. He brushed away the wetness with his knuckle. "Clarissa," he said softly. "Wake now. 'Tis a dream."

Her panting breaths washed against his palm. She struggled with the blankets, forcing them back to her waist.

"Ye're safe."

She clasped his wrist. Then his hand. Her breaths sharpened. She gasped, and her eyes flew open.

"Lass, all is well."

She blinked several times, clutching him harder. "C-Campbell?"

"Aye. Ye're safe."

"Oh, God."

"Ye were havin' a nightmare, by the sounds of it. Fergus wouldnae let me leave until I'd—"

Suddenly, she was plastered against him, her arms coiled like vines around his neck. Full, ripe breasts flattened against his chest. Soft, warm breaths heaved against his jaw. "Campbell," she mewled. Then, she released a small sob.

A fissure around his heart opened.

In one motion, he gathered her close and shifted so she sat across his lap on the bed. His arms wanted to seize. His hands wanted to caress. Instead, he held her as lightly as he could bear, stroking her hair, skimming her skin, soothing her soft, shuddering body.

And ignoring the lustful agony in his own.

"He was doing it again," she whispered. "I couldn't stop him. Why can't I stop him?"

Lightly, Campbell smoothed her long, silken curls. His hands braced her back, but she was so small, his fingers curved along her hips. "Shh, lass. I'm here. I'll nae let him near ye."

She clung tighter, her hands digging into his nape. "It sounded like water. I thought we were safe. He promised. He promised he would stop."

Campbell frowned. "Promised. When?"

She wriggled against him as though she wanted to burrow inside his shirt.

He fought the onslaught, ordering his muscles to freeze. He breathed through the pain. Breathed. Allowed his thumbs to stroke the delicate lines of her spine. Her hair smelled like the lavender fields near his regiment's encampments in France.

Her trembling eased, and her words began to slur. "A letter. Before Scotland. Before …"

He waited.

She softened against him. A dainty hand slid from his nape to his collarbone in a long caress.

Was it intentional? His body thought so. But his mind disagreed. Her warm breaths were long and sweet against his skin. She was falling asleep.

"So warm," she whispered.

He gathered up one of the blankets she'd cast off and wrapped it around her.

She groaned, low and throaty.

The sound shouldn't have ripped through him the way it did. The woman was half-asleep and terrified, for God's sake.

Wait. Were those her lips against his throat?

"Lass," he murmured, gritting his teeth and shifting her gingerly. "Are ye awake?"

A long sigh. A slurred answer. "Dreaming. Forever dreaming of you."

Unwanted lust surged in a tide of fire. Bloody hell, was he being punished?

He tried to move away, but she clung harder. So, he began rocking her as he'd once done with his wee sister. After a few minutes, he felt her go under. Wasting no time, he tucked her back into bed. Her hair fell over her face, so he brushed it back.

Perhaps his fingers shouldn't caress her cheek this way. Perhaps he shouldn't stare at her soft lips or her wee nose or the way her thin shift tightened over the most exquisite pair of—

Damn. What was he doing?

He backed away. Scraped a hand over his mouth. Pivoted and found Fergus. The dog seemed calmer now that she'd gone back to sleep. He fell into step beside Campbell as they made their way downstairs.

The house was quiet. Dawn was still an hour away. As he passed the dining room, his lantern light flickered over the items someone had placed in the center of the table—a ceramic pitcher filled with dried herbs and a wooden bowl filled with apples. As he continued through the kitchen, he noted the shelves beside the garden door had been reorganized. Now, baskets rested in neat rows, lined with blue-checked fabric and labeled in feminine script with their contents. As he paused to gather bread and cider for himself and venison for Fergus, he noticed the curtains on the garden window, yellow-checked cotton printed with wee, dainty flowers.

Already, she'd changed this place. He frowned. Before long, she'd be gone. Returned to England. Married to Teversham, likely.

Bloody *Teversham*. Would she decorate *his* table? Would she organize *his* shelves and dress *his* bloody windows? Would she sweetly sigh his name when he held her after a nightmare?

God, this was stupid. What was wrong with him? The lass needed a husband, and Teversham would treat her well. Not like a wife, of course. Teversham wouldn't bed her unless …

Unless the newly minted earl decided he needed an heir. Which was quite likely. Then, what?

The answer came swiftly: Then, the man who didn't particularly fancy females would do what must be done. And his sweet, bonnie wife would lie back and let him … she'd let him … inside.

Hot pressure built in Campbell's chest. His gut twisted hard.

He slammed his cup onto the kitchen table, retrieved his gun, and made his way outside. Nodding a greeting to the two men assigned to the night watch, he headed for the western rise with Fergus loping alongside.

With long, ground-eating strides, he walked the perimeter, enjoying the bite of cold. He needed it to combat the burning knot inside him.

All his life, Campbell's father had hammered him with warnings about the MacPherson temper. "Men our size cannae afford to lose control, laddie. Ye must never let the rage win. Why? Because men die when we loosen our grip. That simple."

As iron skies slowly lightened, Campbell worked to rid his mind of her. The cooling sweetness of lavender. The silken purity of her skin. The arms that clung and the breasts that pouted for his mouth and the lips that trembled to be kissed. He could want her, aye. But he couldn't have her.

She was not for him. His task was to keep her safe. No more.

Fergus galloped ahead in pursuit of a rabbit. A cow mooed in the distance. Light rain began to fall.

Campbell would do whatever it took to protect her. Training. Vigilance. Hunting Northfield down and making him pay for every nightmare he'd caused her.

Aye, that was the way. Satisfaction began to glow, easing the pressure, giving him focus. He would rid her of her tormentor. Then, he'd send her on her way.

She was not for him, he repeated silently. Too fine. Too soft. Too tempting. No, she was not for him.

He'd tell himself that over and over. He'd carve it into his bedposts and say it like a prayer. He'd repeat it until it stopped sounding like a lie.

Chapter Seven

Clarissa had just finished hanging the third curtain in the front room when Campbell rolled in like a thunderstorm.

"What the devil are ye doin'?" he growled.

She blinked first at his scowling face then at Daniel, who looked nonplussed. "Dressing windows?" she answered.

"Not you." Campbell glared at Daniel. "Didnae I tell ye to take the wagon to the distillery today?"

"Aye, sir. I was on my way out. Miss Meadows needed help with the …" Daniel's prominent Adam's apple bobbed on a swallow. "I'll be off, then." He donned his cap and nodded to Clarissa before escaping through the front door.

She frowned, glancing down at the curtain she still held in her hand. With a click of her tongue, she brushed past the still-thunderous Campbell MacPherson to retrieve the stool from near the fireplace. When she placed it in front of the fourth window and raised her hem to step up, she heard a grunt behind her.

He gave her no other warning.

Enormous hands gripped the sides of her waist. She yelped. Jerked at the ticklish heat. Then, she found herself lifted and set gently onto the floor—precisely as though she were a pianoforte that wanted repositioning.

"Mr. MacPherson!" she gasped when she caught her breath.

He ignored her entirely, nudging the stool aside and plucking the curtain from her fingers. He quickly attached the cloth to the frame using small hooks she'd hidden in the folds. With long, sensitive fingers, he adjusted them into place and draped the fabric just so.

"Where did ye find this, lass?" He fluttered the hem and arched a brow over his shoulder.

"Th-the cloth?"

"Aye."

"I … had a bit left over."

He turned to face her and folded massive arms across his chest. "More than a bit. Ye've dressed every window in the main cottage."

"Well, yes." She brushed at her skirts. "The windows were quite bare."

"Aye."

"And drafty."

"I notice ye havenae answered my question."

She firmed her lips. "The cloth was mine to do with as I—"

He brushed the hem with his finger again. "Ye purchased this for somethin' else, I'll wager."

"Are you displeased with the color? I find it quite cheerful—"

"'Twas meant for a gown, aye? And the hooks were for the bodice."

Her cheeks heated. "Does it matter?"

Eyes of the deepest, darkest brown narrowed upon her. She felt pinned in place, clenching her teeth against the urge to squirm. Finally, he turned to examine the windows, the chairs she'd positioned near the fireplace, and the small seating area at the opposite end of the room. She'd cobbled that assortment together from found pieces—the bench she'd repaired and scrubbed clean; a dining chair she'd covered with a blanket to mimic upholstery; a table Daniel had carried down from one of the bedchambers; the pillows she'd fashioned from worn linens and her trunk full of sewing projects.

He braced his hands on his hips then gave her a glare. "Yer training begins today."

Alarm surged. "Is that really necessary, Mr. MacPherson? I feel quite safe with you and Daniel here to—"

"Call me Campbell. 'Twill save time. And aye. It's necessary."

The first stirrings of panic arose. "Surely you've better things to do. I had a letter from Francis yesterday. He believes he'll be able to return to Scotland before the end of March. That's only, what? Three weeks or so."

Strangely, this did not appease the glowering giant before her. In fact, his jaw was now flickering. "Ye're with me. Outside. Now." He plucked her cloak from the hook beside the door and handed it to her. "Nae more nonsense. Come along."

He ducked through the doorway as though expecting her to follow. As though she were his hound. She wouldn't be surprised to hear him utter Gaelic commands and snap his fingers at her.

Ill-tempered, frustrating Scotsman.

Grudgingly, she followed.

He led her farther from the house than she'd been before—beyond the next two rises, past pastures and fences, past woolly cows munching lazily. As usual, his strides were freakishly long. She had to trot to keep up.

"Mr. MacPherson!"

He ignored her.

She panted with exertion and sidestepped a pile of leavings. "Campbell!"

He stopped. Glowered over his shoulder. "We've a distance to go yet. Best save yer breath for gettin' there."

As she trailed after him, she huffed, "Where are you taking me?"

No answer. A long ramble later, their destination came into view. They topped the final rise to enter a gentle, rolling valley. At its heart, a rocky brook tumbled from between two hills, widening into a large pool before meandering downhill in a southeasterly direction. Here and there along the stream's banks stood clumps of silver birches, their branches swollen with budding leaves. And several hundred yards to the north, where fields of grass and heather rolled gently upward onto a natural plateau, sat a large boulder between two pines and another clump of birch. Campbell headed in that direction.

She halted. The valley was breathtaking. Today, the sky shone wispy blue. A light breeze tossed her curls about, but it felt milder than she'd expected. Sunlight warmed her through her cloak. The air smelled green and bright, as pure as heaven. In fact, she felt as though she stood atop the world. She spun to view her surroundings—all around lay the hills of Scotland looking as if they'd been carved by a giant hand and painted in shadow and light. Their grandeur was stark. Wild. Yet, in this hidden glen with its birch-dappled brook, she felt … protected. She didn't know why. Perhaps it was the distant mountains standing guard around gently rolling terrain. Perhaps the rushing water and riffling grasses soothed her spirit.

Her eyes drifted to broad shoulders and the impossibly tall man ahead of her.

Perhaps it was him.

She'd dreamt of him again last night. He'd held her in his arms after a nightmare, whispering reassurances and making her feel safe. He'd rocked her, warmed her. Such patience. Such tender solidity.

How she longed for that man to be real. But he wasn't. The man now glaring at her as she started toward the boulder barely tolerated her presence. He would not pull her into his lap and hold her like she was precious. She rather thought he'd order her to go back to sleep and leave him in peace.

"Mayhap ye have all day to waste, but I dinnae," he grumbled as she approached.

Several weapons lay on the boulder, she noticed. "Did you forget to eat breakfast this morning?"

He grunted and plucked up a long musket. "No. What's that to do with anythin'?"

She arched a brow. "Oh, not a thing. Did you skip your coffee?"

He withdrew an assortment of supplies from a leather pouch and arranged them neatly in a row. "I awakened early. There was naught to be had."

"Hmm. That explains it."

"Explains what?"

"Your foul temper."

"My temper is fine."

"Then, why are you growling?"

His dark gaze glittered, his jaw flexing. "Ye dinnae ken anythin' about me, lass."

She crossed her arms. "I know you drink coffee rather than tea. I know you prefer your sister's bread to Abigail's and that you take it with jam for breakfast and gravy at dinner."

He grunted and shook his head. While she spoke, he prepared the musket with absent, practiced motions.

"I know you love to read and detest the rain," she continued, watching his hands with fascination. "I know you can make a discarded fence post into a work of art with nothing more than a sharp knife. I know you treat your men like family, and they speak of you like a god. I know you'd rather be surrounded by cows than people. I know your mood goes positively foul whenever you've had too little sleep or gone too long without eating." She paused. Swallowed a sudden lump.

He kept his eyes on his task.

"I know you don't want me here," she finished softly. "I'm sorry this burden fell to you, Campbell. I'm sorry I've brought such trouble to your door."

His mouth tightened. He shoved the ramrod down the barrel with some force. His motions were tight. Angry. Finally, he glanced up. The dark fire in those eyes made her retreat a step.

"Are ye done?" he snapped.

She blinked. He seemed … furious. Why? What had she said?

He offered the gun to her.

"Right. Yes. Ehrm, can't we begin with blades?" She cleared her throat. "Kate and I have had many conversations about the dirk. It seems an admirable weapon for personal defense."

"If a man gets near enough for ye to use a dirk against him, ye've already lost the fight."

"Oh, but surely—"

He lifted her hand and wrapped it around the stock. Neither of them wore gloves, and the contact sent pleasurable shivers up her arm. His fingers were callused, she noticed. She liked the roughness against her skin.

"Accustom yerself to the weight of it in yer hands," he said. His tone was stern rather than wrathful, now, but his expression remained thunderous. He moved behind her and positioned her hands where he wanted them on the gun.

All breath flew out of her body. He was pure heat and hardness surrounding her. Supporting her. Controlling her.

He notched the gun to her shoulder then murmured in her ear, "Now, listen carefully, Clarissa. Are ye listenin'?"

Somewhat. In truth, she could scarcely think. Every part of her seemed to have come alive at once—her bosoms, her hips, her thighs. Her neck and cheek and lips. Everything tingled. Sparkled. Heated and ached.

She managed to nod.

"A gun is a tool. Say it."

"A—a gun is a tool."

"And it's worthless if ye dinnae ken how to use it."

"Right."

"Now, ye're a wee lass. Nae match for a man's strength." One of his beautiful, massive hands slid to her neck. Callused fingers cupped her throat with the lightest pressure.

She nearly groaned. The tips of her breasts hardened and throbbed. Was he *trying* to seduce her?

"I could do anythin' to ye," he rasped in her ear. "Ye'd have naught to say about it." His fingers squeezed, more a caress than a threat. "But if ye have a gun and ye ken how to use it, my strength means nothin'. Yer size means nothin'. The disparity between us means nothin'. Because ye can down me with a shot from dozens of yards away. At that distance, we stand on equal footing. Do ye ken, lass?"

She couldn't speak. By God, the man was intoxicating. She breathed him in—spice and wool, skin and strength.

"Equal footing. Say it."

"Equal footing."

"Aye. Yer goal is to put distance between you and yer enemy. If he draws close enough to shoot, ye shoot him. Dinnae hesitate. Dinnae miss."

Her head was spinning. She licked her lips. "R-right."

"Clarissa."

She loved the way he said her name. "Hmm?"

"Are yer eyes closed?"

"Perhaps."

He sighed and moved away, leaving her holding the gun on her own. "Ye must open them."

She did. Slowly.

"Dinnae be afraid."

"No," she murmured. "I'm not."

He tapped a small protrusion on top of the gun. "This is yer sight. Line up what ye wish to strike with this. Never touch the trigger until ye've aimed properly. Never aim at anythin' ye'd be distressed to kill."

"I don't wish to kill anything." She blinked up at him. "Does that mean we can stop, now?"

He swiped a hand over his mouth. Had that been a smile? "Cheeky lass." He moved behind her again and turned her to face the hillside. "Picture the end of the barrel as a blade stretchin' a hundred yards."

"I believe I just cut that sapling in half, Mr. MacPherson."

This time, when he moved to her side, she saw his smile. It was faint, but it was there. "Campbell," he corrected softly. He held her gaze for a moment before continuing his instruction. "Always treat the gun as if it were loaded. Practice this position over and over when it's empty." He tapped her knuckles where she gripped the stock. "That way, yer hands learn to have a care for yer surroundings when yer mind is otherwise occupied."

Whenever he was near, her mind was always otherwise occupied. That was the everlasting problem.

She'd tried keeping her distance. She'd tried distracting herself with projects. She'd even tried picturing some of her more attractive suitors from last season. That had gone poorly. Mr. Osborne didn't make her tingle. Rather, he'd been the sort of man who formally requested a kiss before formally apologizing for asking.

She suspected Campbell MacPherson—were he the slightest bit interested in kissing her—wouldn't ask. He wouldn't have to. He was her weakness.

"… ready to fire, lass?"

She blinked. Nodded.

"Good. Aim for that log, then. Ye see it?"

Forcing herself to pay attention, she sighted the log he'd mentioned down the length of the barrel. "Yes."

"Use yer thumb to draw up the cock."

Heat surged, making her cheeks prickle. Drat. There went her peculiar problem again. The man was trying to instruct her, not proposition her, for pity's sake. *Focus,* she chided herself. *Focus.*

"When ye're ready, slide yer finger onto the trigger. Then, give it squeeze."

The tip of the gun shook.

"Steady, now." He braced her elbow. "Good lass. Take a breath."

Best to get this over with. She breathed. Cocked the gun. Moved her finger to the trigger. And fired.

The click-and-*crack* of the ignition was loud, the flashing fire too close to her face. She flinched, which spoiled her aim. She didn't know where her shot had landed, but the log remained unharmed. Also, she'd yelped like a deuced ninny.

He lifted the gun from her hands. His gaze glowed with an odd expression. Was it … approval?

"Well done for an English lass, I'd say."

"But I didn't strike my target."

"That wasnae the point."

"It wasn't?"

"Nah." He bent down to prop the musket against the boulder. "How do ye feel?"

Her arms were jellied. Her ears rang. Her shoulders felt stiff from holding the gun so long. But she'd done it. She'd fired a shot.

"Reasonably intact," she replied.

He nodded. "Next, ye'll learn to load."

For the following hour, Clarissa struggled with the paper cartridges full of black powder, the long ramrod and unwieldy barrel, the flashing fire that accompanied each shot, and finding the proper position for her hands. But she found she'd do almost anything to earn that glowing regard from Campbell MacPherson.

Her final shot sent wood flying up from the log. She lowered the gun and grinned her triumph. "Did you see?" She squinted. "Did I hit it?" She turned to him. "I think I did!"

He was staring at her strangely. "Aye. Ye did well."

She laughed, brushing a curl from her eye. "Fancy that." She moved to reload, but he clasped her arm.

"That's enough of long guns for today." He plucked the musket from her hands and bent to retrieve a wooden box from inside his canvas knapsack. He opened the hinged top to reveal the smallest, oddest-looking firearm she'd ever seen.

"This is a pocket pistol," he said, lifting it from its velvet-lined case. "It's useful for carryin' when ye travel or go about yer day. Good for personal protection. John Huxley gave me this one. I modified it for quicker loading."

She frowned. The gun was short—perhaps six inches—and had what appeared to be two barrels rather than one. "Are you certain … I mean, does it *work*? It seems so …" Her gaze slammed into his. Goodness, he was close. "Small."

Standing mere inches away, his heat produced the faint hint of spice she found so intoxicating. "Aye, it's a wee one. Which makes it easier to hide, ye ken?"

"Hide … where?"

He shrugged. "Yer purse."

"My reticule, you mean."

"Aye. Or a sporran. A pocket. A valise. Some lasses even keep one beneath their skirts, strapped to their …" When his eyes dropped below her waist, his neck went a bit ruddy. He cleared his throat. "Ye'll want to store it where ye'd have no trouble retrievin' it, should the need arise suddenly."

"Oh! Such as during a robbery."

"Aye." He angled the pistol this way and that, pointing out various features. "This is an over-under double barrel, which means ye have two shots rather than one. And that's a good thing, because yer range with a gun this wee is closer to ten yards than a hundred." He tapped the twin locks. "These work differently than the musket. I changed the mechanism to use percussion caps. Here. I'll show ye."

Watching him, amusement curved her lips. This was the closest she'd ever seen to Campbell MacPherson behaving with boyish enthusiasm. Although he was as inscrutable as ever, his motions and speech quickened, his eyes sparking.

"Come, lass." He waved her closer. "See this?" His thumb stroked a small metal nub near the hammer. "This is the key." Another stroke of his thumb. "Faster loadin'. Faster firin'. No fashin' about yer primer getting wet." Another stroke and another. "Ye slide this wee cap"—he held up a small metal bit from an open tin—"onto the nipple like so."

Her entire body jolted, squeezed, and quivered. "The—the what?"

"The nipple." He placed another cap on the second nub. Then, he froze. Almost as though he'd heard her thoughts blaring at him, a trumpeting fanfare of indecency.

She was a *lady*, she reminded herself. She should not be having these thoughts. They were inappropriate. Obscene. Picturing his thumb stroking … imagining more, perhaps his mouth upon …

Suddenly, she was sweltering.

He cleared his throat, but his voice remained hoarse. "The rest is much the same as the musket. A couple of balls. Rammin' the rod down …" He cleared his throat again. "Cockin' it." A swallow. "And fire away."

His neck had gone red again. Perhaps her peculiar affliction was catching.

Or perhaps she was so afflicted that she'd crossed into lunacy. Perhaps she was as mad as Northfield, obsessing over a man who didn't want her.

The thought was sobering. She backed away. "Heavens. You've taught me so much today, Mr. MacPherson," she said, injecting as much brightness as she could muster. "Any further lessons, and I'll surely forget more than I retain."

He nodded and rubbed his nape. Then, he carefully returned the pistol and all the other supplies to the knapsack. Finally, he handed her a flask. "Have a drink."

Realizing she was parched, she drank cautiously at first, but found it was simply water, so she gulped it down. When she finished, he was staring at her.

She rubbed her cheek and chin with her wrist. "I must look frightful. Do I have smudges …?"

He took the flask and drank, tipping it back while keeping his gaze on her. When he stuffed it into the knapsack, his motions were forceful. "Ye're fine," he gritted. "Bonnie as a fair spring day."

She blinked. He thought her bonnie?

Hefting the gun and pack, he led her eastward along the brook. His strides now were shorter, more accommodating to her own.

"Tell me about Northfield," he said.

Her stomach twisted. "What—what do you wish to know?"

He cast a dark, inscrutable look over his shoulder. "Everythin'. From the beginning. How did ye meet?"

She blew out a breath as they reached a bend in the stream and slowed to a halt beneath a cluster of birches.

Rubbing her forehead, she worked against the tightness in her throat. The acrid, faintly sulfuric scent of gunpowder remained on her hands.

How much should she say? "I first noticed him year before last. He'd returned to London from his travels in India and Africa. His father and grandfather are renowned hunters. Stephen inherited their prowess."

"Stephen?"

"Mmm. Stephen Northfield. His grandfather is a viscount, but he is a second son, so no title." She waved dismissively. "In any event, he'd been away from London for many years, and when he returned, he made quite an impression on the young ladies. Alas, none of them claimed his notice."

"What about you?"

"Me?" Her cheeks warmed. She fussed away the curls along her jaw. "I was a wallflower. Nobody took notice of me that season."

The furrow between his brows deepened. "Were they all blind, then?"

Something about his reaction made her tingle from head to toe. To distract herself, she picked her way down to the water and stooped to wash her hands. "I was different at the time," she answered. "Plumper."

"What difference does that make? Are Englishmen bluidy daft?"

Warmth joined the tingles. She pressed her lips together as a smile took hold. "You're very kind, Mr. MacPherson, but—"

Another grunt, nearer this time.

She straightened to find him standing beside her.

His eyes flashed as hot as a musket blast. "We'll save time if we cross here. I mean to lift ye."

Oh, good heavens. No sooner had he issued the warning than he scooped her into his arms. The man could have carried her off to a bed of grass and leaves for an afternoon of debauchery, and she would not have uttered a single protest. All the tingles and warmth intensified a hundredfold. Her mind went blank. Her arms went around his muscular neck.

By the time he set her down on the opposite bank, she was weak with longing.

Gently, he drew her arms away and gazed at her with that familiar-yet-strange expression. She couldn't quite define it—part intensity, part curiosity, part pain. Why should it pain him to look at her?

He took her elbow and urged her forward. "When did he take notice of ye?"

As they crossed the wide field, she tried to regain her composure. "Last year. Early spring."

"How did it start?"

"As I said, by last season, I'd changed a fair bit. Kate and Francis brought out the best in me, it would seem. After many seasons going unnoticed, I confess, I was flattered by the new attention. More gentlemen evinced an interest in courtship than in the previous eight years combined."

He muttered something like, "*Courtship.* Right," while his jaw muscles flickered.

"Mr. Northfield was among them. We were introduced at Lady Underwood's soirée. He seemed lovely at first. Polite. Intelligent. Handsome."

Campbell's thunderous mood returned, heralded by the grinding of his teeth. "Describe him."

She shot her giant companion a cautious glance. Perhaps she was improving at reading his moods. Something had sparked his temper; that much was clear. "Brown hair—lighter than yours by several shades. He's tall. Perhaps two or three inches above six feet. Athletic. Fine eyes. A sort of blue-gray, as I recall. Handsome in the usual way of English gentlemen." She grinned, trying to lighten his mood. "But with better teeth. I don't know how that happened. His father resembles the offspring of a hare and a goat."

She thought she spied the corner of Campbell's hard mouth lifting ever so slightly. A small victory?

He offered his hand to help her navigate a rocky slope. Once again, his calluses gave her a pleasurable shiver. "When did ye ken aught was amiss?"

"We were strolling together near the Serpentine. Hyde Park. Have you ever been?"

"Once."

She nodded. "I mentioned a particular song I enjoy. A French tune. He remarked that he'd heard me play it on the pianoforte." She swallowed, recalling Stephen's face at that moment—the overly wide eyes, the disturbing tilt of his head. In his moments of madness, he often appeared to be listening to sounds that weren't there. "I'd only ever played the song at night, alone in my grandmother's townhouse."

"So, ye kenned he'd been watchin' ye."

"Yes. I found it … distressing."

"Bluidy hell," he spat. "What happened next?"

"We saw one another again at a ball the following week. He caused a scene when I consented to dance with another suitor, Mr. Osborne. We argued. He attempted to kiss me. I … I struck him." She shook her head and peered at the horizon. "Afterward, I felt horrid. He apologized and seemed as bewildered as a little boy. Still, his pursuit had become … inappropriate. Thereafter, I endeavored to distance myself. Declined all further invitations for outings. Returned his gifts."

"He was sendin' gifts?"

"Every day, yes. Flowers. Fruit. Gloves and jewels. Perfume." Her stomach cramped. *Steady,* she thought. *Mustn't be sick.* "Even silk stockings, once. They were embroidered with r-red roses." She wrapped her arms around her middle. "His letters grew increasingly urgent and … intimate. He seemed to think I'd consented to marry him, that we were madly in love, and that my grandmother's objections to our union were the only barrier standing between us. He behaved as though we'd—as though he'd already …" She couldn't say it. Reading his words had been bad enough. Repeating them turned her stomach.

Campbell was silent. His face angled away from her as they walked, so she couldn't see his expression. But that big, muscular frame moved stiffly, his tension resonating as she'd never seen it.

"When the season ended, Grandmama and I returned to Ellery Hall. There, his letters continued to arrive, sometimes two or three in a single day. When we spied him in a nearby village, we knew this was not merely a frightful nuisance any longer. He was dangerous. And worsening. So, we accepted an invitation to a house party in Northumberland. We arrived early and stayed long." She shot him a wry smile, but Campbell's face was still turned away from her. "Lady Wallingham was a bit cross with us for overstaying our welcome, but Grimsgate Castle made a splendid sanctuary."

Her smile faded. "We hoped he would lose interest, you see. That a few weeks without seeing me might bring him to his senses. And, for a time, it worked. Upon our return to Ellery, we discovered his letters had stopped. All but one. In that letter, he sounded like a stranger. He apologized for his fits of madness. He said when such episodes came upon him, he'd very little control of his own mind, and that he deeply regretted the distress he'd caused me. He promised never to harm me or those I loved."

Campbell halted a few feet ahead of her.

She stopped, too, waiting for the inevitable question.

"What happened?" he rumbled, his voice grinding like a millstone. He still hadn't looked in her direction.

She drifted closer, needing his strength. "He broke his promise."

An enormous hand came up to scrape over his jaw. "Tell me, lass. Tell me everythin'."

She didn't want to. Even now, the memories made her gorge rise. But she owed Campbell more than she'd ever be able to repay. The least she could do was explain what he was facing.

With a deep breath, she endeavored to answer. "First, I must tell you about a friend of mine. A mischief maker. My staunchest companion." She smiled as the world turned watery. "His name was Dash."

Chapter Eight

Her dream began in the usual fashion—as a nightmare. Thick Scottish fog made it impossible to see farther than the length of her arm. She knew she was near water, for she could hear it licking against rocks. She'd drawn her cloak's hood up around her face. Shivering, she noted the tip of her nose was numb.

He was here. Oppressive. Insane. She could almost hear him sigh.

Clarissa.

Her name was a sinister slide. Close.

Her heart pounded a deafening drumbeat. She waited for him. Why was she waiting? Why would she stand still and let him find her?

You wore red for me, fair one. You wanted to be seen.

Icy fear froze her stiff. She shook and shook. Every muscle wanted to run, but she must stand still. Why? Why, why, why?

Blinded by fog and nightfall, she dared to spin in place. Beneath her feet was green, shorn grass. Near her hand was a fencepost. It had been carved into the shape of an owl. Heart pounding, she ran numb fingertips over damp wood. The feathers softened. Became real. They warmed her hand. The bird took flight, disappearing into the darkness.

Instantly, the dream changed. The hunted feeling lifted. Night brightened into day. Fog receded. Her heart slowed. Her skin heated as if summer had come all at once. She shrugged off her cloak, letting it drop onto the grass.

Fog swirled away, farther and farther. She stood beside blue water lapping at a stony shore. Above, sunlight sliced through the mist in an angling sweep.

Someone drew near. Not sinister. Not a threat. No. The opposite, in fact. This man was safety. This man was firm ground beneath her feet after eons at sea.

He moved behind her, an enormous shadow merging with hers. She leaned back into a hard, unyielding wall and sighed his name. *Campbell.*

Hard arms engulfed her. A square, bristled jaw nuzzled her cheek while firm lips nibbled her neck. "I mean to touch ye, lass."

She groaned, knowing what was to come, knowing because she'd dreamt of him so often. Her body lit on fire. "Yes," she begged, melting against his big, hard frame. "Please."

Enormous, capable hands cupped her breasts. He thumbed her nipples through her gown, making her writhe. Fire streaked from the sensitive tips down to the juncture of her thighs. She reached up and back for his neck, gripping those thick muscles and turning her mouth up for his kiss.

He didn't offer it. Instead, he teased her with his mouth on her neck, his tongue tracing her skin. His hands kneaded her breasts until they swelled and begged for him. He stroked her nipples, squeezing with exquisite pressure. He lowered one hand to draw her skirt up her thighs.

Part of her knew what to expect. She'd dreamt of him a hundred times, felt his touch on every inch of her body.

Another part of her felt virginal, vulnerable. She waited breathlessly to discover the brush of his fingers against her most secretive, desirous center. His fingers hovered there, now. They slid with delicate pressure.

"Here, ye belong to me, lass. Only me." His hand swept down to cup her firmly. His palm pressed and worked gently against her folds. "This is mine. *You* are mine. He'll never have ye. No man will."

He was so enormous behind her, so strong that his hands always astounded her with their control. How many times had he brought her to a blistering peak? How many times had he done things to her she'd scarcely imagined before she'd met him?

And now, every night, she dreamt them. Erotic, forbidden things with a man who would never be hers. This was yet another dream, and she knew how it would end. He'd kiss her. And pleasure her. He'd stroke and tease and do wicked, carnal things until she awakened, her body covered in sweat, her hands reaching for her own breasts, pulsing with remembered satisfaction.

Wanting more. Always, more and more. She'd never be satisfied because this wasn't real.

God, how she needed it to be real.

She shook her head against his chest. Arched her back as he fingered her folds, whispering that she mustn't deny him and he'd never let her go.

Another man had once said these same words, and she'd felt terror. Campbell said them, and she felt blissful longing.

He drove her higher. Circled her tender nub and pinched her tender nipple. She felt the edge of his teeth nipping her ear. "Do ye ken how much ye consume me, love?" He buried his face in her loosened hair. "Christ, I'd kill to be inside ye. I'd crawl on my knees to taste yer sweet cunny when ye come. Would ye like that?"

"I want it," she panted. "I wish this was real."

"Would ye let me touch ye like this, love? Feel how wet ye are." His longest finger slid deep inside her sheath. "Like a hot, soaked silk glove. Ye burn me, sweet Clarissa. Ye drown me."

"Yes. Deeper. Please."

"If this werenae a dream, would ye let me take ye like this?" His free arm squeezed her waist, lifting and lowering her until they were both on their knees amidst the folds of her red cloak. He angled her forward and whispered, "Would ye give me whatever I asked?"

She groaned and drove her hips back, forcing his finger deeper. In her ear, his breathing sounded harsh.

"I'd give you anything, Campbell. Everything. Don't you understand? If you wanted me, I'd be yours."

His head lowered to her shoulder. His chest heaved against her back. "Ye only say that because this isnae real. And because ye dinnae ken the truth."

"No, I—"

He yanked her upright and buried his face in her hair again before gathering the mass in his free hand.

She glanced down to see the goat-shaped fertility charm Mrs. MacBean had given her dangling between her bosoms.

His hand continued working between her legs. His breath fanned hot against her shoulder. He drew her back until her thighs straddled his lap, giving him perfect access to her folds. He released her hair to gently cup her throat. Below, he kept working his finger deeper, pressuring her swollen folds with his palm.

And driving her utterly mad.

"Where did that wee charm come from, eh?"

She couldn't answer. Her head thrummed with heat, her body writhing on the precipice of an explosion. Tighter and tighter the pleasure coiled.

"'Twill never work. What's gone is gone. Some punishments last forever."

What was he talking about? She didn't know. Didn't care. "Campbell. Please."

"Never think I dinnae want ye, love."

She groaned as his words hit her bloodstream. "I wish …"

"I'd bluidy kill and die for ye." He thrust his finger deep, ground his hand against her core, and sent her soaring into the sky.

Sobbing, she clawed his arm, her body undulating as wave after wave broke through her. Ecstasy rippled and pulsed as she collapsed into his arms.

She awakened to the sound of her own gasps. Her chamber was cold. Or, perhaps, she was wet.

She glanced down. Yes, her shift plastered to her body, her nipples tight points beneath damp linen. She'd kicked away her blankets. She'd made a mess of her bed. Pleasure still pulsed between her thighs.

Outside, dawn blushed the sky.

Rolling onto her side, she stared at the changing light, giving her body a chance to recover. From the next bedchamber, she heard a masculine grunt. A low, murmured word to Fergus. A door opening with a faint creak. Then, she heard boots walking away.

And, as she sometimes did after one of her Campbell dreams, Clarissa turned her face into her pillow and wept for what could never be.

Life, Clarissa had decided, was a patchwork of tasks to be done. She stitched her days together one small hour at a time—a bit of sewing here, a pot of tea there. Plotting Campbell's future garden took two hours and formulating the list of seeds took a third. Sorting through his stored carvings and placing them around the cottage took one more.

Unfortunately, she ran out of tasks by half-past two. Campbell had gone to the distillery for the day, which meant a temporary halt to her training, thank heavens. Disciplining her mouth—or any other part—around him required fortitude she didn't have, particularly after the dream she'd had last night.

So, when Rannoch arrived with Stuart MacDonnell in a loaded wagon, she was grateful for the distraction. She threw open the front door, expecting only to greet the two men. Instead, she saw Rannoch lifting a small, cloaked figure down from the back of the canvas-covered wagon. He placed the figure on her feet, and the red-haired Stuart helped her toward the door.

Clarissa's breath caught, gathered into an ache. Sudden joy, like sunlight bolting across the bleak landscape of constant fear, hit her squarely in the middle. "Grandmama?"

Smile-shaped creases and glossing blue eyes curved into a grin. "Dearest," she whispered, holding out her arms.

Clarissa rushed into her embrace. She held her fragile grandmother while Rannoch and Stuart murmured to someone nearby. Clarissa couldn't be bothered to wonder who it was.

She felt like a child again, a child whose world had turned hostile, painful, and dark.

Grandmama kissed her cheek and stroked her hair. "There, there, my darling girl. Shh. I'm here."

Her throat burned. Tears slid. A sob escaped. "I m-missed you dreadfully."

"I know. I missed you, too."

She should be stronger than this. The ache in her chest felt like grief. Fear and grief and unbearable love. For long minutes, all she could do was cling. She'd held herself together for the past ten days. She'd had no idea how close to broken she was. "It's ridiculous ..."

"What, dearest?"

"That I needed you so much." She gasped. Whimpered into her grandmother's rosewater-scented shawl. Caught her breath. "I didn't realize it until I saw you. Good heavens, I'm leaky as a cracked pot."

Grandmama cupped Clarissa's cheeks. Both of them were weepy messes. "We're part of each other," she said, smiling like a sunrise. "Bearing heavy loads requires all parts to be properly assembled and in good working order. So, here I am."

Releasing a watery chuckle as she dug a handkerchief from her sleeve, Clarissa looked her grandmother over. "*Are* you in good working order?"

Grandmama patted her arms. "Yes. Much better, now."

The gray-clad Magdalene Cuthbert approached from the direction of the wagon. She came to stand beside Grandmama with a soft, fond expression. "Her ladyship's cough is much improved, I'm pleased to say."

Clarissa thanked the young woman for her good care and suggested tea. An hour later, chatting around the hearth in the front room, she poured a second cup for Miss Cuthbert while Grandmama described the strange conversation she'd had with Mrs. MacBean the previous day.

"I daresay she may be *slightly* mad," Grandmama said with amusement. "She claimed my dear, sweet Alfie visited her cottage thrice this past week to relay an incomprehensible message about honeycombs, swine, and letter openers. I explained that he's been dead for thirteen years, of course. She asked why being dead should matter." Grandmama chuckled and sipped her tea. "Mad rubbish. Yet, I cannot fault her remedies, for they have worked wonders."

Indeed, Grandmama's voice and color were nearly back to normal. Clarissa found herself reaching for her spotted, fragile hand repeatedly. She hated needing reassurance this much. But for thirteen years, they'd had only each other. Being separated had been … difficult.

"Mrs. MacBean is a gifted herbalist," agreed Magdalene. "She's promised to teach me her formulations and tutor me in midwifery, provided I remain here in the glen."

"Are you thinking of leaving?" Clarissa asked.

Gray eyes lowered then shifted away. "I've considered it. The MacPhersons are generous men, but I shouldn't like to become a burden."

Grandmama scoffed. "A burden? Don't be silly. Everyone here relies upon you. Where else would you go?"

Before she'd finished her question, the door opened. Rannoch and Stuart strode in, removing their hats and nodding their greetings. Stuart carried a sack of onions toward the kitchen.

Looking particularly handsome with his black hair wind-tousled and his chiseled jaw highlighted by slanting light, Rannoch flashed his usual, irresistible grin. "Ladies. Havin' a pleasant blether, eh?" After glancing around at the curtains and newly arranged furniture, he raised a brow and whistled. "Why, Miss

Meadows. Seems ye've added a spot of bonnie to Campbell's sorry, empty house."

She smiled, pleased that he'd noticed. "It's my way of thanking him for all he's done for me. Do you like it?"

"Aye, 'tis lovely. The curtains, the chairs. Well done." When he focused on the carvings Clarissa had placed on the mantel, his head tilted. "What's this? Havenae seen this bird in ages."

Pouring herself more tea, she twisted to admire the black-fired raven. With its wings outstretched, it occupied half the mantel's length. The fish carving and a copper pitcher occupied the other half. "I found them in a crate and thought them too beautiful to be hidden away," she explained.

Initially, she'd considered displaying another of Campbell's carvings—the mysterious beauty with the wild black hair. She burned to know who the woman was and had thought provoking him might satisfy her curiosity. But she'd cut the impulse short. She had no claim on him, no right to entertain such jealousies.

Rannoch wandered closer and traced a finger across one intricate wing. "Reminds me of a pendant our *seanair*—our grandfather—made before he died. Cam wore it for a long time. Years. Refused to take it off. Then, he left for war, put it away. Havenae seen it since. He quit carvin', too, until last year."

Clarissa recalled Broderick mentioning their maternal grandfather had been a metalsmith. Kate's wedding ring was one of his pieces. "Legend has it your grandfather was a renowned craftsman."

"Aye. Some claim he had the sight. Our mam, too. Kenned how a battle would end ere it began. Kenned how to win the favor and protection of the wee folk." Rannoch slid a fingertip over the raven's beak.

"Do you believe in such things?"

Shrugging, he shot her a wry smile. "Didnae stop death, did they?"

A fair point. "Do you remember them well? Your mother and grandfather, I mean."

He shook his head. "*Seanair* died before I was born. Mam a few years later. I only remember a wee bit. She wore white heather in her hair. Sang like an angel when she wanted us lads to sleep." He gave the raven's wing one last stroke and sighed. "Cam remembers her better."

Clarissa eyed the bird's wings, marveling again at how alive the creature seemed, how light rippled along the feathers like an undulation. Such skill it must have taken. Such patience.

After amusing them with an anecdote about one of the distillery's workmen falling asleep in the malt barn and waking up buried in barley, Rannoch focused on

Clarissa. "Have ye learned any Scottish dances yet, Miss Meadows?"

"Only the reel, I'm afraid, though I'd dearly love to learn more. Kate said on All Hallows Eve, the villagers in Glenscannadoo have a gathering called a *ceilidh*. Am I saying that right?"

"Aye. *Kay-lee.*"

"Likely I shan't be here long enough to attend, but it sounds such a lively treat."

"There's dancin' at the Highland Games, too. Competitions, in fact, one for lads and one for lasses." He grinned. "If ye're interested, I could teach ye a wee bit."

"Oh!" Excitement stirred. "That would be splendid! I shouldn't like to be a bother. Perhaps when you next bring Grandmama and Miss Cuthbert for a visit, you could give us all a lesson." She cast a querying look toward the other two women.

Grandmama nodded and sipped her tea.

Red bloomed like a ruddy plume in Magdalene's throat and cheeks. "I've had lessons before," she murmured.

Rannoch shot her a surprised glance. "Ye have?"

She smoothed an imaginary wrinkle from her skirt. "At the orphanage, we learned from a kindly headmistress. Good exercise, she said." A quirk of amusement lit Magdalene's features. She wasn't beautiful. With her long nose and narrow face, even "plain" edged toward flattery. But when her eyes smiled and her full lips curved at one corner, she had the appeal of something rare. "I suspect she simply enjoyed dancing and wanted the excuse. She didn't last long."

Frowning, Rannoch rubbed his nape. "That's the most ye've ever said about the orphanage, lass."

Her smile faded. "My apologies if I've no tales to amuse ye, Mr. MacPherson."

Clarissa blinked at the tart retort. Were they quarreling?

Softly, he replied, "I didnae ask for amusement."

Magdalene's color deepened. A tense silence lengthened.

"And, for God's sake, call me Rannoch," he grumbled. "Mr. MacPherson is my da."

Regaining her equilibrium, Magdalene raised her chin. "Are the supplies unloaded from the wagon?"

"Aye."

"Perhaps ye'd care for something to eat before we return to Rowan House."

Rannoch raked a hand through his hair. "Aye." His smile was wry and weary. "Ye've a keen sense for the

MacPherson appetite, Mouse. I'll see what the maids can find for us in the kitchen."

As Rannoch strode off toward the kitchen, Magdalene's soft, gray gaze followed him like a kitten tracking a bright feather—with painful, fascinated longing.

Clarissa's breath halted in a moment of recognition.

She locked eyes with Grandmama, whose brows were drawn with sympathy. *Yes,* her expression said. *This is how you look at another MacPherson.*

It was true. Clarissa recognized every element of Magdalene's stolen glance: the agony of wanting, the glow of admiration, of helpless adoration. The realization that one would never have what one wanted most.

She'd felt this. Over and over, she'd felt it bloom until it burst out of her in streams of babbling obscenity.

Seeing it in someone else was both kinship and … heartbreak.

On impulse, she offered Magdalene a lifeline. "Next time you come for a visit, you must help me learn the Scottish dances. You simply must. Please say you will."

First came a flummoxed gray blink. Then, a series of rusty squeaks—the origin of Rannoch's nickname for her, according to Kate. Finally, Magdalene answered, "I—I suppose … that is … if ye wish."

"We'll ask Daniel MacDonnell to play his fiddle for us. He's not as skilled as Broderick, of course, but he'll do. Lovely man, Daniel. Stuart's cousin. Works for Campbell. Have you met him?"

She shook her head.

"Very kind. Handsome beard. I'd never fully contemplated the merits of bearded men. Have you?"

Another headshake.

Grandmama cleared her throat as if to say, *My dear, you are pressing too hard. Don't give away the game just yet.*

"In any event, we'll coax Daniel to play whilst you and I practice our dancing. We'll begin with a reel. Jolly fun. Lots of leaping about." Realizing she was rambling, Clarissa forced herself to focus. "Forgive me. I'm afraid if I don't have something to look forward to, I may go stark staring mad. You'll be saving my sanity."

Magdalene's amusement broke past her reticence. For a split second before giggling behind her hand, she revealed her teeth in a full, beaming smile. Magdalene was bashful about her teeth, which were a bit large for her mouth. But Clarissa found her smile lovely. Perhaps, in time, she could persuade her to stop hiding it. "If ye'd care for my company, Miss Meadows, I shall be glad to join ye for a wee bit of dancing."

Of course, Francis would return for Clarissa soon, and she'd have to leave. No dancing at the summer's

Highland Games or the Halloween *ceilidh*. No lengthy campaigns to restore Miss Cuthbert's smile or matchmake for her and Daniel.

Soon, Clarissa would return to England. Soon, she'd leave … him.

Her despair felt ridiculous. She should be glad to go. Everyone would be safer.

Swallowing the ache in her throat, Clarissa summoned her brightest expression for Magdalene. "Splendid," she said, quickly changing the subject. "Grandmama, you should have a look at my plan for Campbell's garden. I'm torn between cauliflower and kale."

Grandmama finished her tea, setting her cup aside with a clink. "Hmm. Have you had word from Teversham, dear?"

She sat straighter. Felt colder. "A few days ago, yes. Francis said all is well. He hopes to return by April."

"Before planting starts, then." Grandmama glanced around the room. "One imagines you'll be missed here. You've a knack for making beauty out of nothing much at all."

Clarissa's throat tightened. Burned. "I'd like to do more. But I can't ask Cam—the MacPhersons to shelter me forever."

Her eyes crinkled. "Can't you? Surely there's *some* recompense Mr. MacPherson would find … intriguing." She sipped her tea and arched a brow.

"I already intend to plant his garden."

"I'd envisioned the arrangement working the other way around."

Magdalene snorted, coughing into her tea.

"Grandmama!"

"Did I ever tell you about my first outing with my dear, sweet Alfie?"

Clarissa sighed. "Yes."

"A sweltering day in August. I wore my most daring bodice."

"Is the teapot empty?" Clarissa lifted the lid. "Perhaps I should take it to the kitchen for a refill."

"We went for a curricle ride round the small village of Alconbury. Alfie drove. Neither of us wished to be there."

Magdalene sat forward to place her cup on the tray. "Why consent to the outing, then?"

"Our families had been scheming to match us for years. Of course, Alfie and I were appalled by the idea. He relished politics, whereas I find the subject loathsome. He preferred London, whereas I'd suffered my first season the way one suffers through consumption. And, whilst I longed for a good husband keen to begin … *gardening*, as it were, he thought himself too young for marriage and fatherhood." Her eyes took on a familiar sparkle. "Our only point of agreement was that marrying each other would be disastrous. And so, a conspiracy was born: We would pretend courtship to pacify our families then stage a parting of ways—for finality, you see. Clever enough, I thought." She paused to smile. "I assumed spending time in his company would be irksome, but without the pressure of expectation, I found myself liking him a *great* deal."

Recalling Grandpapa's quiet intelligence and mischievous humor, Clarissa understood the appeal. "I'm certain he told you one of his farmer-and-hound jokes. Or the one about the talking goose. How could you resist?"

"I couldn't. In the time it took us to travel from my father's house to Alconbury, I'd begun to think him handsome." She angled toward Magdalene. "He wasn't, particularly. But charming? Oh my, yes." Her laugh ended in a sigh. "We stopped for a stroll near the brook. My parasol malfunctioned, and he offered to repair it. Watching him do so was … rather affecting." Wrinkled cheeks pinkened. "I'd just sat down on a log near the water when I felt the first sting."

Magdalene's eyes widened. "Bees?"

Grandmama nodded with a grimace. "A nest inside the log. I leapt up and began shouting, which aggravated them into a swarm. My dear, sweet Alfie raced to help. He was stung four times and I a dozen before he hefted me over his shoulder and carried me into the water. There we stood, soaked to the skin. Cursing. Miserable." Her eyes softened. "Then, we started laughing. Together, at the same instant. When we stopped, he kissed me."

"That wasn't how he told it, Grandmama," Clarissa said wryly.

"Very well, I kissed him. And asked his assistance with my bodice. And I *may* have requested he examine a sting on my thigh. In any event, a door was opened that couldn't be easily shut. We married the following spring. *Gardening* began shortly thereafter."

Magdalene frowned. "Ye changed his mind, then. About marriage and fatherhood."

"No. He still felt he was too young. Only two-and-twenty."

"Then why …?"

"Because we needed to be together." Grandmama caught Clarissa's gaze and nodded toward the carvings on the mantel. "The way fish need water and birds need sky."

Clarissa shook her head. Swallowed a lump.

"Most never find what Alfie and I stumbled upon by accident. Neither of us were willing to toss that away merely because of poor timing." Her gaze remained intent upon Clarissa. "Such a gift should not be ignored."

"And if he hadn't felt as you did?" Clarissa murmured. "If he'd instead looked upon you with pity or indifference, would you still view it as a gift? Or would you think yourself cursed?"

"If I hadn't pressed, I mightn't have realized he felt anything at all." She leaned forward, chin raised. "Sometimes, we must fight, dearest. Even when we most want to hide."

"How I wish it were that simple."

"It is. Not easy, perhaps. But simple."

Their conversation ended when Rannoch returned to the front room, saying the weather was about to worsen and they'd best take their leave. A short while later, Clarissa accompanied her guests outside. Despite feeling bruised from Grandmama's gentle chiding, she hugged her tightly before Stuart lifted Grandmama and Magdalene back into the wagon.

"Not much longer now," she whispered to herself as she watched the wagon roll out of sight. "Not much longer, and this will be over." Even to her, the reassurance sounded hollow.

A sharp breeze cut past her shawl and billowed her skirt. A stronger gust shoved at her, driving her back toward the cottage. She glanced to the darkening sky. Low clouds sent down wispy fingers to brush brown moss and newly sprouting grass. The air smelled of rain. Frowning, she noticed a black bird launching from the roof before sailing high overhead. Suddenly, it swooped down, crossed to the eastern rise, and circled a rocky outcropping thrice.

A deep shiver shook her. Unease prickled her nape. A shadow near the largest boulder was shaped like a man. It didn't move.

Her breath stopped short. Her mouth went dry. She backed toward the cottage door, dread washing her insides with ice.

Was she imagining things? Was that his hand? A gun?

Was he there … watching?

Heart pounding, she reminded herself that Campbell had men posted on both sides of the house. Surely, they would have seen someone approach.

Unless they were in the privy. Or having a nip behind the barn, as she'd seen them do several times. Or drifting off to sleep with their caps over their eyes, as she'd also seen. They were cattlemen, not soldiers.

The black bird circled and circled. Another gust. The shadow moved. Metal glinted.

She scrambled backward. Spinning. Running. Slipping. Gripping the door latch. Thrusting. Slamming. Sprinting. Inside, she raced for the kitchen. The maids rushed forward with worried frowns as she struggled to catch her breath. "D-Daniel. Has he returned from his patrol?"

Jean and Abigail both shook their heads. "What is it?" Abigail asked. "What happened?"

"There was someone … on the ridge … watching the house. I think. I don't know …" She rubbed her forehead. Was she going mad? Perhaps. But her heart still raced. Her skin still prickled a clanging alarm.

What if Northfield had done something to Daniel? What if he'd done something to …?

Panic surged. "Fergus." She gripped Abigail's arm. Shook it. "Oh, God. Where is Fergus?"

The round-faced maid tried to steady Clarissa, murmuring nonsense about staying calm.

"You don't understand. He'll hurt him. He'll …" Her breath caught on a sob. She bolted for the scullery door, both maids calling after her. "Must find him." She yanked it open and dashed outside, shouting toward the barn, "Fergus!"

From behind the barn, one of Campbell's lanky farmhands emerged. He carried a weathered rifle. "Miss Meadows? What's amiss?"

"Where is Daniel? And Fergus?"

He shot her a puzzled frown. "Is there trouble at the house—"

"Just tell me where they are!"

He pointed over his shoulder with his thumb.

Before he could say another word, she hiked up her skirts and ran. She'd only gone a dozen feet when, from behind the barn, stalked a towering, glowering, mountainous male. Fergus trotted at his side. Daniel trailed behind them both.

Instantly, her heart flooded her body with bone-melting relief.

"Campbell." It felt like a bellow but emerged as a sigh. She stumbled to a halt.

He crossed the yard with long, intimidating strides. Dark, flashing eyes locked upon her. "What's wrong, lass?"

She didn't think. She simply ran, stumbling at first then racing. She collided with him at full speed, requiring him to step back to absorb the impact. Her arms latched around his waist. Her face buried in his shirt. She breathed him in.

Steel bands wrapped around her back. A huge hand cupped her nape gently. His fingers were cold and so very, very welcome.

Heavens, he felt solid. Immense. Like shelter.

"Tell me what happened."

"He—I thought I saw someone." She burrowed into him, clinging harder. "I can't be certain." Breathlessly, she described the shadow and the sensation of being watched.

Campbell started to withdraw, but she clutched him with all ten fingers.

"No," she gritted. "If it is him, he'll try to hurt you."

"If it's him, he's on *my* land," came a deep, resolute rumble. Huge, strong hands cradled her jaw gently. "Ye must trust me."

She gazed up at his hard, ferocious face, heart pounding. Aching. "P-please. Be careful."

With stunning tenderness, he brushed his lips along her temple and set her away. "Daniel," he said without looking away from her. "Take her and Fergus to the house. I'll join ye soon."

He claimed the worn rifle from his lanky farmhand and strode away.

She wanted to weep and scream and demand he stay with her. But she couldn't. If Northfield was watching the house, if he had his gun with him, all of them were at risk.

Fergus nuzzled her palm. She patted his neck before she could stop herself.

They returned to the kitchen, where the maids halted their chatter the instant Clarissa entered. Likely they'd been gossiping about her mad ranting. Avoiding their wary, sympathetic gazes, she busied herself preparing meat scraps and pouring water for Fergus. Tense minutes passed while she gathered her composure.

Daniel sat beside her at the table. "I'm sorry I wasnae here when ye took a fright," he said gently. "Fergus was playin' hide-and-seek with a hare. Delayed our return a wee bit."

She nodded, feeling utterly foolish for her earlier panic. Her hands shook as she placed Fergus's bowls on the floor. The dog greedily lapped at the water, snuffling loudly. The need to wrap her arms around him and kiss him between those beautiful eyes seized her until she had to clutch the edge of the table to lock herself in place.

She squeezed it doubly hard when Campbell returned. "Did you find … anything?"

He raised a canvas knapsack like the one he'd carried day before last, only this one was dirtier. Then, he propped a shovel against the scullery wall. Finally, he dug a dingy wool cap from his pocket and hung the hat on the shovel's handle. From inside the scullery doorway, a shamefaced farm hand mumbled an apology.

Campbell glared at the ruddy-flushed youth. "She cannae hear ye."

The farm hand—Jamie was his name, as she recalled—cleared his throat with a rusty squeak. "Very sorry, Miss Meadows. I was diggin' in that area and left my supplies near the rocks whilst I went for a … whilst I … *ahem* … that is—"

"He was havin' a piss." Campbell's crushing glare never lifted from Jamie's woebegone head. "He left the shovel propped against the stones with his cap on the handle. Would have resembled a man at a distance. Likely that's what ye saw."

Strangely, the tight knot in her stomach failed to unravel. She lowered her gaze to Fergus's back then to her own hands. Her knuckles were bloodless. "It was my mistake," she murmured. "I'm sorry to have troubled you all."

The maids' pitying silence merged with Fergus's snuffling to form a mortifying hush. Clarissa's cheeks burned. In brisk tones, Campbell sent Jamie and Daniel back outside to finish their work, then ordered her to follow him into the front room. Reluctantly, she did.

As usual, nervousness spurred her mouth into motion. "I—I wasn't expecting you home so soon. Was your day … productive?"

A neutral grunt. He shrugged out of his heavy woolen coat and crossed to hang it by the front door.

"With so many responsibilities, both here and at the distillery, I'm surprised you find time to visit Rowan House with such frequency. Of course, the food there is lovely. I never considered that putting something Scottish in my mouth could be so pleasurable."

He stilled while removing his hat, stiffened, then hung it on the hook.

"But pleasure it is," she continued. "Hearty, *substantial* fare. Quite filling. Too much so, in all honesty. Having one's body stuffed beyond its capacity may seem pleasurable in the frenzy of the moment, but it's rarely worth the discomfort afterward."

He ran a hand through damp, dark hair. With a roll of his shoulders, he moved to the fireplace and stabbed at the embers. Flames licked upward. Briefly, his gaze settled on the bird carvings. He frowned but held his silence.

She rushed onward. "Still, even for the sake of a delectable meal, riding all that way must be vexing.

Forgive me, but Scottish weather is dreadful. I mean no insult, of course. English weather is also quite dreary. At Ellery Hall, I've been known to plead a headache when I wish to avoid a soaking ride."

He cast her a dark, penetrating look and rolled his shoulders again.

She cleared her throat. "Perhaps your rides offer an exhilarating diversion. Today, I would have welcomed a pounding gallop, I daresay."

He stared at her strangely, his gaze flickering over her bodice. Had she said something peculiar?

She smiled. "Of late, my schedule has been rather sparse, and it's made me restless. Thankfully, Rannoch brought Grandmama for a visit."

He ran a hand over his jaw. "Aye, I asked him to."

"You did?"

He nodded.

"Oh. That was … kind of you." Kind and unexpectedly thoughtful. Had he sensed how much she'd needed it? "Earlier, I was in the drive seeing everyone off, but I didn't see you arrive."

"No, ye wouldnae have. Most days, I take a shorter path along the burn."

"Through the glen where we had our lesson?"

"Aye, the burn feeds MacPherson Distillery. Best water, best whisky."

"I'd enjoy touring the distillery one day. Kate says—"

"Calm yerself, lass."

She paused, noticing her breaths were fast and shallow. "I'm perfectly calm."

Slowly, he moved closer. "Nah. Ye're shakin'."

She dropped her gaze. Her hands twisted together and trembled with a fine tension. She shook them loose and brushed at her skirt. "I'm perfectly fine."

"Clarissa."

"Everything is perfectly fine."

"Ye needn't lie."

"I'm not lying."

He moved near enough that she could feel his heat. "Look at me."

She shook her head and shifted away, wandering toward the fireplace. "I do hope you aren't too vexed that I displayed your carvings." She wadded the fine blue wool of her skirt then released it to brush away the wrinkles. Again. And again. "They're magnificent creations. You should craft new ones and sell them."

"I dinnae like that ye went outside without a guard." His voice was lower. Closer. A raspy rumble. "But when ye saw a threat, ye raised the alarm and ran into the house. That's the best thing ye could have done."

Her mouth went dry. She scrambled to change the subject. "If you were accepting commissions, I would request an owl. Majestic birds. I watched you carve one shortly after I arrived at Rowan House. Whatever happened to it?"

His massive shadow blocked light from the window, surrounding her in heat and comforting darkness. "Dinnae be afraid, lass."

"I'm fine."

"Ye forgot 'perfectly.'"

"Right. Perfectly fine."

Silence intruded, punctuated by the fire's faint crackle, the soft sighing of breath, and the wind's distant groan. She felt his presence at her back, a wall of muscle, bone, and patience. "Ye're safe here."

She shook her head. Her heart thrashed to escape her chest.

"Aye. Ye are." Enormous hands stroked from her shoulders to her elbows, squeezing gently, steadying her. "Anybody tries to hurt ye, he'll have to kill me first. Whole armies have failed to do that."

An unbearable ache bloomed inside her. Heat shimmered down to her thighs, out to her fingertips, and up into her breasts. What she wouldn't give to turn in his arms and draw him into her kiss. What she wouldn't give to claim him as her own.

"I'm such a fool," she whispered to the raven.

"Nah. Ye're fine," he murmured, his breath tickling the wisps along her nape. "Finest thing I've ever seen."

She froze. Had that been a compliment? Before she could ask, he moved away. She turned to see him bracing a hand beside the window, those broad shoulders stiff, one hand cupping the back of his neck as though in pain.

Swallowing hard, she flattened a hand over her middle and scrambled for another change of subject. "Do you prefer cauliflower or kale?"

He twisted to frown at her over his shoulder. "Why?"

"I've only one bed left in the garden. We can't have them mingling. Consider the scandal."

Silence. His mouth twisted into an unexpected curve. Abruptly, he hung his head and shook. Only after she heard deep, resonant chuckling did she realize what had happened.

She'd made him laugh.

Good heavens, it was like coaxing a great, beastly bear to roll over and let her scratch its belly. Pure exhilaration. She wanted more.

"By God, woman. I never ken what ye'll say next."

Happiness took her by storm. "What if Rakish Kale and Careless Cauliflower produced illicit offspring?

We'd have hordes of deflowered Caulikale. Or bulbous, white Pale Kale. Could such an unholy abomination possibly belong in a civilized salad? I think not."

He laughed harder.

She giggled, bouncing up on her toes.

"Cloistered Cauliflower it is, then." He took a deep breath and shot her a glittering look. "Though, if ye add enough butter, even an abomination isnae too bad."

Another dream came for Campbell later that night. First, he saw Isla, though she was obscured by mist this time, and he didn't plunge underwater the way he'd done before. Instead, he stood beside a rocky shore while an owl hooted nearby.

"What in bluidy hell are ye tryin' to say?" he called across the water. His voice was a muffled echo. "I'm done with yer silence. Do ye hear me? Show me somethin' or leave me be!"

Dread swamped him in sticky, icy, sickening sweat. For a moment, he was slighter. Shorter. Confused. His mind flickered strangely from one thought to the next: A dead deer. A white shift. A pair of beautiful lips. An old mill. Darkness. Blood. Rage. Clarissa's sunlit hair.

Red flowers. A broken gate. A sheet on a line. A pair of crows. The scent of death.

Blackness and pain. Pain and blackness. Fear of losing her. Fear of what he might do to her.

Mustn't lose her. Must have her. Own her. Punish her.

Sounds of water pulled Campbell's mind free. An owl landed on a fence nearby. The bird's head pivoted to stare at him with grim silence.

"Sweet bluidy Christ," he rasped. "Was that Northfield?"

The bird didn't answer. It lifted into the sky.

Daylight returned. The sun warmed his skin.

From behind him, a sweet, breathless voice carried across green, shorn grass. "I wondered if I'd see you here again."

He closed his eyes and savored the scent of lavender. "I cannae help myself, love."

She drew near. He turned, soaking in the pure pleasure of seeing her golden curls gleam. Those eyes shone like the sky. Lush lips smiled. Parted. She laughed, the sound of her happiness intoxicating. She ran into his arms as she'd done earlier that day—full speed, no holding back. Only this time, it wasn't from fear.

In his dreams, she was free to want him, and he was free to touch her.

He gathered her close, holding her as tightly as he dared.

"Campbell," she whispered, nuzzling his chest. "If you were mine, I'd spend hours on kissing alone."

His chuckle turned into a groan when she slid her hands from his waist to his belly. "I've a feelin' it wouldnae last that long, lass. One of us would break within minutes."

"Yes. It doesn't seem to matter how often you pleasure me; my appetite is never quite satisfied." A faint quiver in her lower lip caused him a twinge of concern.

"Perhaps I should try harder, eh?"

She shook her head and flattened her palms against his chest. Then, she traced a cross over his heart. "I can't keep doing this, Campbell. Dreaming of feasts will never fill an empty stomach. It only deepens the hunger."

He frowned, puzzled by the melancholy turn. "Clarissa."

"The hunger is devouring me." She pulled away, her voice contorting. "It hurts too much."

"What are ye doin'?"

She moved away, retreating. Retreating.

"No. Dinnae go." He reached for her again, but she'd already vanished into the mist. "Clarissa!" he bellowed. "Dinnae leave!"

But she didn't hear him. And he couldn't see her.

She was gone.

CHAPTER NINE

"I'm goin' after him." The low, resonant thrum of Campbell's fury made the world vibrate in a queer red hue. A fortnight after the dreams stopped, his impatience had grown into a rage.

He'd never felt anything like this. It scared the bloody hell out of him.

Broderick frowned and finished his dram of whisky. "Be sensible. We dinnae ken where he is, and even if we did—"

Campbell leaned into his old, scarred dining table—the one she'd decorated with the first wildflowers of spring. "I mean to track him," he snarled. "And I mean to kill him."

Distantly, he heard Kate and Clarissa laughing in the next room. His gut churned. It wasn't the whisky.

Broderick cast him a speculative look. "Teversham is due to arrive soon. My understandin' is that he intends to wed her."

The rage flared bright. Campbell shoved back his chair and stood up to pace.

"Why not wait? A few days, and she'll be another man's responsibility." Broderick paused. "Another man's wife."

Did he think Campbell didn't know that? Did he think he hadn't been bloody counting?

"Aye, she'll return to England, and ye'll nae be bothered with her. No more bonnie flowers on yer table. No more bonnie lass fussin' at ye to wear a hat in the rain." Broderick shrugged. "For the best, likely. She'll make a splendid countess. Beautiful woman. A wee spot of grace in a man's home." Another pause. "Mayhap her marriage will cause the mad cur to reconsider his obsession."

On the cusp of madness himself, Campbell shook his head. "He has to die."

"Let Teversham handle it. He has funds. He'll hire—"

"No."

"'Tis nearly done. Let her go to a man who wants her."

"He doesnae want her." Campbell's fury drove him to brace his hands on the table and lean across to glare at an infuriatingly relaxed Broderick. "He doesnae," he growled. "Nae like he should. Nae like …"

A smile quirked the scarred side of his brother's mouth. "Like … you?"

Campbell shoved upright, poured himself more whisky, and downed it in a swallow.

"Ye dinnae hide it very well, brother. Nae from me."

"Haud yer wheesht."

"Think ye all those invitations to dine with us at Rowan House were meant to fatten ye up?"

Campbell stiffened. Frowned.

"Kate saw it straight away. Took me a wee bit longer, but sweet Christ, even a man with one eye could spot the attraction." Broderick chuckled. "Dinnae fash. Clarissa thinks riding an hour through pissin' rain twice a week to visit yer brother is *normal* behavior. We didnae explain ye'd *normally* tell me to go to the devil with my bluidy summons."

He wanted to cry rubbish. He wanted to plant his fist in his brother's gut. He wanted to deny everything. But he couldn't.

The truth was worse than Broderick knew.

Broderick sighed. "I did think ye'd come to yer senses sooner than ye have, but what can I say? Ye're Angus MacPherson's son. Stubborn is what built us."

"She's nae for me."

Broderick scoffed. "Aye, right."

"I've naught to offer her."

"That's pure shite, and ye ken it well."

Grinding agony fought his control.

Another peal of feminine laughter echoed from the front room. They were dancing. Clarissa loved to dance.

God, the woman was grace incarnate. He'd taken her to the birchwood glen every day for more training. And every day, she'd impressed him with her dexterity, her awareness of her body and her surroundings. Every day, she'd enchanted him with her natural ease, her sunlight smile, the determined way she nibbled her lip, and the endearing way she laughed at her own failings. Bloody hell. Even her failings made him want her more.

He closed his eyes. Squeezed the edge of the table until his knuckles ached and the wood groaned at the pressure.

"Offer to marry her," Broderick said. "If yer pride cannae bear the confession, ye needn't tell her why."

"My pride has naught to do with this."

"Say it's for her protection. Say it's because ye need a wife and she'll do. Hell, brother. Tell her ye'll wed her for her needlework skills. I've an inkling she'll accept ye, no matter the terms."

Campbell resented the understanding blazing from that single, knowing eye. "She'll want bairns. I cannae give her any." A hollow pain—old, yet no duller for time's passage—twisted him inside. "Think ye she'd accept those terms?"

"Aye," Broderick answered. "I do."

Deep MacPherson voices echoed from the direction of the kitchen. Moments later, Rannoch, Alexander, and Angus entered the dining room, bickering about a new source of barley in Ayrshire. Their arguments halted when they spotted the whisky.

Angus grunted and ran a hand through iron-gray hair. "Well, now, this is a proper welcome, son." Campbell's father clapped his shoulder and pulled up a chair.

Alexander, looking pale, thin, and haggard after his months-long recovery, pulled out his own chair, wincing as the muscles around his wound protested.

Rannoch eyed the half-empty bottle and shook his head. "Pitiful lot. We'll need at least two more." He headed back to the kitchen to replenish the supply.

Angus took a drink and nudged Campbell's chair with his boot. "Sit, laddie. Ye're too big to be loomin' over yer auld da that way." His da refilled his glass. "Go on, now. Drink up."

Reluctantly, Campbell sat and drank.

Angus eyed Broderick. "Did ye tell him?"

"Tell me what?" Campbell demanded.

Broderick rubbed the back of his neck. "We found a hunter's camp a mile north of the quarry."

That was less than a quarter mile from Rowan House. Glaring between his da and his brother, Campbell barked, "Northfield?"

Alexander grunted as he sat forward to pour. "Ye ken the answer. The bugger's here."

"Who tracked him?"

"I bluidy did."

"Then, why isnae he standin' here, where I can do what needs doin'?"

Alexander snagged the bottle and tipped it back for a long drink. "The camp is a week old. Abandoned now."

Campbell snorted his disbelief. "Ye could track a ghost's fart on a foggy night after a month of windstorms."

His brother grunted. Winced.

"What happened?"

"I lost him. That's what."

"How?"

Alexander shot him an acidic glare. "Leave it, brother."

Angus intervened. "Doesnae matter how. We ken Northfield is about. We dinnae ken where. Best ye be watchful, Campbell."

"I should be introducin' that rabid cur to my dirk right now." He glowered past Da at an unkempt, haggard Alexander. "Where is he?"

Eyes even blacker than his own snapped a warning. "Dinnae ken."

"I mean to put him down. I'll nae stop until I do."

"Then do it," Alexander roared. "Track him yer bluidy self!"

"Enough!" Da cuffed both their necks and shook them as he'd done when they were lads.

Rannoch returned with two more bottles and a surprised frown. "What's got everybody's ballocks twisted?"

Campbell worked against the urge to unleash his rage on his brothers. Controlling his temper had never been this hard. It was her. Broderick hadn't been wrong about that.

Rannoch's gaze shifted above Campbell's shoulder, and his frown transformed into a broad grin. Campbell turned to find Magdalene Cuthbert entering from the front room. Rannoch teased, "There ye are, Mouse. Scarcely kenned ye were about, ye're so quiet."

A faint curve touched her lips, though she was careful not to expose her teeth. She smoothed her plain, woolen gown and folded her hands at her waist. "Mr. MacPherson. I accompanied Lady Darnham. She's been very kind."

"I've told ye, we're all Mr. MacPherson," Rannoch retorted. "Ye'll have to be vulgar and call us by our Christian names, or we'll never sort out which of us has displeased ye most."

"Simple enough. You all please me very well." She swept them all with a warm glance before moving to Alexander's side and resting her hand on his shoulder. "Though, I did hope when you left my care, Mr. MacPherson, I shouldn't hear that pained bellow again." She bent closer to murmur at Alexander in her gentle Lowland voice, "Ye've pushed yourself too hard, now, haven't ye?"

"Leave off, Magdalene," he snarled. "I dinnae need a mam."

Angus grunted. "Lad swooned. That's how he lost Northfield's scent. Seven hours straight, soaked to the bone, no rest. He found the camp. Then, the lantern went dark."

Alexander muttered a blistering curse.

"Ah, dinnae give me Christ and crosses, son. Ye should have asked for help. Bluidy daft, riskin' yerself that way."

"Did you reopen your wound?" She moved around to examine his upper chest. "Perhaps I should have a look at it."

He shoved her hand away. "For the last time, I dinnae require yer help!"

Rannoch set the two bottles on the table with a hard clunk. "Mind yerself, brother. Speak to her that way again, and ye'll be diggin' yer teeth out of my knuckles."

"It's all right, Rannoch," she said softly.

"No. It's not, Mouse." Rannoch kept his glare focused on Alexander. "Ye're a black-tempered bastard. Always have been. But she deserves better, especially from the man she's kept alive the past three months."

Alexander scraped a hand down his face and sighed. "Ye're right. Apologies, lass."

Magdalene persuaded him to accompany her upstairs where she could look over his wound, leaving the rest of them to discuss the problem of finding Northfield. They debated strategies while nursing their whisky. Suggestions ranged from staging an all-out hunt to setting a trap with Clarissa as bait—a notion Campbell quickly vetoed.

"She wouldnae be in danger, man," Rannoch sighed. "Be reasonable."

Too many of his brothers had told him to be reasonable today. He drank more whisky and held his silence. Where she was concerned, reasonable didn't apply.

"I still say 'twould be best to wait 'til she's wed," Broderick said. "There's a chance he'll be provoked into showin' himself. Or he'll realize she was never his in the first place and abandon his campaign."

Rannoch nodded. "Mayhap it will wake him from his madness."

"Teversham hopes as much," Broderick replied, eyeing Campbell warily. "Brave man, takin' the risk for her sake. Northfield has already demonstrated what he'll do to a rival. At a guess, I'd say it's more likely he'll view her marriage as a provocation and seek to make her a widow."

Da grunted agreement. "Teversham's a good sort, aye, but this Northfield fellow is a crafty bugger. Dangerous business, puttin' yerself betwixt a madman and his obsession." He slanted a narrow glance at Campbell. "Doesnae bode well for his survival. Or hers."

Campbell ground his teeth. "Which is why we must hunt Northfield down first."

"Or use it to our advantage," Angus replied. "Have ye considered—"

"Dinnae start, Da."

"She'd make a fine wife, son."

"Bluidy hell."

"Wed to Teversham? Damned waste." Angus tossed back the last of his whisky. "Wed to you? Northfield had best be measured for a coffin."

Campbell was about to answer when Clarissa entered, flushed and sparkling. He rose to his feet along with all the other men in the room.

She wore blue today—sky-blue wool with darker blue trimmings at the wrists and bodice. She'd fashioned the wrap around her shoulders from one of his plaids. The soft gray tartan had delighted her so much, he'd caught her rubbing it against her cheek. How could he not offer it to her?

Distantly, he noted Fergus was still following her about, though she continued to ignore him. Poor, infatuated beastie.

Kate and Mrs. MacBean entered behind her, but he couldn't take his eyes from Clarissa. Lately, she seemed … lighter. Her eyes shone with excitement as she greeted Da and Rannoch. Then, she focused on him, and the entire room faded to dun and din. There was only her, deep as blue water, soft as lamb's fleece, bonnie as mist on a fresh-bloomed rose.

Just like that, the rageful, poisonous knot in his chest dissolved. Whisky hadn't done it. Seeing his brothers hadn't done it. But one look at her, and his world came right.

"I've asked Abigail to prepare your favorite dessert," she said, drifting closer and resting her hand beside his on the back of his chair. "No berries this time of year, of course, so I suggested using jam. Kate brought a jar from Rowan House. It's raspberry."

Raspberries were his favorite.

She grinned up at him. By God, she glowed like the moon. "Your sister brought her bread, too. If you walk away from this table hungry, Campbell MacPherson, I'll not be to blame. I've done all I can do." She plucked a bit of straw from his sleeve and smoothed the wool. "You've been visiting the cows again, I see."

He grunted. "It's calving season. We've been givin' the fold supplemental feed." A pause. "Ye could join me tomorrow if ye like."

"Hmm." More brushing of his sleeve. "Their horns are so pointy."

"Aye."

"And they're blinded by that fringe of hair."

A smile tugged against his will. Her excuses were so threadbare, he could see right through them. "Yesterday, ye said their size gives ye a fright."

"Well, yes." Her lashes lowered. Her cheeks hued pink. "Size can be overwhelming."

"Before that, ye claimed the coos offend yer sense of smell."

"A complaint I stand by."

"And before that, ye said ye found them uninteresting because coos are coos, long hair or no."

"If you've smelled one cow, you've smelled them all."

"Clarissa."

She sighed. "Can't we agree I'm a squeamish English miss better suited to serving tea in the parlor?"

He'd agree if he hadn't caught her gazing longingly at the three-week-old calf she'd nicknamed Butter. He glanced toward the corner where Fergus lay sprawled, waiting for a certain English lass to drop a crumb of affection. Fergus did not often waste time with humans who disdained him—not when he had any number of lads willing to play or take him for a ramble.

No, Clarissa Meadows was far from an aloof, spoiled English miss. She obviously fought her own nurturing instincts to keep her distance from Fergus and the coos. He could guess the reason—she'd already lost one companion and feared losing more.

"Ye needn't be afraid, lass."

Blue eyes softened into tenderness. "With you, I almost believe it."

A flash of brilliant red-orange caught his eye. He turned to see his sister, Annie, entering beside her husband, John Huxley. Accompanying them was a much-improved Lady Darnham, who greeted him warmly and tugged Clarissa away to speak with Kate.

Annie waddled forward to place a basket of bread on the table and a kiss on his cheek. "Next time, dinnae wait so long to invite us for a visit. We cannae have ye starvin' for proper bread, great hermit that ye are."

Campbell smiled. "Ye didnae have to do this, sister, but I'm grateful."

Resting one hand on her pregnant belly and the other on John's arm, she snorted. "Gave me somethin' to do apart from complainin' about my achin' back and fat feet." She grinned up at her husband. "Dinnae fash, English. I saved some bread for ye."

John's hand slid atop hers on her belly. "Hmm. I'll have that later, love. Perhaps with a bit of your onion gravy."

"Ye'll have some persuadin' to do if ye think I'll be slavin' away in the kitchen to satisfy yer cravings."

"Fortunately, I've a talent for persuasion."

Huxley was a handsome Englishman—an earl's son and a wealthy man in his own right—who had earned Annie's admiration while training to compete in the Highland Games. He was a good man who took good care of Campbell's wee sister.

But, at the moment, the sight of the Englishman's hand over the bairn he'd helped create drove a rusty spike through Campbell's chest. Their joy in one another was palpable. How much more would they find upon the bairn's birth?

Annie waddled toward the kitchen while John greeted Campbell's father and brothers.

Just then, two more male voices sounded from the corridor. Daniel entered first, carrying a fine gray coat and top hat. Behind him strolled an unexpected—and deeply unwelcome—arrival.

Blond. Lean. Handsomely refined.

Teversham.

The rusty spike from earlier grew claws and teeth.

Teversham searched the dining room, beaming brilliantly as he locked on Clarissa. From the corner where she and Kate laughed with Lady Darnham, he heard her gasp. Then, she murmured, "Francis?"

Campbell's fists clenched hard. His gut clenched harder.

She dashed forward and threw herself into the other man's arms. Teversham lifted her, spun her.

Red so dark it was black intruded on Campbell's vision. Violent urges splintered through him. His muscles contracted. Burned.

Must control it, he thought. *Mustn't let the rage win.*

Quickly, he excused himself and escaped outside. Fergus followed, at last abandoning his hopeless obsession.

If only Campbell could do the same.

He stalked out into the yard beyond the barn, careless of the downpour. Breathing helped, but only at the edges. He braced a hand against the barn's wall. Waited until the red receded. Until he could think.

Only then did he notice he wasn't alone. Beneath a solitary pine, he found Alexander scowling toward the western hills. His brother raised a bottle to his lips and drank deep.

"Mind ye dinnae drown," Campbell muttered, joining him beneath the dripping boughs.

Alexander grunted and ran a hand through black, overlong hair. "Little chance of that."

Ordinarily, it took a great deal of whisky to tip any of the MacPhersons into drunkenness. Their size saw to that. But Alexander had lost a lot of muscle during his recovery. He'd also lost the civilized veneer he'd once had—which had been thin to begin with.

"I didnae mean to insult ye earlier," Campbell said. "Ye're the best tracker of any of us, and I'm thankful. But ye shouldnae have pushed yerself so hard."

Another drink. A slanted glance. "I had good reason."

Campbell frowned a question.

Alexander sighed. "He's been killin' stock, Cam."

Alarm slid up his spine. "Where?"

"North of the quarry. Two of Broderick's coos. A few of Jamie MacDonnell's sheep."

"Ye're certain."

Alexander's gaze was bleak. "Aye. They were shot at range then butchered on site. Left for us to find."

Campbell's blood went cold. Perhaps that explained the wound that had killed one of his cows weeks ago. The puncture near her spine had seemed odd. "Christ on the cross."

"He's a mad bugger. But meticulous." Alexander shook his head and took another drink. "Huxley said Northfield spent much of his youth huntin' large game in India and Africa. America, too. He kens far more than yer average Englishman, I'll tell ye that much."

"What did ye find at the camp?"

Alexander offered him the bottle. "Here. Ye'll need it."

Campbell cursed and brushed it away. "Tell me."

"A lass's shift, fine linen. A lock of hair, blonde. A pair of silk stockings with wee roses on 'em."

Sound slowly muffled beneath a thunderous roar. Red tinged his vision again. "Hers," he breathed.

"Aye, I expect so." Alexander's expression was savage. "Best keep yer lass close, Cam. If Northfield puts hands on her, she willnae fare well."

He didn't bother correcting Alexander's reference to Clarissa as his lass. She wasn't. But right now, that mattered about as much as the fiftieth drop in a deluge. "I must find him."

"Aye. Huxley said the Northfields will come after ye once ye've put him down. I told him ye wouldnae give two shites. He's as good as dead."

Campbell tried to focus on Fergus loping about in the rain. Every time he blinked, an image of Clarissa formed inside the darkness. Her lovely hair spread upon blankets. Her lovely eyes vacant. Her body ravaged. He wanted to retch. He wanted to tear Northfield's head from his shoulders with nothing but his hands. The bloodlust felt foreign and raw—but right.

"Teversham's returned," he muttered.

Alexander stilled. "That so?"

"Aye."

He grunted and took a drink. "I ken what ye're thinkin'." He gestured with the bottle. "Why marry the lass when ye can just eliminate her problem and go back to livin' like a sainted martyr? Wouldnae wish to claim what's yours, now would ye? Might make ye *happy*. Might end this blighted *sacrifice* of an existence ye've set for yerself."

The rain poured harder. He should have worn a hat.

"But there's the trouble. Ye've always been too bluidy honorable."

Campbell shook his head. This was their oldest argument. "And ye've always been too bluidy ruthless."

A faint smile curled a corner of Alexander's mouth. "I'll lend ye some of my ruthless if it'll help ye see reason. Christ, brother. She's been livin' here unchaperoned for nigh on a month, now. If she wants to marry at all, the lass has two options. Ye're the better one."

"She already made her choice."

"Because ye havenae given her another. I'll wager ye havenae even kissed her."

"Leave it."

Alexander chuckled. "Sweet, bonnie lass. Noble bloodline. She and Teversham are both handsome as bluidy sunlight. Think of the bairns they'll have."

The blackness he'd been fighting anchored deep. Caught fire. Bloomed explosively hot until he feared what he might do. He had to shut his brother's mouth. Alexander was provoking him—he knew that. But knowing didn't matter. It worked.

He pivoted until his nose was inches from Alexander's. "Ye're in nae condition to be playin' this game with me," he warned softly. "I suggest ye *haud yer wheesht*."

His brother's gaunt sneer sent his temper teetering. "Or what? Ye'll steal her for yerself? Nah. Ye're too much of a coward."

"Ye bluidy, blackhearted—"

"I've always fancied the fair-haired lasses. Even Teversham shouldnae have trouble tuppin' her. Do ye suppose their bairns will have—"

"Shut yer fucking mouth, Alexander!" His roar echoed like a great beast's maddened cry. His fist struck the tree beside his brother's head with cracking force. "She's mine! Do ye ken? She doesnae belong with him!"

"Aye, I ken. We all ken."

"Speak of her again, and I'll break every part of ye that's still workin'!"

"Offer her marriage. Give her the choice."

He roiled like a wall of fire. "I cannae."

"The fever stole enough from ye. Dinnae let it take everythin'."

"I cannae," he repeated, backing away. His lungs heaved like a bellows. "I cannae do that to her."

"If she marries Teversham, she may go childless, anyway." Alexander's cynical grin was too knowing. "Mayhap that's what ye're counting on, eh? That he'll keep her chaste? Aye, then ye can comfort yerself that ye made the saintly sacrifice and she's still yers, somehow. When do ye fight for what's yours, brother?" He gestured toward the house. "Think ye Isla would want ye livin' this way? Alone in an empty house. Nobody but Fergus for company. It's a bluidy disgrace."

This was torment. He wanted to beat his own brother until he stopped talking. Until the goddamned world stopped burning like the fires of hell.

Alexander's flashing black gaze seared him. "Da insists we should be patient. He says grief takes longer for some. But it's been sixteen years. Ye've punished yerself for no good reason long enough."

"That's nae what this is about."

"No? How long did Broderick resist Kate when she demanded they marry?"

He gritted his teeth. Broderick had been scarred, damaged, and vengeful when he'd met Kate last autumn. Even so, he'd resisted her for all of ten minutes before agreeing to the wedding. He'd been furious. He'd worried his enemy would target her—and he'd been right to worry. But that hadn't stopped him from staking his claim.

"Right," Alexander murmured. "Now, take yer high-minded, daft notions about what Clarissa deserves and what ye dinnae, and add 'em to the pile of shite in the privy. Because that's where they belong."

"I'm nae Broderick."

"No. Broderick has more sense."

"Ye dinnae ken—"

Alexander's laugh was bitter. "I ken if the lass I wanted more than air and whisky was sleepin' under my roof, I'd do whatever it took to keep her there, honor be damned." He finished off the bottle and shoved away from the tree. "I suggest ye do the same before it's too late."

CHAPTER TEN

Clarissa had miscalculated the enormity of planning this dinner. For one thing, five MacPherson men, along with the six-foot-tall John Huxley, would never fit comfortably inside Campbell's small dining room—at least, not without seating the women on their laps.

Then, Francis returned and added to their numbers.

Oh, how she'd rejoiced to see his handsome face again. She'd chattered at him for long minutes, peppering him with questions.

"Tell me everything," she'd demanded breathlessly. "How did you arrive so quickly? How was your journey from Yorkshire? How is George? Did you bring him with you? Oh! And your mother. Is she … why are you laughing?"

He'd chuckled and kissed her forehead. "Let's see. I opted for a lighter carriage this time. Shortened my journey considerably. I left it behind at Rowan House and came here on horseback, a choice I deeply regret. I may have grown gills. George is quite well. He stayed behind to care for Mother, who has improved markedly since becoming a widow." He grinned with affection. "As you predicted."

Kate interrupted to embrace Francis, and the three of them chatted at length. Then, while Kate regaled him with reports on the novel she was writing, Clarissa glanced around the room, searching for Campbell.

She was always seeking him. Always craving glimpses of his endearingly ferocious face. Sometimes, she suspected he'd developed a bit of fondness for her. But it could never equal her fondness for him.

The man was like liquor in her veins. Hot. Intoxicating. Now, she craved another dram, but he'd disappeared.

As she looked around, she could guess why. The small dining room was packed with far too many people. Quickly, she recruited the men to carry the dining table into the front room. She and the other women dressed the table then arranged the chairs.

A short while later, she was finally satisfied, and at Grandmama's behest, she sat for a few minutes to have a bit of cider and chat with her guests. To her right sat Grandmama, Magdalene, Kate, and Annie discussing the best remedy for poor digestion during late pregnancy. Reportedly, less gravy and more ginger root were "measures only a pure dafty would think sufficient." Clarissa wondered whether Annie realized that when she'd married a Huxley male, she'd consigned herself to many, many babies requiring many, many nights of ginger root tea. The Huxleys were, as Kate liked to say, *prolific.*

Clarissa sighed. Where was Campbell? Dinner would be ready soon.

Near the window, Huxley, Francis, and Rannoch discussed the burgeoning shipbuilding industry on the River Clyde near Glasgow.

To her left, Angus and Mrs. MacBean waged a war of opposing facts. Clarissa couldn't decide who was winning.

"Pure rubbish, ye daft auld woman," Angus grumbled. "I've five bairns, nae six. This house never burned down. 'Twas abandoned after auld Rob Robertson tangled with the wrong bull."

"Bull? Och, that one preferred sheep." Mrs. MacBean shook her head. "Some men cannae help themselves. And some sheep can."

Angus grunted. "Regardless, the place was dilapidated before Campbell took possession, but there was nae fire. And for the last time, ye cannae simply claim my donkey as yer own. Bill belongs to me."

Craning her neck, Mrs. MacBean gave him an out-of-rhythm blink. "He favors my company."

"How do ye ken?"

"He told me. On long rides, we have a good blether." She sniffed. "Aye, a chatty fellow. Gassy, too. Are ye feedin' him turnips? I think they dinnae agree with him."

Angus sighed and rubbed his knee. "Ye're mad as a drunken hatter, Mrs. MacBean. But ye do make a fine liniment."

Another blink. Then, a slow smile. "'Tis the least I can do for ye and yer kin. Where would I be if Campbell and Broderick hadnae repaired my cottage? Or if Annie didnae feed me twice a week? Nae to mention Alexander's 'consultations' about his bonnie bride or the fertility preventatives Rannoch purchases in regular bulk deliveries." She clicked her tongue. "If it werenae for the MacPhersons, I'd be starvin' out in the rain, sellin' fertility preventatives and liniment to *strangers.*

No, this is better. Ye're a fine man, Angus MacPherson. All six of yer bairns are a credit to ye."

"For God's sake." He scraped a hand over his face in a gesture familiar to Clarissa. She'd seen Campbell do it often enough—particularly when she'd accidentally said something indecent. "Five. I have *five* children, woman. And Alexander doesnae have a bride."

"*Yet.* Truthfully, the lad could use a father's advice. He didnae inherit the sight from his mam like some." She blew out a wide-eyed breath. "Speakin' of fathers." The woman's gaze suddenly shifted to Clarissa. "Have ye put that charm to good use yet, lass?"

Clarissa froze. She'd only been half-following their nonsensical conversation and didn't care to explain goat-shaped fertility charms to Campbell's father. Fortunately, Alexander chose that moment to return, soaked and glowering. She stood and edged in his direction. "Pardon me, Mrs. MacBean. Mr. MacPherson. I must check on dinner."

"Dinnae wait," the woman called after her. "Time is precious, now."

Relieved to escape, she approached Alexander with caution. He often reminded her of a wounded animal—gaunt, snarling, and defensive. But she'd also seen him control his temper to speak kindly to Grandmama. She knew he'd paid for Magdalene's last two deliveries of medical references—far from a meager purchase. And he'd nearly died trying to save Kate's life after she'd been abducted.

Most importantly, he probably knew where Campbell had gone. And if the scents of bread, onions, and venison were any indication, Campbell was about to miss dinner.

She couldn't have that. This meal had been for him. He needed his family, and she needed a way to thank him. None of her current measures seemed sufficient. He'd said nothing about the curtains, nothing about the furniture or the flowers. He hadn't seemed to notice that she'd asked the lads to light his bedchamber fire an hour earlier each evening, or that she'd asked Abigail to prepare extra meat pies for the men to take with them each morning.

No, he was too busy training her. Like a man possessed, he insisted she learn everything from evasive maneuvers at close quarters to "properly stabbing a man in the kidney" so he couldn't "do aught but bleed and weep for his mam." She found the former similar to dancing. Likely this was the only sort of dancing she'd ever do with Campbell MacPherson, so she hadn't objected. The stabbing, on the other hand, had made her yearn for the return of firearms training. Knives were an uncertain business.

Alexander scowled as she approached the passage where he stood dripping. He ran a hand through longish hair. "Miss Meadows."

Fergus, she noticed, had come in behind him. He was dripping, too.

Avoiding the dog's gaze, she started to ask where Campbell had gone, but Alexander answered first. "He's standin' beneath the tree behind the barn." A subtle smile formed a sardonic curve. "Mind the rain, now. A storm moved in."

On her way through the kitchen, she collected her cloak and inquired about dinner. "A quarter-hour or so, miss," Abigail answered, wiping her forehead with a towel and giving Clarissa a reassuring smile. "Good thing Lady Huxley brought so many loaves, else it'd be later."

Clarissa barely registered the maid's response, so eager was she to find Campbell.

It had been this way for weeks—the longing to be near him, to hear his deep voice and feel his arms around her, even if only for training. Two days ago, they'd sat together beside the brook. She'd been nervous, as she often was around him. Predictably, she'd chattered away about random subjects—her grandmother's recovery from her ailment, the disorientation of having gentlemen who'd ignored her for years suddenly look at her with interest. She'd recounted her fondest memory of her parents, a boat ride that ended with one oar missing, her father swimming, and the three of them laughing until their bellies ached. She'd explained why pineapple was the perfect fruit and satin was too fussy for travel and being plump was akin to being invisible.

He hadn't spoken much. Only listened.

When she'd apologized for her chatter, he'd given her a piercing look and said, "I quite like yer conversation, lass. Though, ye're wrong about pineapple. Raspberries are superior."

They'd spent another five minutes debating whether berries counted as fruit or deserved their own category.

It was silly. And lovely.

Dear heavens, how would she manage when she had to leave him? The beginnings of grief clogged her throat. She shook it away as she exited into the rear garden. Rain was, indeed, pouring. Drawing a breath, she raised her hood and hurried through the downpour.

She found him leaning against the pine trunk. One arm braced on a branch above him. Dark hair dripped onto his coat's collar. A hard jaw flickered as he ground his teeth. He wouldn't look at her.

"Go back inside, Clarissa," he rasped, his voice ominously low.

She halted several feet away. Her stomach panged. Those enormous shoulders vibrated with tension. "Dinner is nearly ready," she said. "Won't you come inside with me?"

"Not now." That was a growl.

Carefully, she rounded the tree to better view his face. "Did you argue with Alexander?"

No response.

She inched closer. "He's bound to be out of sorts, you know. Magdalene said he's in a lot of pain. You mustn't take his ill temper to heart—"

"Dinnae explain my brother to me. I ken him better than most. Ye ken him not at all."

The seething fury behind his words shocked her. "Well, I … I did live in the same house with him for a time. I daresay we are acquainted."

This seemed to anger him further. *"Haud yer wheesht,* woman. Go back inside."

Her own temper flared. No, she would not be quiet. And no, she would not leave until he'd recovered his civility. "What on earth is wrong with you?" She strode forward to stand toe-to-toe with him. "I spent three days planning this dinner. Abigail has been cooking all morning. Daniel awakened early to catch fresh fish. Francis came all this way—"

Suddenly, he pivoted, pressing her back against the tree and bracketing her between powerful arms. She gasped. His eyes flashed black as a thunderstorm. A hot charge flashed across her skin.

"Keep his name out of yer mouth," he gritted.

She lost her breath. Couldn't speak. She'd never seen Campbell like this. His skin stretched tightly over his bones. A vein pulsed near his temple. The cords of his neck strained with tension. And he was looking at her like he was ravenous and she was a raspberry feast.

"Our agreement was that ye'd do as ye're told," he said. "So, let's try this again. Go. Back. Inside."

It took her three breaths to answer. "No."

"Clarissa."

"You've no call to speak to me like this. I've done everything you've asked. More." Her throat tightened to a thread. "Not that you've noticed."

"I told ye never to leave the house without a man by yer side." His gaze roved her face. His massive body simultaneously sheltered and loomed. "Yet, here ye are."

"Yes. With you."

"Aye. With me."

Her chest seized as the grief she thought she'd been managing swelled upward. "Soon, I won't be. You'll be relieved, I'm certain."

A long silence. "Teversham is a fortunate man." His words didn't match his tone. In fact, she'd wager millstones ground up gravel with less resentment.

Again, her temper sparked. His expression was tortured. Was she such a pebble in his boot? Was he that eager to hand her over to another man? Perhaps he was. And perhaps she should let him continue believing that was what he was doing. Campbell didn't want her; he pitied her. She should cut ties and maintain her dignity. Let him learn the truth after she was gone.

His fingers adjusted her hood to better protect her face. His body surrounded hers with heat. But he was soaked, his brows dripping, his lips sheened with rainwater. And he glared as though he hated her with the blackest passion.

"Francis and I will leave within the week," she said tightly. "Your guard duties are coming to an end. Thank you for your hospitality, Mr. MacPherson. Should I acquire sufficient funds, I shall attempt to reimburse you for the expense."

A low, ominous sound rumbled from his chest. "Dinnae *dare* to send me Teversham's coins."

She frowned. "I don't intend—"

"He cannae protect ye the way I can. There's nae bluidy comparison."

"No, I—"

"He's wealthy, aye. Titled. But he'll never want ye."

She didn't understand what was happening. She'd thought at least they'd established a friendship of sorts. Was he *trying* to hurt her? "I know that."

"Are ye willin' to lie with him? 'Tis the only way to give him an heir."

Her head reeled back. "Wh-what business is it of yours? You don't want me, either."

"Answer me," he snarled. "Will ye lie with him?"

"No!" She shoved at his chest, but the blasted giant didn't move an inch. "I've decided against marriage, so there won't be any need."

His eyes flared. His scowl deepened. "What the devil are ye sayin'?"

"He's come to escort me and Grandmama back to England. He'll hire men for our protection. He'll help us deal with Northfield. But we aren't to marry." She drew a shaky breath. "After speaking with Grandmama and corresponding with Francis, I realized I cannot risk his safety for my own—"

"Ye must marry, ye foolish woman."

She raised her chin. "Again, Mr. MacPherson, I fail to see how that is any of your concern."

"Ye'll wed me. That's how."

The constant whoosh of rain must have obscured her hearing. She thought he'd said, "Wed me." How absurd. Obviously, he'd meant something different. Or she'd heard wrong.

"Pardon?"

"We'll announce it today and wed tomorrow. The minister has a nasty gambling habit. I'll bribe him to forge the banns. Nobody will object. Da will see to that."

Briefly, she closed her eyes and shook her head to clear the muddle. But, no, he wore the same ferocious expression, though it was now both calculating and edged with peculiar satisfaction.

"What … I don't … are you …"

"We *could* marry straight away. Vows alone do the job here in Scotland. But as ye're English, I reckon a proper ceremony will please yer grandmother and settle the matter more firmly."

"The matter."

"Aye."

"Of marriage."

"Of you bein' mine." He frowned deeper. Leaned closer. "Mayhap today would be better."

She hooked her hands on his hard, muscular arms. "Campbell."

"Aye?"

"You don't really want to marry me. Why would you offer?"

For a moment, something intensely dark flared in his eyes. Before she could decide what it was, he lowered his gaze to her mouth. "Ye need a husband. A protector."

Disappointment struck, raw and painful. She'd always hated pity.

"And ye'll make a fine wife."

She attempted a smile but lost hold of it. "Do you think so?"

"Ye've a fair hand with a needle."

"Right."

"The curtains are bonnie."

Her head dropped forward between them. "You needn't marry me to keep them. They were a gift."

Silence fell, cloaked by rain. His breathing seemed rough. A bit fast.

Perhaps he was struggling with his conscience, hesitant to leave her without protection, yet far from eager to shackle himself to her forever. She should offer him a way out. One of them had to be sensible.

"We'll wed tomorrow," he muttered. "I can wait. 'Tis only a day."

She raised her chin. Met his gaze. "I thank you for the offer, Mr. MacPherson. But I'm afraid I must decline."

His nose flared. A tiny muscle in his brow twitched. "Nah," he breathed. "Ye'll agree."

She arched a brow. "Will I, now?"

"Aye."

"Enough of this." Her anger swelled, her temper snapping. "I am wholly weary of being the piteous wretch."

He frowned. "Who said anythin' like that?"

"You!" She shoved at him again, and once again, he didn't move. "Let me loose."

"No."

She shoved harder. "I refuse to make you more of a target than you already are. And I certainly will not wed a man who pities me. I'd rather be alone."

"Dinnae be foolish. Northfield—"

A gritted groan of pure frustration escaped. "Damn bloody Northfield! He's controlling my every movement! Every thought. Even my nightmares!" She stifled a rogue sob. "I'd rather run into his arms and meet my death than bear another moment—"

His hand gripped her nape. Dark eyes flashed white-hot. "Here's what ye'll do, instead—whatever I bluidy tell ye. Do ye understand me? Are ye listenin'?"

Her chest squeezed until she couldn't breathe. Everything she'd been carrying suddenly broke her.

"You don't understand," she whispered. "I can't marry you. I can't risk it."

Torturous agony flashed across his features for the briefest second. His hand tightened. His body closed in on hers, flattening her against the tree. "Ye'll do as I say," he repeated. "Ye'll be my wife. And when ye're mine, Northfield willnae be a bother. Ye'll never have to think of him again."

She eyed his rain-wet lips. Heat invaded her belly. Her fingertips dug into the thick muscles of his chest. Anger and despair transformed into something else—hotter, deeper. It tightened and coiled inside her. "You don't want me, Campbell. Not forever. This is mad."

"What I want means nothin'. Ye need a husband. A man who will do what must be done." He grunted his frustration, pressing closer. Hot breaths panted between them. "A man who will keep ye safe. Give ye a home. Care for you and yer grandmother."

"I refused Francis's offer with those very same terms. What makes you think I will accept you instead?"

"Because ye want me very badly."

The truth, spoken in such raw terms, hit her like a fist. She gasped at the impact.

He lowered his head, his hair dripping, his eyes a cauldron. "Ye cannae deny it, lass."

"No," she confessed, her heart breaking. "I never could."

"So, ye'll do as I say." His voice was nothing but gravel. "We'll have the wedding tomorrow. And when the priest asks whether ye'll take me as yer husband, ye'll say aye. And when that's done, and everybody's gone, ye'll take me as yer man in truth."

God, how she ached for him. Even now, with her pride in tatters, she wanted his mouth upon hers. The heat of his body, the strength of his hands, the sheer size and weight of him against her made her weak.

He was her weakness. From the moment she'd first set eyes upon him, leaning in the doorway of Rowan House's drawing room looking like a warrior god with a monk's calm discipline, she'd been lost. Could she walk away? She should. Nothing good could come of a marriage built upon hasty, misguided duty.

But he was right. A husband would solve many problems. And if she'd been asked who she wanted above all other men, there would have been only one answer.

Only one.

Him.

"I can't let you do this, Campbell," she whispered. "I won't—"

A rumbling growl tore free. His eyes blazed bright with ferocious intent. His mouth descended to stroke hers.

Sensation sizzled across her lips, cooled by rain and heated by his kiss.

She gasped. Her fingers clutched the wool of his coat. Fiery lust gripped her belly and hardened the tips of her breasts. "What are you doing?"

"Temptin' ye."

He dipped his head again, taking her mouth with his. Cool lips slid. Angled. Fitted and caressed.

Oh, heavens. She'd dreamt of kissing him so many times—hundreds. But never had she imagined this. The instantaneous combustion. The jellied knees and aching breasts and absolute yearning to explore his mouth with her tongue.

Then, he opened her mouth with his. And everything disappeared. The rain. The chill. Thoughts of dinner or pity or pride.

Everything but him.

His arm slid around her waist, cinching her tighter and tighter until the massive proof of his lust wedged between them, pressing hard against her belly. His tongue glided inside to stroke against hers. His heat was a furnace, firing her hotter.

She clawed to draw him closer. Instinctively raising her thigh along his, she writhed to rub against the parts of him most likely to ease her.

His muscles flexed and hardened. He groaned and drove his hips into hers. His arm tightened around her waist, lifting and wedging her higher against the tree.

Her feet left the ground. She clung and kissed him, devouring his mouth with insatiable hunger. His free hand slid from her nape to her breast.

She moaned as his palm scraped across her nipple. Harsh, brutal panting heaved his chest. He tore his mouth away from hers to trail desperate kisses along her neck, down to the edge of her bodice.

"Bluidy hell, woman," he gasped. "Ye drive me mad."

Cupping his powerful jaw, she yanked at his head until he returned to her mouth. His skin was wet, his whiskers bristly against her fingers. "More," she panted. "Need more."

His entire body went rigid. Still. After several breaths, he pulled back, glaring down at her with a closed expression. Closed, yet ferocious. Resolute. "Do ye want more?"

She sagged against the bark. Aching. Yearning. Melting into a formless muddle. "Y-yes."

"Then ye'll marry me." Dark eyes were savage. "Say ye will, Clarissa. Say the words."

Her head rolled back and forth.

His thumb stroked her nipple. Squeezed.

Her moan caught on her next breath. She clutched his wrist.

"Say it. 'I'll be yer wife, Campbell.' Speak true, *gràidheag*. 'Tis a promise we'll both be keepin'."

Her weakness. He was her greatest weakness.

"Campbell," she whispered. "Please."

His forehead lowered to rest against hers. His lips caressed hers lazily, as though he had all the time in the world and she wasn't dying of rampant lust. "It's easy," he murmured. "Say aye. Yer body needs mine."

He held her nipple captive through layers of gown, corset, and linen. The torturous pleasure of his subtle stroking turned her inside out. "If I agree, I want …"

"Aye? What do ye want?"

"I want leave to touch you. Everywhere."

A low groan echoed in his chest. "God, lass."

Her fists gathered wet wool and jerked him closer. "I'll want to kiss you. Often."

His shoulders heaved as his eyes went pure black.

She panted, thrusting her breast more firmly into his hand. "And you must promise to dance with me at least once. Every year."

"Fine," he grunted harshly. "Now, say it."

"Yes."

"Again," he gritted. "Say my name."

"Yes, Campbell."

"Ye'll be mine. My wife."

"Yes, I'll be yours." Her eyes drifted closed. She swallowed everything—her pride, her dignity, her honor. She abandoned it all for her weakness.

Her eyes opened.

He was the most beautiful thing she'd ever seen. Wet and savage. A hard man in a harsh world gazing at her as though she mattered.

"And you'll be mine," she whispered. "For as long as I can keep you. You'll be mine."

Chapter Eleven

The joviality of Stuart MacDonnell's bagpipes and Broderick's fiddle jangled Campbell's last frayed nerve. Angus gripped his nape with a firm, fatherly hand.

"Patience, son." Da raised his voice to be heard above the music. "Enjoy the chance to admire yer good fortune."

In the center of Rowan House's drawing room, Campbell's bride danced with Rannoch, Kate, and Teversham. Her cheeks were flushed, matching the pink silk of her beaded ball gown. He was glad to see it. She'd been icy-pale throughout the quiet ceremony an hour earlier. The priest hadn't helped matters, questioning her living arrangements and going on about Eve's sinful ways. Campbell had nearly tossed the sweaty parson out into the deluge.

"Do ye recall when I wed Annie's mother?" Da asked.

"Aye."

Lillias Tulloch had been a young widow with a wee daughter and desperate circumstances. Da had proposed marriage within an hour of meeting her.

"She needed a husband. Annie needed a family." Angus's grunt was amused. "You lot needed a mother to civilize ye."

Campbell smiled as he remembered how he and his brothers had been—rough and rowdy with no manners and foul mouths. To be fair, they'd only had Lillias for a year before she'd died, so they hadn't improved greatly with time. But caring for Annie, they'd all gentled. Having a wee sister had been a joy.

"Aye, the marriage was sensible," Da continued before leaning closer. He nodded in Clarissa's direction. "But sensible isnae the reason we cannae look away, is it?"

No. He couldn't look away because she was finally his. It had been three days, not one, since the dinner at his cottage. Since he'd kissed her for the first time. Since he'd abandoned honor and staked his claim.

He'd steeled himself against her beauty after she'd consented to marry him. Rushing her into the house before she could change her mind, he'd announced to everyone—her grandmother, his family, Mrs. MacBean, and especially Teversham—that they intended to wed as soon as possible.

Kate had squealed and clasped a listless Clarissa in a tight hug.

Broderick had clapped his shoulder and uttered, "About bluidy time, brother."

Alexander had given him a dark, silent nod of understanding.

Annie had crowed triumphantly, swatting Huxley's arm and saying, "I told ye, English! Ye thought it'd be another week, but didnae I say 'twould be today?"

John had grinned. "That you did, love. My hearty congratulations, Cam."

Alarmingly, Annie's eyes had welled. She'd cursed and rushed forward to throw her arms around his waist. He'd clasped his sister gently, taking care not to pressure her belly.

She'd kissed his cheek and rasped, "At last, ye'll have the bride I've been prayin' for. Och, ye've made me so happy, I'm greetin' like a wee bairn."

Teversham, meanwhile, had taken Clarissa's hand and murmured, "Are you certain?"

Campbell had wanted to break his arm. He'd wanted to bloody those perfect features and shove the English nobleman away from her.

But she'd replied softly, "Yes, I am." Then, she'd smiled up at Campbell.

And Campbell's anger had unraveled.

Teversham had seemed remarkably pleased, shaking Campbell's hand before insisting that he would be the one to give her away, and she must wear "the pink silk, my darling. You'll be a vision."

Everyone else—Rannoch and Magdalene, Lady Darnham and Angus—had offered joyous felicitations. Everyone except Mrs. MacBean. The old woman had squinted up at Campbell with a glint in her good eye. Then, she'd said, "Make it soon, laddie. Ye've nae more time to waste."

A chill had struck. He'd had the oddest sense she hadn't been referring to the wedding.

Finally, Lady Darnham had approached, asking to speak with him privately. When they'd retreated to the empty dining room, the fragile, white-haired lady had shocked him.

"You should know something about my granddaughter, Mr. MacPherson." She'd faced him, her mouth flat, her customary cheer missing. "She should not be alive."

He'd frowned. What did that mean?

"Her parents adored her. The three of them were inseparable. They took her with them on a visit to her father's family home in Hampshire. On the return trip to Cambridge, there was a dreadful storm. The coach overturned. Two wheels broke, and the vehicle tumbled down a long, steep incline. Everyone was killed. My daughter. Clarissa's father. The coachman and two footmen. The horses." Lady Darnham had swallowed, blue eyes glossing. "Even her new pup given her by her parents."

He'd never asked how her parents had died. And she'd never told him.

"It was a gruesome thing. Dreadful. Yet, Clarissa survived. Likely, her mother's body protected her from the worst of it. Clarissa's legs were broken. Her head had been jostled into unconsciousness. But she lived."

Campbell had cursed beneath his breath. Cold—far deeper than the chill from his drenching—surged through his body.

"The coach was found three days later."

Three days. Christ. Clarissa had been trapped inside a broken carriage with her dead parents for *three days?*

"She was … insensible. It took months for me and my dear, sweet Alfie to nurse her back to health. In that time, she spoke very little." Lady Darnham dabbed her eyes with her handkerchief. "She doesn't remember the accident or the days that followed. She doesn't know how she survived. But when Alfie surveyed the remains of the coach, he told me it was a miracle. That, by all rights, our granddaughter should have died, if not from her injuries, then from exposure."

The old woman had covered her mouth and squeezed her eyes closed in a grieving grimace. Unable to bear her distress, he'd gathered her close. She'd leaned against him, fragile and wee.

"I'm grateful ye told me, my lady."

She'd patted his elbow and sniffed. "It's important that you understand." Blue eyes lifted and held his. "She fought to live. Even when she'd lost everything she loved. For years afterward, she refused the pets her grandfather offered. Then, we lost Alfie, too. And found little Dash. He won her heart, only to become another loss. She's lost far too much. And yet, she continues fighting. For my sake. For her friends and, yes, for herself. That is the woman you seek to marry, Mr. MacPherson. That is the woman who will become your wife." She'd given him a final, teary pat. "I trust you will love her accordingly."

Now, as he watched his wife—the woman who'd lost too much, who'd fought to live and agreed to be his—his guilt receded beneath a tide of triumphant satisfaction. He hadn't behaved honorably. Some would say he'd been ruthless as the devil, and they'd be right. But something about this woman had slowly cracked apart the man he'd been, revealing what lay beneath: the man who wanted her more than air and whisky. The man who would do anything to keep her, even tell scurrilous lies and use her desire against her. He had no excuses. And no regrets.

"Aye," said Da, casting a dark, familiar look at another blonde woman seated on the opposite end of the drawing room, chatting with Lady Darnham and Magdalene Cuthbert. "Sometimes, honesty will do naught but frighten a skittish lass away. So, we use whatever excuse will serve."

The elegant woman Angus was eyeing like a plate of venison and gravy was Eleanora Baird, an Inverness widow and Annie's dressmaker. She'd come at Annie's request to help Clarissa with her wedding-day ensemble. Campbell suspected Nora's frequent visits to the glen had less to do with dressmaking than with her affection for certain members of the MacPherson clan.

"When do ye suppose ye'll be makin' an honest woman of her, Da?"

The old man released a growling snort. "She'll never sell her dress shop. Bluidy hell, she even refuses to sell that rickety trinket she drives about. A gig? Nah. An invitation to be robbed; that's what it is. Impossible woman. I dinnae ken why I bother with her."

"Aye, ye do."

Da sighed and drank his cider. "Aye. I do."

Campbell smiled despite his black mood. He'd had four hours of sleep in the past two nights. His body was in constant torment, relentlessly hard and needful. He only hoped Clarissa didn't balk at his size. And that he'd be able to control himself with her. And that she'd cease dancing in ways that made her breasts jostle and quake.

He ran a hand down his face. Draining his cup, he stood and left the drawing room to find Alexander. His brother was arguing with Mrs. MacBean in the entrance hall.

"… patience, laddie. Make good use of the waitin'." The old woman patted Alexander's ribs. "Hire a cook to feed ye proper. More meat and less whisky. Rebuild that braw strength. Aye, she'll fancy that."

"For the last time, auld woman," he grumbled. "I'm askin' ye to make me some of Broderick's liniment. I never said aught about a bride, delayed or otherwise."

"Yer house is a fine one. But she *must* have a garden." The old woman squinted and gave him another pat. "Focus on buildin' her one with walls. Deer are pests before they're dinner. I'll bring ye some rowans. Mayhap a willow or two. Oh, and dinnae build the gate just yet. I've somethin' in mind. Do ye fancy goats?"

Alexander rolled his eyes and sighed.

"No? Hmm. Mayhap a badger, then. Suits yer temperament."

"Liniment. I fancy liniment. Any chance you could make me some?"

"Of course. Why didnae ye say so?"

Campbell approached the pair. Alexander's kilt—the red MacPherson tartan—matched Campbell's. But he noticed how loosely it fitted around his brother's waist. Mrs. MacBean was right. Alexander needed to focus on recovering his strength. Instead, he'd been making daily forays into the east hills to track Northfield.

That was about to end. "Did ye see anythin'?" he asked.

Alexander glanced up and shook his head. "He's nowhere about."

Mrs. MacBean turned her half-blind gaze upon Campbell. "Ye'd ken where he is if ye bothered to listen, laddie."

Campbell frowned. "What does that mean?"

"Yer grandfather isnae pleased with ye."

He stiffened. "Our grandfather has been dead since I was wee."

"Aye. Dead. Nae blind."

The old woman's nonsense was beginning to chafe. He turned to Alexander. "We'll begin the hunt tomorrow. Have ye the new rifle ye purchased in Edinburgh?"

"Aye."

"Good. Meet me at the house. An hour past sunrise."

Alexander nodded before stalking away, presumably to find more whisky.

Campbell turned to Mrs. MacBean. "I've a suspicion ye gave Clarissa somethin' to encourage fertility. Dinnae do it again."

A blink. Then, her milky eye went strangely bright. "Such power," she breathed. She touched his wrist with a single finger. "Such pain."

He jerked away. "And dinnae mention my grandfather again. He's gone. So is our mam."

"Nae gone, son." Her voice sounded layered. Her eyes glowed. "Waitin'."

A shiver floated across his skin. His curiosity got the better of him. "For what?"

"For ye."

"To die?"

"No, laddie. To wake."

His gut hardened. "I'm as awake as I'll ever be."

She gave a small smile. "They're pleased with yer bride. Pleased ye gave her one of their rings. Bonnie lass. Valiant heart. She'll be the sun in yer sky, lad. But we must save her first." Suddenly, she seized his fingers in a crushing grasp. *"Listen,* Campbell. Listen."

Everything inside him tightened. Went cold. "There's naught to hear," he replied softly.

She continued in that queer, layered voice, "When was the last time ye called upon the wood, laddie?" Her left eye glowed white. A trick of the light? Had to be. Then, she clicked her tongue and gave his chin a tap with a gnarled finger.

Just as his grandfather had always done.

"Too long," she breathed. "Too long."

He reeled back, heart kicking. He tore his hand from hers.

Her frowning blink fluttered. When she refocused on him, she seemed confused. "What's amiss? Ye're lookin' peely."

He didn't reply. He couldn't. His throat was too tight.

"Ah. In a wee bit of a wedding night swither, are ye? Naught to fear." She dug into the leather pouch tied around her waist, withdrawing a brown bottle. "Here." She squinted at the label, shook her head, and quickly tucked it back into the pouch, withdrawing a second, larger bottle. "Here. This will help. Dinnae use it all in one night. Ye'd be surprised how scarce caterpillar fungus is this time of year. And dinnae ask how I came by the milk." She blew out a breath. "That goat may never forgive me."

Through three dances, Clarissa had felt his gaze upon her like a warm, tingling weight. Halfway through the fourth dance, however, the feeling vanished. When Broderick and Stuart played the final notes of the reel, she searched the drawing room.

He was gone. Disappointment clogged her throat like cold ash.

Kate clasped her arm. "You realize we are sisters now, don't you? This means I'm permitted to borrow your green kid slippers."

Clarissa stared at the empty chair beside Angus. "I suppose it does," she replied. "But not the half-boots. You ruined my last pair."

"Who puts red silk lining in white cotton half-boots? They were bound to turn pink someday."

Clarissa hummed a diffident response.

Kate gave her a squeeze. "Don't look so bereft, dearest. Likely he's arranging the carriage to take you home."

She glanced at her friend, whose expression shone with gentle sympathy. "Home," Clarissa breathed. "Right."

"We must name your house. Something lovely and fanciful, I think." Kate clicked her tongue. "Stonecroft Farm, perhaps. Sunny Hill Farm?"

Francis joined them with a wry grin. "How about Hairy Coo House?" Blue eyes danced with humor. "Appropriately Scottish."

Kate laughed. "I know! Gingham Heath. For the curtains. No? Oh, well. We'll think of something."

Mrs. Grant approached to inform Kate she'd received a package. Clarissa took the opportunity to search for her new husband.

Husband. She still couldn't quite believe it.

The past few weeks had tossed her about until she didn't know whether the sky was up or sideways. First, she'd made the wrenching decision to decline Francis's proposal—which had only been possible because Grandmama had suggested they sell every painting, chair, and marble tea table left inside Ellery Hall to hire men who would deal with Northfield. Next, Clarissa had planned the dinner for Campbell, wanting to thank him for everything he'd done before she must say goodbye.

Then, he'd gone mad. And insisted they marry. And *kissed* her.

Oh, how he'd kissed her.

Nothing had seemed real since.

Their wedding, if one could call it that, had been performed by a sweaty, disapproving priest. Her bridegroom had loomed like a thundercloud. Rain had poured outside the drawing room, splattering the windows in waves. Her ring—a wide gold band dotted with pearls and etched with ancient symbols—had something wrong with it. Even now, it felt hot and tight on her finger.

She and Campbell had stood facing one another before the fireplace, she holding a nosegay of bluebells and daffodils, and he glaring hot enough to set her flowers on fire. Everyone had cheered when the ceremony ended. Campbell had promptly ordered the priest to leave.

Afterward, she'd been too nervous to eat more than a few bites of the delectable breakfast Kate had served—smoked haddock and eggs, herbed lamb, buttered peas, apple tarts, and spiced cake. She'd been too nervous to drink more than a sip of whisky from the *quaich,* a two-handled silver cup she was meant to share with

Campbell. She'd been too nervous to look at him, too nervous to speak. For her, that was very nervous, indeed. When Kate had rallied Broderick and Stuart to play, she and Francis had coaxed Clarissa to dance.

Clarissa didn't know why she'd assumed Campbell would want to dance with her. She'd gazed up at her bridegroom like a moonstruck ninny, admiring his red kilt and ash-gray coat, his strong jaw and dark eyes, growing warm as she imagined those massive arms and beautiful hands guiding her through a reel.

In response, he'd cleared his throat, buttoned his coat, and stalked away without a word. Then, he'd downed several glasses of whisky without pausing for breath.

Rannoch had offered to dance with her.

Rannoch.

He was a superb dancer with a charming grin, but he wasn't her husband. She didn't know whether to be vexed, insulted, or grateful. Rannoch had implied Campbell rarely danced. Clarissa had decided that was a poor excuse. If he was a bad dancer, she would give him lessons. And perhaps teach him better manners.

Meanwhile, however, she must find him. She first asked Angus, who pointed her toward the entrance hall. There, she found Mrs. MacBean wearing a bewildered frown. In her hand was a brown bottle.

"Och, lass." She placed the bottle in Clarissa's hand. "Take this. Ye'll need it."

Automatically, Clarissa read the label. *Everlust Unguent* was underlined several times. Beneath were smeared sketches of a worm, a goat, and a flower. "What is …" She squinted at the worm. *Was* it a worm? Her cheeks heated. Perhaps not. "Oh, dear."

"Aye, ye'll thank me. Now, where did I put that rabbit charm?" She wandered away, muttering to herself.

A shadow blocked the light from the windows. "Had enough of dancing, eh?" came Campbell's deep, rumbly voice from behind her.

She spun. Her stomach swooped. A warm flush bloomed. Good heavens, he was devastating in a kilt. "I thought perhaps you might join me."

He edged close, taking the bottle from her hands and tucking it into his coat pocket. "I'd rather take ye home, lass."

Heart pounding, she swallowed and sighed. "It—it's still raining."

"Aye. Da lent us his carriage."

"Oh." Heavens, he was close. And warm. And big. "Not even one dance?"

He started to answer, but Kate entered from the drawing room accompanied by Mrs. Grant and the lovely dressmaker, Mrs. Baird. All three women were frowning in a concerned fashion. Mrs. Grant held a long box with a loosened ribbon.

"Clarissa, dearest," Kate murmured, nibbling her lip. "Did you, by chance, purchase items from a milliner's shop in Inverness?"

Frowning, Clarissa drifted closer. "No. I haven't visited Inverness in weeks."

The ladies cast each other concerned glances.

"What is it?" Campbell demanded.

Mrs. Grant offered him the box. "It arrived early this morning by courier. I assumed 'twas for Mrs. MacPherson, but she kens naught of it."

Mrs. Baird added, "I recognized the packaging. It's from a shop near mine. A milliner named Mrs. Kennedy. Quite talented, actually. She's a friend."

Chilling shivers coursed over Clarissa's skin, sinking deep as she eyed the box with the blue ribbon. "H-have you opened it?"

Campbell clasped her shoulders and gently pulled her back into his body.

She was thankful for his warmth, his strength. But she needed to know what was in that box.

She plucked it from his hand and tore it open. There, amidst brown paper and white netting, lay the gift meant for her. A black bonnet, black veil, black gloves, and black lace shawl. Widow's weeds. Atop a pair of black silk stockings was a small white card bearing three simple words: *Soon, my love.*

Her hands shook. Her knees turned to water.

The ladies gasped and murmured in shocked tones.

Campbell's arm braced across the front of her shoulders, holding her upright. He handed the box to Mrs. Grant and ordered her to take it away.

"He means to kill you." Clarissa's words were soundless, for her lungs had flattened. She wheezed in a breath. "We must recall the priest. We—we must deny the marriage."

"No."

"Campbell. Let me go." She struggled against his hold. "I'll leave. I'll … I'll draw him away. He'll kill you. He means to kill you."

She tried to turn, but he held her fast while instructing Kate to inform Broderick what had happened. Then, he bent to Clarissa's ear and said, "I'm takin' ye home, *gràidheag*. Brace yerself. I mean to lift ye."

The word he'd used sounded like *gry-eck*. He'd used it before. She didn't know what it meant, and she couldn't gather her thoughts to ask. Panic had taken hold.

He scooped her into his arms. Gently. Carefully. "Put yer arms round my neck." His voice was rough but tender. "There's a good lass. Now, it's rainin', so ye'll want to … aye. Tuck yer head in just like that."

She buried her face against his thick, strong neck. Scents of wool and clean male skin filled her lungs. Her head felt detached, as though it floated two feet above her shoulders. She was panting. Her chest tightened. Squeezed harder and harder. A dry sob shook her.

"Almost there. Into the coach we go."

Light dimmed. He'd placed her on his lap. He held her tightly and tucked a blanket around her shoulders.

"He means to kill you," she gasped. "Campbell." She clung harder, as though she might bind him to this life. To her. "You cannot remain my husband."

"Lass."

"No. NO!" She clung desperately hard, her fingers digging into his muscular nape. "I won't let him hurt you. I won't! Cast me aside. I'll leave Scotland. I'll disappear."

"*Wheesht,* Clarissa. Calm yerself."

"It's not too late. We must find the priest. He can't have gone far."

His hands stroked her back, smoothed her hair. "Dinnae be foolish. 'Tis done. Ye're mine, now."

"No. I'm not the foolish one. He—"

"He'll be gone soon. Ye've naught to fear."

She froze. Straightened. His expression was calm and implacably hard. But his eyes were dark fire.

"What does that mean?" she asked.

"Precisely what it sounds like, lass."

"Y-you intend to …"

"I intend to take ye home." His eyes lowered to her mouth. His thumb caressed her cheek. "Then, I intend to take ye."

Her belly swooped. Her heart thudded.

"We're married," he continued in granite tones. "Ye cannae change it. Neither can he."

Chapter Twelve

Sitting on the edge of her bed—which would soon cease being hers if her husband had his way—Clarissa poured more oil on her left hand. "Blasted, dratted ring." She twisted it around and around her finger, but it refused to budge past her knuckle. "Why won't you come off?"

She tugged. Twisted. Tugged some more.

It was no use. The band was too tight.

The entire carriage ride back to Campbell's house had been a pitched battle. She suspected Campbell thought he'd won after carrying her bodily into her bedchamber and barking at her to stay put until he returned.

She would not stay put. She would not stay in this house or in this marriage. She would not risk his life so that she could have what she wanted.

Snuffling sounded beneath her door. She blew out a breath and wiped her hands on a towel. "Not now, Fergus."

More snuffling. Then, the squeaking of the latch.

She closed her eyes and released a breath. *Tap, tap, tap, tap, tap.* A warm weight on her thigh. She opened her eyes.

There he was, calmly resting his scruffy gray head on her lap. His tail wagged. He sighed.

Her heart seized painfully, twisting and demanding until she couldn't bear the ache. "Why must you do this?" she whispered. "Why?"

Another sigh. His warm breath wafted across her hand.

She could not fight a war on two fronts. She could no longer resist both him and Campbell. Slowly, she moved her hand to stroke his head. Wiry gray fur was softer than it looked. She slid her palm down his neck, sifting fur through her fingers.

"You and your master are equals in one respect," she murmured as the dog continued warming her legs with his chin and long, heavy frame. "Equally stubborn." Her throat burned. "How am I meant to love you when I'm certain to lose you in the end?"

Fergus raised his beautiful face and licked her cheek. Just like that, her heart slipped. She gritted her teeth, cupped his face, and bent forward to rest her forehead against his. A soulful sigh. A nuzzle. She wrapped her arms around him. His head came to rest on her shoulder.

She petted him for long minutes, letting him climb onto the bed and curl up beside her with his head in her lap. "This must be our secret, you understand?" she murmured. "No one else can know."

Her ring flashed and glowed in a shaft of light from the window as she found a particularly good spot behind Fergus's ear for making his leg twitch. He rolled over onto his back, wearing a broad smile.

"Oh, now you want your belly rubbed, do you?"

A shuddering sigh and a lolling grin of adoration.

"Very well." She went to work. "Again, I must stress, this remains between us. Outside this room, we are strangers."

As she reached his furry chest, he licked her wrist.

"Yes, well. I suppose strangers might occasionally lick one another, provided one of them is sufficiently bold."

She scratched beneath his long chin. His whole body shuddered. A small whine emerged. His head rolled back in ecstasy.

"Hmm. I thought you might like that. This beard of yours is forever damp. Have you considered a kerchief?"

He grunted and snuffled then rested a paw on her arm as though to prevent her withdrawing.

"Perhaps we'll fashion one for you. Do you fancy yellow gingham?"

"I'd be surprised if ye had any left, *gràidheag.*"

She shot to her feet and spun to face the door. Fergus clambered off the bed and trotted to Campbell's side before her husband gave him a pat and sent him on his way.

He'd changed out of his kilt, she noticed. Now, he wore only a pair of deerskin breeches, a loose shirt, and an inscrutable expression.

He stepped inside the chamber and closed the door. "Are ye hungry, lass?"

She drew a shuddering breath. Heavens, his shoulders were massive, his arms thick as trunks, muscles rippling with every flex of his hands.

Hungry? She was famished.

"No," she rasped. "Campbell, we must discuss the matter of severing our union."

He started toward her, eyes roving from her hair to her toes. They locked upon her bosom.

And burned.

"We—we cannot stay married." God, her throat was dry. And her gown was tight, particularly across her bosom. And her belly was effervescing, her skin dreadfully hot. "The risk is far too—"

"Ye've let Fergus dirty yer gown."

She glanced down. Several faint, muddy smears marred the pink silk. "It will wash. Really, Campbell, for your sake, we must—" She felt his heat an instant before she raised her head. He'd moved within inches. Her pulse quickened. Her eyes locked on the center of his chest, right where the V of his shirt revealed crisp, black hair over warm male skin.

"Mayhap I could help ye," he said, low and rumbly. He held up his hands and wriggled his fingers. With a quirking smile that turned her knees into jelly, he gave her a considering look. "I'm good with my hands."

Her entire body pulsed as though she'd been struck by pleasurable lightning. She released a breath, retreating until the bed frame brushed the backs of her thighs. She clasped the foot rail. "Oh, God. Don't do this."

He arched a brow. "Do what?"

"Tempt me. You know … you know how much I …"

He closed in upon her.

She shook her head. "Please, Campbell."

"Does it fasten with hooks, then?" He stretched those long, thick arms around her. A long finger traced a whispery caress down her nape.

She shivered. Shook. Moaned.

"Here, now."

She felt those nimble fingers tickling her spine. A cavalcade of tingling sparks rippled across her back, reaching her scalp and hardening her nipples until they ached.

"Better, eh?"

Her eyes were closed, her lips pressed together. Everything inside her was a hot pool. And the scent of him was driving her mad—like fresh air, clean skin, and subtle spice. He smelled like heaven itself.

"Now, ye keep talkin' rubbish about ending this marriage when ye havenae given it a proper chance, *gràidheag*. Mayhap ye'll be glad to have wed such a great beast." He stroked her cheek with his knuckle. "I'm harder to kill than ye suppose."

A sob formed inside her chest, half despair and half need. "You don't understand. I never see him coming. The only warning I have is the one he gives me." She opened her eyes to meet his. "You must distance yourself. We'll pretend to have a row. We'll declare the marriage void."

"Nah, we'll stay married."

This was a repeat of their conversation in the carriage. "I say we won't."

"That's nae what ye said this mornin'."

"Don't be ridiculous. Those were the vows. I spoke them because you insisted. And the priest was standing right there, expecting the same."

"So, ye lied."

"No." She released a frustrated breath. "I received an unmistakable message from someone who means to make me a widow. It changed the calculus considerably."

"Right. And ye dinnae trust me to protect ye."

"I don't want you to *die.*"

"That makes two of us." A little smile curled one corner of his lips. "There. It's settled, then. Now, would ye like some help removin' yer gown, or would ye prefer to undress yerself?"

She grunted her annoyance. "You are maddening. I'm not removing my gown."

He grasped the hem of his shirt and drew it off over his head.

She might have swooned. Not entirely, mind. Just enough to pay homage to the most fascinating sight she'd ever seen.

Campbell MacPherson was a *magnificent* man. Endless shoulders flexed and straightened. Arms thicker and far more muscular than her thighs rippled as he tossed the shirt away. And his chest was … a work of art. A tapered mat of dark, crisp hair covered great slabs of muscle. A ridged belly appeared carved from wood or marble. Except that he was warm. Hot, even. And so enormous that she couldn't breathe.

"Dinnae ye wish to satisfy yer curiosity, lass?" He hooked a thumb into his waistband.

Which drew her gaze down past his belly. Past his hand. To his thighs. Where a long, impossible ridge stretched his breeches with even more impossible force.

Dear God. The man was enormous *everywhere.* Magnificent *everywhere.* How had she not noticed before? But then, he often wore long coats, even with his kilt. She'd seen him buttoning one earlier.

She collapsed against the bed. "This … you … dear God."

He glanced down at himself. "Aye. He's a wee bit intimidatin' at first. Dinnae fash. We'll go slow."

"How—how am I supposed to …" She shook her head, staring like a ninny. "Impossible."

"If ye remove yer gown, I'll let ye touch me however ye like."

Her body lit aflame. Her breasts swelled, nipples tingling into hardness. She could scarcely catch her breath. "No, I … we cannot stay married. It's not safe for you."

"Touchin' isnae tuppin', *gràidheag*."

Her eyes flew up to his. "You would allow me to touch you without … consummation?"

His gaze was purely black, now. His nose flared. He licked his lips. "Aye. I ken how much ye want to."

"But, if you touch me in return, I'll lose my head," she confessed.

He glanced at his hands. "Then, I promise nae to touch ye. Not until ye ask."

The problem was twofold: She wouldn't ask; she'd beg. This was precisely how he'd coaxed her into marriage in the first place.

Secondly, she had a second point. What was it? She couldn't recall.

God, he was beautiful.

"Very well," she whispered to her weakness. "But I'm keeping my gown on."

"Fair enough."

"And you must sit on the bed so I can reach you. With your hands on the bedframe."

He grunted. "Trews on or off?"

"On," she rasped reluctantly. "Less temptation."

"Hmm, that doesnae leave much territory for a curious lass to explore."

She licked her lips, eyeing the rust-hued male nipples peeking through his chest hair. "It's enough."

"Aye, then." He slid closer until she could smell the rich spice of his skin and feel the wash of his breath upon her hair. Then, he slipped past her and sat on the bed. He positioned himself with his back against the headboard and his arms outstretched to the two posts. He looked like a warrior god expecting his nymph to pleasure him.

"I want to kiss you," she confessed.

"Ye'll have to come closer, then."

He'd loosened the fastenings of her gown earlier, so the bodice slipped as she started forward. She gathered up her skirts, huffing her frustration as one of the sleeves slid off her shoulder.

Campbell's molten gaze followed the movement, shifting between her shoulder, her bosom, and her lips.

She climbed up on the bed, crawling to reach his side. His eyes glued to her bosom, on jostling display before she sat back on her heels. "Would you mind if I kissed you?" she asked his lips.

"Not at all, *gràidheag,*" they answered. "But it will be easier if ye straddle me."

It was a fair point. She shifted her skirts, pulling them up her thighs so she could climb onto his lap. Then, she rested her hands on his shoulders, savoring the heat of his skin. She'd always adored his neck—so strong and thick. Her fingers slid there next, exploring the sinews of his shoulders along the way.

"Come closer, lass," he murmured softly. "Dinnae fear. Ye'll feel me between yer legs. But it will feel good."

Her breathing quickened as she gripped his neck. With shimmying movements, she scooted forward until her thighs truly straddled his hips. The impossibly large ridge of his male staff pressed hard against her folds. Nothing separated them except his breeches. It felt like he'd always belonged there, like they were fitted to one another.

Her aching breasts pressed into the hard contours of his chest. And now, their faces were nearly touching. Even with her sitting astride him, he loomed above her. His eyes burned like coals. "There. Now, kiss me."

She sank into his mouth, all but grinding their lips together. He opened for her, stroking her tongue with his. Her fingers dug into his hair, thick and faintly damp. The scent of rain and fire and man flooded her senses. She found herself mewling in pleasure, rubbing her breasts against his hard chest. Her cravings all multiplied at once.

She ground her hips into his. Her hands cupped his hard jaw to trap him for her mouth's pleasure. She played with his tongue, gripped his shoulders and rode him hard. Over and over. He was a thick ridge fitted to her perfectly. He was heat and muscle, spice and strength. He let her touch him everywhere—the flat male nipples, the bones at the base of his throat, the crisp hair arrowing down his belly. He said nothing, only breathing harshly and burning her alive with his gaze.

He offered himself without demand. If she didn't already want him with every inch of her body, that would have done it.

Her hands delighted in him. Her mouth devoured him. Her nipples demanded more of him. More and more and more.

There was so much more she could have, her desire whispered. So much.

Her hips worked harder as the thought took flight. Oh, how gloriously that massive staff pressured upward against her. How soft and hot and sensitive she felt everywhere. Especially *there.* In that sweet, slick, swollen center. Rippling pleasure started in waves. She was wetting his breeches. She was using his impossible hardness to quench the relentless ache in her core. Still, the fire didn't die. It expanded. The heat between them burned too hot to be real.

A deep, agonized groan rumbled in her ear. Wood gave an ominous creak as he gripped the bed. She scarcely heard it.

She was lost. "Campbell," she sobbed, frantically kissing his jaw and then his neck, tasting the salt of his sweat as his body shook and heaved beneath the onslaught of hers. None of it was enough. She needed … him. "I'm dying."

"Tell me what ye need, *gràidheag.*" His voice was shredded.

"More. You."

Wood creaked again as his hands flexed and gripped. "Be specific. Do ye need my cock?"

She nodded, her face burning as she clung tighter.

"Ye must take it out, then."

"I can't. I can't bear to move." She writhed against him, her head falling back as pleasure burst upward with explosive heat. It wasn't enough. His body alone wasn't nearly enough. "Oh, God. Please."

"Do ye want my hands?"

"Yes. Please. Pleeeaase."

"Do ye want me to touch ye?"

"Yes." She panted like a horse run too hard. "Touch me. I'm begging you."

"If I do, then ye must take me inside. And once that happens, ye're mine forever. Do ye ken, Clarissa? Nod if ye ken."

She nodded. "Anything. I'll do anything."

His chest heaved. Powerful arms wrapped around her back, crushing her against his body. A low growl rumbled as long fingers tugged at her hair, forcing the length to tumble down her back like a waterfall. He pressed the mass to his nose, inhaling deeply. His knuckles tickled her back. Without further warning, he ripped her bodice free and tumbled her back onto the mattress.

He braced himself above her, a dark god with burning-coal eyes and a lock of black hair falling over a heavy brow.

"I want ye naked. Now."

She bit her lip and nodded, but he wasn't waiting for permission. Without another word, he stripped her of every scrap—beaded silk gown, corset and stockings, cotton petticoats and linen shift. Half the items would need repair. The stockings would need replacing.

She didn't care a whit. The man she'd wanted from the first moment she'd seen him was lying above her, and finally she could see him properly. Those deep, endless eyes devoured her. She glanced down to see what had his attention.

Her breasts. They were swollen and flushed. Nipples that were usually the pale pink of seashells stood like beaded berries, fiery rose and achingly hard. Should she be embarrassed by how much her body wanted him? Perhaps. She felt wanton. Desperate.

Should she fret that he'd be disappointed by the curve of her belly or the width of her hips or the fine, silvery lines that marred both after years of plumpness?

She didn't fret. She didn't feel embarrassed. She didn't have a chance.

His eyes shifted to hers. And there it was. There *he* was. The piece she'd been missing when she'd thought his body would be enough. Black fire burned away any thought of separation. How foolish she'd been, thinking she could touch him without losing herself. That she could leave him behind or that he would let her.

"Campbell," she whispered, reaching for him.

He clasped her wrists and pinned them above her head. "My turn," he rasped. "It's my bluidy turn, Clarissa."

"Yes."

"Lie still and let me luik."

She sighed. Arched her back. Fought the urge to squirm.

A long, low groan sounded. A powerful jaw flickered. He eased up until he sat between her spread thighs. He scraped a hand over his face. Those burning eyes traveled down her torso, down and down to the place where damp curls and pink folds told the tale of her desire.

She couldn't decipher what he was thinking, but he looked tortured, as though she was tearing him to pieces. "Campbell," she pleaded. "Touch me. God, I need you so much."

"What do ye need, hmm?"

"Your hands. Your mouth."

"My hands," he murmured, sliding both palms along her outer thighs, onto her hips and waist. He traced her ribs with his fingers and stroked her navel with his thumbs.

Fire chased shivers and gooseflesh. Her nipples tingled and hardened further. She arched again. Writhed. He held her still.

"My mouth." He lowered his head to kiss the bone between her breasts, directly over her heart. His jaw nuzzled the swell of her right breast. His tongue traced a sleek, wet trail to her areola. Then stopped. He did the same to the left breast, halting before he reached the sensitive tip.

Groaning a protest, she clenched her teeth against the urge to beg again. He seemed determined to torment her. Was this what happened when a woman wanted a man more than he wanted her—he took his sweet time while she perished from unrequited lust?

"Campbell—"

"What else do ye need, lass?"

"Please. God, this is—"

"Say the word, now."

She lay there for a moment, head spinning. She didn't understand. "What word?"

"Ye long to be mine. Say it."

"Yes, I do," she whispered.

"Tell me ye want me inside ye."

"Dear heaven. You know I—"

"Because it will hurt this time, *gràidheag*. No help for it. I'll go gently as I can." He moved his hand between her thighs and slid two fingers down the crease of her folds.

Astonishing pleasure bloomed outward, shaking her entire body.

"But ye're tight here." Long fingers slid down. Then, one slid inside.

She jolted. Her thighs tightened automatically, stopped from closing by his hips.

He inserted a second finger.

She felt a stretching pinch, brief but distinct. His fingers were thick. Even one seemed large. Two were uncomfortable—nearly painful. Suddenly, she understood why he was taking so long to prepare her. Her eyes fell to his groin. To the thick, massive stalk tenting his fall.

Good God. He would never fit. His staff was enormous.

His thumb danced over the tiny nub at the center of her sex while his opposite palm slid over her belly and up to her solar plexus. Finally, he stroked upward and cupped her breast.

She groaned.

"Easy," he soothed. "Dinnae fear. I'll always take care of ye, lass. Always."

Soon, heated pleasure rocked her in waves. The sensations tightened as his fingers began to pressure and pulse inside her. His other hand began caressing her nipples, thumbing them and squeezing them in rhythmic harmony.

As though she were an instrument and he a master musician.

Between her thighs, discomfort dissolved into aching heat. It coiled into binding ropes. Into a knot of fire.

"Oh, God," she panted, arching high into his touch. "Campbell. I'm going to—"

"Aye. Come for me."

She gripped the wool blanket beneath her. Writhed to force his fingers deeper. Threw back her head and gasped when he swept them over a hidden pleasure center. Her body tightened. Harder. Bursting. Light exploded behind her eyes as her entire being flew up and out, shattering into pieces.

She heard her own pleas for mercy, along with repeated incantations of his name. Slowly, as she floated down in a shimmering cloud, her body went limp, savoring the sight of his hands upon her—between her thighs and upon her breast. She let herself soak in the connection to him as he stared down at her.

"God, ye're bluidy glorious, *gràidheag*. Someday, ye'll ken how I see ye. Someday, ye'll understand what it cost me to …" He shook his head.

She noticed his cheeks were flushed, his lips swollen from their earlier kisses. He kept his fingers inside her, still stroking, though his motions were gentler now. He couldn't seem to tear his eyes away from her breasts and her sex.

His free hand unbuttoned his fall. Then, he took out his cock. It was darker than the rest of him, heavily veined and viciously red, hard, and swollen. It arched up from a nest of black hair and a set of proportional ballocks.

Her body had been temporarily sated, but the coil of lust was already tightening again. She licked her lips, wondering how the translucent bead welling on the head of his cock tasted.

He withdrew his fingers and slathered the head of his cock with her juices. Then, he forced the massive stalk down to caress her swollen nub.

She moaned his name. Even the sight of such contact sent her careening toward another peak.

"Shh, easy," he rasped. "Yer body is wee, but ye were made for me. Relax yer thighs. Let them fall wide. Good."

The large, rounded head traced and teased through her folds for long moments before notching at the opening it sought to invade.

Her heart pounded. Her thighs stiffened. "Campbell."

He was focused on their joining, but when she said his name, he glanced up. His eyes were purely black. Purely savage. "Take me inside," he ordered, grasping her knees and forcing them up toward her shoulders. Then, he braced himself above her, thrusting his cock an inch or two inside her passage.

Her eyes widened. She shook her head. She was slick and wet where they'd begun joining, but all her fears about his size had merit. He was huge. The stretch felt impossible.

"Stay with me, lass," he whispered, playing with the hair at her temples as his lower half continued pressing forward. Deeper. Deeper.

She gasped as the painful stretch continued. "Dear God. I'm not certain I … Campbell. We don't fit."

"We fit." He gave her more. "Ye're so wet for me, it's nigh impossible to resist poundin' away at ye. But I will." He clasped her chin gently. Kissed her hard and gave a small thrust. "I will. Now, let yer muscles relax. Aye. That's the way." More intrusion, more of that sharp, pinching pain and deeper, aching fullness. "Take more."

She panted, writhing to adjust the angle. "I'm trying."

"Aye, I feel ye." He drew her legs up around his waist. Thrusting deeper, he continued kissing her in slow, sensual sweeps.

She arched into him and cupped his jaw. She held his gaze, falling into a black abyss of need. The heat of his cock was incredible. She felt scalded. Invaded. Claimed.

When he was seated fully, lodged deep inside her, his eyes flared and lit. "Feel me there?"

She nodded. Strained.

He began thrusting. Out and in. In and out. Slowly at first. Then, firmly. Steadily. Rocking deeper. Harder.

She scarcely knew what to do. It was both uncomfortable and distressing. Hot and provoking. Too much and not enough.

"Yer body needs mine," he gritted, his eyes burning. "Nae other man's. Mine." His hips thrust with deep motions, driving higher and harder inside her. He seemed bent on proving his point.

She gripped his neck and arched to accommodate him. "Campbell."

He adjusted his angle, forcing the long, slick stalk to drag across her swollen nub with the next thrust. It caused her sheath to seize and squeeze and ripple with lightning force. She released a long, keening moan. Pleasure swallowed every hint of discomfort, bursting outward and sizzling across the ether.

He grunted. Groaned. Quickened his pace as she begged him to do it again. Anything. She'd do anything if he'd only go deeper. Harder.

"Please, Campbell. Please. Oh, how I need you."

"Aye, ye do," he growled, so hoarse his voice sounded doubled. Layered, somehow. "Take me. Take me into yer body. Down to the root. Take yer pleasure, wife."

Like the click-and-crack of a trigger, the words "pleasure" and "wife" fired her high into the sky. She clawed and sobbed as her body seized upon his. So furiously did she grip him, she heard him cursing. Grunting her name in her ear. Then, he took her in rough, pounding strokes. His hand gripped her hair. His lips buried against her throat. His body strained as he rode her.

Rode her.

Rode her hard and deep.

Faster and faster.

Until the galloping end, when he released a long, loud bellow against her skin and erupted inside her in a scalding tide. Somehow, his pleasure became hers, and they merged. One body. One skin. One soul.

Perhaps because he held her so tightly.

Perhaps because she loved him so much.

Perhaps because she needed him the way fish need water and birds need sky.

She didn't know why, only that this was real. They were bound. And, as she cradled his head against her and felt his hard muscles ease toward sleep, she prayed that the price of having her heart's desire would not be his life.

CHAPTER THIRTEEN

With every fiber of her being, Clarissa longed to punish her husband until he begged for mercy. He'd certainly shown her none.

Her body had never been this sore. She could scarcely sit. But that was a minor irritation, the cost of a night of transcendent pleasure. A cost she paid gladly.

No, her wrath was due to his absence. He'd left her shortly after sunrise. Briefly, she'd awakened, a limp, drowsy mess, when she'd felt him leave their bed. All she remembered was a fierce kiss, a whispered "Go back to sleep, *gràidheag,*" and a feeling of blissful contentment.

Arrogant, reckless man.

She slammed a cup of cider onto the kitchen table and cast her brother-in-law a scathing glare. "This is rank idiocy, Alexander. Your brother is the thickest, most obstinate, insufferable arse in all of Scotland. All the world!"

He wiped the sloshed cider from the table and took a drink. "Now, now. Rannoch isnae so bad. I've met a few Frenchmen who are worse."

"I meant Campbell, as you well know." She tried to sit and had to wince before settling more gingerly.

"Aye, I ken." He quirked a small grin. "He's a lot to manage when he sets his mind on somethin'."

"A lot to manage? He's impossible!" She blew out a breath and petted Fergus absently. The dog always seemed to sense when she needed comfort. "As I explained, Stephen Northfield is the grandson of Viscount Northfield. Who is bosom companions with *three* ministers in the current government. Who will happily hang any daft, intractable, infuriating Scot who dares touch a hair upon Stephen's head."

Alexander cast her a dark glance over the rim of his cup. "Ye're assumin' there will be enough of Northfield left for his kin to mourn."

She scoffed. "Exaggerations aren't helpful."

He didn't answer, only raised a brow and drank.

"What are you saying?"

He glanced inside his cup. "Have ye anything stronger? Whisky wouldnae go amiss."

She poured him more cider and shoved a plate of fresh crowdie cheese across the table. "You need food, not liquor. Now, I should like an answer, if you please."

He sighed, popping a bite of cheese in his mouth. "What would ye like to hear?"

"The truth, of course."

"Nah." He chewed before continuing, "Truth sounds like a fine thing 'til ye ken it. Then, all ye want is for that beast to go back in its bluidy cage."

She rolled her eyes and plucked a square of ham from her plate for Fergus. The dog was gentle as he nibbled from her fingers. She scratched his ears as a reward. "What nonsense. Campbell should not be hunting Northfield. I don't care that he took Rannoch along. It's too dangerous."

"Aye. For Northfield." His gaze narrowed on her. "What has Cam told ye of his time in the Highland regiment?"

"Nothing whatever. Kate mentioned he was once a soldier, that he'd seen battle on the Continent and returned to Scotland after Waterloo. That's all I know."

He nodded. "Did she tell ye I joined at the same time? That we served together?"

A frown tugged. "No."

His mouth twisted. "Ye've naught to fear, lass. There's a reason Campbell left the battlefield after only a few years."

"Why is that?"

"Same reason I left." He took a swig of his cider. "We're good at killin'."

A chill shivered over her skin. "I should think that would make you both quite valuable to your commanders."

"Oh, it did."

"I don't understand."

He braced his elbows on the table and gave her a slow, cold smile. "A good man isnae good because he's harmless. He's good because he kens how to manage his darker nature, which is easier if he never lets it get out of hand."

She considered his point. "Being good at something can be heady. Like dancing. The thrill of mastery, the challenge of it. It tempts you to indulge more deeply."

Black eyes flashed. He seemed surprised at her understanding. "Aye."

"I'm dreadfully worried for him, Alexander." Her throat tightened. She hugged Fergus's neck and kissed him between his sweet eyes. The dog smiled and settled down to lie beside her chair. "I've tried to explain how dangerous Northfield is, yet Campbell seems to regard him as merely a nuisance."

"Ye're underestimating Cam. Gather a hundred dangerous men in a room, and I'll tell ye which one to fear. 'Tis the one who stays calm when the guns fire. The one who makes other men scatter like rats in daylight."

Frowning, she examined Alexander's hands. They were relaxed. His whole body was. He often held himself very still, she'd noticed. Even injured and in pain, he moved with smooth, ghostly grace.

"I wish you'd gone with him," she whispered.

"That makes two of us, lass."

She glanced out the window at the ominous gray day. It wasn't raining, but it was about to. "What made you follow him into the regiment?"

A long pause. "Thought he'd decide living was better than dyin' if he had a brother to look after. It worked."

Shock rippled through her. She studied Alexander's calm features as he took another drink. "He—he joined because he wanted to … die?"

A single nod.

"Why?"

He ran a hand over his unshaven jaw. The gesture was so familiar, it made her heart ache. "Now, that's somethin' ye'll have to ask him." Alexander shoved to his feet and started toward the garden door.

"Was it a woman?" she asked softly, though she wasn't certain she wanted the answer. Wasn't certain she could bear it.

He stiffened. Glanced over his shoulder. Then left without another word.

Campbell was beginning to think Northfield was a phantom. They'd spent the first half of the day escorting Nora Baird back to Inverness, where she'd helped them question her friend, the milliner.

Mrs. Baird had gently prodded the pinched, dark-haired Mrs. Kennedy, "Surely ye saw his face," to which the milliner had replied, "Nae surely about it. Never met the man. He arranged the order by message. Seemed proper enough. The note was left for me in that slot, there." She'd nodded to a brass letter slot in the shop's door. "Some gents prefer this method over visiting the shop in person. More private."

Campbell had demanded to see the note. She'd handed it over with a frown. He'd recognized Northfield's writing from Clarissa's letter, but this one had no postal marks. It had been hand-delivered, probably by Northfield himself. Which meant the man was close enough to Inverness to deliver messages and close enough to the glen to slaughter livestock on MacPherson land. Yet, nobody had seen any strangers about, never mind a tall Englishman.

"Are ye certain ye dinnae recall aught else?" he'd asked Mrs. Kennedy. "Where he's been lodging or where he'd go for a pint? Anythin'?"

"All I ken is he pays in coins and pays promptly, Mr. MacPherson. Would that all my customers did the same."

They'd spent the rest of the day combing every wee village within ten miles of Glenscannadoo. The fourth village they searched was no more helpful than the previous three.

Now, the sun was nearly down. And his mood had gone black hours ago. He adjusted his hat and mounted his horse as soon as he and Rannoch exited the village's lone tavern.

"Do ye reckon he's camped this whole time?" Rannoch asked as they headed southwest toward the fifth village.

"Nah," Campbell answered. "Alexander would have found him, were that the case. Besides, he'd need supplies. Ammunition. Food. Paper for his bluidy notes."

Rannoch grunted and shifted in his saddle, squinting as they rode through a shaft of red sunlight. "Mad bugger. Imagine bein' that obsessed with one lass."

Campbell didn't answer.

Rannoch glanced his direction as they took the road toward Dalgrudie. "Nae to say she isnae bonnie. Because she is. A fair beauty with a kind heart. I've always thought so."

He focused on the road ahead. It was little more than a rough path through rocky terrain dotted by short pines and clumps of thistle.

"Did I ever tell ye she embroidered my plaid with a wee acorn?" Rannoch continued. "I left it behind after dinner one evenin', and when I retrieved it a few days later, the work was done. I asked why she'd bothered. She said, 'Oh, I thought it suited you.' Then, she spent a long while explainin' how I was similar to an acorn, as it contained such 'immense potential.'" He laughed and shook his head. "Aye, she's a charmer, yer wee bride. A true lady." He huffed. "Ere long, she'll want a finer place than that auld pile of thatch and stone ye call a house. 'Tis clear she's done her best to make improvements, but damn, man. A wife needs more than Rob Robertson's castoffs to make a proper home."

He gritted his teeth and glared ahead.

"I predict ye'll soon be crackin' the seal on all that money ye've been storin' up. Does she ken the size of yer fortune—"

"Haud yer wheesht, Rannoch."

"No, then."

The silence that followed was unfortunately brief.

"She fancies dancin', aye? Mayhap I'll teach her a few more Highland dances before the Glenscannadoo Games this summer. She could enter the lasses' competition. Aye, she'll be a true MacPherson, then. Of course, I'll have to take my time with her. Trainin' requires long hours and a firm hand."

"Nah. Ye'll keep yer bluidy hands to yerself if ye aim to keep 'em attached."

Rannoch grinned wide then broke into laughter. "Broderick said ye were far gone. I didnae think it was this bad."

It wasn't this bad. It was worse. Twelve hours since he'd left her sleeping in the warm nest of their bed, and he couldn't draw a clear breath. He'd had chest wounds that were less painful.

"Ah, brother. Ye should be home with her."

"Not until I find Northfield."

"Have ye considered that's what he's after? A shot at ye?"

Of course he'd considered it. He wasn't an idiot. "Doesnae matter. Bastard has to die."

Rannoch glanced around at the dwindling light and lengthening shadows. Rolling his shoulders, he at last fell silent.

A half-hour later, Campbell was grateful for his youngest brother's uncanny talent for seduction. The buxom barmaid at the Three Swans Inn seemed likewise appreciative, as she started spilling secrets the moment Rannoch grinned in her direction.

"Och, no. Havenae seen any Englishmen to speak of," she said, running a finger down Rannoch's biceps. "Though, I do think it a wee bit strange, ye askin'."

Rannoch played with a lock of the lass's hair. "And why's that?"

She grinned and leaned across Rannoch to place Campbell's ale on the table, thrusting her bosoms beneath Rannoch's chin. "Last month, Ed Ramsay claimed his nephew was visitin' from England for a hunt. Then, he asks about you."

"Me?"

"Well, the MacPhersons, at any rate. I didnae think ye were acquainted. A week later, Ramsay comes in to buy more blankets, and when I asked after his nephew, he denies he ever mentioned it." She snorted. "Peculiar thing to say. He's auld, nae daft." She squinted. "Come to that, 'tis a peculiar thing for Ed Ramsay to leave his house, the poor auld man. Hasnae come round much since his wife took ill."

Campbell's spine prickled. "Where does he live?"

The barmaid sniffed and raised her chin. "Well, now. Why should I tell ye?"

He sat forward, glaring.

Rannoch smiled calmly and told the maid, "Best ye answer, lass. He's had a long day."

She swallowed. Eyed Campbell's shoulders and his expression. "Take the main road north. Turn at the mill. 'Tis the farm just past the bridge."

Campbell finished off his ale, tossed a coin on the table, and stood. The barmaid scurried back several steps.

"Yer ale is shite," he uttered before striding out to the inn's yard.

Rannoch followed, but he waited until they'd both mounted and started down the main road before commenting, "Ye didnae have to insult her ale."

"Was I wrong?"

A sigh. "No."

It didn't take long to find the place. The stone farmhouse sat at the end of an overgrown lane, isolated amidst a stand of pine and ash trees. The two-story structure was flanked by stone fences and a wooden stable in poor repair. A goat munched away in the garden. A pair of ravens cawed from the roof. Otherwise, there were no signs of life—no smoke from the chimneys, no light from the windows.

"I dinnae like the look of this," Rannoch murmured, laying his rifle across his lap.

Campbell slowed their pace. "Aye."

They routed into the tree line, dismounting and tying the horses. Then, he assessed what he could see of the property in the faint moonlight. "See what ye can find in the stable. I'll work my way round the house to enter from the garden. If ye find Northfield, damage him all ye like. But dinnae kill him. That's for me."

Rannoch cast him a grim stare. "Christ. I'm glad ye're on my side, brother."

They each approached the house from different directions, keeping to the shadows and staying clear of the line of sight from the windows. Campbell palmed his pistol and dirk then moved around the back of the house, noting the bedsheets hanging on a slumped clothesline. They were covered in rusty stains. He moved to the garden gate, which was wedged open at a crooked angle. The goat bleated. He stepped out of its way, and it ran past him.

He listened, watched for signs of Northfield or Ramsay. Nothing.

The garden door was unlocked. He opened it. Immediately, he recognized the stench. He wouldn't find Ramsay or his wife here—at least, not alive.

Cold fury gripped him. He forced it down, moving silently through the scullery and kitchen. A deer carcass was laid out on the table, largely intact. Blood puddled the floor, but the carcass wasn't stiff, so the animal must have been killed days ago.

Venturing further inside, he discovered Mrs. Ramsay in the lower bedchamber. She lay in her dressing gown and mobcap staring sightlessly at the window, her hands folded over her chest, her mouth agape. She'd been dead at least a day or two.

He searched the house room by room, finding evidence of a "guest" having slept in an upstairs bedchamber—woolen blankets piled in the corner, a washstand with whiskers remaining in the bowl. He found no other possessions—no guns or ammunition, no clothing or shaving soap.

Grim certainty crystallized: Northfield had been here, but he wasn't any longer.

Campbell finished searching the house and met Rannoch outside the stable. Rannoch's expression was bleak and ominous. "Likely Northfield is gone, Cam. At least a day or two."

Campbell nodded. "Any sign of Ramsay?"

Rannoch stepped back and gestured to the stable doors. "Aye."

Inside the stable, an old man with a white beard dangled from a rafter. He hadn't been hung by the neck. Rather, he'd been tied, strung up, and bled out like hunted game.

Cold, grinding sickness filled Campbell's body. "Christ on the cross."

"I must admit, I'd hoped yer lass was makin' a fuss over naught. But I fear it's the opposite. Murderous bastard."

Campbell nodded and scraped a hand over his mouth. He pulled his dirk from its scabbard and cut Ramsay down. Rannoch helped him lower the old man's body onto a pile of straw. Then, they found a blanket and covered him.

"How do ye reckon Northfield persuaded Ramsay to help him?" Rannoch asked.

"Ramsay's wife was ill. Likely Northfield threatened to kill her, which gave him control of Ramsay. She's been dead a day or two longer than Ed, here. I suspect she died of her illness, which left Northfield naught to hold over Ramsay. The poor man attempted an escape. Northfield killed him."

Rannoch sighed. As they made their way back to their horses, he observed, "He's clever. An Englishman would be noticed round here straight away. So, he finds a local man to fetch supplies and give him shelter. But not too local, eh? Dalgrudie is an hour's ride from Glenscannadoo, well outside MacPherson territory, and ye only pass through here if ye're headed to Dingwall. Ramsay was a perfect target." Rannoch paused. "Northfield might be mad, but he thinks like a hunter. A predator. Bluidy dangerous."

If Campbell could speak, he'd have made the same observations. Bloody dangerous was right. But, at the moment, all he could do was urge his horse to travel faster.

"Why would he abandon the house?" Rannoch mused as they passed the mill and turned onto the main road. "He could have buried the Ramsays. Could have kept livin' there, huntin' his food, nobody the wiser."

Campbell swallowed a sick, cold knot. "He doesnae need the house any longer. His hunt is ending. He means to take his prize." That was why he'd sent the widow's weeds. Clarissa had said the only warning she ever received was the one Northfield gave her. The warning had been issued. Northfield was coming for her.

Rannoch was silent for a long while. Then, he said, "We'll keep her safe, Cam. Whatever it takes. MacPhersons protect our own."

Campbell nodded his thanks. But, inside, his instincts were howling that even an army of MacPhersons might not be enough.

Two hours later, he entered his house through the scullery after ensuring the men on watch hadn't spied anything unusual. Exhaustion made every muscle ache. The smell of death still haunted him. And the wretched ale from hours earlier remained a bitter memory in the back of his throat.

But God, it was good to be home.

He sighed when he saw Alexander drinking whisky in the kitchen.

"Ye're late, brother." In the lantern light, Alexander's eyes were red but sharp. He looked as haggard as Campbell felt. "Did it take all day to bury the man?"

"I didnae find him."

Alexander poured him a dram, sliding it across the table. "Aye, he's a slippery fish, that one."

Campbell washed away the memory of bitter, musty ale with the golden fire of MacPherson whisky. "I discovered where he's been hidin'."

Alexander lifted a brow. "Where?"

In blunt terms, he described what he and Rannoch had found.

Alexander ran a hand over his unshaven jaw and cursed. "We'll have to inform the constable."

"Rannoch will do it in the morning." Campbell paused, his head swimming circles around the one thought that never left his mind. "How is she?"

A faint smile. "Vexed with ye. Frettin' about yer safety."

He gritted his teeth. The need to see her was a grinding ache.

"Go on," Alexander said softly. "She's asleep, so probably willnae mind ye starin' at her like a pure dafty."

Campbell grunted as longing speared his chest. He moved toward the passage, eager to find his wife. At the entrance, a twinge of concern made him turn. In the firelight, Alexander's features were starker than usual. He looked like a man who'd seen heaven but resided in hell. "Get some rest, brother," he commanded. "I'll need ye strong for the fight to come."

Casually, Alexander finished his whisky and shoved to his feet. "Aye. Ye will," he replied as he retrieved his rifle and opened the garden door to head outside. "But there's no rest for the wicked, eh?"

Frowning, Campbell wondered if Alexander's wound was all that plagued him. His brother seemed … he didn't know. Broken, somehow. A woman? He wondered.

Right now, Campbell had his own woman to worry about. The thought drove him forward, taking the stairs two at a time. He halted in front of her door, trying to calm his heart before he bloody frightened her. He clenched and released his fists. Swallowed. Felt the rise of anticipation. Gently knocked and opened her door.

The bed was empty.

"Bluidy hell," he muttered. Where was she? Cold panic snaked up his spine. Alexander had said she was asleep. There wasn't even a fire in the hearth. Instantly, he started for the stairs—and paused when he passed his own chamber door. Had that been a creak? It sounded like his bed every time he rolled over.

He thrust the door wide, his heart pounding. There in the center of his bed, wrapped in his gray plaid with her arm draped over a sprawling Fergus, lay his sweet, bonnie wife. The world shifted, forcing him to brace against the door casing. He breathed his relief. Wandered closer.

God, how he needed to hold his lass.

Fergus snuffled and raised his head. Tail wagging, the dog sat up and hopped down from the bed to greet Campbell. After a few pats and quiet praise, Campbell sent him to lie on his pallet. Then, without another thought, he stripped down to his trews and climbed into the bed to lie beside Clarissa.

She mumbled sweetly and reached for him, though she appeared to be asleep. He took her in his arms, cradling her body against his. Then, he granted himself permission to touch her.

Her hair, soft as silk floss, delighted his fingertips. Her shoulders and back felt so dainty and wee. Her pale cheek tempted his lips. Her lips hardened him to the point of pain.

The warm cushion of her body was miraculous. How he craved her. How he needed those laughing eyes teasing him about his black moods. How he longed for the words to explain what she was to him.

But he'd never been good with words. Broderick was better at explaining things, and Rannoch could charm a lass out of her skirts with devilish efficiency. Even Alexander was more articulate, though he understood Campbell's struggle better than the others. He knew more about Isla, more about the past.

Campbell stroked his wife's sweet features, tracing her pale brows and delicate nose. When she shifted and clasped his wrist, he gathered her in tighter, molding his strength around her as her palm slid up his chest.

"Campbell?" she murmured sleepily.

"Aye," he whispered, kissing her temple.

"You're home." Thick lashes fluttered. She sighed. Blinked up at him. Caressed his jaw. "Never leave again."

His heart turned inside out. By God, this woman was his. Would that ever fail to astound him? "No," he rasped. "I'll never leave ye."

She frowned. Her lower lip trembled until she firmed it. "I missed you. I worried. Alexander said I shouldn't, but I can't help it."

"Dinnae distress yerself, *gràidheag*."

Her fingers dug into his muscles, kneading him like a kitten. "And now I want you again. It never ceases."

Fire shot through his cock, which stood hard and ready, despite his exhaustion. His body was ungovernable where she was concerned.

"I'm … indisposed, so we can't …" She sighed. "Dratted courses. Such a bother. Perhaps it's for the best, though. Every time I'm near you, I feel as if Mrs.

MacBean fed me a fertility tonic. Ridiculous." Her eyes drifted closed as she snuggled into him. "I'm ridiculous."

"Nah," he rasped. He wanted to tell her she was the furthest thing from ridiculous, that he'd stumbled into paradise after wandering across a vast, barren moor. But he couldn't speak. His throat was tight, his chest tighter.

Before Clarissa, he hadn't realized how withered and cold his existence had become. Then, last Christmas, he'd seen a breathtaking English beauty staring at him across his brother's drawing room. Those boundless eyes had flared wide, darting to his hands and thighs, and she'd blushed the bonniest pink. He'd been a long-dead man suddenly yearning to take a breath. The more he'd seen her, the deeper his need had grown. It became a craving. Then an insatiable desire. He'd tried to satisfy it in his dreams, but that had never been enough. His desperation had been evident to his brothers, though he'd only begun to recognize it himself when he'd learned she was in danger.

"Ye're my Eden, love," he confessed to her now, his voice rough. "Perhaps I'm a thief for claimin' ye when I've no earthly right, but what's a man to do when he's handed a miracle? Keep it, that's what. Guard it with his life. Cherish it with everything he has."

She didn't reply. With her head tucked between his shoulder and neck, she merely hummed and relaxed into sleep.

Only as he surrendered to exhaustion did he realize he'd finally spoken his heart's truth—aloud—to his bonnie wife. But he'd spoken in Gaelic.

CHAPTER FOURTEEN

"Ye cannae be serious." Campbell leaned back in his chair with a frown. "The man's killed two people. Strangers. He must be stopped."

Clarissa poured her husband's second cup of coffee and drew his gray plaid—now her plaid—tighter around her shoulders. "I agree."

"I mean to kill him. Dinnae give two shites what his kin thinks about it."

"Which is why *I* must care about such things." She sat down across the kitchen table from her husband and poured herself some tea. Gesturing toward the sideboard, she explained, "Like napkins."

"Napkins?"

"Think how empty and disorganized the baskets would look without matching napkins."

He glanced over his shoulder.

"A woman notices things a man doesn't," she clarified. "The need for proper labeling, for example."

His eyes resettled on her and narrowed.

"There's a fine line between austere and barbaric, you know. Corks in a rusted tin are decidedly the latter."

In lieu of a reply, he snorted and drank his coffee.

"I'm not complaining."

"Nah. 'Course not."

"My point is that you shouldn't dismiss my concerns."

"I didnae dismiss ye." He gestured toward the baskets. "I've let ye make whatever changes ye cared to, aye?"

"Well, not *all* of them."

"What else would ye like?"

"Windows that don't whistle off-key, for a start."

He rolled his shoulders. "New windows. Fine."

"A fireplace that doesn't douse itself."

"Do ye mean the one in yer old bedchamber? Ye're sleepin' in my bed, now. Ye havenae any use for it."

She tapped her teacup's chipped edge and arched a brow. "A proper tea service wouldn't go amiss."

"Fine."

"A fence for the garden. A new bed for Fergus. Apple trees. Oh! And an owl. I should like you to carve me an owl."

"Enough, lass. Once Northfield's dead, I'll change the whole bluidy place, if ye fancy it. For now, he's my main concern."

"You can't kill him. His family will come after you. They'll want to see you hang."

"I ken."

"No, I don't think you do. Northfields have seeded themselves *everywhere* in aristocratic society. Every noble family has at least one Northfield bride or Northfield cousin or Northfield by-blow. My cousin Rupert's son married one. So did Kate's sister Annabelle." She sipped her tea absently. "Though, Robert is a Northfield by blood, not name. His grandmother, I think." Another sip. "Which only proves my point. They are *everywhere.*"

Realizing she'd forgotten the honey, she started to rise, but Campbell snagged the jar from the sideboard with his impossibly long reach. He set it beside her cup.

She blinked. "Thank you."

He grunted.

She spooned honey into her cup and stirred. Her courses were nearly done, but whenever they came, she preferred things sweeter. "Now then, where was I?"

"Hanging."

"Right. Lord Northfield won't care a whit about Stephen's misdeeds or whether he was killed in defense of my safety. Whoever kills his grandson—"

"'Twill be me."

"Campbell," she chided.

"The matter's settled."

Her spoon clinked into her mismatched saucer. "The constable was suitably outraged by the murders of poor Mr. Ramsay and his wife. He recognizes the threat Stephen poses." When Rannoch had reported their deaths a few days ago, the young, sharp-eyed constable from Inverness had stopped by the house to question her and Campbell. He'd departed a short while later, promising to recruit his "best men" to join the search for Northfield. "I found Mr. Gillespie's determination heartening. Perhaps the pomade was a bit overdone, but he seemed earnest."

"He looked like a larded ham," Campbell grumbled.

"All I'm saying is we should give the constables a chance to find Northfield before we go embroiling ourselves in a murder trial. At best, you'll be transported to Australia. I've no wish to reside in Australia."

"Those lads couldnae find their ballocks with a mirror and a map."

"What would it harm to let them try?"

He drank his coffee and swept her bosom with a scorching black gaze. "Let's say they find Northfield. They'd have to bring him before the magistrates. Judges can be bought." Another sip. "Happened before. Broderick would have lost Kate if matters had been left to the law. Nearly lost her anyhow." He drained his cup. His eyes ensnared hers, making her belly flutter. "I'll nae trust yer safety to incompetents, *gràidheag*."

After catching her breath, she clicked her tongue. "Why are you being so unreasonable?"

He shoved away from the table, his chair scraping across the floor. Rising to carry his cup into the scullery, he frowned at the honeypot near her wrist. "How much longer?"

Her cheeks fired hotter than her tea. "T-tonight, likely."

The past four nights, he'd returned from long days of managing cattle and hunting Northfield to climb into their bed, where he'd held her until morning. No intimacies while she was indisposed, of course. Just the two of them lying together, soaking in each other's warmth, and slowly falling asleep. Though his body's desire for hers remained obvious—his size made it difficult to hide—he hadn't voiced any frustration.

Until now.

With a nod, he started for the doorway. Then halted. Then spun and stalked back to her. Suddenly, he cupped her nape, bent in half, and kissed her hard. A long, silken slide of his tongue teased her senses. Hints of coffee and a heady blast of delicious man sent her head spinning, her heart pounding. She reached for him.

He broke the kiss, breathing fast. "Cannae stay. Too much to do."

She cupped his jaw. "We haven't finished our discussion."

"Aye. We have." He kissed her one last time before striding away.

"Campbell!"

The scullery door opened and closed.

She blew out a breath. Blast, the man was infuriating. And tempting. And a masterful kisser.

And infuriating.

The maids had the day off, so for once, the house was quiet. Too quiet. She tapped a fingernail against her teacup. Fire crackled in the hearth. Wind whistled beyond the window. Her tea began to cool, though her wedding ring remained warm.

Here she was, sitting again, waiting again, hiding again. How utterly useless she felt.

She twisted her ring on her finger, round and round.

She couldn't persuade Campbell to protect himself, no matter the argument. He was determined to kill Northfield and damn the consequences. *Infuriating* man.

Round and round.

Clearly, she could do nothing to stop him.

Round and round.

But could she protect him?

She squinted toward the kitchen window and resumed tapping her teacup in a quickening tempo.

Perhaps. But she'd need a countermeasure. And a great deal of help with a great deal of influence.

Minutes later, she'd donned her cloak and headed outside to the cowshed. "I wish to visit Rowan House," she announced to her husband, who paused while pouring a bucket of water into a trough. A giant cow lowered her head to drink.

"For what?" he grumbled.

"For a visit." She braced her elbows on one of the rails and ignored the calf trotting toward her. His fluffy face was *not* the cutest thing she'd ever seen. It wasn't. It *wasn't.* "I wish to go, and I want you to take me."

He muttered something beneath his breath. It sounded like, "Bluidy dyin' to take ye," but he was swiping a hand over his mouth, so she couldn't say for certain.

The calf nibbled her cloak. She tried to ignore him, but he gamboled away merrily then returned for another nibble. She refused to engage with his heart-melting eyes and sweet, woolly face and busy pink tongue.

Another tug.

"Butter," she hissed. "Stop it."

He nuzzled her hand.

She sighed and gave him her finger. "Just this once." He latched on for a lick and a suckle. "Your mother is right there, you know."

Campbell arched a brow in their direction. "I think he prefers you, lass."

She clicked her tongue. "Silly boy." She scratched his head and withdrew to pet his face. "One day, you'll be too big for this."

Patting the cow's hindquarters, Campbell exited through the gate to stand beside Clarissa. "Some creatures are never too big for petting."

She slanted a glance at her enormous husband. "So, will you escort me to Rowan House?"

"Tell me why."

"I must speak with Francis before he leaves."

A muscle in his jaw flickered. "Cannae spare the time. Calving season keeps me busy—"

"Never mind, then. I'll ask Daniel instead."

He glanced away, cursed beneath his breath. "Nah, I'll take ye. Da wants me to return his coach anyhow."

Two hours later, her out-of-sorts husband lifted her from the coach and carried her into Rowan House's entrance hall.

Clinging to his muscular neck, she assured him, "I can walk, you know." All the while, she secretly savored the strength of his arms, the absolute safety they offered.

Carefully, he lowered her feet to the floor but kept a hand on her waist. "Ye have an hour. Dinnae leave the house without me by yer side. Do ye ken?"

She patted his chest, trying not to notice how good he smelled. "An hour is insufficient. I'll require at least two."

"One."

"I think two. McInnes's shortbread must be savored slowly."

"God, ye try a man's patience."

"Don't be silly. This will be your chance to consult with Broderick. Commiserate about English wives. Compare notes on growling techniques."

"I dinnae growl."

She smoothed his wool with repeated strokes. "Of course you do. Now, give me two hours, hmm? Show patience now, and I shan't object to a little *impatience* later."

His nose flared. Black eyes went molten a split second before he glanced away. "Woman, ye drive me mad."

She arched a brow. "Oh? Do you find me infuriating?"

"Frustrating, aye."

"Good. The sentiment is mutual."

A short while later, Campbell disappeared into Broderick's study while Clarissa sat in the drawing room nibbling Mr. McInnes's tender, buttery shortbread and explaining the purpose of her visit to Francis. Kate and Grandmama listened with fascinated expressions.

"It's a considerable boon, I grant you," Clarissa acknowledged to her dear friend, nervously sweeping crumbs from her brown wool skirt.

Francis braced an elbow on the pianoforte and snorted. "Blackmail a friend of the Prime Minister? No, no. Think nothing of it."

"I wouldn't ask if I weren't desperate. I know how you loathe discussing your father's … indiscretions."

"I loathe discussing my father's anything. His affair with Kitty Northfield and the likelihood that

Northfield's heir is not of his loins? I'd rather attend a session of Parliament sober. Or ride naked on Rotten Row during the fashionable hour. Or attend Parliament naked and sober. In February."

Kate sat forward and held up a hand. "Pardon my ignorance, but how do you *know* Silas Northfield was fathered by Lord Medford?"

Grandmama patted Kate's hand. "To whom does he bear a greater resemblance, dear? Stephen?" She nodded toward Francis. "Or Teversham?"

Kate blinked. Sat back. "Oh. Yes, I see." Silas Northfield was blond, blue-eyed, and handsome as a sculptor's masterpiece. He didn't look like a Northfield. He looked like Francis's father. And Francis. "But are we *certain* Mrs. Northfield dallied with Lord Medford? She doesn't seem the sort."

With a faint smile, Grandmama replied, "We're certain, dear."

"How do we—"

"Kitty Northfield birthed Silas eight months after a visit with her bosom friend in Yorkshire. Mr. Northfield did not accompany her."

Kate's eyes flared wide. "Bosom friend. Who?"

Francis answered, "My mother."

"After Silas's birth, a rift formed between Lady Medford and Mrs. Northfield," Grandmama explained.

"Some observers speculated that Lord Medford's wandering eye had strayed into Kitty's … *garden,* as it were. However, when Mr. Northfield claimed parentage without objection, the matter was soon forgotten."

Clarissa stood and approached Francis, who leaned against Kate's grand pianoforte with studied nonchalance. She wasn't fooled. "I understand what I'm asking."

Francis's blue eyes flashed. "No. You don't."

"It will reopen your mother's wounds. It will invite a dreadful scandal just when you've a chance at real happiness."

"My happiness is of least concern. Attracting Lord Northfield's scrutiny, his enmity, risks exposing … too much." He grimaced. Sighed. "His connections are—"

"Everywhere. I know. But this secret doubly damages him. Remove Silas and Stephen, and no heirs remain beyond their father. The line ends ignominiously. He won't risk such an outcome."

"You're terribly certain he'll concede to our demands. What if you're wrong?"

She might be. The Northfields did genuinely love Stephen, and grief might drive them to take retribution against Campbell regardless of pressure.

"It's possible Lord Northfield will resist persuasion," Grandmama interjected. "I would suggest approaching Mrs. Northfield first."

Clarissa shot her a puzzled frown. "Why?"

"When I wrote to Lord Northfield warning him of Stephen's behavior, he refused to take action. Northfields are loyal to their blood first and foremost. But Kitty is Silas's mother as much as she is Stephen's. She'll be grieving, but she won't endanger Silas's inheritance. We'll need an ally in that family."

Clarissa nodded. "Mrs. Northfield first, then." She turned to Francis. "Will you help?"

Francis's gaze shifted to Kate. "I should have departed yesterday. Why did I let you persuade me to wait for better weather? This is Scotland. The weather does not *improve.*"

Clarissa reached for his hand. "They'll hang Campbell, Francis. If he kills Stephen, they will kill him." Her throat tightened to a painful thread. "We must do something."

After a few moments, he relented. "Very well. I shall try. But I must warn you, if Mrs. Northfield proves unreceptive, I cannot follow through on my threat. The damage would be too great for no discernible benefit." He squeezed her fingers. "I'm sorry, darling. This bluff may not work."

Kate joined them at the pianoforte. "We can aid the effort from another direction, as well." She looped her arm through Clarissa's. "I'll write my father and sisters at once and ask for their support." Kate's father was an earl, and her brothers-in-law included two earls, a future marquis, and a powerful duke. "With such united opposition, Lord Northfield must certainly hesitate to demand charges."

Tears pricked Clarissa's eyes. She'd never been so grateful for her dear friends. "I was hoping you would offer. Thank you."

"Campbell is dear to me, too." Kate grinned. "Besides, I was planning on writing my family for another reason." Her eyes lit and twinkled as she flattened a palm on her belly and fluttered her fingers.

Clarissa gasped. "No."

An excited nod.

Filled with joy for her beloved friend, Clarissa threw her arms around Kate. Together, they squealed and danced on their toes. Her excitement was for Kate and Broderick, who had survived a nightmarish ordeal and deserved every happiness. But she also felt a tug of longing.

In all the madness of the past month, she hadn't allowed herself to contemplate what it meant to be married. Now, she pictured the babes she might have.

Sweet little boys with square jaws who would grow into men as strong and honorable as their father. Adorable girls with dark eyes, whom their "Da" would carry everywhere and protect with all his might.

Heavens, she would love to see him dancing with his little girls the way her father had danced with her.

Her heart squeezed hard enough to make her gasp.

She wanted to make memories with Campbell, make a home—feeding her family around a scarred table. Laughing together as Fergus waited for the children to drop a scrap or two. Rocking a cradle carved by her husband's hands. Making love to him on blustery nights after the children were asleep.

She wanted his children. His heart.

She wanted him to love her as fiercely as she loved him.

Later that afternoon, as he lifted her onto his enormous bay horse and mounted behind her, she could scarcely breathe for the longing. He hadn't said much after meeting with Broderick, who had promised to return the coach to Angus. Now, with Campbell's arms locked around her and his chest at her back, Clarissa gazed across the silvery waters of Loch Carrich and the misty grasses flanking the road. Clouds hung low, but the rain had stopped for a while. She shivered.

"Are ye warm enough, *gràidheag*?"

"Yes." She glanced down at the horse's neck, petting the long, black mane. "What's his name?"

"Dunmore."

She sifted the long strands through her fingers and gave the stallion an approving pat. "He's very big."

"So am I."

"Right."

Silence lengthened. He guided Dunmore past a thicket of pines onto a new road heading up into the western hills. "This is the way to the distillery," he rumbled. "I'll show ye how I go home most days."

She nodded, but her mind was elsewhere, circling the question of foremost concern: How did one lure a man into falling in love?

In the past, she'd assumed it involved beauty. A bit of charm. Fluttering lashes and a goodly display of bosom. But she'd employed all those tactics during her last season, and results had been mixed, to say the least.

"Did ye have a pleasant visit, then?"

She paused in her ruminations to answer, "Mmm. The shortbread was lovely."

Campbell did seem to want her—a point in her favor, surely. Should she launch a campaign of seduction? Could she make him forget the mysterious woman in his past and form a deeper affection for his wife?

A squirrel darted across the road. "Not far now," he murmured, turning onto yet another road branching southwest along a small brook.

Seduction couldn't hurt, she decided. To the best of her knowledge, men quite enjoyed lovemaking, and her wedding night had proved Campbell was no exception. She frowned. Did *she* enjoy it too much? Perhaps he'd prefer a more decorous wife, one who didn't beg or shout his name at such volumes.

"Lass?"

She nibbled her lip. What if the reason he'd been so patient with her—sleeping chastely, waiting for her courses to pass, limiting kissing to once or twice a day—was because he found her no more desirable than any other female? Perhaps he preferred a slenderer wife with a smaller bosom. One who didn't bear signs of her struggle against plumpness. One with wild black hair.

"Clarissa."

If lovemaking wasn't her best strategy, she must think of another way to unlock his heart. But what? In truth, she'd spent too many years being ignored by men. One successful season was insufficient training. Her efforts to enchant him with her wit had failed. Flirtation had failed. Whatever her claim to beauty, that had failed. For the first month of their acquaintance, she'd aimed her entire arsenal in his direction, and the entire arsenal had fallen flat.

It hadn't helped when the erotic dreams had begun, resulting in her little vulgarity problem. She suspected he'd found it amusing, but had her outbursts given him the wrong idea? What if he thought her a trollop? Perhaps she should tell him the truth.

Drat. She was overthinking things. He didn't seem reluctant to perform his husbandly duty. Really, the more he did so, the better her odds of conception. And she thought he rather liked seeing her naked.

Behind her, he shifted in the saddle as though deeply uncomfortable. "Bluidy hell."

She leaned forward then wriggled her hips to rebalance her seat.

His arm cinched her waist like a vise. "Be still," he growled.

She huffed. "Heavens, your temper has been foul of late."

"If ye're vexed with me, then say so."

"Very well. I'm vexed with you. Don't bark at me in such a way."

"That's nae what I—bluidy hell. I didnae bark."

"You certainly did. Why can't we have a pleasant ride together?"

He grunted and smoothed a hand over her belly. "I thought we were. Then, ye went quiet. I dinnae like when ye go quiet."

She blinked. Lost her breath for a moment as the heat of his palm spread across her abdomen. "That's the first time a man has ever said that to me."

A deep chuckle ended raspy. A hard jaw nuzzled her hair. "I like yer conversation."

Her muscles heated. Weakened. Ached. She relaxed into him then wriggled to find a more comfortable position.

His groan rumbled through her back. "Christ, lass. Be still, I'm beggin' ye."

"Well, if your pistol weren't constantly wedging against my hip, shifting wouldn't be necessary."

A pause. "That's nae my pistol."

She frowned. Then froze. Then realized. "Oh."

He sighed. "Mayhap ye could distract me."

First, she'd have to distract herself. Her skin was blazing hot. "What should I …?"

"Tell me what sort of house ye'd fancy, if ye could have anythin'."

Slowly, she relaxed against him, considering her answer. "I've never thought about it, really. Wherever I land, I've always just made the best of things."

His jaw nuzzled her temple. "I ken." Then, he muttered something low in Gaelic before continuing, "But if ye didnae have to make do, would ye want a grand place like Ellery Hall?"

She huffed out a chuckle. "Oh, I shouldn't think so. A house that size becomes a burden if you haven't the funds to maintain it. All those empty rooms …" She shook her head. "They echo, you know. Once you sell the carpets and draperies, they're just cold, dark boxes. Even the ones that smell like Grandpapa have nothing to offer but emptiness. Truthfully, I prefer a smaller house, though not too small. Rowan House is lovely. Your father's house, too." Angus's home was a warm, sturdy farmhouse nestled at the juncture of twin valleys Glenscannadoo and Glendasheen.

He held her tighter and guided Dunmore around a fallen limb before leaving the road and cutting uphill along a dirt path. She noticed the trees around them becoming sparser the farther they traveled. Woodlands now mixed with open meadows and rocky terrain. Soon, she heard trickling then rushing water. He slowed the horse as they approached a cluster of boulders beside a lone pine tree. "Let's walk a bit, eh?" He dismounted then lifted her down. Along the length of his body, she slid to the ground.

She noticed his hands lingered longer than normal around her ribs, and his neck had gone ruddy. When she met his eyes, they burned hot as coals.

Her breath quickened. His body felt huge and hard against her.

Abruptly, he stepped back to lead Dunmore away. Coldness seeped in to replace him.

Shaking off her strange sense of loss, she braced a hand against the pine. The bark was whorled and rough. She looked closer and saw a face. Tingling shivers danced up her spine.

"Campbell," she called.

"Aye."

"There's an owl in this tree."

He chuckled. "Aye. There's another like it on Broderick's land."

She examined the strange configuration—whorls forming the head, a small protrusion forming the beak, longer swirls of bark forming the wings. She traced a finger over its eyes. Her fingertips sparked, even inside her gloves. "It feels magical."

"Nah," he said. "I suspect a stag had a go at it once or twice. Parasites came in, as parasites do. Scots pines are resilient. Plenty of sap. It repaired itself, but those battles leave scars."

"Why an owl, do you suppose?"

"I think we see what we care to see. 'Tis just a random set of shapes, ye ken?"

She clicked her tongue. "You're spoiling my sense of wonder."

"Apologies, lass."

She turned to wander in his direction, up onto a small rise. Only then did she notice where they were—on top of the world. In that moment, she lost her breath. She stood on a ten-foot knoll above their little birchwood glen. Having arrived there from a different direction, she hadn't realized. But there was the tumbling waterfall, the swollen brook, the wide pool, and the fallen tree she'd peppered with practice shots. From this higher perspective, in the distance, she could even glimpse Loch Carrich and the deep carpet of green in Glenscannadoo's southerly end.

"Oh, heavens! You can see everything from here. The whole valley."

He gave Dunmore a pat as the horse drank from the brook, then he retraced his steps to join her on the knoll. "Aye. 'Tis a grand spot."

She slid her hand into his, which seemed to startle him. But he didn't pull away. "I love this place," she sighed, snuggling against his arm. "It feels … safe."

He repositioned her with her back against the front of his body and wrapped his arms loosely across her shoulders and waist. "Ye must be pinin' for home. Mayhap this summer, I'll take ye to England for a visit."

"Actually, I find myself rather enchanted with craggy mountains and little waterfalls tucked away where only the sky can see them."

"'Tis a harsher life, here."

She squeezed his wrist. Did he worry that she'd be unhappy living with him? Nothing could be further from the truth. His house was small and rustic, to be sure, but minor changes could make a big difference. "One of the ground-floor chambers could be rearranged for Grandmama," she said. "And if you repair the hearth in my old bedchamber, we could turn that room into a nursery. Then, we'll have everything we need."

His body tensed along the length of hers.

More reassurance was in order, clearly. "I shall plant the garden soon. Mrs. MacBean offered to find saplings for us. A grove of apple trees will be lovely on the south side of the house, I think. Oh, and raspberries." She closed her eyes. "Picture it, Campbell. Each summer, the children and I will pluck basketfuls. Their little fingers will be stained red from the juice." She laughed lightly. "That reminds me, we should purchase a proper bathing tub. Between Fergus and our babes, doubtless we'll need it."

The arm across her waist hardened to steel. He drew her in tighter.

Frowning, she looked around for trouble. "What's wrong?"

His head lowered until she felt his breath heating the side of her neck.

"Campbell?"

The long silence deepened. He seemed to be struggling with something. Then came his answer, low and pained. "There willnae be any bairns, *gràidheag.*"

Shock ripped through her. Why would he say such a thing? "Well, perhaps not straight away, but—"

"Not ever."

She tried to twist to look at him, but he held her fast. "That's impossible to know." She tugged at his arms, which had flexed until they were almost painfully tight. As if he feared she might flee.

"It's true."

"Don't be silly. I may be eight-and-twenty, but with persistence, I should think—"

"Not because of you, Clarissa. 'Tis me. I cannae give ye bairns."

"You're being ridiculous." She plucked at his arms. "And you're holding me too tightly."

His arms loosened, but he didn't let her go.

She blew out a sigh. "What makes you think you can't father children?"

A moment ticked by filled only with the sounds of rushing water, his breath, and her own heart. "'Tis a long story. Are ye certain ye wish to hear it?"

"I'm certain I'd like an answer."

"Very well." His chest heaved. "When I was nineteen, I fell ill. It started as a fever. Then swellings. Couldnae do my work. Couldnae leave my bed. Da summoned a healer from Dingwall. Marion Cormick. She brought her daughter along to help care for me."

"You must have been very ill. I've never seen you laid low."

He grunted. "I was out of my head. Fever dreams. Pain."

"What was the illness?"

"The mumps. Alexander had it first. Didnae affect him too badly. Broderick and Rannoch came through with naught but a wee complaint or two. But my case was severe. Marion couldnae do much apart from feedin' me broth and herbs, so she asked her daughter to keep me company during the worst of it."

A prickle of unease rippled across her skin. This was his second mention of the daughter. "How old was she? What was her name?"

Several heartbeats passed before he answered, "She was my age. Her name was Isla. Isla Cormick. She was the bonniest thing I'd ever seen."

Unease tightened its fist until her heart felt pierced. Crushed.

"Isla sat with me for many hours. Cared for me. Talked with me. When the fever broke, I was weakened. We spent a fortnight together whilst her mother tended others in the village. She had a spark, ye ken. A sharp tongue but a kind heart."

And black hair. Clarissa could see her face—perfect features with a perfect beauty mark and wild black hair. He'd loved her. She could hear it in his voice. The way he said her name—with soft reverence.

"Her fever started soon after mine was done. She didnae say aught about it. Then, her face swelled. She couldnae eat. Too weakened. Too bluidy sick. By the time she grew insensible, I kenned she wouldnae live. Tried to save her. Couldnae." His voice thinned to a thread. "We summoned the physician from Inverness. He said the fever had gone into her brain, her blood. Rare, but he'd seen it twice before."

This was the woman he'd loved. Isla Cormick. A girl who had helped heal him and had died for her efforts. Clarissa didn't want to hate her. The girl had done nothing wrong. But the sick, piercing jealousy might as well be a blade through her middle. She could scarcely breathe.

"She died, then?"

"Aye." His arms tightened around her again, pulling her back hard into his chest. His jaw nuzzled her ear.

"W-Would you have married her, had she lived?"

A long silence. "Aye."

She'd known. The moment he'd spoken Isla's name, she'd known the truth. And the truth was crushing her, heart and bone.

"We shared a … connection," he said. "She had a wee bit of the sight. Said it was stronger here in the glen. Many others have said the same. Mrs. MacBean. My mam. During my fever, Isla would visit me in that place."

Clarissa tried to swallow, but she felt choked. Broken. "Where? The glen?"

"Nah. There's an in-between place ye go when ye dream. That's where she'd meet me. That's where we …"

Fell in love. He didn't have to say it. Clarissa had fallen in love with Campbell in her dreams, too, though those were entirely her own fabrication. A pitiful, needy invention from a heart desperate to have him.

"Kate says your mother and grandfather had the sight."

"Aye."

"Do you have it?"

More silence. Then, "I did. Once. After Isla died, she continued to visit me that way," he explained. "She railed at me about my intentions to join a regiment. Said she wouldnae stand by and watch me risk my neck for foolish reasons." His chest heaved on a sigh. "I'd killed her, and still she sought to protect me."

"You didn't kill her. That's absurd."

"Might as well have done. She died of the illness I gave her."

She shook her head. "You tried to save her."

"Aye. And I failed. Everything failed. The carvings. The dreams. I couldnae hold her here." His voice roughened. "What good is the bluidy sight if I cannae save the people I love? Useless bluidy visions. So, I let her visit me for a time. Then, I stopped listenin'. That was when she told me what my punishment would be."

Clarissa's blood turned cold. "Punishment?"

"Aye. Her fever had taken her life." His jaw pressed against her cheek. "My fever had taken my bairns. All the bairns I might have had. Forever."

Tears sprang up, turning birch leaves, mossy stones, and pooling water into a blur of greens, browns, and grays. "No. You dreamt all this. Perhaps the bit about your infertility wasn't real."

"Clarissa."

She gripped his arms, the pain in her chest churning a panic. "Guilt over her death has made you see things in a peculiar light. She helped her mother tend the sick, yes?"

"Aye."

"Like Magdalene or Mrs. MacBean, she would have been exposed to illness routinely. That is the risk one takes when caring for others. My grandmother's illness could have killed me. That certainly would not have been Grandmama's fault."

"Fine. Mayhap it was merely a consequence of the fever, not a punishment." His arms tightened. "But it is real, *gràidheag*. I've had sixteen years of proof."

She didn't want to hear this. There was only one way to prove he was infertile, and it involved other women. Jealousy was bitter, sour, painful, and ugly all at once. It crouched inside her like a demon. It burned everything it touched. "What makes you so certain?" she choked out.

"Dinnae ask about that. Ye must trust me—"

"Just tell me, Campbell." It took everything she had not to sob. "Tell me the truth."

"Very well. I was with a woman for a few years, a widow with a son. She had her own brewery. We saw each other from time to time. At first, she only wanted comfort, nae marriage. After a year or two, she began thinkin' differently. She asked if I might want to marry her, as she was near thirty and wanted more bairns. I told her what I'm tellin' ye—that I couldnae give her any. She pretended to accept it, but she kept tryin'. Three more years, never conceived. I left her so she might have the family she wanted."

"And did she?"

"Aye. She wed a cooper from Perth. Last I kenned, she had two more laddies. Her husband's a good man. His casks are some of the finest in the Highlands."

The burn of jealousy cooled into a raw wound. He'd spoken of the widow the way she might speak of a friend who'd moved to another county—fond but distant. He hadn't loved her. He'd loved Isla, and Isla was dead.

Which left Clarissa.

How did he feel about her? Fond enough to stand between her and a madman. Fond enough that he held her tenderly in their bed, plucked honey from the shelf without needing to be asked, and let her wrap herself in his plaid on cold nights.

But love? No. If he loved her, surely he would have told her the truth before they'd wed. Surely he'd have wanted her to know that in choosing him, she'd be choosing a life without children of her own. He'd offered the widow that courtesy.

How much less must he care for Clarissa?

She closed her eyes. "Let go of me," she whispered.

A deep, rumbling groan echoed from his chest, resonating through her back and along her cheek where his jaw pressed against her. "No."

She gritted her teeth. Clawed at his arms. "Let. Go. Of me." She wedged her elbows inside and shoved with all her strength. "Let go! Let go, let go, let go!"

His arms fell away, and she ran down the hill. She only stopped when she reached her favorite tree at the edge of the pool. Her reflection wavered and swirled inside the water. She bent and found a stone then threw it at herself. The water swallowed it up, resuming its eddy without a pause.

She buried her face in her hands.

"Clarissa." He stood behind her, a massive man blocking the wind. "I only wanted to … God, *gràidheag,* I never wanted to … But first ye were set on marryin' Teversham, and then ye said ye wouldnae marry anybody, and I … needed ye safe. I wanted ye safe. I should have told ye the truth then. But ye wouldnae have agreed to—"

"I'm going home," she muttered before dropping her hands. Her palms came away wet. She wiped them on her skirt and wiped her face on her sleeve.

"Clarissa."

"I'm going home!" She traveled along the edge of the pool to where the brook narrowed enough for her to cross it. Just as she felt him approach to lift her, she snapped, "Don't touch me," and hiked up her skirts. Then, she picked her way from stone to slippery stone, icy water filling her boots.

"*Gràidheag,* ye must let me help. For God's sake, lass, let me fetch the horse—"

"I don't want the horse. I want to walk. Now, leave me alone!"

"I cannae do that. Ye ken I cannae leave ye without protection."

She halted. Tried to breathe. Shivered and wadded damp skirts inside her fists. "Fine. You may follow me. I shall wait."

Heaving silence began to feel thunderous, as though his temper had finally caught fire. "Dinnae move," he growled.

Moments later, she heard Dunmore cross the brook behind her, and she started forward. With fury driving her pace, they arrived back at the farm swiftly. He took Dunmore to the stable while she entered the kitchen cold, wet, and miserable. With the maids absent, the house was quiet and still. The kitchen lads had kept the hearth burning and a pot of beef stew simmering. With angry motions, Clarissa removed her cloak, yanked a chair away from the table, and sat with a graceless plop. Then, she folded her arms on the table and laid her head on her wrist. Breathing the smell of wood and old onions and peat smoke, she tried to reconcile the pain of loving a man who would never love her.

Fergus trotted in from the front room. She hugged his neck and rubbed her forehead against his. "Hallo, my boy," she whispered, scratching him beneath his chin.

He sighed and licked her chin in return.

Despite her misery, she smiled. "You never gave up, did you? Even when I ignored your affections."

He groaned and grunted, his long, lanky body waggling.

"My sweet, persistent boy." She kissed his face and busied herself refilling his water dish. As she set it on the floor, everything she'd learned about her husband circled in her mind. She twisted her ring, which continually felt hot to the touch and stubbornly refused to be removed. She'd once tried to give him his freedom from this marriage, and just as stubbornly, he'd refused.

But why should she let him go? She was his wife. Yes, in his youth, he'd loved Isla, and he'd cared for the widow enough to walk away and give her a chance at the family she'd wanted. Very well. Perhaps he would never care for Clarissa the same way. Perhaps she'd never have little ones of her own.

But all the way back from the birchwood glen, she'd heard her grandmother's words in her head, repeating and repeating: *Sometimes, we must fight, dearest. Even when we most want to hide.*

Sometimes, we must fight.

Clarissa had hidden long enough. She'd accepted the crumbs others offered and made the best of things too often.

No more.

She stood and started for the scullery, taking the buckets beside the garden door in each hand. Outside, she stalked to the well and began filling. One of the kitchen lads offered to help. She handed him the second bucket.

Soon, between the two of them, she filled the giant kettle on the hearth and stoked the fire to get it boiling. Then, she went into the small chamber off the scullery—the one warmed by the back of the hearth—and dragged the largest washtub to the center of the floor. Back outside for more buckets. Her shoulders burned and her arms ached by the time she was done pouring both cold and heated water into the tub.

After retrieving a few supplies from her bedchamber, she returned to the small room with its tiny window and tinier yellow curtain. Then, she closed the door and stripped away every scrap of clothing. The tub was scarcely big enough to sit hugging her knees, but the heat did its work, and soon, she was sighing at the relief. Taking up a tin of her favorite lavender soap, she washed her entire body, pausing a moment as her hands slid over her belly. She glanced down. Saw the imperfections. Recalled the battles she'd already won.

"I'm alive," she whispered to no one in particular. "I'm still here."

And, as long as she was his wife, she had something worth fighting for.

She washed her hair, rinsed it with pitchers of fresh water, and dabbed her face with a towel. Then, she plucked up a small brown vial from the stool beside the tub, uncorked it, and downed the contents, wincing at the bitter taste. "Oh, that is foul," she muttered. She'd have to ask Mrs. MacBean what precisely went into a fertility tonic. Or perhaps she didn't wish to know.

After her bath, she donned her shift and a fresh gown. Then, she brushed out her wet hair to dry, took a deep breath, and looped the ivory charm around her neck. It rested next to her mother's cross.

He might love Isla. But he did not *belong* to Isla.

Campbell MacPherson belonged to Clarissa. And, whether he liked it or not, she intended to stake her claim, hold her ground, and fight with everything she had.

With her mind resolved, she arranged a few items on the kitchen table, penning a note that he couldn't miss. As she finished her work, she paused to give Fergus a scratch. Here was her inspiration—a loving heart who hadn't given up on her.

"No going back," she murmured. "You have what you wanted. Now, you're mine forever."

Happily, Fergus seemed pleased with the terms of her surrender.

CHAPTER FIFTEEN

The first thing Campbell noticed upon entering the house was the scent of lavender. The second was her note. He stood in the doorway of the scullery, staring at the little white tent of paper bearing his name in looping script.

His blood drummed in his ears. Desire he'd tightly leashed for the past five days slammed against his control. Cracks formed. He willed them away, tensing against the ache. No doubt she'd want to sleep separately. Likely she was still wounded and furious. Her pain had torn him to pieces earlier. He hadn't known what to do, apart from granting her the distance she'd demanded. In truth, any amount of distance from his wife was too much.

Scraping a hand over his jaw, he plucked up her note and examined what she'd left for him on the table—a hot bowl of stew, a pitcher of cider, and half a loaf of Annie's bread. Even when she was furious with him, his bonnie wife made certain he was fed.

He unfolded the paper.

Husband,

Make use of the bath in the scullery. Eat well. Then, come to our bed. I have much to say, and I shall expect your full attention.

Your wife,

Clarissa

In the washroom off the scullery, he discovered a tub filled with fresh, steaming water, a pile of clean clothes, and a round of soap. He bathed as quickly as possible, ate just enough stew and bread to quell his lesser appetite, and climbed the stairs to the drumbeat of his greater appetite.

Outside the bedchamber door, he breathed to dissipate the need. His skin pulsed with it. His muscles thrummed.

She sat on his bed, gray plaid wrapped around her shoulders. Pale blonde hair draped over one shoulder, drying into lovely, looping curls. Deep blue eyes peered up at him, soft, solemn, and resolute.

His breath caught in his chest. His hands curled against the longing to touch her. He closed the door. Crossed his arms. Waited for her condemnation.

"Did you have enough to eat?" she said softly.

"Aye. Did ye?"

She nodded. "I ate a little."

The sight of her turned his knees to water and his cock to stone. Lust was a monster he'd kept well caged until now, but the damned beast battered his insides. "Ye shouldnae have hauled that water yerself," he said. "That's what the lads are for."

"I wanted a real bath." She shrugged. "I didn't mind doing what was necessary."

"I mind." He felt a growl building in his chest and worked to keep his tone gentle. "Ye're too fine for such work."

Her cheeks flushed. Her mouth tightened. "Is that what you think? That I'm 'too fine'?"

"Aye." He paced closer, raking a hand through his hair. "Too fine for this place. Too fine for me."

Her eyes flashed fire. "So, I shall always come up wanting, in your eyes. Is that it?"

What had sparked such a daft notion? "No."

But she wasn't listening. She scrambled off the bed and charged him, giving him a hard shove. She was wee, so it didn't have much force behind it. But it did surprise him. Clarissa was, as a rule, easy-tempered. At the moment, however, she was a tea kettle set to scalding.

"Too fine, am I?" She tossed away her plaid, revealing a sheer shift and not much else. Another shove. "Well, too bad, you great Scottish lummox!"

Lust sank new talons into his ballocks as her breasts heaved beneath the linen. Hard, flushed nipples scrambled his mind. He supposed she was panting out of temper, but it didn't matter. The sight of those round, soft, glorious mounds and ripe, beaded nipples was pure witchcraft.

"I am your wife!"

He shook his head to clear it. What were they arguing about? "Lass."

"Don't you 'lass' me." She wadded a handful of his shirt and yanked him closer—or rather, yanked herself closer. She was too small to pull him off balance. "We are wed. At *your* insistence."

What was this babbling nonsense? Of course they were wed. He'd broken every one of his own rules to see it done. "Aye," he agreed.

"I tried to release you, but nooo. Campbell MacPherson takes his guard dog duties ever-so-seriously."

This time, his "aye" was low and cautious. He'd seen his wee sister Annie in a similar state before—high dudgeon, Huxley called it. But Clarissa didn't have Annie's hot temper. So, he wasn't certain how to handle her unusual behavior.

Apart from finding it inappropriately arousing.

"As your wife, I *demand* your consideration."

He was considering her. Every bonnie inch of her. He clenched his fists to keep from taking hold of his woman. God, she smelled good. Lavender fields and honey-sweet Clarissa.

"Isla is dead. *She* is not your wife and never will be."

He wondered what she would do if he kissed her. On one hand, she might darken his daylights. On the other, he'd be kissing her. It might be worth it.

"Your former mistress is wed to another. She, likewise, is not your wife and never will be."

If he slid his fingers along the neckline of her shift and gave a wee tug, he could split the thin fabric with minimal effort.

"I will have the same concessions you gave them."

Or he could toss Clarissa on the bed and draw the shift over her head. It would save her the trouble of mending later.

"You granted Isla the chance to capture your heart. I want the same chance." She straightened her shoulders, thrusting her breasts harder against her shift. "I *demand* the same chance."

He could be inside her in minutes. If he was gentle and deliberate. If he gave her the control she wanted, as he'd done on their wedding night. But could he last that long? Ah, God. He could feel her tight sheath now. The wet, pulsating pleasure.

"You granted your mistress the chance to try for a babe."

He was fairly certain he'd never been this hard. Perhaps on their wedding night, but not any other time. All the blood in his veins seemed to have gone into his cock. He'd have to manage her carefully. She loved to pet him and rub that sweet body all over his.

"I *demand* the same opportunity." She tilted her head to a stubborn, challenging angle. "You will grant me leave to get myself with child."

That statement centered his focus like a shot fired out of the dark. Every muscle, bone, and fiber inside Campbell's body froze. The hair on his nape lifted. Lust warped and darkened. Deepened. Grew blacker and redder. He stared down at his wife, scarcely believing what she'd just said.

Grant her permission to lie with another man? To leave Campbell's bed and grow another man's bairn in her womb?

"Nah," he breathed, the room pulsing red and black. Red and black. "I wed ye so no other man could have what's mine."

Blue eyes rounded, flaring bright with alarm.

Which meant he'd spoken aloud a truth he'd meant to keep hidden. So be it. Perhaps it was time she knew. "If ye let another man touch ye, *gràidheag,* best ye be prepared to watch him die. Because I'll tear his head from his neck with my bare hands." He moved into her, driving her back toward the bed. "Not quick, ye ken. I'll take his ballocks first. Naebody enjoys hearin' a man scream like that. Especially him."

"Campbell!" she squeaked. "What—"

"If I told ye to remove yer shift, would ye do it?"

"I—you're …" She sputtered to a breathless stop. "Campbell!"

"I dinnae wish to frighten ye. Northfield's done more than enough of that. But I cannae play civilized any longer." He rubbed his jaw. "And I'd very much enjoy strippin' yer shift from yer body. Just a wee rip.

Ye'll have to mend it later. But mayhap ye willnae mind."

"I didn't say I wanted to conceive with someone else. As if that would even be possible, given my feelings for …" Her breasts were heaving. Tempting. Her hand came up to slide across his chest. "I want to try with you."

He could scarcely think for the red, pounding monster that had taken control of him. But her words did return some of his sanity. "I told ye, lass. I cannae give ye bairns."

"I know what you said. I want to try anyway." Her chin went up again. Her eyes grew fierce again. "I *demand* to try."

His heart twisted hard. "Clarissa, there's naught to try for."

"There is." She clasped his hand and laid it flat over her belly. "You must allow me to hope."

"Every month, ye'll grieve the loss of somethin' that cannae be." He caressed her soft belly, wishing with all his heart that he could give her what she longed for. "Hopin' for the impossible brings naught but pain."

Her delicate jaw flexed. "Hope is what kept me alive, Campbell. Long past the point I should have died."

"Ye mean with Northfield?"

"No. Before that. When I was a girl." She sat on the edge of the bed. "My parents and I traveled from Cambridge to Hampshire. It was a route we'd taken many times before. During our visit, a cousin brought a new pup that I played with obsessively. My father asked if I wanted one, and, of course, I did. On our way home, we took a detour to visit a friend of his, a breeder with several new litters." She swallowed hard. "I was allowed to choose which pup I wanted."

"What did ye choose?"

A wee smile touched her lips. "A white one. I don't recall the breed. Only that he had white fur and a black nose." She clung to his hand, squeezing it tighter. He laced their fingers together and stroked her wrist with his thumb. "A bad storm caused one of the main roads to be impassable," she continued, "so we took a different road through some remote hills. The horses took a fright. They sc-screamed. Bolted. Later, my grandfather said one of the wheels caught on something. A downed log, I think. The coach overturned, tumbled down a steep embankment."

He stroked her hair. "Aye. Yer grandmother told me."

"I don't recall very much. The silence that came after. The smell of death. The weight of my mother. How stiff linen becomes when the blood dries."

He sat beside her, brushing his knuckles along her cheek. "'Tis over now, *gràidheag.*"

She nodded. "For years, I blamed myself. If I hadn't wanted a dog, we'd never have been there. I live with that knowledge, the same way you live with Isla's death. Perhaps we'll always carry these burdens, whether they are rightfully ours or not." She caught his eyes and held him fast. "But I am here because every moment inside that coach, with death all around me, I believed I would be found. I *knew* I was loved." She hesitated, her eyes filling then falling to her lap before she confessed in a whisper, "Someone came to comfort me there. A woman. I thought her an angel at the time because whenever she appeared, the smell of death vanished, replaced by the scent of flowers. I still remember the things she said—that I had a purpose. That I would have a family of my own one day and that I mustn't give up." She smiled, wiping away a tear. "I've never told anyone about that."

He didn't doubt her recollection. He'd witnessed too many things that defied common explanation. Although many years had passed since he'd closed the door upon it, his sight wouldn't allow him to make assumptions about which visions were real and which were not.

She shook her head. "Hope is important, Campbell. I'm asking you to let me do this."

He cupped her bonnie face and kissed her bonnie lips. "Very well, lass. Ye may have yer way with me as often as ye like."

"Not good enough. I want your full cooperation."

"Oh, I'll give it to ye. Likely more than ye'll find comfortable." He eyed her bosom. "Now, about that shift."

"One last thing."

He stifled a groan. "Aye?"

"You must attempt to fall in love with me."

At many points during this conversation, he'd found himself at sea. But nothing she'd said was so bewildering as this. However, if it set her mind at ease to make nonsense demands, he'd be easy about it. "Done."

She must not have heard him, because she shoved to her feet and paced to the window. Linen billowed and caressed womanly curves.

Like an animal, all his senses coalesced upon the same point—her.

"I know you loved Isla."

He licked his lips, wondering how often she'd let him tup her now that she was bent on a mission. Thrice a day? More?

"But I want your heart to be fully mine." She held up a hand. "I can be patient. Take the time you must."

Once her wee body was well accustomed to him, he could simply toss up her skirts and take her in any location he pleased—against a tree or a stable wall, over a chair or the bed, on the floor in front of the fire. She'd demanded he apply himself, after all, and he'd never been one to shirk his duties.

"If it helps, I've been in love with you from the first."

He blinked. "Ye have?"

She nodded. "I assumed you knew."

He'd known she wanted him. He'd known she had a fascination with his body—his hands in particular. "That's good, lass. I'm pleased ye love me. Now, if ye come stand here between my knees, I'll help ye with that shift."

Her lovely features tightened with irritation. Blue eyes flashed fire. "What is wrong with you? I'm pouring out my heart, and you're behaving as if we're discussing what to have for breakfast."

He rubbed his nape and sighed. "How would ye prefer I respond?"

"By indicating that you heard me."

"I hear ye fine."

"And?"

Rising, he forced his muscles to relax before he frightened her. With a skittish lass, it was best to appear at ease even when he was burning alive. "And I'd like to see ye naked, now."

"Campbell. I just told you that I love you."

"Right."

She huffed and threw her hands out to her sides. "Unbelievable."

"I ken I should have told ye I couldnae father bairns before we wed."

"Yes. You should have."

He approached her slowly, the way he'd approach a difficult mare—with a gentle tone and respect for her temper. "But if I had, ye might have balked. I couldnae risk it."

She rolled her eyes then covered her heart in a mocking gesture. "All for my safety. I'm honored. Thank you, kind sir, for the *noble sacrifice*."

He laughed, the sound dry and rusty. In fairness, he'd never been this close to breaking. It was the damnedest thing to be married to one's downfall. "Ah, ye have me all wrong, *gràidheag*. When I took ye as mine, nobility was the first thing to go."

Before she understood why he'd moved so close, he dipped, slid an arm beneath her buttocks, and lifted her high against him until their noses touched. She squealed and clung to his neck. Startled eyes and lush lips rounded on a gasp.

He saw his opening and took full advantage. Sliding his mouth against hers, he invaded with his tongue, stroking and grinding, plunging deep. He waited until she deliberately rubbed her nipples against his chest before giving her a chance to take a breath.

"Now, ye asked to be tupped," he rasped. "Dinnae complain when I oblige." He hauled her to the bed and lowered her onto her back. Then, he split her shift from neck to hem. And there she lay, his woman, flushed pink with excitement amidst the tatters of linen. Between her breasts rested a familiar pendant. He'd suspected Mrs. MacBean had made one for her.

"Aren't you going to ask about this?" She fingered the leather cord.

"Nah, I've seen it." He nudged it aside and lapped a berry-ripe nipple with his tongue. She tasted like lavender candy. The need to devour her gnawed inside him.

She jerked and plunged her fingers into his hair. Clutching. Arching. Moaning. "God, I'm mad for you," she gasped. "What do you mean—dear *God.* More. Harder. With your teeth … like that … yes." Wee, feminine fists yanked at his hair. "What do you mean you've *seen* it?"

The world was on fire and his cock felt like a bloody cannon, so he replied without thinking, "In our dreams." He yanked his shirt off over his head, dispensed with his trews, and spread her thighs wide. "I mean to kiss ye here, *gràidheag*." He traced a single fingertip down through soft, pink folds that opened like a flower for him. "Dinnae be alarmed."

"Wh-what? Wait. Oh, heavens."

He shoved her higher on the bed and dropped to his knees, scooping up her hips and dragging her to his mouth. Then, he began feasting. Groaning at her sweet taste. Lapping that beautiful, tender bud that swelled for his tongue. Her petals glistened and wept. Her thighs strained. Her hips writhed in his hands. He spread her wide with his thumbs and suckled that sweet, bonnie center hard and deep.

She screamed his name. His barbaric soul howled its satisfaction. Again and again, he pressured and suckled, ignoring his own throbbing cock, ignoring her pleas for mercy. By the time he slid a finger inside her sheath, she'd come against his mouth twice. As he inserted a second finger, testing her readiness, her bud stood brilliant red and flagrantly swollen above her folds. He soothed it with light strokes of his tongue.

He glanced up across her belly and breasts, both of which tempted him with quivering undulations.

Rubbing his jaw against her satiny inner thigh, he hooked his fingertips inside her, searching for that wee, sensitive place that sent her soaring. He brushed it. Applied a bit of pressure.

"Campbell!" Her shouts were threadbare, her body arching and gasping and choking on incoherent ecstasy. Pride at watching his woman come, knowing that he was the cause, washed through him in a triumphant surge.

Gently, his fingers pulsed and rubbed inside her tight, rippling sheath to keep her pleasure high and steady. With his tongue, he savored the sweet, salty nectar she gave so generously, laving her swollen folds and kissing her inner thighs.

"Not again," she sobbed. "I can't. Please, Campbell. It's too much."

Like a man possessed, he gripped her knee and pulled her in tighter. "I told ye, *gràidheag*. I'd crawl on my knees to taste ye here." He licked her swollen bud, giving it a wee suckle. "Now, all I want to do is feast."

"Come inside me. I need you."

He nuzzled her thigh, closing his eyes and breathing lavender-scented desire. "More than my fingers?"

"Yes," she panted.

"What do ye need?" He glanced up the length of her body and smiled. "Say the word, now."

"Y-your cock."

"Aye." He rewarded her with a thrust of his fingers and more pressure. She arched high, her breasts flushed and lustrous from her exertions. "Ye love those rough words, dinnae ye? Shall I fill yer sweet cunny with my cock, *gràidheag?"*

Those wondrously blue eyes, lambent and dark, begged him before her lips opened to whisper, "I want that so badly, my love."

There she was. Aye, he had her. The hunter in him locked on. "Ye're such a wee thing," he rasped, working his fingers harder, stretching her a bit. "I may still feel too big for ye, great beast that I am. We've had but one night. Are ye certain ye can take me?"

"Yes. Pleeease, Campbell."

"I like when ye call me yer love."

She reached for him, stroking his hair. "You are. My one and only love. How long I waited for you."

He rewarded her with another pulse, watching with savage satisfaction as his wife came for him again, drenching his hand, gripping his fingers, and easing something raw inside him. Commanding her pleasure was the closest thing to paradise he'd ever experienced. The hitching cries, the beauty of her pale curls sliding across pink nipples, the uncontrolled ripples of her belly as she surrendered herself.

Slowly, he slid his palm along her thigh, easing her legs down as he withdrew his fingers. He kissed her knee. Then her hip. He pushed himself to his feet, aware that he loomed above her and that this level of arousal made him monstrously huge. "Luik at me, *gràidheag,*" he ordered.

She opened her eyes, her lips parting on a little gasp, her pink tongue swiping as she took him in. Her hands were splayed out beside her head. Her nipples were hard and flushed. They hardened further the longer she stared. She began panting. Then nibbling her lip.

"This is for you, my wicked lass. All this desire. All this need."

She moaned. "I want you so much."

"Enough to let me take ye as I like?"

A frantic nod.

"Might be a bit rough. Are ye certain?"

Another nod.

"Very well. Sit up."

A little pucker of confusion, then she scooted into a sitting position, folding her legs to one side in a sweetly feminine pose.

He smiled. "Now, I dinnae want ye to be surprised, so I'll ask ye to repeat what I'm about to do to ye."

Her eyes widened and dropped to his cock. Little teeth nibbled that plump lower lip. "I—I suppose that's acceptable."

It was more than acceptable. This was the key to his lass. From the start, she'd responded to filthy, erotic talk the way most women would respond to a stroke or a kiss—with bone-melting desire. He'd discovered it first in his dreams, suspected it from her conversational slips, and confirmed his suspicions on their wedding night. Now, he'd use it to full advantage.

He sat beside her on the bed. "First, ye'll go to yer hands and knees."

"I … what?"

"Say it, now."

She blinked and nervously played with her pendant. "First, I'll go to my hands and knees."

"Then, ye'll brace yerself so I can mount ye proper."

She licked her lips. Eyed his chest and his shoulders and his cock. Her fingers slid down to the swell of her breast. "I'll brace myself …"

"So I can mount ye."

"So you can mount me." Her breathing quickened.

"When I'm certain ye can take me nice and deep, I'll lift ye up so ye're astride me."

"You'll make certain I take you nice and deep"—*pant, pant, pant*—"then position me astride you."

"Aye. Then, ye'll watch while I show ye how well we fit."

"Oh, God," she whispered. "I'll see how well we fit."

"And I'll tup ye hard, pleasurin' those sweet nipples that remind me of raspberries atop a bowl of cream."

"Campbell," she groaned, her fingers sneaking away to caress one of those nipples.

"Say it."

"You'll take me hard, putting your beautiful hands on my nipples."

"Aye. On yer knees, now. There's a good lass."

She positioned herself before him on the bed, her lovely backside facing him, her wet, pink folds blooming an invitation. He caressed one of her soft buttocks, thumbing the small of her back. Then, he rolled onto his knees, took his cock in his hand, and stroked her drenched sheath with the tip. He propped himself over his wife, nudged aside her hair, and nuzzled her ear. "Brace yerself, lass. I mean to come inside."

A long, low groan sounded from her throat, followed by, "Yes. Please, my love. Please."

The first inch nearly killed him. She was so tight, he was sure he'd either come immediately or burst into flames. Her hips worked to take him, to push him further inside. He had to grip her nape to control the motion. "Easy," he muttered, more to himself than her.

He went deeper. At first, he controlled the pace, but soon, she grew demanding. Her sheath pulled him with greedy pulses. Before he knew it, the agonizing inferno of his lust took the reins, and his thrusts grew harder. Deeper. His cock claimed new territory with every sawing breath. He buried his face in her hair and his cock deep and hard inside his wife. Her pleasured cries were a balm to scars he'd long forgotten existed.

"Ye like how I stretch yer wee cunny?" he rasped in her ear, kissing the delicate whorls and relishing the softness of her skin. "It's nae too much, now, is it?"

She shook her head, thrusting against him and arching her back to take more. "It feels so huge and yet so good, I can scarcely breathe."

He grinned. "Good lass. Now, take more." He gave her a firm thrust that wedged the head of his cock against the mouth of her womb.

She gasped and stiffened. "Oh, my God. Oh."

"Aye, now ye ken. Try to relax. Just a wee bit more."

Her arms and shoulders trembled as he pushed her as far as he dared.

"How does that feel, *gràidheag?*"

"So much." She released a long, throaty groan and lowered her head between her arms. "The pressure is so deep, it … aches. I don't know if I can … Campbell. I'm not sure I can …"

"Aye, ye can." He banded an arm around her waist and gently drew her up until she straddled him with his cock buried as deep as he could go. She tried to lift up to relieve the pressure, but he controlled her movements, keeping her firmly in place. He swept aside her bonnie blonde curls and kissed her neck. Then, he slid his hands up to her breasts and began to play.

She sat stiffly at first, gripping his arms and struggling to accept their new position.

Rhythmically, he strummed her right nipple with his knuckles while cupping her left breast and squeezing that nipple between his fingers. "Luik down, Clarissa," he murmured.

She did. Her sheath squeezed him hard and bathed his cock anew. She saw what he saw—his conquering invasion of her wee body, the glistening evidence of her welcome, and the flagrantly swollen response of her breasts and clitoris. Those bonnie thighs clenched and trembled alongside his. She sobbed and threw her head back against his shoulder, reaching back to clasp his neck and turn her face into his kiss.

And kiss her he did. He sank into her mouth as his fingers began working her nipples, squeezing and stroking and loving the most exquisite breasts he'd ever set eyes upon.

Perhaps he hadn't the proper words to explain what she was to him. Perhaps she'd never understand how far he'd go to keep her safe and happy. But he could give her this pleasure. He could claim pure mastery over her body. He could fill her so full, she'd feel empty without him inside her.

As he pleasured her breasts, his knuckles brushed against the amulet. Made of antler, it portrayed an ancient fertility god once worshipped by their Celtic ancestors. He'd seen the symbols before, but with his head swimming and his ballocks aching, and his wife driving him bloody mad, he couldn't recall where. He couldn't even remember his own name.

"Campbell," his wife panted.

Ah, yes. Campbell. That was it.

"I'm going to … I'm reaching my peak … again. This is lunacy."

He wanted to fill her with his seed. He felt the urge rising in his cock, felt his own peak quickening along his spine.

She laced their hands together over her left breast. Her ring was hot to the touch. Something about that tickled the back of his mind, the same way the amulet had. He slid their joined hands over the amulet, which rested over her heart.

She arched and clawed at his neck. His right arm seized her waist and angled her forward again onto her hands and knees. That was when he began to unravel. Her sweet moans and the warning ripples of her impending climax hurtled him into a mad frenzy. He withdrew a few inches and drove back inside. Longer strokes followed. Soon, he was pulling back to the tip and driving fully inside her with deep, powerful thrusts. Each one rocked her forward and made the bed groan at the force. He suckled her neck. Slammed inside her. Set a rhythm far more punishing than he should have.

He had no excuses. His control was gone.

Gripping her hand harder and forcing his cock deeper, he growled in her ear all the things he shouldn't say. All the things that might frighten his wee, bonnie lass if she knew the truth.

But something had broken inside him. Some sort of barrier. He couldn't piece it back together. He couldn't stop the flood.

"The first time I saw ye, I kenned ye were mine." He was dying and being reborn inside a cauldron of fire. "I fought it." He rested his forehead on her shoulder. "Christ, how I fought."

"Campbell," she choked, gripping the coverlet with her bracing hand.

"Might as well have fought breathin'. Nearly killed me."

"I couldn't fight it, either," she panted. "Even my dreams were filled with you."

"Now, I want to make bairns with ye."

"Yes."

"I want to fill yer womb and see ye dance with our wee ones."

"Yes. Oh, heavens. Yes, yes, yes."

"I dinnae ken if it's possible. But for you, I'll do anythin'. 'Tis a cold place I've wandered without ye. Dark and cold. Ye're the sun in my sky, *gràidheag*. I'd change the whole bluidy world if it would make ye shine."

She groaned through gritted teeth, deep and long. Sweet, tightening pulses of her sheath squeezed him hard. Her release built and broke free in an instant. She arched. Seized around him. Sobbed her pleasure to the rhythm of his pounding. Her plaintive, blissful cries sparked his quickening.

It climbed. It gathered. It commanded his surrender.

And he gave in gladly. The explosion rocked him to his root and sent him soaring. With deep, bellowing shouts and long, forceful thrusts, he filled his wife with everything he had, let her body have what it wanted. No sense fighting. He'd lost his heart from the first. Claiming her as his own had given him back a piece at a time.

As they collapsed together in their bed, he held his lass close with their joined hands nestled over her heart, their joined bodies edging toward sleep. And finally, after a long winter alone, he felt the sun in his sky melt away the last of the cold.

Chapter Sixteen

Something had changed. Clarissa stopped at the end of the new garden bed and braced a hand on her hoe. Shading her eyes, she peered across the sunny yard to where Campbell unloaded a wagon full of straw and supplies. He was grinning at Alexander. Then, he laughed—a small chuckle, but still. Unusual.

"Does Mr. MacPherson seem different to you?" she asked.

Daniel straightened from planting seeds and lifted his cap to scratch his head. "Aye," he said cautiously.

She frowned at her friend. "What do you suppose it is?"

He cleared his throat. Swiped a hand over his beard. Cleared his throat again.

"Daniel?"

"Er, some men find their wives … pleasin'. Particularly after bein' unwed for a long time."

Oh. Her cheeks heated. That wasn't what she'd meant, but she supposed their frequent "tupping" had lightened Campbell's mood. For the past ten days, he'd glowered less often and even revealed a playful side from time to time.

As Daniel resumed sowing cauliflower, she nibbled her lip and contemplated her husband's massive, flexing shoulders. He hefted a cider cask that normally took two men to lift. Casually, he chatted to Alexander as though it weighed nothing. The man was tireless.

In more ways than one.

After her demand that he attempt to sow some seeds in her garden, as Grandmama might say, he hadn't given her the slightest quarter.

She awakened each morning with him sliding inside her. She fell asleep each night with him spent but still half-hard inside her. During the days he was home, he took every opportunity to "find" her in odd places and perform his "duties."

Two days ago, she'd been searching for another footstool in the barn when he'd come up behind her and slid a hand over her backside. She'd huffed that this wasn't the proper place and swatted his hand away, but he'd growled low, filthy things about wicked lasses who must stay wet for their man if they didn't wish to be sore. She'd melted into a puddle. He'd taken her hard right there on top of the blasted crate, muffling her cries of ecstasy with his mouth.

Yesterday, he'd taken her to the birchwood glen for more shooting practice. After much discussion of priming and nipples and ramrods, she'd only managed to fire her pistol twice before he'd tossed the weapon aside, backed her against a tree, and dropped to his knees. Then, he'd lifted one of her legs over his shoulder, gone under her skirts, and brought her to climax twice. She'd chided him afterward, insisting on returning the favor.

Her new favorite pastime was worshipping the parts of him that gave her the most pleasure—his hands, his mouth, and especially his cock. Oh, she'd explored that particular delight from ballocks to tip. By the time she'd discovered the taste of the tiny bead of fluid that signaled the heights of his arousal, he'd lost his patience. Then, he'd tossed her skirts up, wedged her high against the tree, and filled her with his massive cock. He'd ordered her to lower her bodice and suckled her breasts until she'd seized upon him and screamed his name to the heavens. Only after playfully admonishing her loss of control did he begin thrusting. By the time he'd released inside her, she'd lost all strength in her limbs, half of her voice, and most of her mind. He'd had to lay her down on the plaid he'd spread upon newly scythed grass so she could recover. After a half hour, he'd rolled her onto her hands and knees and taken her again as though he hadn't already spent himself inside her three times that day.

It was ridiculous. Not the lovemaking, of course. She adored every moment of that. But the frequency and intensity of her desperate, unrelenting desire overwhelmed her sometimes. It was dizzying. A little embarrassing.

Additionally, he still confused her. Coaxing him toward explanations about his "sight" or the oddly familiar things he'd said both in her dreams and during their real lovemaking was a herculean task. Every time she'd asked, he'd shrugged it off. "They're dreams, lass. Naught to fash about."

Finally, last night, after she'd tormented him with her mouth for long, blistering minutes, he'd confessed the truth. "Sweet Christ, woman. Fine. Yer dreams about me were real—in a way."

She'd squeezed his cock and given him a slow stroke as a reward, reveling in his agonized groan. "Explain how that can be, my love."

Abdomen heaving on rough breaths, he'd gripped her hair and gazed down at her with tender, possessive fire. "I wanted ye. Couldnae have ye."

"Why couldn't you?"

"Ye ken why. Ye deserved a chance to have bairns."

"I'll have the chance with you." She'd fingered her amulet. "I'm certain of it."

He'd shaken his head. "Determined lass. I couldnae have ye as I wanted. But *there*, I could. I've always had better control in dreams than others have. In that place, I could touch ye as I liked."

"Very well. But how did your dreams become mine?"

He'd stroked her cheek with his knuckles and her lip with his thumb. "I didnae ken that was happenin' at first. I thought I'd bolted the door on those abilities long ago. I'd been tryin' to restore them for Broderick's sake since last year, but it hadnae worked. Then, ye said somethin' at breakfast one day. Somethin' about plowin'."

"Because you'd said it in my dream the night before." With a slow grin, she gave him a lapping caress. "It was on the tip of my tongue."

His chuckle was hoarse. "Aye. That's when I kenned that I'd gone travelin' a wee bit far afield."

"You seduced me. Over and over and over."

"Wasnae intentional."

"But once you knew we were sharing the same dreams, you didn't stop, did you?"

Those black eyes had gone ferociously hot. He'd gripped her hair in his fist and licked his lips. "Nah."

"Why not?"

"Because makin' ye come is my bluidy right."

Their conversation had ended abruptly when he'd decided to demonstrate his point at some length.

She now believed he was in love with her—his descriptions about feeling she belonged to him from the first might as well have been her own words to him. She'd like to confirm her suppositions, but she didn't want to push him too hard.

In the best of times, Campbell wasn't the sort of man to wax poetic about his innermost thoughts. And right now, he was managing a great deal, with calving season and the distillery and securing defenses on the farm and hunting Northfield. His sister, Annie, had experienced two bouts of false labor in the past week, requiring both Magdalene and Mrs. MacBean to remain at Glendasheen Castle. Angus had visited the farm once to warn Campbell about more slaughtered sheep, which had darkened his mood despite his happiness at seeing his da.

She'd held onto her remaining questions for her husband, giving him the time he needed to complete his work. For now, she was content to pleasure his body and be pleasured in return. More than content. She'd never felt such happiness before, as if she floated along a stream of sparkling light, all while being held in the strongest arms on earth. Safety and joy, the firm ground she'd never thought she'd reach. That was her love for Campbell and his for her.

Now, as she completed her planting and put away her tools, she fanned herself with her gloves. The whole week had been warm and dry, unusually so for late April. But that wasn't the reason for her sudden flash of heat. No, that was due to her husband's hands. He'd started pitching straw from the wagon into a wooden bin near the cowshed. His hands gripped the handle of the fork with that loose, deft touch she'd grown to recognize.

Blast, she was thirsty. Hot, thirsty, and counting the hours until bedtime.

She entered the kitchen to find Rannoch flirting with both Jean and Abigail as they prepared dinner. The handsomest MacPherson seemed to flirt reflexively with every female between twenty and sixty. Notable exceptions included Magdalene Cuthbert, whom he treated like a nun, and his two sisters-in-law, whom he treated like sisters.

She assumed he'd been warned away from Kate by Broderick. Likely Campbell had done likewise regarding Clarissa. Campbell's threats to dismember any man who touched her had sounded both casual and deadly, as though he'd killed many men and another would be no trouble. Rannoch was wise to be cautious. But then, he'd treated her like a sister since the day she'd arrived in the glen.

Which made her wonder, how long had he known Campbell's true feelings? Had they all suspected? She frowned. Had Kate?

"Ah, there's my bonnie sister-in-law now," Rannoch said with a grin. He dug a note from his waistcoat pocket and came around the kitchen table to hand it to her. "Mrs. MacBean sends her regards. She wanted to come, but Bill the Donkey was feelin' poorly. She claims he cannae tolerate turnips."

Clarissa examined the note. Then, she read it again. And again. It still didn't make sense.

Tell Campbell the anchor is in the blood. Bone of your bones. Flesh of your flesh. Find the circle that burns and chase it.

Remember to cut the grass short and feed it deeply. Stags will run free. Rabbits will never perish again.

When you return for your purse, forget the long barrel. Two is better than one.

Houses are boxes. Some are empty. Some are full.

The letter opener is sharp enough. Just use it and stop complaining.

If you find three, you'll find four.

It will be a lassie first, a lad second, and seven to follow.

I might be wrong. It could be eight. Use the unguent.

Tell Angus to stop feeding Bill turnips. They make him gassy.

As long as a heart beats, there is hope to be found.

"What nonsense did she write to ye?" Rannoch asked.

Clarissa shook her head. "I don't really understand any of it. Well, the part about the turnips, perhaps."

"Dinnae fash. Everybody kens she's mad as coo on moonshine. Last month, she told me to hang upside down with my hat on. When I asked her why I should do such a foolish thing, she said 'twould tickle the fancy of the only two lasses who matter." He snorted. "She keeps after Alexander about buildin' some fancy walled garden with a gate when he should be mendin' that hole in his shoulder. And all those rowan trees she planted outside Broderick's house will be a pure mess come autumn. Birds swarm for the berries. There'll be naught but leaves, red berries, and bird shite as far as the eye can see." He shook his head and popped a bit of bread in his mouth. "Daft auld woman."

She folded the note and tucked it into her sleeve. "Are you here for the wagon?"

"Nah. Dinner."

An odd sensation struck her belly. She rubbed her abdomen. "Rather a long ride for dinner. You're most welcome, of course. We're always happy to see you."

He grinned, his eyes twinkling amusement. "Ye've a wee bit of somethin' on yer cheek, lass."

She rubbed her cheek.

"Ye missed it. Here, let me."

He took a napkin from the table and wiped the area beneath her eye. Just as he was finishing, boots sounded in the scullery.

"Rannoch," came a low, soft rumble. "What did I say about keepin' yer hands to yerself?"

Rannoch's hands went up. He backed away two paces. "Better, brother?"

Huge and thunderous, Campbell crossed the kitchen in three strides. "'Twould be better if ye did as I instructed." He slid a long arm around her waist and glared at his youngest brother. "Did ye bring it?"

"Aye."

"Good." Campbell bent and kissed her with shocking thoroughness. Using his tongue. In front of everybody. "I mean to have a wash before dinner, *gràidheag*. Join me if ye like."

She nodded. After he left the kitchen, she frowned at the younger MacPherson male, her senses ringing with suspicion. "Rannoch. I've two questions for you."

"Aye, lass?"

"First, what does *gràidheag* mean?"

"Ye dinnae ken?"

"I've been meaning to ask, and now I'm curious."

He shrugged. "Closest thing might be callin' ye 'love.' Or mayhap 'sweetheart.' Nah, 'beloved' is better. Beloved woman."

Her heart turned over at least three times then heated like a furnace. He loved her. She'd suspected, but suspicions weren't knowing. He'd loved her from the first, the same way she loved him.

"What's yer second question?"

Once she'd caught her breath, she asked, "What are you really doing here?"

While reaching for another bite of bread, he stilled for a moment. His eyes sobered then twinkled with a feigned smile. "I told ye. Dinner. Mayhap some whisky."

"Don't fib. You brought something. What is it?"

He rubbed his nape. "A rifle."

Another queer sensation fluttered in her belly. She rubbed a palm over it and sighed. "You're here because of Northfield, aren't you?"

"Ye should speak to Campbell about this."

"I don't want you getting hurt. I don't want any of you …" She covered her lips, fighting tears. She'd nearly forgotten. Amidst her sense of safety and her happiness with Campbell, she'd nearly forgotten the threat that hung over all their heads.

"Listen, lass." He reached for her shoulders then thought better of it. "None of us is blind to what Northfield is. We ken the risks. We ken what must be done."

She eyed the man before her. At times, he seemed so much younger than his brothers, lighter and perhaps sweeter, that one could be forgiven for thinking him a different breed of man altogether. But right now, he was pure MacPherson—tough as steel, big as the Highlands, generous as the sky.

"Thank you," she whispered. "Are you to be my nursemaid, then?"

His smile was gentle. "Aye. I'll wear a wee, ruffled cap and serve ye oatcakes with yer tea."

"Mmm. And extra naps. I've been a bit weary of late."

Upstairs a few minutes later, she entered the bedchamber to find her husband waiting. He wore nothing but a towel around his waist. She went lightheaded. "Dear God."

"What's wrong?" He glowered as she closed the door. "Did Rannoch try to touch ye again? I cannae break his hands just yet, but in a day or two—"

"No," she sighed. "You're just … heavenly."

He glanced down at himself. "Ye must fancy a great lot of hair, *gràidheag.*"

Heat swirled around her lower belly. She pressed a hand there to tame the ache. "I fancy a great lot of man."

He grinned. "Well, I can give ye that."

She felt a tingling rush and nearly swooned. "I love you, Campbell."

His smile faded. He tossed aside his towel and came to brace both hands against the door on either side of her. "And I love ye, Clarissa."

"I know." She rested her palms over his heart. "I also know you've found Northfield."

His sigh was deep and shuddering. He leaned closer, his head hanging down between them. "Alexander tracked him to a spot south of the quarry.

He's camped there before, but now he's returned. We'll head out before first light. Rannoch will stay with ye."

This was the difference she'd noticed in him earlier—purpose and anticipation. Campbell had his target in his sights at long last. Northfield's hours were likely numbered. "I wish I could help protect you. Something more than sending Francis off to attempt blackmail."

"Ye mustn't fash about me. I'll be fine."

She slid her arms around his waist and laid her cheek over his heart. The rhythmic thud was reassuring. "Please come back to me safe." She clung tighter, her fingers digging into his muscular back. "I can't bear the thought of ..."

He wrapped her up tight, one massive hand cradling her head against him while the other slid down to her lower back. His thumb traced little circles on her spine. "Whatever comes, ye must know this, *gràidheag*. Before ye, I was dead. Seein' ye felt like breathin' for the first time. A wee bit painful, at first. Then ... pure joy." He kissed the top of her head and pulled her in tighter. "A man will fight to his last scrap to keep such a miracle safe. Because without ye, I'm dead anyhow."

Heart pounding, she turned her mouth up to find his. He kissed her hard, as he'd done in the kitchen, sliding his tongue deep and controlling her with his hand on her nape. Soon, their kiss turned desperate, two mouths trying to merge and pleasure and quench, all at once. Acutely aware of his naked arousal, she clutched his hair and all but climbed him to get closer. He lifted her skirts and hefted her higher against the door.

She groaned. Wrapped her legs around his waist. Felt the urgency rising. Too fast. Too fast. So fast, she couldn't catch her breath. "I need you. God, Campbell. I'm aching."

His mouth slid to her throat, nibbled to her neck. Hot breath and hotter man set her on fire. "Are ye wet for me?" he whispered. "Can ye take what I give ye?"

"Yes," she panted. "Give me everything."

He bent his knees and slid the length of his cock along her folds. She gasped. Arched. Carefully, he notched the head at her opening. "Ah, ye're afire, my bonnie Clarissa. Have ye been thinkin' wicked thoughts today?"

The initial stretch taunted her desire. She clawed his neck and kissed his lips, writhing for more. "Need you. Inside me. All the way. Please."

He held her tighter against the door, positioning her so she couldn't look away. Dark eyes blazed into hers. "Luik at me while I take what's mine." He slid deeper.

The fullness somehow always managed to shock her senses. Ripples of sensation worked outward from their joining. Heat and tingling pleasure zinged across her breasts and belly.

"So wet. Tight." He gritted his teeth. "Need to … go deeper." He slid deeper. "That's it. There's a good lass."

She clawed his neck and arched her back. The flowery cotton of her gown had felt light while she worked in the garden, but now, it was too much. She was sweltering. Yearning. She needed to feel his skin against hers. "Take my gown off," she pleaded.

His eyes narrowed. "Are ye makin' demands, wife?"

"Yes."

A slow grin. A deep, penetrating thrust.

She groaned his name as the pressure exploded into pleasure.

"Now, then. I mean to take ye to our bed and ride ye hard. Mayhap after ye've come for me like a good lass, I'll strip ye naked and do it again." He nibbled her neck. Nuzzled her ear. Whispered, "But slower."

She released a hitching moan and buried her face against his neck. Then, she felt herself being carried. Lowered onto the bed. Covered by her husband's heat and strength. Filled with his cock to the fine edge between too much and perfect pleasure.

He lay fully atop her, raising her knees higher, stretching them wider. Sinking deeper. He nuzzled the kerchief she'd tucked inside her neckline. Licked a bead of sweat from between her breasts. Then, he began thrusting deep and hard. The pace was steady at first. Long, deliberate strokes.

He pressed her knees nearly to her shoulders and angled his cock to drive her mad. His eyes burned into hers as the tempo quickened. Intense bursts of pressure coiled her pleasure tighter. Tighter. Deep inside, a tempest built. She was sobbing his name. Begging for release.

His face was a ferocious sight, his jaw flexing, the vein near his temple distended. But his eyes told the full story—he'd do this forever if he thought it would please her. He'd forestall his own release to give her everything she needed.

She reached up to cup his jaw. Drew him down into her kiss. Whispered against his lips, "Give me everything, my love. I demand nothing less."

His brow crashed into a pained glower. His groan was pure agony. His hips jerked, forcing his cock harder against the very depths of her core. Then, he rode her with a grinding, pummeling fury.

The pleasure billowed into an explosion so vast and consuming, her vision blurred into shimmering light. Her body quaked. Shook for long, boundless seconds as the paroxysms rolled on and on. Even as the pleasure passed its crescendo, she took everything he gave and demanded more. She demanded *his* completion. When his thrusts quickened into a final frenzy, he gave her that, as well.

Her big, rough Scot held her desperately tight as he shot his pleasure deep inside her, filling her in a scalding flood. Every ragged groan in her ear was either her name, a curse, or "I love ye so bluidy much, *gràidheag.*"

In the end, as he gently withdrew to lie beside her, wrapped around her from behind, and tenderly kissed her ear, he murmured something in Gaelic. His voice was shredded, so it split in half, sounding layered.

Drowsy and still reeling from the storm's power, she caressed his jaw. "Tell me in English, my love."

He sighed. "'Twas a prayer." His hand slid over her belly, warming her, soothing her. "May God watch over she who carries my heart."

Her eyes filled. She slid her hand over his. "And may the man who carries me return safely to my side."

He grunted. "Victorious, eh?"

She chuckled. "Yes, my fierce Highlander. May you return to me victorious."

"I'll expect ye to reward me thoroughly when I do." He kissed her nape and nuzzled her hair. "Now, about that gown."

Chapter Seventeen

His dream was clearer than any he'd had since he was a wee lad. The sun shone bright as gold. The ground was wet after a rain. Earthy scents of mud and grass filled his senses. The clank of metal striking metal filled his ears.

He stood in the village outside his grandfather's old smithy. He hadn't seen it in years. It had burned down while he was away at war. But it looked the same as when *Seanair* had been alive—long and low, made of gray stone with a slate roof. Wide doors stood open most of the day to let the heat of the fires escape.

His grandfather wandered outside, chatting with Campbell's mam as if this were any other day. Sunlight glinted on the russet highlights of his mother's hair. She was a tall woman, long and lean with a throaty, ready laugh and generous eyes. She carried a bundle of blankets in her arms.

When she spotted him approaching, her smile widened into a glorious grin. She rushed forward to throw one arm around his neck, kissing his cheek with three pecks, as she'd always done. "Campbell!" She hugged him harder and kissed him again—one, two, three pecks and a laugh. "Ah, my son, how glad I am to see ye!"

His chest tightened as he held his mother in his arms. "Mam, I've missed ye."

"Och, I'm always about. Ye've only to come by for a visit from time to time."

A roughened voice came from near the smithy doors. "Is that my wee laddie? Ah, nae so wee anymore, eh?"

He drew back to greet his grandfather, who was now six inches shorter and three-stone leaner than Campbell. "*Seanair*. By God, 'tis good to see ye again."

The old man grinned and tapped Campbell's chin with his finger. "It's been too long. I thought ye'd forgotten the way."

He hadn't forgotten. He'd been lost. Exiled. But Clarissa had given him the light he needed. She'd guided him home, step by step. "I'm wed now," he said proudly. "Ye should see her. Bonniest lass. Her eyes are the blue of Loch Carrich on a summer day."

"Oh, aye. We were there at the weddin'. Bonnie, indeed. A beautiful bride." His grandfather smiled at Mam with that sparkling twinkle Campbell had only ever seen echoed in Rannoch. "Ye're a very fortunate man."

"Aye." He glanced around, wandering toward the smithy doors, curious if the workshop was the same as he remembered. The interior was darker, but light from the windows glinted off his grandfather's work—cups and plates of embossed metal, jewelry ranging from fine crosses to thick, braided bracelets. Bronze and silver dominated, but a copper cup caught his eye. On the side, a relief stood out—a deity with antlers.

"That's Cernunnos," said his grandfather. "He's one of the auld ones, a lord of wild things. Still offers a wee bit of magic in certain areas of life. Good for quick breedin'. Of course, he cannae overcome power like yers. Ye built a sturdy prison, son." *Seanair* tapped Campbell's chin. "Naebody could unlock those chains but you."

He turned to his mother, almost afraid to ask the question his heart begged to answer. "Have I done it, Mam? Clarissa asked me to let her hope. But I dinnae ken if it's possible …"

Her smile lit her up from the inside out. She beckoned him closer. "Come. Have a luik." Then, she shifted the blankets in her arms, flicking aside a corner to reveal a tiny, sleeping bairn. The infant yawned sweetly and rubbed its eyes with tiny hands.

His heart nearly exploded with joy. Light brightened and flashed until the air turned white. The smithy disappeared, as did his mother and grandfather. Suddenly, he stood inside swirling mist. He heard the trickling of water. Out of the mist, rushing at his head came a great bird. It swooped low, forcing him to crouch and swipe. The bird landed beside him. Its head swiveled. Its eyes blinked. In quick succession, he felt crushing dread, a sharp streak of pain across his forearm, a quivering in his hand, and a thick, burning sensation in his abdomen. The owl launched and flew away, but as its wings scattered the mist, Campbell glimpsed a flash of something red. Not blood. Cloth. Red, like Clarissa's cloak.

Everything went black, and he shot up out of a dead sleep. The bedchamber was dark but for the moonlight streaming through the window. Immediately, he knew Clarissa was gone, though he also sensed she was safe. Fergus was gone, too, and that dog wouldn't let anything hurt his favorite lass.

Running a hand over his face, he tossed aside the blankets and wrapped a plaid around his waist. Then, he retrieved a gift he'd meant to give her, donned a shirt, and went in search of his wife.

He found her in the front room. Limned in the ethereal blue of a midnight moon, she stood barefoot in her white shift, long curls swaying down her back. A scruffy, lanky, besotted hound stood with his front paws on her shoulders.

Dancing.

She was dancing with Fergus in the moonlight, humming sweetly and keeping her steps small for the dog's sake.

He rubbed a hand over the agonizing fullness inside his chest, wondering how he was meant to contain this much love. He couldn't, he supposed. Perhaps instead, he was meant to pour it out as an offering to her.

"A wee enchantress, ye are."

"Oh!" She spun, causing Fergus to land on all fours. She bent to kiss his head and scratch his ears. As she straightened, her eyes turned teasing. A mischievous smile touched her lips as she swayed and danced lightly in Campbell's direction. "It seems you've caught me with another suitor. A scandalous turn of events." A wee giggle escaped. "In fairness, Fergus is rather dashing, and a surprisingly good dancer." She spun on her toes and halted before him. Her face angled up toward his. "Kiss me," she whispered.

And he did. Gently. Chastely. A reverent brush of his lips across hers. Then, he held his gift for her up and let it dangle in front of her eyes. Even in the moonlight, he could see her delight. Her eyes glossed. She covered her lips. "Campbell," she choked. "It's exquisite."

The owl was wee, less than two inches long. He'd carved it from the oldest rowan wood, incorporating symbols of the auld spirits best suited to guarding precious things. He'd strung it on a fine silk ribbon Rannoch had fetched from the village haberdashery. It was the blue of her eyes. The ribbon would lay softly against her skin and, if he'd estimated the length correctly, settle the owl just above her heart. He looped the necklace over her neck, gathering her hair gently to slide past the ribbon. As he'd expected, the wooden pendant settled slightly above her fertility charm and slightly below her mother's cross. He nudged the antler of Cernunnos. "Ye may not need to wear this one much longer, *gràidheag.*"

She beamed. "Do you think so?"

"Aye."

"Oh, I do hope you're right." She fingered the owl, tracing it with loving strokes. "I confess, when I saw the carving you made of Isla, I was jealous. I know you loved her, but seeing it manifested in such beauty from your hands was … tormenting."

He frowned. "Clarissa, mayhap I havenae been clear. I did love Isla. She was a kindhearted lass, and our affections had a purity that only youth and death can bring. But I didnae carve her face out of love. I did it to lay her to rest. I wanted to bury her where she belonged—in the past."

She wouldn't look at him, her eyes trained on stroking the owl's wing.

"Must I say it plainly?"

Her throat rippled on a swallow. "I suppose you must."

"Nothin' in all my days compares to what I feel for you. Not my time with Isla. Nor my time with any other. Ye're paradise for me. A bluidy Eden with gingham curtains and wee flowers everywhere."

Her eyes lifted, glossy and startled. "You like the curtains?"

He laughed, his heart flooding its banks again. "Aye, ye bonnie, maddening woman. I love the curtains. And I love my bride." He held out his hand. "Now, be a good lass and dance with me."

More startled blinking. Then, a slow, wondrous smile. She sank into a graceful curtsy and slid her hand into his. He pulled her close, bent and scooped her up with an arm beneath her knees and one at her back, loving her squeak of surprise and clinging hands.

She laughed as he took light, sliding steps around the room. Fergus danced alongside. Clarissa hummed a melody only slightly off-key. And Campbell spun through shadows and moonlight holding paradise in his arms.

With morning came fog. Dense, blinding fog. Campbell cursed as he crouched beside Alexander, trying to see the camp below. They couldn't see much. A few rocks. A gnarled pine. But, mostly, a blanket of whitish gray mist as thick as old McInnes's skink.

In the stillness, however, they could hear sounds. The trickle of a wee burn that winnowed down from the upper hills. The crackle of a campfire. The cawing of crows.

Alexander shifted his rifle slowly from his shoulder to his lap.

"Can ye see anythin'?" Campbell asked in an airless whisper.

Alexander shook his head.

Bloody hell. This mission had gone to shite.

Last night, after his dance with Clarissa, he'd taken her back to their bed and made love to her again. Before she'd fallen asleep, she'd shown him the note sent by Mrs. MacBean. The old woman's sight might be stronger than his, but he couldn't decipher her mad ramblings. Apart from the bit about the turnips. Bill the Donkey was a gassy creature. He'd have to remind Da to change his feed.

Below, the crows grew louder, their cries more frequent. Something near the camp huffed and grunted, breathing heavily. Northfield?

Blast, he couldn't see. Then came a knocking sound. *Knock, knock, knock, knock.* Long grass rustled as someone moved in sporadic bursts. Perhaps the man's mind was gone, and he was thrashing about as madmen were wont to do.

Campbell would gladly put him out of his misery.

He gestured to Alexander instructions to flank the camp from either side of the rocky outcropping above Northfield's camp. Alexander nodded. As they each made their way down the slope, the crows' cawing grew constant, drowning out some of the thrashing. He closed in on Northfield's position, following the grunting sounds through the fog.

When he heard Alexander's signal—the distinctive squeak-and-pop call of the capercaillie—he halted in place and whistled two sharp, upward notes. Alexander's request irked Campbell a wee bit. He'd wanted to kill Northfield himself. But if the bugger was in Alexander's sights, he had only one reply: *Fire away, brother.*

The shot echoed with a sharp *crack!* Chaos reigned. What must have been hundreds of crows took flight, scattering the mist and creating a deafening noise. Beneath that was the thrashing, knocking, and deep grunts of a life about to end. Then came a splitting whine—wood or branches being torn, perhaps—and someone raced away at a pounding pace.

Campbell gave a single upward whistle before taking off at a dead run. If Alexander's shot had either missed or merely wounded Northfield, Campbell would be the one to find the bastard. He would be the one to bring him down.

He raced after the sounds, using his longer strides to close the distance. Soon, he saw the trail of blood. By God, the rabid dog had been hit. A surge of satisfaction thrummed through him. He ran harder, hearing Alexander behind him.

Ahead, the arrhythmic thudding of Northfield's footsteps slowed. Stuttered. A wheezing grunt sounded strange and muffled. The metallic odor of a bloody demise reached him just as the footsteps ceased on a final *whump*. He slowed his pace and approached with caution, following the trail of blood.

When he saw its source, he halted. Ice bloomed inside his veins. Spread outward in a relentless tide of dread. It deepened. Hardened. Filled him until he was drowning.

Alexander came to a halt alongside him, breathing heavily. Then, he began cursing with the foul blackness Campbell wished he could manage.

He couldn't speak at all. He couldn't speak any more than the poor stag that had been trapped in a net, staked out near the camp, and shot by Alexander's rifle. That animal couldn't utter a sound. Because that animal was lying dead on the ground at his boots.

And Northfield was very much alive. Not here. But alive. Likely closing in on Campbell's wife as he stood there, watching an innocent creature's blood drain into the long grass.

Alexander bent forward at the waist then straightened and stared up at the sky. "Bluidy bastard!" he roared. "I'll cut your fucking throat for this!"

Campell's cold sank deeper. Every muscle hardened with a new purpose. "Nah," he breathed. "I will." He clamped a hand on his brother's nape and gave him a shake, as Da had always done. "We must go, now. He's hunting her. We must get to him first. Ye ken?"

Alexander nodded, though his breathing remained heavy and his eyes furious. "Let's go."

They raced for the horses, mounting at a run and urging their mounts to a gallop. The quarry was in the east hills at least an hour's ride from his farm. But at a run, they could shorten the ride by half. He didn't know if the horses could take such a punishing pace, but it didn't matter. Nothing mattered. If he had to, he would run it on foot.

She was in danger. That stag had been a decoy, tied and tangled, likely bound loosely enough that it could escape if it thrashed hard enough and long enough. Which would happen if it was shot. But the bastard hadn't been content to merely sacrifice the animal. Its newly sprouting antlers had been sawn off, its snout bound with wire so it couldn't scream.

Northfield must have known they were coming. And the only way he'd know is if he'd heard Campbell and Alexander making plans in the yard. Which meant he'd been close enough to hear their voices. Which meant he'd been near her. Watching.

Christ on the cross, had he been there the whole time? How? Campbell had established regular patrols. He'd surrounded the farm with traps and men. He'd sent Fergus out scouting with Daniel twice a day. He'd taken every conceivable precaution, and it hadn't been enough.

His horse began flagging. Alexander's fell behind. Campbell leaned forward, murmuring reassurances to the exhausted animal. He promised oats and rest. He promised mares aplenty and a pasture all to himself if Dunmore would just get him home in time.

"My female is there, old friend," he said in Gaelic. "I need you to help me save her." The large stallion heaved and put on a new burst of speed.

They didn't bother taking the northerly path, instead veering south through thick brush and woodlands. The fog was denser around the loch, limiting visibility to about ten feet, but he and Alexander had explored every inch of the glen before they'd sprouted whiskers. They drove their mounts at a reckless pace, leaping over fallen logs and ancient stone walls. On they raced up into the western hills, taking the road when it was faster and cutting through raw heathland when his patience lost the battle with urgency. By the time they topped the rise above the farm, smoke was an acrid omen.

And the queer, glowing nimbus below was the arrival of hell.

Black smoke filled the sky in a towering plume, but the farm remained enveloped in fog, creating a massive ball of pulsing orange surrounded by white.

Dunmore balked. Campbell slid from his back, grabbed his rifle, and ran toward the shouts of his men and the devouring roar of fire. Distantly, he heard Alexander shouting something behind him, but he ignored it. Instead, he ran, driven by the encompassing dread.

Time is short, he thought. The old woman had told him time was short.

He'd only just taken his first breath after a long death. Clarissa couldn't be gone. She couldn't. He'd feel it.

Aye. He'd feel it if she were. *Bone of my bones. Flesh of my flesh.* Words spoken by Adam about his Eve. *The anchor is in the blood.* His bairn, perhaps. Inside her womb. Safe and wanted and loved. His hope, given to him by his wife.

He'd inherited his sight through blood ties, his grandfather and Mam. Perhaps a similar tie to his child would be strong enough to find her. Save her.

He raced toward the largest blaze—the barn. Fire had turned it into an inferno. The roof had collapsed. He veered past escaping cows and soot-stained men, shouting for Rannoch. He was out of air, his lungs burning from the smoke as much as the exertion. "Rannoch!" he roared.

One of his men found him. He carried two buckets and offered Campbell one. Seeing the wet kerchief over his man's face, he tore off his shirtsleeve and doused it in the bucket before tying it over his mouth and nose.

"Rannoch's with Daniel, sir! They're on the wagon just past the stable. Daniel was shot."

Ah, Christ. How many had been wounded? How many had died?

Bloody hell, he couldn't think about that now. He must find his wife. Clarissa was the bastard's prize. She would be his true target.

He staggered into the yard surrounded by flames, smoke, and chaos. His men fought the blaze as best they could, but the buckets of water might as well be a sprinkle of dog piss for all the good they did. The cottage's thatch roof shot up flames twelve feet high. A booming crack signaled the collapse of the cowshed. Finally, amidst the madness, he spotted his brother standing by a wagon thirty feet beyond the burning cottage. The nearby stable was the only building spared.

"Rannoch!"

His brother turned. His face was blackened by soot, his right hand roughly bandaged with a strip of wool. "Cam," he rasped.

On the back of the wagon sat Daniel, his blood oozing down into his beard from a wound near his temple.

"What happened?" Campbell demanded. "Where is Clarissa?"

Rannoch nodded toward the stable. "There. With Fergus."

He sprinted for the stable door. Inside, it was dark and strangely quiet. Too quiet. Too still. "Clarissa?" Frantically, he searched every stall, hoping he was wrong. When he wasn't, his heart collapsed. There was nothing. Except, on the floor at his feet lay a leather collar tied to a rope. He staggered against the railing, a wave of dizzying sickness assaulting him.

Back outside, he ran, ignoring the burning in his stomach, the fear gnawing at his bones. "She's gone." The words emerged without sound, forcing him to repeat them in a roar. "Rannoch! My wife is *gone!*"

Rannoch shook his head. "No. She was here. Right here." What Campbell could see of his brother's face lost all color. "Ah, God, no. Not again."

Campbell charged forward and grasped his brother's nape, forcing him to focus. "Tell me what happened." He gave him a shake, his lungs heaving and aching and burning. "And, for God's sake, be swift about it. Time is short. If she dies, it's the end of me. Do ye ken? The end of me."

"I ken, brother. I'll help ye find her. Ye're not alone in this."

Fury like he'd never known blazed upward from the blackest depths of his soul. It split him down the center. It broke his voice in two. "I'll find her. Then, I'll tear him apart. Nothing will stop me."

Rannoch's eyes flashed into wariness. He swallowed. Nodded. Then, he calmly explained how Campbell's paradise had been stolen and replaced with hell. "It all started with tea and oatcakes."

Chapter Eighteen

On the day that changed everything, Clarissa awakened with a craving for oatcakes and honey with a strong cup of tea. Outside, crows were creating a wild cacophony. That must have been what disturbed her sleep, she thought, because she could have slept on for another hour. She stretched in bed, feeling the remnants of her night with Campbell—a magical night filled with dancing and pleasure and love. She sighed blissfully at the memories.

Then, she laughed as Fergus trotted over to wash her face with his tongue.

"Eww, Fergus!" She pushed him away and rolled onto her feet. Wrapping herself in her gray plaid, she opened the door to let him out. "Go find Daniel, hmm?"

The dog trotted merrily into the corridor before loping toward the stairs.

She closed the door and started to wash and dress. She noticed the fog hadn't yet lifted. When Campbell had kissed her goodbye before dawn, he'd cursed the nuisance weather but said it should burn off by noon. She glanced at the small clock on her dressing table. Half eleven.

After tying a shawl over her sprigged cotton day dress—the blue one with the white roses—she sat on the bed to roll on knitted wool stockings rather than the silk ones she'd originally selected. If the weather meant to be chilly, then she meant to be comfortable.

Of course, "comfortable" was a condition of degrees. Her inner thighs were sore from both overworked muscles and whisker-chafed skin; her bosoms flashed fire at every brush of fabric; and her womanly bits had been thoroughly pillaged by a ruthless marauder.

Campbell "The Marauder" MacPherson.

Blast, the man was relentless. And magnificent.

She grinned and fingered her owl necklace. Thank heaven he was hers.

Downstairs a short while later, she entered the kitchen to find Rannoch munching on buttered bread and chatting with a rosy-cheeked Abigail. He paused to give Clarissa a wickedly charming grin as he slid a plate of oatcakes across the table. "Good mornin', sister. I promised ye oatcakes and tea." He poured steaming water from the kettle into the teapot then placed it on a trivet. "And here ye are. Oatcakes and tea."

She chuckled. "Indeed, you are a man of your word." She nodded toward the sideboard. "Fetch me that honeypot, won't you? I've a craving."

He plucked it up, frowned, then peered inside. "'Tis empty."

"Oh, aye," said Abigail, wiping her hands on her apron. "Apologies, Mrs. MacPherson. I used it all for the honey cakes. They're a special treat I was plannin' for this evenin' after … well, when Mr. MacPherson comes home."

Clarissa's belly twinged with worry as she recalled the risk he was taking. "Very thoughtful, Abigail. Thank you." She pasted on a bright smile. "Rannoch, I believe there's more honey in the larger crate on the supply wagon. Perhaps you could carry it inside for me?"

He finished the last of his bread and dusted his hands. "Straight away." He reached for the rifle propped beside the potato bin. "Stay here, ye ken? Mayhap pour us some tea. I'll only be a moment."

She nodded then sat at the table arranging cups and waiting for the tea to steep. Fergus slipped inside through the scullery before Rannoch closed the door behind him. The dog came to beg scraps from Abigail, who fed him a plate of chopped beefsteak. Clarissa smiled to see her hound being so spoiled.

Before the meat was halfway gone, he stopped. Snuffled. He paced away from his plate toward the scullery door.

Clarissa glanced at his half-finished beef and frowned. It wasn't like him to leave any food whatever behind. "Fergus?"

He stared at the door, each breath ending in a tight, low huff. The fur on his back lifted. Growls followed, long and quiet at first. Then, several deep barks.

Her nape prickled. A chill chased down her spine. She went to him and stroked his head. "What is it, my boy?" she said gently. "What's wrong?"

More growling. Tension stiffened his body.

A loud *crack* came from outside.

Abigail screamed. Jean yelped and dropped a tin of almonds. Fergus's growls erupted into snarling barks.

Confusion sent Clarissa's head spinning. Had that been a gunshot? It had sounded strange. And the crows were cawing so loudly, she could scarcely think. Concern for Rannoch and the men helped her shake off her disorientation. She ordered Abigail and Jean away from the windows and shooed Fergus away from the door.

Minutes later, Rannoch entered carrying a limp, unconscious Daniel over his shoulder. Daniel was dripping blood from his head. Because Daniel had been shot.

The kitchen faded to misty gray.

"Clarissa!" Rannoch barked. "Help me, lass. Dinnae swoon, for Christ's sake. I need ye."

Light sharpened.

"Breathe, now." He'd lain Daniel out on the table. Abigail sobbed into a towel. Jean looked ready to retch. Fergus remained near the scullery door, hackles raised and growling sporadically.

Clarissa took a deep breath and smelled something odd. Acrid. Like soot or … smoke.

"Look, the bullet grazed him here," Rannoch said, pointing to the part of Daniel that oozed blood into his beard. "Shouldnae be too bad if we clean him up a bit and put a bandage on it." He cuffed Daniel's shoulder and took his rifle in hand. "Good lad. Take care of him, now, Abigail," he said to the teary maid. "Shouldnae marry a man if ye cannae tend his wounds."

Frowning, Clarissa watched Abigail smile and nod. What in blazes? Abigail and Daniel? When had this happened?

Noticing his beard caked with blood made her gorge rise. Near the door, Fergus continued growling with increasing menace.

"The next time that door opens, he's bound to bolt," said Jean, dropping strips of linen into a pot of boiling water.

He would. Fergus would bolt. Clarissa needed to retrieve his collar. She'd rarely seen a faster dog than Fergus. If he bolted, she'd never catch him.

Abigail bent over Daniel's face, turning her cheek above his nose. "He's breathin'." She clutched his head to her bosom. "Ah, thank the guid Lord!"

"Stay here and clean him up. If he awakens, make sure he's steady before he stands. I—I must go upstairs," Clarissa muttered. "Fergus needs his collar and I left it ..." Head spinning, she wondered if she might be sick right there. The ground seemed to be rolling beneath her stomach, forcing it up into her throat.

She rushed upstairs and managed to deposit the meager contents of her stomach in the wash basin, rather than on her gown. "Huzzah," she whispered. "So tidy. Grandmama would be proud." She covered her eyes and laughed. Fought a sob. Covered her mouth with a towel and screamed.

This was her fault. All of it. She'd drawn the madman here. She'd put all of them in danger. For what? She'd wanted to be more than a wallflower. She'd wanted to be beautiful for a season, to stand in the light and be noticed.

Well, she had been. She'd been noticed by Stephen Northfield. And he'd turned everything around her into blood and death. Had her vanity been worth it?

She rocked back and forth on her toes, a grinding, keening fear swallowing her whole. Was Campbell safe? If he wasn't safe, she couldn't imagine what she'd do. Lie down and never rise again, likely.

She could almost hear her grandmother admonishing her. "This is no time to fall apart, dear. Why, when my dear, sweet Alfie died, I lay in bed for three months, and not a single thing improved. Well, perhaps the weather. He passed in winter, you know."

She wiped her eyes and rinsed her mouth. She searched the small chest at the end of the bed for Fergus's leather collar. It lay beside her leather reticule. The one where she kept her pistol with the twin barrels. She glanced toward the wall, where Campbell's musket rested on a wooden rack.

When you return for your purse, forget the long barrel. Two is better than one.

Mrs. MacBean's note. Had she meant two guns? Or two barrels?

Clarissa decided if one gun was good, two were better. She began loading the pistol with shaking hands. She slid it inside the purse and looped it alongside Fergus's collar over her wrist. She was preparing to load the musket when Rannoch burst in.

"Time to go."

"Go? Where?"

He clasped her upper arm and hauled her to her feet. "Out. The house is on fire." All but tossing her toward the door, he paused only long enough to pluck her red cloak from its hook and drape it around her shoulders before scooping her up and carrying her down the stairs at a stunning pace. As they passed by the front room, she glanced over his shoulder and saw a wall of fire devouring her yellow gingham curtains.

He didn't set her down until they'd reached the stable. Only then did she notice Rannoch's face was stained black with soot.

"Stay here," he warned. "Fergus will protect ye. I'm right outside. Daniel is awake." He clasped her head between his hands and kissed her forehead. "All is well. Nobody has died. Even the coos are safe."

Her heart turned over. "Butter?"

He lifted a brow. "Are ye hungry right now, lass?"

"No. Butter is a calf. He's just a little one. Not even t-two months."

Stroking her hair, he held her gaze, looking so much like Campbell that her heart nearly broke. "He's safe. They're all out wanderin' the pasture, munchin' grass and stayin' clear of that big, orange ball of flame."

Her chest shook on an inward breath. "Dear God, Rannoch. What happened?"

Grim fury shone in his eyes. His jaw hardened. "The shot was a diversion. His real aim was to set the fires, which he did. Every building except this one. It's possible he was thwarted when all the men swarmed the yard." He ran a hand through his hair. She noted it was bandaged.

"What happened to your hand?" she whispered.

He glanced down. "Burned it. Some fires dinnae want to be put out."

She swallowed and nodded, noting that Fergus had been tied to one of the stall rails. She went to her dog and slid his collar around his neck before retying the line properly to make him more comfortable. "Did you find where the shot came from?"

"Aye. A rocky spot atop the eastern rise."

Her skin prickled. The same place she'd thought she'd seen him weeks ago. "Was he there? Did you find him?"

His mouth tightened into a grim line. "He wasnae there."

Her breathing quickened as her stomach lurched again. "How did he fire a shot without being there?"

Rannoch sighed and braced his hands loosely on his hips. "He set up a contraption. A timer, of a sort. The trigger was attached to a string. Which was attached to a weight. Which was suspended on a scale. Which slowly unbalanced."

She swallowed reflexively, begging her stomach to calm. There was no basin here. *This is no time to fall apart, dear.* "What did he install as the counterweight?"

A long, reluctant pause. "A rabbit."

Her eyes slid closed. Visions of well buckets filled her head. She wanted to howl her anguish. But she mustn't fall apart. There was Campbell to think about. She must be strong for Campbell. "He let it bleed, didn't he? And as it drained, the weight lowered and tripped the trigger."

"Aye."

"And shot Daniel."

"*Grazed* Daniel. He's awake. A mite crabbit. But awake."

Tears swirled. She nodded. "Good."

"I must speak with him for a wee bit. Will ye be all right, here?"

"Yes."

He gave her forehead one last kiss then stepped outside.

She wandered to the doorway, tightening her cloak around her. The leather pouch swung against her thigh, reminding her of the weapon inside. She secured it tighter to prevent any accidental firing.

Beyond the stable doors, she saw Rannoch speaking with Daniel, whose head had been bandaged. Her gaze drifted across the yard to the bizarre sight of her home burning. The thatched roof was a roiling blaze. The drafty windows were splintering under the heat. Her curtains were gone. The barn roof had collapsed. Campbell's sculptures doubtless would already be ash. Even the privy had caught fire. Everything was being devoured by a hungry, growling force.

"Everything," she whispered. "Everything. Gone."

She braced her hand against the rough plank wall. How had it come to this?

A concussive *boom* rocked the yard. She ran outside to see what had happened and saw the kitchen wing of the cottage collapse. Her kitchen. The table where Campbell drank his coffee and fetched her honey. The scullery where she'd prepared their baths and decided to hope. All of it gone.

For what? Her vanity?

Rage she hadn't recognized billowed up like the blaze before her. It deepened and grew. It took root inside her guilt and broke apart the foundation.

No. By God, no. This was *not* her fault. This was madness. Roaring flames and slaughtered animals and bone-quaking terror were not the consequence of vanity. They were the consequence of a deranged mind, a mind that couldn't distinguish between casual flirtation and wholesale ownership.

"Clarissa!" Rannoch shouted. "Back inside the stable, lass. It's not safe out here. The ash is fallin' and settin' things on fire."

She glanced up. Sparks and ash billowed upward with the smoke, falling here and there like snow. She backed toward the stable.

She didn't deserve this. She never had.

Nobody deserved to have their life destroyed for the sake of one man's obsession. Campbell had been right. The only way to end the threat and save her own life was to end Stephen Northfield.

When she entered the stable, she didn't see Fergus. She blinked. There was the line tied to the rail. There was his collar lying on the ground. But no Fergus. It took her long, agonizing seconds to understand what had happened.

Fergus had bolted.

Dear God, no.

Fergus was gone. Fear and dread rocked her. She stumbled out of the stable, frantic to find him. She was gathering up enough air to shout his name when she heard a bark in the distance. Without another thought, she charged after him, running through thick fog toward the sound of her beloved hound's snuffling growls.

Heart pounding a panic, she ran with all her strength. He mustn't be harmed. She couldn't bear it. Not after Dash. Not after she'd surrendered her heart.

She scrambled over rocky, mossy ground. Searching. She halted, trying to hear past the chaos behind her. Trying to see through the mist and smoke. She longed to call his name, but she didn't want to alert Northfield to her location. So, she followed the sounds.

There! Another bark. She veered left, stumbling over a shin-high boulder and cursing as her toes collided in a glancing blow. The mists were swirling. Moving. She was on higher ground. The smell of smoke was fainter. She stopped. Blood pounded in her ears. Her lungs burned. She bent forward and coughed in wrenching gusts. Bracing her hands on her knees, she dropped her head and listened. Somewhere to her right, a cow mooed. In the distance, the fire roared on in a dull thunder.

She closed her eyes, listening past her sawing breaths. There. A faint bark. Another. Closer. She turned in that direction and ran. Soon, she recognized the fences and rocks. She recognized the sound of water. A trickle. Then a rush.

She was near the birchwood glen. She staggered to a halt.

"Where are you, my boy?" she whispered, her panting edged with love and panic. "Please. Show me where you are."

Quiet reigned, broken only by the trickling whoosh of water. A dense wall of mist swirled strangely, and she felt suspended in cold white. Out of nowhere, the mists parted. A flock of black birds cawed and flapped just above her head. A larger bird swooped low. Brown. A raptor's wingspan.

She lost her breath. An owl. She blinked at the sight. The owl flew in tandem with the crows, veering off to her left. Fiery prickles inched down her spine. She started in that direction, noticing the water becoming louder. Then, she heard the bark. Short. Sharp.

Deep, menacing snarls followed. Ferocious. Loud.

Fergus was attacking.

Her heart leapt. She raced toward the sounds, gathering her gun purse close and opening it wide to reach for her pistol, taking the familiar weight of it into her hand. She couldn't see much, but if Fergus was attacking Northfield, she would help wherever she could. That dog was hers. She would fight for him and for herself and for everything the rabid devil had taken from her.

Scrambling blindly over a rise, she peered past the shifting fog and glimpsed a dark figure flailing near the fallen log. Fergus's clenched snarling sounded promising—as if he'd sunk his teeth in deep. Mists closed off her line of sight, but hoarse male shouts of pain told the tale just as well. Oh, yes. Fergus was a born and bred hunter.

With his family, he was gentle as a lamb. Mellow. Lazy, even. But on the hunt? Fergus was a hundred-plus-pound force of nature.

Pride in her hound squeezed her throat. She dashed along the edge of the brook, searching for her usual crossing point. The mossy boulder, yes. The trio of birches, yes. There. She started across, one stone at a time. *Careful not to slip,* she thought. *The water is cold.*

Just as her wet boot touched the muddy bank, she heard another broken cry from Northfield. Then, she heard a sound she'd been dreading.

A loud, pained yelp from her hound.

"Nooooo!" The scream was wrenched from the depths of her soul.

The thud of a hundred-plus-pound body hitting the ground.

A faint whimper. Silence.

A crow cawed mournfully. Her heart screamed louder than her voice, though that was deafening in the quiet glen. *"Fergus! Ferguuuuss! Nooooo!"*

She stumbled over rocks and shorn grass. She fell to her knees beside her hound. Fergus lay on his side, his lanky body struggling with every panting wheeze. Blood coated his muzzle and the wiry gray fur above his shoulder. His wound looked like a gash from a blade.

Dizzy and sick, she covered it with her hand. Fergus whimpered and struggled to breathe.

"You bloody bastard!" she screamed at Northfield. "I will kill you for this!" She bent over Fergus, touching her forehead to his and stroking his beloved face. "Don't you leave me. Don't you go."

A shadow was her only warning. A long, hard arm seized her around her throat. She was choking. Being dragged upward along a body much bigger and stronger than hers. She clawed and fought for air, but the man who held her was unrelenting, his grip crushing.

"Ah, my fair one," he whispered in her ear. "You wore red for me."

She thrashed in his hold, using her boot heels to grind at his legs, using her fingernails to claw at his wrist. Black dots floated amidst swirling white. She was losing her grip. Fergus's bite had mangled Northfield's arm, and blood slicked her hands. She still held the pistol, but she couldn't grasp it properly. Wet fingers fumbled. The gun tumbled to the grassy ground. Despair gripped her harder than Northfield.

"How you love to be seen." The deep, crooning tones of her tormentor echoed her nightmares. "I'm always watching, my sweet Clarissa. I can't look away. I took care to stay hidden, of course. Our enemies want to keep us apart. Your grandmother is well guarded by the one-eyed man. She must die later. First, I will slay the giant. For now, we will defy them all so that I may have you." A long, low groan. Hot breath on her neck. A sickeningly aroused madman at her back. "I must have you. I can wait no longer." The arm banding her waist slid upward. A shaking hand gripped her breast, the pressure starting tentative then turning painful as his excitement grew.

Sound dimmed. Light darkened to gray. She couldn't breathe past his hold on her throat. And she was weakening.

Suddenly, his injured arm loosened. She sucked in air, seeing flashes of light swirling. His other hand dropped away from her breast to fumble with her skirts and, presumably, release his fall.

Campbell had taught her to look for openings, moments of opportunity when a man was vulnerable. This was her chance. She wheezed in a breath and, using a move she'd learned from Mademoiselle Durant, she dipped and spun in the circle of his arms then moved into him. Startled Northfield eyes flared above her. His face was black with soot, his head covered with a woven grass hood. He smelled like the cows. He looked like a woodland demon, garbed in a robe of grass, leaves, and twigs. Around his waist was a belt with a scabbard for a knife. The knife dripped. He tilted his head curiously. "Are we dancing, Clarissa? You know I don't approve."

She mustn't waste time. Viciousness was her best chance. She heard Campbell's voice in her head: *Go for the ballocks, lass. They're an easier reach than the eyes on a tall man. Take hold, give 'em a twist, and have nae mercy when the weepin' starts. Once ye're free, run.*

The problem was that his bizarre robe made locating the ballocks with any precision a difficult task. So, she improvised. "Yes, we're dancing," she rasped. "Here. Let me show you my arabesque." She swung her knee up with a dancer's force, simultaneously sweeping her arms in an arc that collided with his injured arm. The knee landed a withering blow to his aroused manhood.

Her other strike dislodged his hold on her. Harsh bellowing was a delight to her ears, but she didn't wait to hear more. She danced away, crouching to retrieve her gun.

Then, she ran. But she felt him behind her. She spun. Took aim. Fired.

He didn't even flinch.

Ah, God. She'd missed.

Stumbling backward as he advanced on her with heaving breaths and maddened fury, she cocked her second shot. Her foot slipped on a patch of mud. She reeled. Just as she caught her balance, he reached her. Reclaimed his hold. Growled like a snarling, rabid beast. Lifted her and slammed her against a tree with bone-rattling force. Pain exploded through her spine and chest. Air abandoned her in an instant.

His hand gripped her throat, his face swerving close to hers. He bared his teeth, eyes flaring sickeningly wide. Then, he roared incoherently before snarling, "You are mine! Why must you always let others stand between us? Don't you understand what I will do? The giant built a bloody *fortress* around you." His head shook oddly, his eyes winking closed and open, closed and open. "I couldn't penetrate it. Had to fire blindly. Had to burn the world to flush you out. Had to plan. Plan and plan. Patience, son. Father always cautioned patience. You were there in the stable, and I was close. I could almost smell your hair."

He withdrew his knife, long and bloody. He used the tip to snag a lock of her hair. Drawing it loose from the pins, he cut the lock free and tucked it into his belt.

"The dog gave chase," he continued. "One admires a determined hound. But the giant. He is not easy. I long to take him down, too, but he is not easy. Neither was the tracker. Even with him wounded, I could never find the right shot." A frown of confusion. A crumpled grimace of pain. "Clarissa? My head pains me again, fair one. Hold me, won't you?"

She finally gained enough air to steady her hand and wheeze out a reply. "Yes," she said gently. "Let me hold you."

He lowered his head to her shoulder. She tucked the double barrel of her pistol against his ribs.

And fired.

He lurched. Staggered backward. Stared at her with disbelief as his wound bloomed red over his grassy robe.

"What have you done?" His frown was bewildered. "I love you. You are beautiful to me. So beautiful."

She'd hit him just above his scabbard on his right side. He still held the knife, and he hadn't gone down. One shot was clearly not enough. Two would have been better. Still, she was glad she'd brought the pistol instead of the musket. Low visibility would have made a long gun's superior range virtually useless.

"I've killed you," she answered, her voice a wincing croak. "Slowly, perhaps. But I've killed you like the rabid monster you are."

He looked down at his wound, bending inward as pain weakened him. When his eyes lifted again, confusion contorted into eerie blankness. Then his face became a mask of rage. "Your defiance begs punishment. I will not be parted from you."

He charged her. His blade lifted. With her left hand, she covered her belly. Her ring turned hot enough to burn. With her right hand, she swung her empty gun. Metal struck metal. The blade sank with half the force, but it would have pierced her heart if she hadn't been wearing two amulets and a cross, all of which layered upon each other beneath her bodice.

Frustrated, Northfield reeled back for another stab.

A savage roar sounded through the mist, doubled and echoing. Fog parted. Her giant of a husband rushed in like a warrior god unleashing the fury of the heavens. He gripped Northfield like a great bear. Lifted the two-hundred-pound man with no more effort than he lifted a cask of cider. Then, he slammed him to the ground with so much force, she heard bones crack.

She didn't wait to see the rest. Her husband had come for her. He would deal with Northfield. That was all she needed to know.

Instead, she ran to where Fergus lay, still and bleeding. On her knees, she stroked his sweet face and whispered her love. Tears flowed freely. She buried her face in his fur, grateful that at least she would be there to comfort him in his final moments. Gently, she rested her cheek against his side. Heard the faintest heartbeat.

As long as a heart beats, there is hope to be found.

Hope surged. She removed one of her wool stockings and wadded it into a pad. Then, she tore away two strips of her hem and tied them together. She packed the wool pad against Fergus's wound. She meant to tie the strips around the dog's body to secure the makeshift bandage, but when she slid her arms beneath him, she struggled with his weight. She managed to tie it off, but clearly, she wouldn't be able to carry him herself.

Behind her, the sounds of Campbell's vengeance—punishing blows, loud cracks, and gurgling rattles—reached a crescendo. A final crack. A final roar. Then silence.

She dared a glance behind her. What she saw left little doubt about Stephen Northfield's fate—the madman lay in pieces. Her husband calmly straightened, spat upon the remains, and said something in Gaelic. Then, he strode toward her with torment and worry and love shining in his eyes.

She sobbed with relief. "Campbell. Oh, my love. You found me."

"Always," said her man of few words.

"Fergus … He's too heavy. We must take him back to the farm. We must stitch his wound. Please. Can you carry him?"

He crouched beside her, gathering her close and kissing her hair. "Aye, *gràidheag*. Can ye walk?"

She nodded. Rested against his heart for the briefest respite. Then, she stood.

He scooped up their hound in his powerful arms. "Follow me, then. Let's take him home."

Chapter Nineteen

Clarissa kept her vigil by Fergus's side for seventeen days. That was how long it took him to regain his appetite and wag his tail when she scratched his chin. Early on, she insisted he must lay beside her on the bed she shared with Campbell. Her husband held her, and she held Fergus, throughout the first two days and nights.

Later, she agreed to move him closer to the window for his comfort. They'd brought a sofa upstairs from Rowan House's library and covered it in soft blankets. She'd allowed it to be placed a full four feet from her bedside, but no more.

Throughout each day, either Campbell, Broderick, or Angus would come to lift Fergus so he could be fed and tended by Clarissa, Magdalene, Kate, and Mrs. MacBean. She'd never seen a dog so beloved, but then, Fergus was a rare hound.

Her own health slowly improved. A bruised throat and ribs healed enough to cease causing her pain. Grandmama fed her soup and held her hand and shared anecdotes about Grandpapa's back injury after a peculiar mishap on a library ladder. Clarissa suspected there had been more to the story. Grandmama rarely blushed.

On their third morning at Rowan House, Kate entered her bedchamber with a pair of shears. "Good morning, dearest," she said with a loving smile. "I thought you might like a bit of a trim." Tenderly, Kate snipped and sifted to even out the part Northfield had cut away. When she was done, she wrapped slender arms around Clarissa's shoulders and held her fiercely tight. "I'm so very glad you're safe," she whispered. "Thank heaven you came here to Scotland. This is where you belong."

Clarissa quite agreed. She embraced her friend in return, tears flowing freely as they'd done since the day her home had burned to the ground. Kate and Broderick had taken in all the refugees from Campbell's farm. Daniel still wore a bandage beneath his cap, and Magdalene was still applying salve to Rannoch's burns twice a day, but nobody had been killed, apart from Northfield. Many hands made light work, but Rowan House was full to bursting.

Now, she thanked the woman who had helped Clarissa find her firm ground after twenty-eight years adrift. "I can never repay you, my dearest Kate. For telling me to dance. For offering me sanctuary. For insisting Campbell visit far more frequently than was sensible. For seeing how much I needed him. For protecting Grandmama. For being my friend when I had so few. I would not trade you for a hundred others."

"Even though my singing is abominable?"

She'd laughed. "Even though."

On the seventh day of their stay, news arrived of the birth of John and Annie Huxley's first babe—a son they'd named Finlay, or Fin, for short. Angus, Alexander, Broderick, Rannoch, and Campbell had all celebrated with copious rounds of whisky and drunken toasts to Huxley fertility and Annie's venison with onion gravy.

Clarissa hadn't quite understood the connection, but Campbell had assured her that one taste of Annie's cooking had been all it had taken to keep John Huxley coming back for more. "Bargain was set after that. Poor man couldnae stay away."

On the tenth night at Rowan House, Clarissa lay tangled with Campbell in their bed. A soft breeze from the window washed over their naked skin as an owl hooted in the distance. Tenderly, Campbell kissed the bruises over her breastbone left by the force of a madman's rage. While all three of her necklaces had protected her, Cernunnos had taken the brunt of Northfield's blade, splitting the antler charm down the middle and saving Campbell's owl from similar damage.

Now, as she caressed her husband's muscular neck, her heart was finally at peace enough to ask, "How did you find me?"

He nuzzled her breast and slid his palm over her belly. They'd made love for the past hour, yet she felt him hardening against her hip.

She smiled. Her husband was tireless. "Campbell?"

"I'm concentratin', lass."

"On what, precisely?"

He grunted. "I think yer nipples are a wee bit darker than before."

She rolled her eyes. "You are obsessed."

"Aye."

"I know you find explanations about your visions trying."

"I've visions of takin' ye again soon. Do ye suppose ye'll come before or after I'm inside ye this time?"

"Campbell."

"I ken how much ye like my hands. But ye also seem to fancy my cock a great deal."

"Oh, for the love of—"

"Ye're right. 'Twas a daft question. The answer is both. I'm a very fortunate man."

She laughed. Sighed deeply. Stroked his square jaw and traced his lips with her fingers. "Do you mind explaining a bit? I don't wish to press you, but I am curious how you knew where I was when nobody possibly could."

He sobered. Loved her with his eyes. Kissed her softly. "My sight comes through my bloodline—*Seanair* to Mam to me. Mrs. MacBean's message spoke of the anchor in the blood and the circle that burns." His hand laced with hers over her belly then traced her ring with his thumb. "I pictured my Eden. Imagined the ring my grandfather had fashioned for her. The owl I had fashioned to protect her. And the wee life she and I had fashioned together. Flesh of my flesh. Bone of my bones. I found the line. And I chased it."

Her eyes filled with tears. They made the moonlight dance. They spilled over and tickled her skin. "You found me. Found us."

"Aye. Always, *gràidheag*."

By their fourteenth day at Rowan House, Clarissa grew suspicious that Campbell was planning something in secret. But every time she asked, he brushed her off or seduced her. Not that she minded the latter. Her husband's arms were a sanctuary without equal.

But all the maids stopped chattering every time she entered a room, and nearly all the footmen and farmhands had disappeared. Additionally, Alexander, Angus, and Rannoch stopped visiting around day nine, and Broderick suddenly decided around the same time to spend long hours at the distillery. Campbell himself also claimed to be needed at the distillery and, although she had Grandmama and Kate to keep her company while she tended to Fergus, she missed her husband dreadfully.

On their eighteenth day at Rowan House, she discovered Campbell's secret. Because he showed her.

First, he awakened her at sunrise with her first surprise of the morning—his fingers hard at work discovering the changes to her breasts while he entered her from behind. She approved of such surprises and expressed her satisfaction at considerable volume. He'd offered his tongue to keep her mouth busy.

His second surprise had required that she leave the house. She'd hesitated to leave Fergus when he'd just resumed walking steadily. But Campbell had ordered her to dress for "a wee excursion," and she trusted him without question, so she had done it.

Now, she sat in front of him on Dunmore's back as they approached the ruined remains of their home. Rain had taken two days to fully douse the smoldering timbers. But, since then, much of the debris had been cleared. As they arrived at the stone shell of the cottage, she expected him to stop and let her explore. She asked him why he hadn't. He continued up the rise, saying, "Naught left to see, lass. We've better things ahead."

By the time she realized where they were going, her belly was a tangle of knots.

He nuzzled her ear. "Be easy, *gràidheag*. Ye're safe."

She breathed the air, sweet and soft. She closed her eyes and felt the cool damp and his warm arms. Then, she looked out over ancient mountains at the top of the world. Beauty surrounded her. A Highland sky sheltered her. And her magnificent husband loved her with every scrap of his wondrous heart.

The knots unraveled. Her lungs breathed. Her dark memories receded.

Fortunately, as they crossed the brook into the birchwood glen and Campbell lifted her down onto shorn grass, she saw all remnants of that horrible day had been cleared away. She didn't know what he'd done with Northfield's remains, and she didn't particularly care. Her nightmare was over, all traces gone.

But here, she noticed other, less pleasing changes. "Where is my log?" she asked. "Someone's removed it."

"Aye."

She paced toward where it once had lain. "I worked very hard to pepper that log with holes, Campbell."

"I ken."

She huffed and pivoted. A second change became immediately apparent. "Where the devil is my boulder?"

"Gone."

Outraged, she glared at her husband, who seemed to be fighting a smile. "I see nothing amusing about this. You've cut down the pines. I loved those pines." She stomped to where the ground lay turned and bare like a field about to be planted. "You even removed the stumps. What were you thinking?"

"That mayhap ye wouldnae want boulders or stumps in yer drawin' room."

"My …" She lost her breath. Then, she spun in place, looking upon the little glen with new eyes. "Oh."

He crossed to her, pulling a leather envelope from his pocket. Untying the string, he offered it to her without explanation.

Burning with curiosity, she opened the flap and withdrew the folded papers inside. When she saw the sketches, she covered a gasp. "It's a house."

He hummed agreement.

"It—it has *windows,* Campbell. Lots of them."

"Aye." He chuckled. "These ones willnae whistle."

"We'll need so many curtains." She shuffled through the papers, her excitement mounting as she saw the arrangement of the third and second floors. "*Twelve* bedchambers? Oh, heavens. A nursery, maids' quarters. Our bedchamber. My, that's sizable. Will it look out upon the brook?"

"'Twill look out upon the whole glen and Loch Carrich besides." He pointed at the promontory with the owl tree. "That's how high the first floor will be. The second will be much higher."

Shaking her head in wonder, she glanced down. "And a bathing room with a fireplace. Oh, dear. The kitchen lads will certainly have a great deal of hauling to do up all those stairs."

"Nah. There's springs everywhere in these hills. We'll have cisterns and pipin' like we do at the distillery. Finest water in the Highlands. Nae haulin' required."

She flipped to the first floor and gasped. "Oh, Campbell! A music room *and* a ballroom?"

"For dancin'. Ye must have a grand place to dance, *gràidheag.*"

"A sitting room. A library. A study. That will be yours, of course. A quiet place to read and work on your carvings. Not to worry. I shall insist the furniture is properly sized."

Finally, she turned to the last page. Her eyes welled. "Campbell," she whispered. "Ah, my love. It's perfect." The ground floor had everything she could have dreamed—a kitchen they'd need three tables to fill, a dining room running half the length of the house, a drawing room the size of Rowan House's, a scullery and larder and servants' quarters rivaling Ellery Hall's. And, toward the front of the house, on the quiet side tucked between a small parlor and a room labeled simply as "Hounds Quarters," was a suite of rooms for Grandmama. She'd have her own sitting room, bathing room, and bedchamber with a door out to a small, private terrace.

"You've thought of everything. It's quite large." She glanced up. "Costly."

"Dinnae fash. I've a wee bit set aside."

She quirked a wry grin at his tone. Knowing her husband as she did, he likely had more than a "wee bit."

"When did you do this?" she asked.

"Started sketchin' after yer first lesson."

She sniffed, knuckling away joyful tears. "But that was … that was before we …"

"Aye." His grin was slow, his eyes glowing. "What can I say, lass? Ye set me to dreamin'."

She leapt at him full force, wrapping her arms around him with desperate, passionate, all-consuming love. He cupped her face and held her steady for a deep, tender kiss—which escalated a great deal faster than she'd planned. By the time she heard the jangle of horses and the clatter of wagon wheels arriving, she was contemplating the merits of shorn grass as a cushion for her knees.

"*Mmmph.* Blast. I think someone's here." She tugged Campbell's hand out of her bodice and spun to stand with her back against his front just as Kate and Broderick rolled past the owl tree in one of the distillery wagons. "Er, Campbell?"

"Aye?"

"Is there a road there, now?"

"Aye. Rain made it take a wee bit longer than I'd hoped. Ten days to cut in. Four to make it passable. Broderick's men helped. Made the work go easier."

Good heavens. "A remarkable feat."

"We'll need a proper road. This way, I'll spend less time travelin' to the distillery and more time with ye."

"What about the farm?"

"Barns can be built anywhere. Cowsheds and stables, too. We'll use what's left of the stone on the old farm to construct quarters for the men. Huxley has some slate left from his castle renovations."

"We'll need a place for Butter."

He sighed. "Ye're spoilin' that calf, Clarissa. He'll be unmanageable once he's grown."

"Mmm. If we feed him extra hay in winter, do you suppose he'll grow bigger horns? I think very large horns would be dashing."

He sighed. "Lass."

"I want a good-sized garden."

"Right."

"And chickens."

He grunted. "Fine. But nae roosters. They're a pure nuisance. Wake ye at dawn, strut round actin' territorial, and turn aggressive if ye get too close."

"Hmm. I quite like a good cock, actually."

"Christ on the cross, lass. Ye're beggin' for trouble."

She grinned. "Later, perhaps. We have company."

Kate squealed, waving excitedly. By the time Broderick lifted his wife down and placed what appeared to be a picnic basket in her arms, she could barely contain herself. She dashed down the slope to greet them.

"Are we having a picnic?" Clarissa laughed. "I didn't bring a blanket."

"No picnic, I'm afraid." Kate shot a grin up at Campbell. "May I?"

"Aye, Katie-lass. Show her what's inside."

With a gleam of anticipatory delight, Kate opened the basket's hinged top. Something inside was moving. Something white. Furry. Something that grunted and released a tiny whine. A black nose poked above the woven edge. Round, black eyes and a sweet, scruffy face followed.

Her heart skipped a beat. Campbell reached past her to scoop out the little pup. It fit inside his hand with room to spare. "She's a terrier. A man I ken in Argyle procured her for me." He scratched the little pup's ears and brought her close enough for Clarissa to pet. "Do ye like her?"

She couldn't speak, so she settled for nodding.

"Would ye care to keep her?"

She nodded again. Another tear escaped.

He cradled the pup near her heart. She stroked the tiny head and released a watery laugh when the dog tried to gnaw her finger.

"What would ye like to call her?"

Her heart squeezed. "Hope." She reached back to draw him down for a kiss. "I'd like to call her Hope."

His grin dawned slowly, his eyes lighting her sky. "Hope it is, *gràidheag*."

Epilogue

June 28, 1827
Ellery Hall
Cambridgeshire, England

"She was drunk as a lord when I arrived. Offered me iced cakes and gin." The handsome new Earl of Medford leaned against the bookshelf in Grandpapa's study, his expression both outraged and disbelieving. "She wants me to go riding with Silas. Riding. As though we're two young scamps with new ponies." He shook his head. "Ridiculous. She might has well have pinched my cheek."

Clarissa coughed as dust plumed from the canvas she was sliding off one of Grandpapa's crates of paintings. "What did you say in your letter beforehand?"

"Nothing! I was quite cryptic." Francis moved to help her, plucking a cobweb from her hair before shooing her toward a chair. "Simply mentioned I'd like to speak to her regarding her son. I didn't even specify which one."

"You didn't mention Stephen at all?"

"I didn't have a chance. She stained my cravat with her tears. She insisted on telling me everything. Positively *everything*. I now know the most intimate details of my father's peccadilloes. It was ghastly."

She met George's eyes, and they shared an amused smile. "Well, you must have alerted her somehow. A woman doesn't confess a secret of this magnitude without prompting."

Francis finished folding the canvas and added it to the stack in the corner. "Perhaps seeing my new title stirred her regrets for the past. Regardless, from the moment I entered Mrs. Northfield's drawing room to the moment she showed me sketches of Silas as an infant, blackmail was out of the question."

"Yes, a public pronouncement does make blackmail slightly less effective."

Francis snorted. "Slightly."

"Perhaps this is for the best." Clarissa plucked a hinged silver box from the shelf near her elbow. Grandpapa had stored all sorts of bits and bobs in all sorts of boxes throughout the house, but they'd yet to find what they were looking for. They'd saved his study for last. "I've been feeling queasy about tangling you up in such a scheme, honestly."

"*Now*, you're queasy? The woman described Silas's conception in some detail. She then described her night of passion with her husband two months later. She said Mr. Northfield knew the truth from the beginning and that Silas's birth brought them closer. Went on and on and *on* about her love for the man. Quite a forgiving chap, I daresay." He blew out a breath and retrieved a pry bar from the floor before applying it to a nearby crate. "I cannot unhear such things, Clarissa. I cannot now wash my mind clean."

"I'm sorry, Francis."

"She wants me to arrange a reconciliation with Mother. She said her fondest wish is for her son and her oldest friend to forgive her. Evidently, her husband has no plans to renounce his heir, so I expect Silas will come round eventually."

She grimaced. "I know you didn't wish to distress your mother any further. Did Mrs. Northfield say anything about Stephen?"

"No. The Northfields now believe him to be traveling abroad. America, I think. Or Canada. George, which one did we decide on, in the end?"

George glanced up from searching a box of paste jewelry. He handed Clarissa a brooch. "Newfoundland. You thought it suitably remote, and Mr. MacPherson concurred."

"Ah, yes. Now, I remember. The ship departed from Liverpool last week. Stephen's effects will be discovered sometime near end of summer. Dreadful bear attack. Or wolves. George?"

"Wolves." George's eyes twinkled with affectionate exasperation. "How much whisky did you drink that night?"

Francis arched a brow. "MacPherson challenged me. To decline the invitation would have been the height of rudeness. Besides, my prize was five bottles of the best whisky in Scotland. Blessedly light on the peat smoke. He says next year's vintage will be even better. I'd like to taste that for myself."

Clarissa smiled and slid a hand over her belly, which was just beginning to show signs of mounding. "You shall. By then, the house will be complete and our nursery well on its way to filling up. I'll expect regular visits from you and George, and my children will expect yearly gifts from their Uncle Francis."

Although her plan to protect Campbell from any future retribution over Stephen's death had fallen through, Clarissa had decided to take her husband's advice and try to stop fretting over it. Francis had learned upon his return to England that the Northfields had been unaware of Stephen's presence in Scotland, and they remained unaware of his demise.

There was always a chance they would learn the truth—many residents of the glen knew his name and that he'd earned MacPherson wrath. Perhaps one day, rumors would escape and find their way to Northfield ears. She'd shared her concerns with Campbell late one night in May, and he'd answered simply, "There's naught for anybody to find, *gràidheag*."

"But what if there is?"

"There isnae. I made certain of it. The crows did the rest."

"I must *know* that you're safe, my love. I cannot abide a single doubt."

He'd sighed and stroked her hair. "Very well. We'll write Teversham in the mornin'. Northfield was fond of decoys. Mayhap that's where his tale should end."

A month later, on their way south to settle some important matters at Ellery Hall, they met Francis and George in Yorkshire. A few items from Stephen's camp were shipped off to Liverpool shortly thereafter, along with a generous bribe to an old friend of Campbell's from his days in the Highland regiment. The friend worked for a shipping company transporting goods to America and Canada.

Clarissa had been comforted by the plan, but she'd still wanted more reassurance, so she'd asked Francis to visit Mrs. Northfield and test the waters for future blackmail. To protect Campbell, she would invent secondary plans for her secondary plans. She would do whatever it took.

But now, it seemed clear she'd have to live with some uncertainty. Campbell had been telling her she worried for nothing. Perhaps she did. Time would tell.

Out in the corridor, Grandmama directed Campbell toward the study. "My, that does look heavy, dear. Is it heavy?"

A deep grunt. "Aye."

"Now, then, where shall we put it?"

Clarissa watched her husband carry the massive trunk across the room as easily as other men might carry a snuffbox. She sighed. Melted.

"Oh, not there, dear. A little to the left."

Campbell bent and lowered it precisely into place.

Grandmama beamed and patted his cheek. "Perfect."

Clarissa went to her husband's side as Grandmama opened the large barrel-topped trunk with shaking hands. Inside lay a miscellany of items from the past—Grandpapa's painting supplies and smaller canvases, three blankets the moths had decimated, a child's wooden horse, a bronze bust of some long-forgotten Roman general, and a collection of smoking pipes.

Grandmama dabbed her eyes with her handkerchief and brought one of the pipes to her nose for a delicate sniff. "Ah, he loved this one." She grinned wide, her creases smiling with her.

Clarissa's heart turned over watching her grandmother relive her most cherished memories. She found Campbell's hand and brought it to her lips. "Thank you for this," she whispered. "Grandmama hated leaving her keepsakes behind."

Campbell nodded. "I just hope we find what we're lookin' for."

So did she. Grandpapa had gone to a great deal of trouble, after all.

Over breakfast one bright spring morning, Campbell had described a dream in which a "quiet sort of Englishman" invited him into a library to discuss the intricacies of managing a large estate. "Felt like I was bein' interviewed for a steward's post," Campbell had grumbled to Clarissa. "Then, he starts on with some rubbish about bees, sayin' how honey lasts forever if ye take care with it, and pigs deserve everythin' they get." His frown had turned into a disgruntled glower. "When the man lit up his pipe, I kenned I was in for a long blether."

The mention of a pipe had, of course, given Clarissa a jolt. She'd quizzed him at length and, after discussing the details with Grandmama and consulting with Mrs. MacBean, they'd decided a return to Ellery Hall was in order. Today was their second day searching through Grandpapa's old belongings.

"I remember this," Grandmama said, pulling a small painting from the trunk's corner. "Clarissa, do you remember the pond in Alconbury?"

She peered over Grandmama's shoulder at the painting. "Nothing but lily pads and frogs, as I recall. Quite loud in summer."

"There's a companion for this one. Alfie liked to paint in series. Now, where is it?" Grandmama sorted through the stack, frowning. Then, she paused. Her fingers hovered. Trembled. She traced the edge of a walnut frame.

Curious, Clarissa moved to help her, lifting the framed canvas from the corner where it was wedged. The painting depicted a wide, straight brook beneath a leafy tree. On the bank was an old, fallen log. In the lower corner, resting on a blanket near Grandpapa's signature, were two bees and a pot of honey.

A tingling flush made her gasp. She covered her mouth as tears pricked her eyes. "Oh, Grandmama. Do you suppose …"

Grandmama's eyes found hers. They were shining. "Let's find out, dear."

They spent several minutes examining the painting, exploring the frame, and puzzling over what, precisely, Grandpapa had meant for them to see.

As Campbell, Francis, and George debated the best method of taking apart the frame—with Francis arguing against Campbell's suggestion of brute force—something moved in the corner of Clarissa's vision.

A streak of gray darting past the study's open door.

She turned to look, but the corridor was empty. She refocused on the painting. George was quietly suggesting they find a letter opener and gently pry the frame loose.

Another streak.

Clarissa spun. What was that? The maids were away at the market fetching supplies for dinner. There shouldn't have been anyone else in the house. She wandered toward the doorway, looking left and right. Nothing. She was about to turn away again when she saw it.

Dark gray. Waving just beyond the corner of the passage to the billiard room. Back and forth. Playfully, it shook like a furry gray finger.

Her heart seized.

The tail disappeared. In its place popped out a round face with dense gray fur and enormous copper eyes. "Mrow." The cat pounced into a pool of sunlight, and her heart leapt. Twisted.

"D-Dash?" she whispered.

A second cat leapt atop the first. She blinked as they rolled together, swatting one another. A third joined in the antics a moment later.

She covered her heart, which felt like it might burst. From the direction of the main wing, she heard one of the maids chattering. The girl scurried down the corridor looking harried. "So very sorry, Mrs. MacPherson. I didn't mean to let them inside. We've been feeding them outside the garden door, so that's where they come most mornings. When we returned from the market, they slipped in beneath our feet."

She questioned the girl about the kittens, which appeared to be several months old. The maid said she'd found them in the stable six weeks after Clarissa's departure for Scotland and had been feeding them ever since.

Something must have alerted Campbell to her turmoil, because suddenly, he was there. "What's wrong?"

She wiped away a tear. "Nothing." She gave him a watery beam. "Everything is wondrous."

His frown deepened. He glared at the maid and eyed the trio of cats playing in the corridor. Then, he sighed. "Are we addin' three more to the household, *gràidheag?*"

She sniffed. "Perhaps."

A fourth cat leapt out of the shadows to collide with its siblings before darting toward the billiard room.

She patted her husband's arm. "Three or four."

Behind them, Grandmama warned Francis to take care with Grandpapa's letter opener, as it hadn't been sharpened in some years and might injure him if he tried to force it beneath the frame.

Finally, Francis crowed in triumph and handed the letter opener to George with a dashing flourish and a brilliant grin. "My rapier skills are quite superior, I'll have you know."

They all gathered around as Grandmama separated the canvas from the frame's backing and retrieved the envelope secured inside. Together, they read the letter signed by Grandpapa, Rupert Stimson, multiple solicitors, and several witnesses.

The letter specified that all income from the Ellery estate must be reserved for the sole use of Rosamond Brightwell Stimson, the Dowager Countess of Darnham, and her granddaughter, Miss Clarissa Meadows. It stated that Rupert Stimson, as the heir to the Darnham title, would be awarded five percent of said income for his kind service as an advisor to Lady Darnham on estate matters. It stipulated that, if ever Rupert Stimson reneged on his obligations, the estate in its entirety would be withdrawn from its current trust and transferred into a new trust under full control of Lady Darnham and any agent of her choosing. All funds inappropriately dispensed to Rupert Stimson would be repaid to the estate in full, with a ten percent penalty added for every year of delinquency.

The letter was numbered as the third of three copies.

Clarissa assumed Rupert had managed to burn the other two.

"Well, my darling Clarissa," said Francis. "It seems your Cousin Rupert is about to be thoroughly beggared. Perhaps I should inquire if he'd care to sell his house in Brighton. George quite fancies the sea air."

Grandmama dabbed her eyes. "I should have known my dear, sweet Alfie wouldn't leave anything to chance. He was quite the skillful negotiator."

Clarissa squeezed her hand. "And he loved you with all his heart."

"As he loved you."

Her eyes filled. Campbell wrapped his arm around her waist and tucked her against his strength. She sniffed and accepted the handkerchief he offered. "I can scarcely believe it. He was watching over us the whole time."

"That's just the thing, dear." Grandmama kissed Clarissa's cheek then beamed up at Campbell. "The best husbands always do."

Watch for the next book in the
Midnight in Scotland series

COMING SOON!

MIDNIGHT IN SCOTLAND: BOOK FOUR

THE WICKEDNESS OF A HIGHLANDER

BY

ELISA BRADEN

More from Elisa Braden

Be first to hear about new releases, price specials, and more—sign up for Elisa's free email newsletter at www.elisabraden.com so you don't miss a thing!

Midnight in Scotland Series

In the enchanting new Midnight in Scotland series, the unlikeliest matches generate the greatest heat. All it takes is a spark of Highland magic.

The Making of a Highlander (Book One)

Handsome adventurer John Huxley is locked in a land dispute in the Scottish Highlands with one way out: Win the Highland Games. When the local hoyden Mad Annie Tulloch offers to train him in exchange for "Lady Lessons," he agrees. But teaching the fiery, foul-mouthed, breeches-wearing lass how to land a lord seems impossible—especially when he starts dreaming of winning her for himself.

The Taming of a Highlander (Book Two)

Wrongfully imprisoned and tortured, Broderick MacPherson lives for one purpose—punishing the man responsible. When a wayward lass witnesses his revenge, he risks returning to the prison that nearly killed him. Kate Huxley has no wish to testify against a man who's already suffered too much. But the only remedy is to become his wife. And she can't possibly marry such a surly, damaged man…can she?

The Temptation of a Highlander (Book Three)

Hunted by a madman bent on possessing her, English beauty Clarissa Meadows flees to a friend's house in the Scottish Highlands. With nowhere left to run, she accepts the protection of rough, solitary giant Campbell MacPherson. But falling for her bodyguard puts him in a predator's sights, forcing an impossible choice: stay with the man she loves or save him from the wolf she's brought to his door.

Rescued from Ruin Series

Discover the scandalous predicaments, emotional redemptions, and gripping love stories (with a dash of Lady Wallingham) in the scorching series that started it all!

EVER YOURS, ANNABELLE (PREQUEL)

As a girl, Annabelle Huxley chased Robert Conrad with reckless abandon, and he always rescued her when she pushed too far—until the accident that cost him everything. Seven years later, Robert discovers the girl with the habit of chasing trouble is now a siren he can't resist. But when a scandalous secret threatens her life, how far will he go to rescue her one last time?

THE MADNESS OF VISCOUNT ATHERBOURNE (BOOK ONE)

Victoria Lacey's life is perfect—perfectly boring. Agree to marry a lord who has yet to inspire a single, solitary tingle? It's all in a day's work for the oh-so-proper sister of the Duke of Blackmore. Surely no one suspects her secret longing for head-spinning passion. Except a dark stranger, on a terrace, at a ball where she should not be kissing a man she has just met. Especially one bent on revenge.

THE TRUTH ABOUT CADS AND DUKES (BOOK TWO)

Painfully shy Jane Huxley is in a most precarious position, thanks to dissolute charmer Colin Lacey's deceitful wager. Now, his brother, the icy Duke of Blackmore, must make it right, even if it means marrying her himself. Will their union end in frostbite? Perhaps. But after lingering glances and devastating kisses, Jane begins to suspect the truth: Her duke may not be as cold as he appears.

Desperately Seeking a Scoundrel (Book Three)

Where Lord Colin Lacey goes, trouble follows. Tortured and hunted by a brutal criminal, he is rescued from death's door by the stubborn, fetching Sarah Battersby. In return, she asks one small favor: Pretend to be her fiancé. Temporarily, of course. With danger nipping his heels, he knows it is wrong to want her, wrong to agree to her terms. But when has Colin Lacey ever done the sensible thing?

The Devil Is a Marquess (Book Four)

A walking scandal surviving on wits, whisky, and wicked skills in the bedchamber, Benedict Chatham must marry a fortune or risk ruin. Tall, redheaded disaster Charlotte Lancaster possesses such a fortune. The price? One year of fidelity and sobriety. Forced to end his libertine ways, Chatham proves he is more than the scandalous charmer she married, but will it be enough to keep his unwanted wife?

When a Girl Loves an Earl (Book Five)

Miss Viola Darling always gets what she wants, and what she wants most is to marry Lord Tannenbrook. James knows how determined the tiny beauty can be—she mangled his cravat at a perfectly respectable dinner before he escaped. But he has no desire to marry, less desire to be pursued, and will certainly not kiss her kissable lips until they are both breathless, no matter how tempted he may be.

Twelve Nights as His Mistress (Novella – Book Six)

Charles Bainbridge, Lord Wallingham, spent two years wooing Julia Willoughby, yet she insists they are a dreadful match destined for misery. Now, rather than lose her, he makes a final offer: Spend twelve nights in his bed, and if she can deny they are perfect for each other, he will let her go. But not before tempting tidy, sensible Julia to trade predictability for the sweet chaos of true love.

Confessions of a Dangerous Lord (Book Seven)

Known for flashy waistcoats and rapier wit, Henry Thorpe, the Earl of Dunston, is deadlier than he appears. For years, his sole focus has been hunting a ruthless killer through London's dark underworld. Then Maureen Huxley came along. To keep her safe, he must keep her at arm's length. But as she contemplates marrying another man, Henry's caught in the crossfire between his mission and his heart.

Anything but a Gentleman (Book Eight)

Augusta Widmore must force her sister's ne'er-do-well betrothed to the altar, or her sister will bear the consequences. She needs leverage only one man can provide—Sebastian Reaver. When she invades his office demanding a fortune in markers, he exacts a price a spinster will never pay—become the notorious club owner's mistress. And when she calls his bluff, a fiery battle for surrender begins.

A Marriage Made in Scandal (Book Nine)

As the most feared lord in London, the Earl of Holstoke is having a devil of a time landing a wife. When a series of vicious murders brings suspicion to his door, only one woman is bold enough to defend him—Eugenia Huxley. Her offer to be his alibi risks scandal, and marriage is the remedy. But as a poisonous enemy coils closer, Holstoke finds his love for her might be the greatest danger of all.

A Kiss from a Rogue (Book Ten)

A cruel past left Hannah Gray with one simple longing—a normal life with a safe, normal husband. Finding one would be easy if she weren't distracted by wolf-in-rogue's-clothing Jonas Hawthorn. He's tried to forget the haughty Miss Gray. But once he tastes the heat and longing hidden beneath her icy mask, the only mystery this Bow Street man burns to solve is how a rogue might make Hannah his own.

About the Author

Reading romance novels came easily to Elisa Braden. Writing them? That took a little longer. After graduating with degrees in creative writing and history, Elisa spent entirely too many years in "real" jobs writing T-shirt copy ... and other people's resumes ... and articles about giftware displays. But that was before she woke up and started dreaming about the very *unreal* job of being a romance novelist. Better late than never.

Elisa lives in the gorgeous Pacific Northwest, where you're constitutionally required to like the colors green and gray. Good thing she does. Other items on the "like" list include cute dogs, strong coffee, and epic movies. Of course, her favorite thing of all is hearing from readers who love her characters as much as she does. If you're one of those, get in touch on Facebook and Twitter or visit **www.elisabraden.com**.